# A BANNER IS UNFURLED

## VOLUME 1

# A BANNER IS UNFURLED

## VOLUME 1

MARCIE GALLACHER

KERRI ROBINSON

Covenant Communications, Inc.

Cover image: illustration © Cameron Gardner, reference photography by Brett Thelin.

Cover design by Jessica A. Warner, copyrighted 2005 by Covenant Communications, Inc.

Published by Covenant Communications, Inc.
American Fork, Utah

Printed in the United States of America
First Printing: October 2005

13 12 11 10 09 08 07    13 12 11 10 9 8 7 6 5 4

ISBN 13: 978-1-59811-593-2
ISBN 10: 1-59811-593-6

*To Julia Hills Johnson, our third-great-grandmother,
and to our children, the jewels in our crowns.*

# ACKNOWLEDGMENTS

Heartfelt thanks to our husbands, Gray Gallacher, tour guide extraordinaire, and Brent Robinson, chief wordsmith and computer whiz. Not only did these wonderful men keep the home fires burning, but they also spent hours researching, traveling, and initially editing this story. We would also like to thank our parents, Tal and LaRae Huber, for their support and encouragement.

We feel deeply grateful for the many individuals who made this work possible. We are indebted to Dale R. Broadhurst for the tremendous research he has done, for his willingness to share his vast collection of historical documents, and for his kind and timely answers to our questions. Thank you, Carol Holmes and Lisa Jensen, for giving your time and talents to this project. There are so many individuals who we don't know personally—Johnson family researchers and genealogists over many generations who have passed on; historians both within and outside the Church, whose research taught us so much. Thank you to the many Johnson cousins who shared with us their insight and family stories, including Dale LeBaron for his wonderful book *Friend of the Prophet,* Marla Homer and Greg Brown for posing as Julia and Ezekiel, and Preston Johnson, David Stapley, and Loni Gardner from the Benjamin Franklin Johnson Family Organization who befriended, encouraged, and helped us in so many ways.

Last, but in no way least, how we appreciate Shauna Humphreys, Christian Sorensen, and the entire Covenant staff for sharing this dream and vision with us.

# PREFACE

In each of our lives, we hear stories that touch us with such force that we desire to share them with others. The Ezekiel and Julia Johnson story is one such tale—brimming with passion, sacrifice, tragedy, and hope. Yet it is not simply the story of one family. The members of this family were very prolific and wrote a great deal about events and individuals in early Church history. Today, some of these events and people are little known by the general Church membership. There were early leaders who consecrated all they had to the newly restored gospel and lost their lives in the effort—without the opportunity to write their own histories. Don Carlos Smith, the youngest brother of the Prophet, the powerful missionary Joseph Brackenbury, and Lyman Sherman, whom Heber C. Kimball referred to as "Joseph's right hand" in Kirtland, share their testimonies through the eyes and hearts of those around them.

The early wives and mothers in the Church may not have been called to positions of authority, but they were leaders in their families. Sometimes the spark of faith burned first in their hearts, and they led their husbands and children to the waters of baptism. There were single sisters, with or without children, who walked the path of faith alone. We found that so many of these voices were silenced by death due to hardship and exposure. We wondered if these women would have embraced the gospel had they known the sacrifice. Yet, if the candle of their faith sometimes wavered, it never went out but burned with steady warmth as the Lord sustained them through their trials. Their love and strength has influenced each page of this story. We honor their lives.

Finally, these great men and women worshipped their Savior by following the leadership of a young man—Joseph Smith Jr. Each of Julia and Ezekiel's fifteen children accepted Joseph as the Prophet of God. Some of them knew him intimately and recorded in moving detail their interactions with him. None of them turned against their beloved Prophet or left the Church for even a brief period of time. As we came to know Brother Joseph through the eyes of this family, their love and gratitude for him became our own. We understood more deeply his unique calling in a historical context. We felt overwhelming gratitude for his human qualities—his merriment, his humility, his courage, his faith, and his kindness.

Although most of the narrative has a historical core, there are a few purely imaginative segments, such as those involving the fictional characters Kathryn Clay, Elijah Handy, and Hope Randall. Notes accompany each chapter so that readers will know where imagination and history intersect. The story brings situations and characters to life.

We believe that the novel is an art form and art is an attempt to record the actual feel of life. Willa Cather wrote that art is created because life is "too strong to stop" but "too sweet to lose." We hope each reader will feel the sweetness of this family who actually lived, the strength of our collective latter-day history, and the true greatness of the Prophet Joseph Smith.

*Marcie Gallacher*
*Kerri Robinson*

# EZEKIEL AND JULIA HILLS JOHNSON FAMILY
## 1828

Joel Hills [b. 1802] [m. Annie Pixley, 1826]
    Julianne [1827–1829]
    Sixtus [b. 1829]
Nancy Maria [b. 1803]
Seth Guernsey [b. 1805]
Delcena Diadamia [b. 1806]
Julia Ann (Julianne) [b. 1808]
David [b. 1810]
Almera Woodward [b. 1812]
Susan Ellen [b. 1814]
Joseph Ellis [b. 1817]
Benjamin Franklin [b. 1818]
Mary Ellen [b. 1820]
Elmer Wood [1822–1823]
George Washington [b. 1823]
William Derby [b. 1824]
Esther Melita [b. 1827]

*The dates in this chart represent the actual dates of the Johnson family.*
*For plot considerations, some ages have been changed in the novel.*

# PROLOGUE

*High on the mountain top*

*A banner is unfurled.*

*Ye nations, now look up;*

*It waves to all the world.*

—Joel H. Johnson, from "High on the Mountain Top"

*March 1787*

Fourteen-year-old Ezekiel Johnson threw the last forkful of hay to the livestock on his stepfather's farm a number of miles outside of Ashford, Connecticut. It was a cool evening. Through the slats in the barn roof, he saw the sky turning pink from the setting sun. As he worked, his wide mouth formed a grim line over a smooth, youthful chin. The boyishness of his chin contrasted vividly with his experienced and somber, gray-blue eyes. It was as if the boy's features were young but a part of his soul was old and worn.

The boy sighed. The daylight hours had been better than most, but he feared the evening. Isaac Chapel, his stepsister's husband, had come to help clear the new field. Isaac's presence had kept Zeke's stepfather, Jonathan King, in check. But Isaac wasn't staying for supper. Zeke figured King's meanness was stored inside from being nice all day and would blow out of him tonight.

He unlatched the barn door and pushed it open. The high, thin clouds glowed crimson. Patches of new grass grew among layers of mud. A chill breeze blew his hair into his eyes.

"Zeke, my boy!" Isaac's pleasant voice startled Ezekiel. A husky man in his early thirties, Isaac had unruly black hair and merry green eyes. He jogged up to Zeke, grinning. "Lizbeth and I are taking my niece Mary to the circus next Thursday. We'd sure like it if you could get away and come with us."

Zeke looked down. "Isaac, you know Mr. King'll never let me go."

"I mentioned it to him, Zeke," Isaac encouraged. "He said he'd let you go if he could spare you. I think it's worth you asking. I'd best be heading home now."

Ezekiel had difficulty finding a time to speak with his stepfather about going to the circus. Finally, on Tuesday morning, he blurted out the question.

Jonathan King answered carefully as he itched his red beard, "Boy, you should have mentioned this days ago. I told Isaac you could go only if I could spare you. The new field isn't plowed yet or ready for planting."

"What if I get it plowed?" Ezekiel asked.

"Then I'll let you go," Mr. King stated as he raised his eyebrows, knowing that it would be impossible for the boy to finish the task.

Still Ezekiel's heart leapt at the possibility. Zeke figured he had two days, and though his stepfather was harsh, his word was law, an unbreakable iron fist.

All Tuesday, the boy labored, shouting at the horse Bill to hurry up as the two moved the plow through the hard ground. Yet by dusk, only a fourth of the earth was turned and ready for seed. Ezekiel lay in his bed that night, staring dejectedly out the window at the full moon. *A full moon!* The thought exploded in Ezekiel's mind. When he was certain his mother and King were asleep, he slipped quietly to the barn and harnessed Bill, driving the confused gelding to the field. Bill worked faithfully through the hours—trusting Ezekiel and only spooking once in the shadows—as if he were mindful of the boy's wish.

At dawn, Zeke hurried back to the barn, fed Bill, and did the milking. He was at the table by breakfast. No one suspected he had been up all night. While Mr. King and Zeke's mother went to a neighbor's to help shear sheep, Zeke continued plowing. It wasn't long before the horse became so exhausted that he could scarcely move. The boy resorted to whipping the tired animal. At first Ezekiel hated striking Bill. But eventually he hardened to the task, finding the strength to beat the horse by turning his mind to a day at the circus.

Zeke worked past sunset. King arrived home and found him in the field finishing the plowing under a darkening sky. Zeke watched anxiously as his stepfather stared at the field dumbfounded. King wouldn't have praise for him, but that didn't matter. Zeke would go to town.

"How'd you finish this?" King asked, stroking his beard, his green eyes narrowing.

"I worked hard. The field's ripe for planting. I'll go see Isaac tomorrow," Ezekiel stated, glancing sideways at Bill, whose sides heaved and whose nose was almost to the ground from exhaustion.

"Put the horse away and come in the house," King snapped and turned away.

Although nearly too tired to stand, Zeke cared tenderly for Bill that evening, rubbing his legs with liniment and giving him the greenest, most inviting hay. When Zeke finished, he walked slowly toward the house. He figured he'd eat a little bit and go to bed. Then tomorrow would come, his own day.

Zeke had scarcely stepped inside when King throttled him from behind and dragged the boy to his mother, Sethiah, while exclaiming, "The devil has worked beside your unholy, misbegotten child! How else could he have plowed so quickly?"

With halting shouts, Zeke insisted that he and Bill had been up all night working. "You gave your word. It is my right to go to town," the boy shouted, struggling to catch his breath with the man's fleshy arm around his throat.

But Jonathan King would not be assuaged. "Your heart is black, boy! Your bonny looks will not spare you a beating."

King whipped Ezekiel in the kitchen while his mother, with bent shoulders, silently stirred mush over the fire. Ezekiel hated them both at that moment—his stepfather for his lies and cruel treatment and his mother for watching silently. To endure the beating, he imagined the father he had never known. He pictured him tall and strong with clear blue eyes. He imagined him thrashing King for calling his son *unholy* and *misbegotten*. He remembered a winter evening long ago when his mother had tucked him into bed. He had asked about his father. She had whispered that Zeke must not believe anything Mr. King said about him, that his father was a good man, a patriot who lost his life at Bunker Hill. God himself had sanctioned his parents' union. Ezekiel wanted to believe her but felt some doubt at the moment. If it were true, why didn't she shout it out for Jonathan King to hear? Why would she let him beat a hero's son?

Then, as the horsewhip fell on Zeke's shoulders once more, King shouted, "I'm beating you, boy, same as you beat my horse."

Thoughts of the boy's father shattered as the image of the horse, Bill, rose in his mind. Ezekiel broke. A racking sob shook his young body. It was the sign Jonathan King waited for. The whip stilled, and a single, choking breath escaped the quiet Sethiah. But although Ezekiel cried in part because of the pain, he cried most bitterly because a new hatred had entered his soul. Ezekiel hated himself. He hated himself for becoming like his stepfather, for beating the animal who labored for him.

"Pray, boy," his stepfather said, sucking in breath as he leaned the horsewhip against the wall. "Go to the barn and pray for forgiveness. Perhaps God will be merciful even to an illegitimate child."

And so young Ezekiel limped out to the barn. Instead of praying, he went to the gelding and hugged his powerful neck. "I'm sorry, Bill," he whispered. Then Ezekiel made a promise to himself. He would never strike an animal or child as long as he lived. He would not be cruel like his stepfather or weak like his mother. He would be strong like his real father. Strong enough to leave this place. Strong enough to be a hero someday.

Two weeks later, after milking and other chores, Ezekiel sat down for breakfast at the sturdy beech table. Outside, a steady rain beat on the fields and trees. Sethiah filled her son's plate and set it before him. She was a thin woman of average height with high cheekbones and even features. Her brown hair was pulled back in a tight bun. She was just over thirty years old, making her twenty years her husband's junior, though she did not seem young, her blood-streaked eyes devoid of the buoyancy of youth.

Yet her step was lighter than usual this morning, for her husband was in town bartering with the cooper and gunsmith. The farmhouse smelled of smoked pork, steamed potatoes, and boiled eggs. Ezekiel fingered one of the eggs. He didn't feel much like eating. He dreaded the thing Jonathan King had told him to do today. He was to take the horse to a neighbor and sell the animal for thirty dollars.

For Zeke, Bill's sale meant losing one of the few joys in his life. When Zeke rode Bill, it was as if a miracle occurred. The boy felt truly alive, suspended for a moment in time in absolute partnership with a powerful and noble creature, outside and above the drudgery of existence.

Ezekiel stared with hatred at the old rawhide purse sitting on the table. The name *James King* was stamped on one side in gold leaf. Ezekiel fingered the purse and turned it over. The date *April 1742* was stamped on the other side.

"Did that purse belong to Mr. King's father?" Ezekiel asked.

"I s'pose," Sethiah answered.

"I wonder if James King was as ugly as his son," Zeke said violently. "I'm thinkin' on taking a knife and shredding the pouch."

With effort, Sethiah sought to turn the tide of the conversation. "Mr. King's never trusted you with his purse before today," she commented as she grated suet for the meat pies she would make later. "I think it's a sign of better times. Strive to be worthy of that trust."

"He's selling Bill because I care about him," Ezekiel exclaimed. "Because he knows it will hurt me, break me like a horse or something."

"Thirty dollars is a lot of money, Zeke. A person can buy two colts for thirty dollars. A person can live quite a while on thirty dollars." She paused and added, "Your food is getting cold."

For a moment, Ezekiel considered refusing to eat, though his stomach twisted from both turmoil and hunger. It would show her how much he hated the life she had given him. But lack of nourishment would deplete his strength, not anyone else's. He ate mechanically, unaware of the calming peace his appetite gave to his mother.

"There weren't many eggs this morning," Sethiah commented as she refilled Zeke's plate with pork and potatoes. "Jezebel's in a stew because of the rain."

"That hen is always in a stew. Her red feathers make her mean," Zeke stated.

"The color red has nothin' to do with meanness," his mother countered.

"It does in this house," Ezekiel stated.

"You've got to try, Zeke." Sethiah poured her son more milk. "Mr. King has fed and clothed us for eleven years now. Try not to raise his ire."

Zeke ground his toe into the wood floor. It was rare that King was gone, that Zeke could safely speak. "He hates me, Mother. He would kill me if he weren't afraid it would send him to hell. Why am I so easy to hate?" Ezekiel's question hung desperately in the air.

Sethiah felt pain in her forehead. Her hand shook as she laid it on her son's shoulder. Ezekiel reached up and took the hand to steady it. Sethiah spoke. "God has not given Mr. King and me a child. Mr. King thinks it is because of my sin. But to me, you are easy to love, impossible to hate."

Ezekiel's heart pounded. What was she saying? He knew she was trying to comfort him, to explain . . . but he was filled with confusion. How had she sinned? Was he an unholy child as Mr. King claimed? What of his father who died in the war? "What was your sin?" The question leapt from the boy.

"My sins are my own," Sethiah whispered stiffly.

"We could leave this place, Mother," Ezekiel nearly shouted. Strange thoughts and questions coursed through him. "We could take Bill and never come back."

"Zeke, what would we eat?" Sethiah's voice came out low and fearful.

"I could work hard. I could take care of you."

"Zeke, you are a lad."

"Almost a man, Mother. One day, I will leave here and never see Jonathan King again in my life," Ezekiel's words tumbled out. "Who will you choose, Mother, your son or your husband?"

"Zeke, Zeke," Sethiah moaned. Her hand trembled violently in his, and her voice became high with fear. "Son, why do you tempt me? It is a terrible sin for a woman to leave her husband. I cannot commit such a crime. I must think on the times Mr. King is decent to me despite my sin."

"Then you choose to live in this misery?" Ezekiel's voice rose in confusion.

"I choose to live in heaven someday," Sethiah said with strange intensity. "I can never leave my husband."

Ezekiel moved his hand. Sethiah's fingers remained on his shoulder, fluttering like the wing of a dying bird. The sound of rain on shingles filled the silence between them. King had built this house, this sturdy, well-built, terrible place. Ezekiel imagined he heard Jonathan King's hammer above the clap of the storm.

The boy gulped down his milk. He felt a driving force rising within him, a need to be away from here. "I'd best be going," he said. His voice sounded like a man, not a child.

"Son, take Jonathan's other coat," Sethiah responded. "It's warm." The boy took the man's greased and waterproof coat off the peg and put it on. The long sleeves stretched past his hands. He donned a wide-brimmed hat to keep the rain off his face and put Jonathan King's purse in the pocket.

"I've made you lunch," Sethiah added as she took a meat pie from the larder and wrapped it in a pudding cloth. She scanned his face as if she hoped to remember every feature. "Put a rug on Bill to keep him dry."

Ezekiel nodded. "Good-bye, Mother."

"God go with you, son." Sethiah handed him the pie and reached out and touched the boy's cheek. Zeke turned and put the food in a knapsack. His heart quaked at her touch, for he knew it would be the last. He dared not think much of leaving her or Bill. He looked back at her once more and saw a tear on her cheek. Did she know he was going? Did she know that the things she had said at breakfast seared like lightning in his mind? *A person can live quite a while on thirty dollars . . . Mr. King thinks we do not have children because of my sin . . . I can never leave my husband . . . To me, you are easy to love, impossible to hate.*

Twenty minutes later, Ezekiel Johnson walked through the New England rain toward Jacob Wheelright's farm with water streaming neatly off his coat and the horse in tow. Thoughts clicked through his mind like tallies on a ledger. After the sale, he'd make like he was going home, then duck into the woods at the same place the children cut through on their way home from school. Their footsteps and the rain would erase his tracks. Then he'd head to town to have a word with Isaac. After that, his business would be done in Ashford, Connecticut. Forever.

The rain was easing up as Isaac Chapel stood in his shop inspecting the rake he had just finished. The teeth of the rake fit perfectly into the head. The haft was strong and sure, smooth in his hands. Isaac heard a knock at the back door. He put down the rake and opened it. For an instant, he didn't recognize Ezekiel standing there, water dripping from the hat that angled over his eyes and shaded his young features.

"Zeke, is that you?" Isaac grinned.

Zeke nodded quickly. "You're alone?"

"Just me and the cockroaches." Isaac stretched his arm around the boy, pulling him in out of the rain. "What brings you here today? Does our stoic Mr. King fancy a new rake? If he sent you here this late, he must mean for you to spend the night with me and Lizbeth. I will see you laugh before morning, my serious young priest."

Zeke blew out a sharp breath and moved away from Isaac's arm so that he could face the man squarely. "He didn't send me here, Isaac. I've run away. I want a word with you."

Isaac looked intently at the boy, his smile fading. He thought of how he had left home to join the army when only a few years older than Zeke. Although he came through the revolution unscathed physically, memories of comrades who died and those whom Isaac killed still troubled him. When a man cried in terror, Isaac felt his own soul tormented.

"Mr. King can be cruel, Zeke. But the world is a harsh place for a penniless boy."

Ezekiel did not flinch.

"You are set in this," Isaac asked.

Ezekiel nodded.

Isaac continued, "Then I will give you what money I can."

"I don't need money, Isaac. I have thirty dollars from the sale of Bill."

Isaac raised his eyebrows. He thought of Sethiah and her tired, gray eyes. "Ezekiel, your mother will suffer keenly if you leave."

Zeke shrugged and shook his head. He didn't want to talk about this.

"Zeke, you must consider her," Isaac pressed.

"She won't come with me," the boy muttered.

"She knows you are going?"

Zeke's voice crescendoed with emotion as he spoke. "I told her that someday I would go, that someday she must choose. She told me she will never leave King."

The boy was shaking. Isaac knew of the beatings, of the ill-use he had suffered at King's hands. "Sit down, son," he said gently, guiding Ezekiel to a chair.

Zeke sat down, but there was tension in him.

"Where will you go, Zeke? To the sea?"

Zeke shook his head. "I don't hanker to work on some slave ship. I can learn a trade or work hard in the fields."

"There are masters as cruel as Jonathan King," Isaac muttered as he paced across the floor. "Zeke, wait here while I go home and get you food and my horse."

"No," Zeke responded. "King will come here first. I can't wait. I came here to ask you to watch over my mother. I won't come back. Never."

"Never is a long time," Isaac said wisely. "But I'll watch over her. Always."

"Isaac, if you break your word, my ghost will come back and haunt you."

At this, Isaac smiled gently. "Boy, I'm older than you. I figure I'll be the first one dead." Then tenderness filled Isaac, and he embraced the boy, repeating the words his own father had said when Isaac left home. "Child, may God go with you."

Zeke moved carefully away. "God's got no use for me," he muttered.

"Boy, you've learned all the wrong things about God," Isaac said quietly. Then he walked to the fire. As he spoke, he fingered his shotgun, which hung nearby. It was a beautiful piece. Trimmed with silver, there wasn't a finer gun in New England. "Zeke, make your way to Albany, New York. Find a man there by the name of John Pilling. He knows smithing and carpentry. Tell him I've sent you and he's to find a place for you. I knew John in the war." Isaac picked up the gun and placed it in Zeke's hands. "Take this, son, and be safe."

Tears gathered in Zeke's eyes as he stared at the gift.

"Only use it for defense or food. Never unjustly kill a man."

Zeke nodded. "I promise," he said gravely.

He looked so young to Isaac as he stood there trying not to cry. Isaac wanted to cheer him. He grinned and clapped Zeke on the shoulder. "Since it will be your only companion for a while, give it a name, Zeke, a woman's name. Something soft and pretty."

Suddenly Zeke grinned through his tears. "Betsy," he said. "Bess for short, after our cow."

Isaac laughed out loud. He found the ammunition, then took an apple and some honey out of a drawer and packed the items in Zeke's knapsack.

"Go now, my boy," Isaac said gently.

As Ezekiel hoisted the knapsack to his shoulder, he asked one more question. "Isaac, do you know anything about my father?"

Isaac shook his head. "No. But there was a letter once that your mother wrote to a woman in Grafton, Massachusetts, by the name Esther Hills. I delivered it there when I had some business that way. Mrs. Hills told me she has known your mother all her life."

Ezekiel nodded and repeated the name. "Esther Hills from Grafton, Massachusetts." Zeke put on his hat. "Good-bye Isaac," he said. "I'll try to become a man as worthy as you."

Isaac put his arms around Ezekiel for the last time. "You already are," he said. This time Ezekiel returned the embrace. Isaac walked the boy to the back door of his shop and watched him as he disappeared into the woods.

*September 1798*

It was a windless day in Grafton, Massachusetts, as fifteen-year-old Julia Hills poured molten soap into molds. Julia whispered a silent prayer thanking the Lord for giving her the energy, strength, and skill to work. The Savior she loved noticed the sparrow's fall.

"Ho, Jule," her older brother Joel entered the tidy New England kitchen. He lowered his lanky frame, allowing a load of firewood to fall from his arms into a metal bracket.

"Such a fine day." Julia smiled at him. "I'm tempted to be idle today with everyone else gone. But idleness is a sin."

Joel grinned. "A sin I embrace! A quiet afternoon to read!"

Julia raised her eyebrows at Joel.

There was a knock at the door. "Attend to it, Jule," Joel said, getting up and winking. "I have an appointment upstairs with a certain book of essays."

"You still have the chicken coop, barn wall, and roof to fix," Julia called after him. "And it would be better for you to read the Bible."

"Beware," Joel called down from the top of the stairs. "You're my sister, not my mother. As a son I obey; as a brother I torment."

Julia shook her head. Joel was lucky he had a kind heart. Though he was two years older, Julia often felt his senior. She hurried to the door and unlatched it. Her eyes widened at the young man before her. He was of average height, his clothes stained and worn from travel. He possessed a fine build and a way of standing with his head slightly cocked that gave him a look of attentiveness. His hair was a soft ginger brown and curled at the ends. His eyes were the blue-gray of ice on a lake in the winter. His nose edged toward prominence, and his brows were arrow straight.

"Miss," the young man addressed Julia, "I'm looking for Mrs. Esther Forbush, formerly Mrs. Hills."

"You've come to the right house, sir," Julia said politely. "I'm Julia Hills. My mother married Mr. Forbush five years ago."

Joel came back downstairs with his book. He stepped up next to his sister. "Hello, I'm Joel Hills," he greeted the stranger with a handshake. "The rest of our family is in Upton looking at a team of oxen. May I ask what business you have with our mother?"

"My mother was an old friend of Mrs. Forbush."

"Our family will be home late this afternoon," Joel explained. "Stay and have dinner with us. Mother is partial toward old friends."

Julia saw weariness beneath the man's strength. "Sir, would you like to eat and rest?"

The man looked gravely at the tall and lovely girl. Her deep brown hair was plaited into shiny braids arranged in a knot at the nape of her neck. Her eyes were colored so dark a brown that her pupils were barely visible. Yet despite the darkness of her eyes and hair, her skin was fair. "You are most kind, Miss Julia. But, I have lunch in my pack. I'd be much obliged if I could water my horse, then I'll do any work you need before dinner."

"This is good news," Joel exclaimed. "The roof of the chicken coop needs fixing, and one of our horses kicked a hole in the barn wall. Jule, I might be able to finish my book!"

Julia glanced sideways at Joel, then spoke pleasantly to the stranger. "Sir, you won't do my brother a favor by working for him. He must learn that labor is a Godly burden."

The man answered with a slight smile. "But if your brother reads to me while I labor, then the work is done and my mind has been enlarged. A much needed improvement."

Julia couldn't keep herself from glancing at the gentleman's face. She decided that his eyes were like the sky in the spring, the weather changing each time she looked into them.

Joel laughed. "Well said. If my sister had her way, we would both work while she read the Bible aloud to us. Though I love God and keep his commandments, sometimes His word is a bit tedious." Joel yawned.

"But your sister's voice—that would not be tedious." The young man glanced at Julia.

"You don't know my sister well," Joel teased. "Her lectures and scolding are exhausting."

Color rose to Julia's cheeks. She ignored Joel and smiled politely at their guest. "Sir, you have not told us your name, nor where you are from."

"Ezekiel Johnson. I've lived in many places, most recently Albany. But I was born a stone's throw from here in Uxbridge."

"I've never heard of an Ezekiel Johnson from Uxbridge," Joel commented.

"I left when I was a babe," Ezekiel explained. "I have not been back until today."

"Then you have come home," Julia stated.

Ezekiel let out a short, bitter laugh. "Home to a place I know nothing of?"

Surprised by the bitterness in his voice, Julia sought for something to say. "Did you bring a wife or children with you?"

"I have no family," he said shortly.

"Really?" Joel's voice was light. "No mother and father. No sisters and brothers. I am envious if all of your days are as peaceful as this one."

Ezekiel's face hardened. "Boy, you don't fathom what you say."

Julia heard pain in his voice as clearly as if she had seen a wound bleed. His family must have died. Words rushed from her as she reached out and touched his arm. "Mr. Johnson, Joel meant no offense. If by wishing or praying, Joel or I could bring back your family, we would."

At these words, the man looked down and studied his worn boots. Embarrassed, Julia knew she had no right to be so familiar. She focused on the apple orchard and yearned for its shade to cool the hotness of her cheeks.

But within Ezekiel, her kind words struck a chord that reverberated. He had come on his own lonely business, expecting nothing. As he stood there staring at the ground, tears pooled in his eyes, and his restless nature trembled and halted.

"Excuse me, Mr. Johnson. I must start dinner," Julia said stiffly.

"Thank you, Miss Julia," Ezekiel looked up, blinking as if the sun were too bright.

After she left, Ezekiel gathered his thoughts. He had come here to ask an ugly question. Instead, he had found this lovely girl. Her words shone with such innocent compassion—the balm of hope on a stranger's weary wounds. His intention to inquire as to the legitimacy of his birth wavered for a moment. He felt an intense desire to know Julia better, to rest in the steady warmth of her kind, confident brown eyes. Yet if he anchored himself to someone so precious as this girl, he would be in perilous waters. To lose such a gift could destroy him. Ezekiel shook his head to wake himself up. His eyes met Joel's. The boy watched him quizzically.

Ezekiel thumped the boy on the back. "Come, Joel. Let's get to it. Work is a godly burden, as your sister so kindly told us."

"Would that she were less kind," Joel joked.

"I wish so as well," Ezekiel stated, leaving the boy to wonder at the sudden defeated tone of this stranger's voice.

Julia spent the afternoon in the kitchen preparing supper and resolving not to think of the stranger. In the late afternoon, the meal was nearly finished, and Julia heard noise in the yard. She hurried to the front door and opened it. Her family was home with two oxen in tow. Joel was introducing Ezekiel Johnson.

Julia's stepfather, the short, bald Enoch Forbush, climbed out of the wagon seat. "Why Mr. Johnson," he boomed. "There is always room for a weary traveler at my table. Especially one who helped old Joel work so industriously!" Thirteen-year-old Nancy gaped at the handsome, beardless stranger. Joel hefted four-year-old Enoch Jr. onto his shoulders. Mr. Forbush lifted a sleepy little girl out of the wagon bed.

The children's mother, Esther Forbush, stepped out of the wagon with a baby in her arms. She studied the young man. Her eyes were dark and calm—much like Julia's but bordered by fine wrinkles. Her dark hair was streaked with gray. She stood shorter and rounder than her daughter. "Ezekiel Johnson," Esther thoughtfully repeated the stranger's name as she looked into the gray-blue eyes. "I am so pleased you have come to Grafton and my home."

"Mr. Johnson," Mr. Forbush asked at supper. "What is your trade?"

"Right now I sell cowbells. But I'm a housewright as well, sir. Someday I hope to buy virgin land, divide it, build cabins on it, and sell it to settlers for a substantial profit."

The older man grinned. "I wish you luck, laddie. Are you here to sell *me* something?"

Ezekiel hesitated for an instant. "No, sir. I was born in Uxbridge but left long ago. I'm alone now and have come to ask Mrs. Forbush what she knows of my history."

"Tell us his history, Esther," Enoch's voice boomed down the table to his wife.

Julia and Nancy paused in their serving, not wanting to miss a word. Little Enoch looked up from his food, sensing something important about to transpire. Esther wiped her mouth on her napkin and placed it back in her lap. She smiled at her husband. When she spoke, her tone was calm and clear. "Dear husband, privately I'll tell Mr. Johnson whatever he wishes, for I loved his mother. Then he may give his story to whom he chooses."

Esther's refusal to obey her husband caused Ezekiel to flinch. Involuntarily, he stiffened, thinking Enoch Forbush's face would contort with anger.

But Enoch Forbush beamed at his wife fondly, then turned to Ezekiel. "There you have it, Mr. Johnson. My wife is a woman with her own mind. You should hear her tell the minister just what she thinks of the doctrine of the elect. But when she keeps a secret, she keeps it. When her mouth is closed, it is closed."

"And she swallows no flies," Joel added.

The younger children burst into laughter.

"I have a smart, opinionated wife and children I dare not let out in society," Forbush boomed. "What do you think, Mr. Johnson? What's a man to do?" Then Forbush's laughter filled the dining room, tumbling as free as water over a fall.

After supper, Esther invited Ezekiel to walk outside with her. A brisk wind blew from the north as the sun edged behind distant hills. Esther pulled her cloak closer around her. *The past exists in every breath and heartbeat,* she thought, *in what grows and what dies, in the babe who once was the young man next to me.* As they passed the garden and gained the orchard, the colors of the sky deepened. Esther spoke. "Most of this orchard was planted eleven years ago. The year Mr. Hills died. The peaches bore fruit in four years, the apples in six. The children and I ate our first apples the year I wed Mr. Forbush. He has been a kind stepfather to my first three children and a doting father to the next three."

"You are fortunate indeed," Ezekiel commented.

Esther spoke earnestly. "Were you fortunate, Ezekiel? Was Jonathan King kind?"

Ezekiel shook his head and looked in the distance "No. He was harsh, unbearably harsh. I ran away when a lad of fourteen. Eleven years ago—the same year Mr. Hills died."

"A dark year for both of us," Esther remarked as they walked slowly forward. "Poor, sweet Sethiah. What became of her, Ezekiel? Did she have more children?"

Ezekiel shrugged. "None when I left. Last week, I tried for the first time to find my mother, but she and King have moved to Canada. None of the neighbors know where."

"Did your mother tell you of me?"

Zeke shook his head. "No. My stepsister's husband, Isaac Chapel, gave me your name on the day I ran away."

Esther stopped walking and stood deep in thought. She could not blame Sethiah for wanting to keep the circumstances of Ezekiel's birth a secret. Indeed, that would explain why she had never told her son of Esther. But the past was not a stone box to be buried. Yet Sethiah's past was like Pandora's box brimming with horrors. For an instant, Esther hesitated to open it. She prayed that young Ezekiel would find hope left after all else blew free.

The young man standing beside Esther shuffled his feet, reminding Esther of a horse pawing. Esther spoke. "Years ago, Mr. Chapel brought me the only letter I ever received from your mother. With the letter was a lock of your hair and a baby tooth you had lost."

"Did you know my father?" Ezekiel asked.

Esther did not answer immediately, but asked a question of her own. "What has your mother told you about him?"

Ezekiel felt suddenly irritable. "Why does it matter?"

"It matters a great deal to me," Esther replied. "When I was young, your mother worked for my mother, tending us children. She was about twelve years old when she started and I a lass of eight. She sang songs with us. We ran races and wove flowers in our hair. When my entire family was sick with fever, it was your mother who attended my bed and nursed me back to health. Sethiah was as a sister to me."

Zeke answered simply. "She told me God sanctioned their union. She told me he was a patriot and died at Bunker Hill. She told me I am named after him."

"Come, Ezekiel," Esther said gently. "Sit with me on the garden bench and I will tell you all I know."

The sky darkened and the stars came out one by one. Esther began, "When your mother was about my Julia's age, a young man named Ezekiel Johnson lived in Grafton. He was a dashing and reckless patriot. He was present at the 1770 Boston Massacre. He spoke constantly of freedom from the chains of England.

"He became enamored with your mother and asked for her hand. Ebenezer Smith, your mother's stepfather, feared Ezekiel's reckless patriotism and refused him as a suitor. Brought up as an obedient daughter, Sethiah yielded to her stepfather's will, though it grieved her heart. How Sethiah loved Ezekiel! To her he was as dear as the air she breathed.

"Then, one day in late spring, Ezekiel brought a note to me and begged me to carry it to Sethiah. He had an assignment from the Sons of Liberty and must leave soon. This was his final chance to contact his beloved. With a girl's romantic heart, I gave it to my dear friend, not fathoming that the note contained the instructions for a rendezvous that night. Thus it happened that under the stars on the last day of May 1772, Ezekiel Johnson convinced Sethiah Guernsey that he loved her as no man had loved a woman before. He told her that she was his wife in God's eyes. Then, in the beguiling disguise of gentle love, he recklessly took from Sethiah her youth and innocence.

"When Sethiah realized she was with child, Ezekiel was gone. Afraid and confused, she would not tell anyone who had fathered the infant. Sethiah's irate stepfather and distraught mother kept her situation secret for as long as possible.

"A few months before you were born, a traveler stopped by my house to tell us of the Committee of Correspondence that had been formed in Boston. He explained the steps each American must take to resist British measures. He also asked if we were acquainted with a fellow Son of Liberty from these parts named Ezekiel Johnson. He said that this brave young patriot was now living in Holliston and was engaged to Rachel Merrifield. The next morning, I ran to your mother and told her she must tell Ezekiel of her situation before he married Rachel. The color fled from her cheeks, and for days she would not eat or drink. She felt that God was punishing her. She became very ill and both feared and hoped she would lose the baby. But you, who were destined to live, hung on to life tenaciously. Despite her agony, Sethiah would not go to Ezekiel. She had grown up knowing Rachel, and she would not cast the shadow of her shame on the girl.

"After you were born, Sethiah was forced to answer to the Grand Jury for the crime of fornication. The court insisted Sethiah name the child's father. She refused, and no one could bend her will. She was found guilty of fornication, of concealing her pregnancy, and of bringing into the world an unholy child. Sethiah was fined five shillings to be paid to the king. My father and mother felt compassion for Sethiah and paid the fine."

Esther stopped speaking for a moment. The young man next to her stared out into the night. He wasn't wearing a coat. "Are you cold?" she asked. He quickly shook his head. Esther gently touched his hand, and it felt like frozen clay. She drew her hand away and continued. "Sethiah worked for my mother while I tended you. You were the most exquisite and wondrous little being. Sethiah hadn't given you a name, and so we called you Little One.

"Summer passed and winter came. On a clear day in December, Sethiah and I were in the wagon on an errand. Sethiah drove the mules while I held you, nearly a year old now, in my arms. You were bundled in blankets and fast asleep. Your father, whom we had not seen for a year and a half, rode up to us. Your mother stopped the mules. I thought I saw her heart beating through the layers of clothing. She beckoned me to give you to her and handed me the reins. Her gloved hands trembled.

"Ezekiel Johnson jumped from his horse. He was disheveled. Word had reached him that Sethiah Guernsey had borne an illegitimate son. He demanded to know if the child were his. When she answered in the affirmative, he tore at his hair, and agonized sobs rent his frame. He begged her forgiveness. He swore he would go mad if he married Rachel knowing that Sethiah and his son suffered in silent shame. But Rachel was also with child.

"He told Sethiah that he would go to Boston and participate in an uprising planned against the British Tea Act. He would seek death in the fight for American Independence, praying his blood atoned for his sins. Weeping, he begged her to tell her son that his father died fighting for freedom.

"She reached out to him and held his head in her lap next to his babe. She bathed his hot forehead with her tears. Finally, he kissed his son's cheek and left us. That was the last word Sethiah ever heard from Ezekiel. From that day forth, your mother called you after your father, Ezekiel Johnson."

After Esther finished speaking, darkness and silence encircled the two like a thick mist shutting the world out. An owl winged through the sky. Finally Ezekiel spoke. His teeth clenched tightly against the warm vapor of his words. "So King spoke the truth."

"I knew Jonathan King," Esther commented. "He was not worthy to marry your mother."

"Why do you speak of my mother as if she were a saint?" Ezekiel burst. "She was weak and dishonest! She told me my father was an honorable man. Yet he was the worst of scoundrels. My name, my very existence, reek of shame."

"Oh, Ezekiel," Esther rejoined, her voice as warmly passionate as his was icily bitter. "Your parents' sins do not shame you. Our Lord was born to earth through the line of David and Bathsheba. The very Bathsheba who was the wife of Uriah, the man David purposely sent to death in battle. What a grievous sin David committed. Yet through David and Bathsheba came the Son of God—the Christ who freely forgave the woman taken in sin and told her to go and sin no more. We are not responsible for our parents' sins any more than we are condemned because of Adam's sin. Our own sins are enough to bear.

"Ezekiel, this is a new country. Aristocrat and laborer have the same rights as citizens. There is freedom and abundant hope for a young man like you."

Ezekiel's voice was bitter. "Not all are free. There are slaves in this country. Parents' sins follow their children. Mrs. Forbush, a kind lady such as you would not wish for a man with my background to woo or marry her daughter."

Esther was quiet for a moment, and Ezekiel knew that the arrow of his words had found the mark of truth. Yet when she spoke, her voice was sturdy. "You do not know me, Ezekiel Johnson. If your heart proved gentle, loving, hardworking, and loyal, then I would welcome you as a suitor to my Julia."

"And if it did not?" Ezekiel asked, his voice barely audible.

"Then I would ask Mr. Forbush to tar and feather you before driving you from town," Esther remarked with a twinkle in her voice. "But I trust that won't be so."

"You are the noblest, kindest woman I have ever met," Ezekiel whispered brokenly.

"Oh, dear young man," Esther said as she put her hand over his. "It is easy to seem noble when one has been blessed as I have been. But if I had lived Sethiah's life, I fear that I would not seem so noble."

# 1

*Since then I have listened to strains of sweet music*
*The sweetest that nature or art could produce,*
*The song of the birds, the harp organ or viol*
*The sweetest of singing, but then 'tis no use*
*To compare with the notes that I heard in my childhood*
*On that bright sunny spot in the place I was born*
*Give me back the sweet strains of that dear cherished music*
*My mother to blow it, the old Dinner Horn.*

—George W. Johnson, from "The Old Dinner Horn"

*December 1828*

Julia stepped outside her cottage to blow the dinner horn. She paused for a moment to briefly admire the beauty of the afternoon. It was nearing one o'clock, and the windswept sky shone clear and blue. Shifting her weight, she placed her hand on her back to more comfortably bear the burden of her unborn child. Seven months along with her sixteenth child, forty-five-year-old Julia relaxed her shoulders, thus surrendering her usual regal carriage to rest in the quiet of the moment.

These brief seconds of solitude were precious indeed. With winter approaching and each day's light diminishing, Julia felt deeply thankful for the containers of preserves, dried fruit, and cider filling the kitchen cellar. Dried meat hung from the ceiling, and bins overflowed with grain. The endless and nearly back-breaking labor of every able-bodied member of the family had yielded ample fruit.

She glanced past the orchard and down the hill toward Canadaway Creek where thick foliage grew. The once leafy trees stood mostly barren now with the scarlet and yellow leaves molding on the ground. Five of her children tramped somewhere in those woods, making a contest of gathering nuts and a game of finding rocks for candle dipping.

Julia pivoted, and her dark eyes drank in the northwestern view. Beyond the woodland, she could make out the whitecaps of Lake Erie mingling with the gray-blue sky. Listening closely, she heard the sound of voices in the forest where Ezekiel and her older sons labored chopping wood for the winter. Two of these sons, Seth and David, were grown men now but unmarried and living at home. Julia's oldest son, Joel, named after her brother, had his own family and lived a few miles away. Julia's three oldest daughters, Nancy, Delcena, and Julianne, were inside putting the finishing touches on the meal. These six siblings who had tussled when they were young were now very close.

The joy of these grown children filled Julia as she stood on the porch. If this pride was sinful, she did not know how to overcome it. Hard-working, God-fearing men and women, they were noble jewels in her eyes. She loved them, rejoiced in them, and feared for them. She had discovered that the concerns of motherhood did not end when children reached adulthood; they only became more difficult to soothe. And yet what a satisfaction to watch fully formed individuals emerge from her seed and nourishment. That she and Ezekiel had a part in their being amazed her. Yet she knew they were God's children first and her children second.

Julia breathed deeply and straightened her back. The moments of contemplation ended as a gust of wind caught her stray tresses. Julia pushed back those strands of black hair, now streaked with gray. There was no more time for quiet thought. Today was a day for life and work. Julia lifted the dinner horn hanging near the door and blew it loud and long. She remained on the porch, waiting to greet her tribe.

A few moments later, noise filled the yard. They came from the wildwood and the creek bed, these whom she treasured, each with a story to tell. She kissed them as they passed the threshold— first gangly, bossy nine-year-old Mary, her apron turned up to hold a quantity of nuts, then the rambunctious little boys, George and William, with grimy hands and rocks in their pockets, and finally Baby Esther who was not yet two, her face flushed and heart beating fast in the struggle to keep up.

Once the little ones had kissed their mother, sixteen-year-old Almera and fourteen-year-old Susan whisked them away to wash their hands and faces before dinner. Next, adolescents Benjamin and Joseph rushed toward the door, grinning as they dodged their mother's kisses. Finally, Seth and David entered, chatting together about fixing Joel's roof that afternoon. Each bid their mother a cheerful hello.

There was only one left to welcome, her husband, Ezekiel. Julia sighed, thinking of how strain rather than companionship defined their relationship lately. She recalled three nights ago when Ezekiel had stayed late at the tavern drinking. Exhausted from her pregnancy and knowing he would come home intoxicated, Julia had left a quilt for him on the rocking chair and gone to bed, barring the door to block his entry into their bedroom. She had known that Seth, who was reading by candlelight, would wait up for his father. A few hours later, Julia had awakened at the sound of a door slamming and Ezekiel's loud and drunken voice. Then she had heard Seth gently coaxing his father to lie down and rest. That night, Seth had given his father his own bed and slept on a hand woven rug in front of the fire. An inebriated father was a heavy burden for this twenty-three-year-old son.

"My Julia," Ezekiel's voice called to his wife. He gained the porch and stood before her, his skin ruddy from wind and work. He reached behind her and closed the door to give them privacy. She knew that despite her age and pregnancy, he found her lovely. She placed her hand gently on his cheek. Julia looked into his eyes and felt a glimmer of hope for today. They were clear and blue-gray, not reddened from drink. His hair was gray too, but his arms were muscular from years of taming primeval forest. The wrinkles on his swarthy cheeks did not diminish his manliness. Then Ezekiel spoke the words he had uttered countless times since the day of their marriage. "I love you, Julia Hills Johnson, more than the heavens above and the earth beneath."

"And I love you most of all," Julia answered.

"More than God even?" Ezekiel challenged.

Julia lowered her eyes and did not answer. *More than peach brandy even?* she would have questioned had she not known that it would splinter this moment. She loved this man, and yet, even after over thirty years of knowing him, she did not fully understand him. If only he could find strength through God rather than escape through intemperance. Ezekiel pulled her close and kissed her. She breathed in the essence of him. He was her strength and her weakness, her joy and her pain. He was her husband, her Ezekiel.

A knock sounded at the front door just as the dishes were cleared and a dessert of cornmeal pudding with maple molasses was brought out. Delcena's light brown eyes darted toward the sound. Her deep brown hair curled in shiny ringlets around her face. Today, she was the only sister dressed in her Sunday clothes. With heart pounding, Delcena knew who stood at the door. Lyman had promised that he would come to ask for her hand. Calming herself, she thought of how Pa was sober and of how her mother had assured her that her father bore Lyman Sherman goodwill. Still, Delcena feared. She remembered Nancy's experience two years ago. When the widower Sam Granger had asked for Nancy's hand, her father, with drink in his belly, had shouted that no daughter of Ezekiel Johnson's would wed a man who beat his dog to death and whipped his young child. Nancy had bent to her father's will like a willow in the wind. But if her father refused, Delcena would not lose Lyman. Delcena uttered a silent prayer, asking that her father would see her as a twenty-two-year-old woman rather than as his little girl.

Little George and William flew to the door and answered it. Baby Esther would have been there too if she had not, after a few bites of pudding, climbed onto her father's lap and fallen asleep. Shouts of "Hello, Mr. Sherman," "Delcie, Mr. Sherman's here," and "Are you gonna talk to Pa, Mr. Lyman?" filled the room.

"Come in, Lyman Sherman," Ezekiel's voice rang out over the group. "Have some pudding."

Nancy and Seth quickly made Lyman feel welcome. Tall, gentlemanly Seth stood and embraced his friend, leaving an empty spot on the bench next to Delcena. Nancy went to the pantry to get Lyman a bowl of pudding. After shaking Ezekiel's hand and admiring the sleeping child in his lap, Lyman took his seat. Without looking at his intended, Lyman felt for Delcena's hand and, at the feel of it trembling, stroked her palm with his thumb.

Lyman's purpose today was clear, for he was dressed in a dark broadcloth suit and a stock tie. His wire-rimmed glasses magnified his expressive, brown, long-lashed eyes. His cheeks were reddened from the cool, outside air, and his beardless face bore a flawless complexion, causing him to appear younger than his twenty-four years. Of average height and build, his features were very pleasing, and Nancy had once told Delcena that her beau had the look of an angel.

For a moment, all was quiet as the Johnson clan watched Lyman gently let go of Delcena's hand and begin eating his pudding.

Eighteen-year-old David spoke, his brown-gold eyes gleaming merrily. "Lyman, old man, why don't you come with Seth and me to put a new roof on Joel's house this afternoon? We could use a hand. That is unless you're busy today."

Delcena shot a look of warning at her teasing brother, but Lyman remained undeterred.

"I would, David," Lyman smiled, "but I have other business here today. If the roof can wait until tomorrow, I shall be there before the sun rises."

"Mr. Lyman isn't dressed for *working*," twelve-year-old Joseph added with a conspiratory wink at David.

"There are many kinds of work, Joseph," Julia said, sensing her daughter's discomfort with her brothers' merriment. "Some of the most difficult is done in one's best clothes. Think of preachers and schoolmasters."

"Here, here," Seth, who was the local schoolmaster, agreed.

"Speaking of preachers, Mrs. Johnson," Lyman said as he reached into the pocket of his suit and pulled out a newspaper article. "My cousin Philastus Hurlbut sent me an interesting and troubling article from the *Niagara Courier.*" With that, Lyman proceeded to read an article that told of an illiterate young man from Palmyra professing to have seen an angel who had shown and delivered up to him an ancient book of hieroglyphics on plates of gold, along with huge spectacles for interpreting the characters. From these plates, the young man had purportedly translated a new Bible. One of the few believers was an honest and industrious farmer from the area named Martin Harris, who had agreed to finance the publication of the book.

"I'm not surprised that Doctor Philastus has served up an article full of rubbish," Ezekiel said when Lyman finished reading.

Julia gently chided her husband. "Philastus is Mr. Sherman's kinsman and thus deserves our respect."

"A man's actions, not his birth, command respect," Ezekiel countered. Then he looked directly at Lyman. "Philastus's father was a great friend of mine in Vermont and has my respect. But when young Philastus visited a year ago, he told my daughters to call him Doctor Hurlbut and bragged of his powers of healing and discernment. The man is full of himself."

"Papa, please," Delcena begged.

"No, Delcena," Ezekiel countered. "Your young man will know the lay of the land in this household."

"I appreciate your forthrightness, Mr. Johnson," Lyman said thoughtfully. "When Philastus was a child, my aunt called him

Doctor, and told him he was her seventh son and, thus, blessed by heaven with power. I fear this has affected Philastus and made him proud from childhood. Yet, Mr. Johnson, I would ask for your patience with him. Philastus studies the Bible diligently and has a generous heart. It is my hope that God will help my cousin overcome his weakness. A year ago, Philastus introduced me to Delcena. For that most choice blessing, I am in his debt."

Ezekiel studied young Lyman Sherman. The man spoke well and earnestly. Ezekiel remembered his own first dinner with Julia's family. Enoch Forbush had treated him with great kindness and hospitality. Esther Forbush had given him bitter truth and the brightest hope. He nodded approvingly at Delcena's young man. "Well said, Lyman. But when a man's flaw is his very nature, as I fear is the case with your cousin, I have never seen it overcome."

"But Husband," Julia said earnestly. "Aren't we all dual-natured and subject to faults?" She thought of Ezekiel's drinking and her own impatience. "Surely God is the master surgeon, and through faith in the sacrifice of His Son, any man's flaw or weakness can be miraculously overcome."

Ezekiel gazed at his wife, but did not answer.

"Ma," eleven-year-old Benjamin cut into the conversation. Dark-eyed Benjamin's nature was earnest and, at times, brooding. "Why would anybody have special power just 'cause they are the seventh son?"

Joseph, intelligent and talkative, laughed. "Good point, Ben. Will's the seventh son and look at him!" All eyes fell on little William, his face covered with food, as he intently placed rocks from his pockets into his pudding.

David chuckled. "Superstition tells us that the seventh son has powers of creation, and William is creating a town in his pudding."

Laughter skipped across the table, but Benjamin wasn't about to be put off.

"Mother, why is the seventh son so important?"

Julia turned to Ben. "Son, superstition abounds. Some people believe that because the world was created in seven days and because God has ordained the seventh day as the Sabbath, that a seventh son in a family is endowed with great power for good or for evil."

"Do you believe that, Ma?" Ben questioned.

"No, Benjamin. I believe that every person has the power to choose good or evil, and we are blessed in God's eyes when we keep the commandments and when our hearts are filled with love for His Son, Jesus Christ."

"But, Ma," the boy continued, "remember when Seth and David saw that fireball cross the sky that night they were hunting coons?"

Julia nodded. "And I told you, Ben, that I thought it a sign of the near approach of the coming of Christ."

"Then couldn't that newspaper article be true? Couldn't that man have really seen an angel? Couldn't that be a sign of Christ's coming as well?"

Julia answered, "This Joseph Smith is likely one of the false prophets that the scriptures tell us will arise in the last days. Whether the young man lies of himself or is deluded by Satan, I don't know. In either case, my heart is troubled for his soul."

"Benja," Seth added, "in Acts, chapter five, the apostles Peter and John are put into prison and the council considers slaying them. A wise Pharisee named Gamaliel speaks out. He reviews the lives of a number of false prophets and explains how in a few short years, these men's followers were scattered and came to naught. Then he suggests leaving Peter and John alone, for if their work is of men, it will also come to naught. But if the work is of God, the council cannot overthrow it because they will only fight against the Almighty. This story teaches us a lesson, Ben. If this Smith is a false prophet, as I believe, he will come to naught. If perchance he speaks the truth and is engaged in God's work, then we will hear more of him and know him by his fruits."

Ben nodded, his question answered.

Joseph spoke up. "Seth, with your way of explaining Godly things, you ought to have been the seventh son."

Ezekiel restlessly arose from the table with baby Esther in his arms. Julia's and his children's religiosity caused him unease. He had seen too much of hypocrisy and fanaticism in his stepfather's home all in the name of the Almighty. This chasm separated him from his wife and children. He felt a driving need for a drink of brandy, but for the moment he battled the desire out of respect for his wife and daughter.

"Mr. Sherman," Ezekiel said, "after I put my babe to bed, I'll be back. If you have something to say to me, you'd best get ready to say it. My Nancy and I have a colt to break this afternoon."

When Ezekiel returned and sat back down at the head of the table, every eye turned to him. Anticipation hung in the air like living breath.

"Mr. Johnson, should we go into the sitting room to talk privately?" Lyman questioned.

"Whatever you have to say, Mr. Sherman, my entire family can hear," Ezekiel countered. Delcena ached inside. Her father wasn't making this easy.

"Mr. Johnson, I have come today," Lyman said steadily, "to beg the privilege of your daughter Delcena's hand in marriage."

"Will you cherish her and treat her right?" Ezekiel asked.

"Every day of my life," Lyman answered.

Ezekiel spoke thoughtfully. "Remember, son, that if you ever raise a hand against my girl or any of her children, I'm as handy with old Bess there," Ezekiel nodded toward his gun on the mantel, "as my wife is with her Bible on the stand."

A smile broke forth, radiating through all of Lyman. "You have nothing to fear from me, Mr. Johnson. I would want no less protection from the father of dear Delcena."

"Then you may have my daughter's hand with my blessing," Ezekiel announced with emotion, adding, "if it is Delcena's will."

"It is, Papa, it is," Delcena declared with tears in her eyes.

The family burst into cheers.

Ezekiel stood as Lyman and Delcena came to him. He embraced Lyman first and then hugged Delcena tenderly.

"I love you, Papa," Delcena whispered.

"And I love you, princess," Ezekiel said as Delcena rested her head against Ezekiel's chest. Her father touched her cheek with his callused finger and saw Delcena smile for joy.

After this exchange, Julia sighed with both relief and exhaustion. Ezekiel had behaved nobly, and Delcena's dreams were coming true. Julia already held Lyman in great esteem. Joel had married well too—Annie was a dear. She only prayed her other children did as well. With moist eyes, Julia watched the couple move around the table hugging each brother and sister. Then her turn came to embrace her daughter and future son-in-law.

"I'm so happy, Mama," Delcena said softly. "Should we stay and help with the work?"

"Go and enjoy the afternoon with your beau." Julia laughed. She hugged Delcena tightly, feeling the babe inside kick at the pressure.

"Thank you, Mrs. Johnson, for the pudding and more." Lyman grinned.

Julia watched the young couple nearly skip through the door hand-in-hand. One by one, members of the family left for their various tasks, leaving Julia, her daughters, and the littlest boys. Julia began clearing the table, though her limbs felt like they had been dipped in molasses.

"Mama," perceptive Nancy ventured, noticing Julia's fatigue, "why don't you rest? Almera and Susan will scour the trenchers while Julianne takes the little boys upstairs to nap. I'll sweep before I meet Pa in the barn."

"Nancy, catch George," Julianne said with a grin as she tossed Nancy a damp rag. "I'll chase down Will."

A moment later, Julianne and Nancy held the little boys firmly as they wiped hands and mouths. "Hold still, Wily Will!" Julianne laughed. Then she addressed her sister, "Nance, Seth left out his trousers and boots for you to wear when you ride."

"Oh, Nancy," Julia moaned. "I shudder at the thought of you wearing a man's clothes. What do you suppose the neighbors think when a lady dresses like that?"

"It saves my dresses," Nancy replied with a soft laugh as she let go of George, who spun away only to be reined in by the firm hand of Julianne, who then guided George and William up the wooden steps with the promise of a story. Nancy hugged her mother. "I'm a stronger rider sitting astride than sidesaddle. I'll pin my hair up under a palm leaf hat, and any passerby will think I'm one of the boys."

"And I'll cut off the ends of my hair," Julianne teased from the top of the steps. "We'll stick it under Nancy's nose with corn syrup. When neighbors go by, she'll look to all the world like Seth."

The little boys broke into peals of laughter. Mother Julia sighed in defeat. Nancy was old enough to make her own choices. Aching pain radiated from Julia's back down into her legs. "I do need a rest," she admitted. "But there is so much to do. Winter is coming, and a wedding and a baby."

"I know how you feel Mama," Almera blurted, her black eyes luminous and her cheeks red as she scoured a pot with ashes. Artistically gifted, the endless toil of frontier life made the intensely lovely girl restless. She added, "Mama, the work never ends. Sometimes, the thought of it drowns me. How I envy Delcie off with her beau! With her luck in love, she ought to at least share the work today."

Susan, a quiet, observant girl, thought Almera had nothing to complain about. Almera had more than her share of luck. Young men were always looking Almera's way, never Susan's.

Julia placed a hand on Almera's shoulder and said gently. "Try not to covet Delcena's joy on her engagement day. Yours will come soon enough when Delcena is laboring in her own household. Marriage is the beginning of a new life, but it is also the beginning of new burdens."

Almera shook her head and let out a quick breath. Sometimes the house felt so small and her longings so intense. She continued scouring the trencher.

Once alone in her room, with the babe moving within, Julia could not sleep. She thought of how just ninety minutes ago she had stepped outside to simply blow the dinner horn. With a wedding to plan and the delivery of her babe growing nigh, Julia wondered what tidings tomorrow would bring.

*Teach me, O Lord, to know Thy ways*
*To keep Thy statutes still,*
*That I may serve Thee all my days,*
*And do Thy holy will.*

*Establish, Lord. Thy word in me—*
*In Thy poor servant's heart,*
*That I may know none else but Thee,*
*And ne'er from Thee depart.*

*May my delight be in Thy word;*
*Oh, quicken me with grace!*
*That I may do Thy will, O Lord,*
*And live to see thy face.*

—JOEL H. JOHNSON

As David and Seth drove the wagonful of firewood to their brother Joel's place, clouds thickened in the sky. Upon arrival, their eyes were drawn to the red shingles piled near the south side of the rustic log cabin. "They are finely made," Seth commented. "Joel's rude cabin will have a royal roof." The shingles had been cut from white oak and dipped in resin to preserve them, hence the deep red hue.

"Joel! Annie!" David energetically called as he swung down from the wagon. He unhitched Cephas, allowing the elderly horse to graze unhindered in Joel's yard. "We have news today."

Annie opened the door and shut it behind her. Her thick auburn hair lay tucked beneath a white bonnet. She was a small, sturdy woman with expressive hazel eyes. She pressed a forefinger against her lips, and a smile dimpled her full cheeks. "Shh, David. Sixtus is asleep."

"Then I'll wake him and play with him." David grinned as he hugged his sister-in-law, who was more than a full head shorter. "Where's that brother of ours?"

"Joel went with my father to meet with Judge Houghton. He should be back soon. Come in, you two. I made a spice cake yesterday. Just speak quietly. Sixtus kept us awake last night."

"I'll throttle my little brother if he speaks too loudly and wakes the baby," Seth whispered with a smile.

"I'd be much obliged," Annie chuckled. Seth thought of how it was good to hear her laugh. He felt as close to Annie as to his own sisters. Four years ago, Annie had been a dear friend of Sophia, Seth's fiancée. When the delicate Sophia died from a kitchen burn turned gangrenous just three weeks before the wedding, Annie had comforted Seth with stories of Sophia's girl-hood and of Sophia's childlike joy in Seth's love. In turn, Seth had stayed with Joel and Annie after their two-year-old girl, Julianne, passed away last summer. Seth had harvested Joel's crops, nursed his ill brother, and counseled the stricken Annie with his testimony of eternal life.

The three sat down at the table, and Annie cut both young men a piece of cake, which neither refused, though they had finished dinner just an hour ago. She offered them a small glass of cordial. David accepted with a twinkling eye. Seth declined the spirited drink, requesting water instead.

"Now for the news," Annie declared after she had served her guests.

"Guess," David grinned at her slyly.

Annie paused. "Hmm. Your brother Joseph discovered buried treasure at the bottom of Canadaway Creek?"

David shook his head earnestly. "Try again."

"David, you have hooked a young woman?" Annie exclaimed.

Seth smiled at the banter between the two.

"I hook them, but they twist free and escape my net." David laughed.

"Not so. You toss the poor things back into the creek," Annie countered, thinking of how David was such a handsome lad at six feet three inches tall, with powerful shoulders and legs. His curly, light brown hair and brown eyes flecked with gold complemented his engaging laugh. He would break many hearts.

Then Annie's eyes widened. "Mother Julia hasn't delivered her babe, has she?"

"Not yet," Seth said.

"A hint," David added. "A member of our family has landed her own fish."

"Hmm." With elbows on the table, Annie rested her chin in her hands. "Lyman and Delcena are engaged."

David snapped his fingers and loudly proclaimed, "Right! How do women know these things? Do you send thoughts to each other over time and space?"

Annie laughed. The baby fussed for an instant, then let out a wail.

Annie pointed a forefinger at David. "Throttle him, Seth."

As Seth reached for his brother, David jumped up and darted toward the door. "I think I'll fix the shingles before it rains," he called as he exited the cabin.

Seth stood. He was an inch shorter than David and slender, with dark eyes and black hair. Scholarly and deeply religious, Seth was manly and elegant, a gentleman in every sense of the word. He taught the winter school in Pomfret and was loved and revered by the community.

Seth paused for a moment as he watched Annie pick up her son. Sixtus quieted and closed his eyes at his mother's touch. Annie sat in the rocking chair with the child in her arms.

"He's beautiful," Seth admired as he cleared the table. Then he walked over to the two. He reached a hand out to touch the babe's bald head, feeling the incomparable softness of an infant's skin. The child stretched, made a sucking motion with his mouth, and closed his eyes.

"Joel says I mustn't pick him up so quickly," Annie commented. "He fears I'll spoil him. Yet I can't help myself. Only Sixtus calms the ache in my arms for Julianne. Seth, do you think God will let us keep him?"

"I pray so. Yet, we must strive to trust in God's wisdom, Annie," Seth said gently.

"Sometimes God's wisdom confuses me," Annie uttered as quick tears filled her eyes. "Still, I thank Him every day for this child."

"May I hold him?" Seth ventured.

Annie smiled and handed Seth the baby.

Seth cradled Sixtus in his long arms. The child fussed. His uncle moved the infant to his shoulder and sang.

*Poor world . . . what wilt thou do*
*To entertain this starry stranger?*
*Is this the best thou canst bestow?*
*A cold, and not too cleanly, manger?*
*Contend, ye powers of heav'n and earth,*
*To fit a bed for this huge birth.*

*Proud world, said I, cease your contest,*
*And let the mighty babe alone.*
*The phoenix builds the phoenix' nest.*
*Love's architecture is his own.*
*The babe whose birth embraves this morn,*
*Made his own bed ere he was born.*

As Seth's soft baritone filled the room, Annie's heart swelled for this brother-in-law. Soon Sixtus slept once more, and Seth carefully laid him in the cradle.

Annie spoke. "I would that Sophia were here, Seth. That the two of you had a babe and cabin of your own."

"It is God's will, Annie. I think Sophia was too lovely for this world. Yet my mission on earth is not yet complete."

Seth and Annie's eyes met. Seth smiled softly. She had a loving heart, and Joel was a lucky man. Outside, they both heard the tapping of the hammer as David pounded shingles into the roof. "I'd best go help him," Seth commented.

Seth and David finished half of the roof before Joel rode up. He dismounted, tied up his horse, and walked over to his brothers. Well over six feet tall and rail thin, Joel looked up at them as they labored. His dark, receding hair lay thin and lank on his brow, and his square, beardless face was gaunt in the waning daylight. Joel appeared considerably older than his twenty-six years.

"How are you, Brother Joel?" Seth greeted him.

"Been better," Joel commented as he shrugged and coughed. "The roof looks good. Thank you." Then he noted that the pile of shingles on the roof was running low. He bent down, picked up a bunch, stepped onto the ladder, and handed them to David. Nodding and grunting, David reached for the shingles, set them near him, then took a nail from between his teeth and continued working rapidly.

Seth paused for a moment and glanced at Joel. "How'd it go with Houghton?"

Joel shook his head. "Not well," he blurted, his long hands clenching the sides of the ladder. "The creditors won't stop. They have my house, land, and half the rights to my shingle cutter. Supposedly I'm still in debt for the materials I bought on credit to build the mill. Foolishly, I insured the dam for a year, and the workers are suing as well. Annie's father tried to talk some sense into Houghton, but the others are intent on destroying me. They demand all proceeds from the sales of my shingle cutter."

David spit the nails into his hands. Sweat glistened on his face and forearms. His eyes smoldered at the injustice. A couple of years ago, Joel had purchased a farm on credit and had been hired to build a sawmill to pay the debt. Then a spring flood had torn the milldam from its foundation. Joel's creditors took his land. Then ten months ago, Joel had invented and patented a shingle cutter that could cut forty to fifty shingles in a day. Now the same men were trying to swindle Joel out of the proceeds. David felt a driving need to protect his oldest brother, who looked frail and broken. David struck the roof with his fist. "How can men be so evil?"

Joel lessened his grip on the ladder. His face was lined with weariness rather than anger. The hail of discouragement had doused the fire in his soul. Joel thought of how David was eighteen now and needed to know the way of men in the world. Joel's voice was low as he told David the story. "It's an old grudge, David. Some of these men are Universalists. Several years ago, shortly after I joined the Free Will Baptist Church, the Universalists were having great success in this area. I disagreed with their tenets, feeling that they were a far cry from the pure religion I read of in the New Testament. I wrote a poem called Anti-Universalism that put a damper on their proselytizing. This poem delighted the Presbyterians, who then offered me a college education if I would embrace their doctrine and become a preacher. I declined and explained to them that I yearned for the gifts of the Spirit that Paul described. I saw little of that in Presbyterianism. Leaders of these denominations thought me proud. I should have taken the Apostle James's advice and bridled my tongue. Instead, I made many enemies. Now they have no mercy."

David ferociously pounded the nails. The passion in his voice punctuated each hit of the hammer. "Our fathers fought for religious freedom and the right to speak freely. Mother is a Presbyterian, you and Nancy are Baptist, Annie, a devout Methodist. Father is without religion, and we fear for him. Yet, we all respect and love one another. What is wrong with these men?"

Seth spoke calmly. "Many who claim to know Christ do not follow His example. Thus they are not truly men of God. I too long for those spiritual gifts of old. Yet I think that in these days, spiritual gifts may not belong to any one sect, but to all of those who purify themselves and become the saints of God."

"We'd best discuss spiritual gifts another time," David said, raising his eyebrows as he looked up. "It's going to rain."

The three men worked in silence for a time. The adroit David laid two shingles for every one his brothers laid. Racing the weather, they finished the roof.

As they climbed down and began unloading the wood from the wagon, it started to sprinkle. Joel spoke. "I'm considering moving to the Ohio."

"I think you should," David stated. It was what he would do if he were Joel. "A new start far away from all of this."

"But our family is here. And Annie's too," Seth countered.

"You should come, Seth," Joel pressed. "I fear my creditors will come after you if I leave. They have hold of a partnership document we signed a couple of years ago. Come and find a girl in the Ohio. Start a family. Leave these memories. The land is fertile and beautiful. With the canal system reaching the Ohio River, people and goods come from all over. There is ample opportunity."

Seth shrugged but didn't answer. "I'll come," David volunteered, thrilled at the hope in Joel's voice, the renewed energy in his brother's pale face. "An Ohio girl sounds just fine to me."

"Have you talked with Annie?" Seth asked.

Joel shook his head. "No. I fear it will upset her. She and Sixtus are doing well, and I don't relish leaving the family. I may wait a year and see if my prospects look up here. Last night, I dreamed that my path was dark. Then I turned and saw the Ohio shining in faraway sunlight. Perhaps the dream was from God. Seth, if I go, come with Annie and me. David, you too."

"I won't leave Mother," Seth sighed and shook his head. "Not with Pa's intemperance. But go, Joel, if you believe it is God's will. I don't fear your creditors."

A chill rain began to fall. Seth turned to David. "Let's get home. By nightfall, this rain will turn to snow."

Seth harnessed Cephas while David thumped Joel on the back in parting. "All is well, Joel. You have a tight roof on your house. Your boy has a hearty scream. Your wife is round and pretty. Delcena and Lyman are engaged. My advice is to forget your troubles and look to the Ohio."

As Seth and David drove the wagon home, wet snowflakes fell on the men's hair and shoulders. David laughed and blinked the snow from his long lashes. Cephas plodded faithfully forward. The sky darkened. David sang aloud, his voice warm and steaming in the cold. Seth, giving way to his brother's youthful joy, joined in.

> *I prithee send me back my heart,*
> *Since I cannot have thine;*
> *For if from yours you will not part,*
> *Why then shouldst thou have mine?*

Earlier that afternoon, while David and Seth were securing Joel's roof, Nancy met her father outside the barn. Leo, a two-year-old colt whom Nancy had named for his bold heart, was tied with a loose rope to a hitching post. Leo pawed the ground, eager but not afraid. Nancy watched as Ezekiel gently ran a short riding whip over the colt's back, sides, belly, and haunches. Leo danced at first, then settled, tolerating the massage of the crop.

"We want him to respect the crop, but not fear it," Ezekiel explained. He leaned the whip against the post. "It is a reminder, not a punishment."

The colt was a lovely, deep bay with black legs, mane, and tail. Already bigger than Katy, his dam, he stood over sixteen hands high. "He's a spirited fellow, but his eye is kind," Nancy commented as she rubbed the colt's ears. Leo leaned closer to her, and Nancy cradled his head in her arms.

"We'll see how he does under saddle," Ezekiel commented as he hefted the riding saddle off the post.

Nancy grinned, her face awash with life as she admired the colt.

"You're partial to this fellow, and he's partial to you," Ezekiel stated as he looked at his daughter. When they worked the horses together, Nancy reminded him of the little girl who had fed the animals with him, with apple-red cheeks and gray eyes alight with anticipation. This spirited horsewoman seemed a far cry from the ladylike, proper eldest daughter who graced his hearth. When Ezekiel spoke, his voice was firm and matter-of-fact, hiding the smile behind his eyes. "I know you're hankerin' to ride him. But he's not broke yet, and I don't want you hurt. He's a beast of burden and has to learn to work like the rest of us."

"He'll bear me, Pa. I know it."

"First, we'll pony him beside Katy so he gets the idea. You ride the mare, and I'll ride the colt. If he does all right, you can try him."

Nancy saddled Leo while her father bridled the mare. The colt hardly flinched when she tightened the girth. The family only owned one saddle so Nancy would ride Katy bareback. Her father gave her a leg up and suggested she warm-up the mare by riding around the field while he bridled the colt.

Nancy loved the feel of the horse beneath her, the scent of the noble creature. In the house, she felt tall and loose-jointed, too wide-faced and prominent nosed—like the old maid she feared she was becoming. But on a horse, she was whole, young, and lighthearted—a part of nature and meant to be here on this earth. Her mother did not understand this feeling, but her father knew the pulse, the movement, the heartbeat, and the joy.

While Nancy rode the mare, Ezekiel adjusted the headstall and warmed the metal bit by rubbing it between his bare hands. Then, leaving the halter on, he put the reins over the colt's neck and attempted to slide the bit in Leo's mouth. For a moment, Leo resisted, barring his teeth and tossing his head. Ezekiel pressed his thumb into the corner of the horse's mouth. The animal released his jaw, and the man slid the piece of metal in. Immediately, Ezekiel lifted the headstall over Leo's crown, gently worked it over his ears, and adjusted the brow band. He stroked Leo's neck and praised him.

Nancy rode Katy up and halted. Ezekiel attached the rope to the colt's halter and handed one end to Nancy. While making a low trilling sound with his tongue to calm Leo, Ezekiel placed one foot in the stirrup, then he pulled himself up so that his weight lay across the animal's back. Finally, he swung a leg over and sat erect in the saddle, the reins in his hands. The colt stood alert, a bit nervous, but not angry. His ears angled back, attentive to the man on him, not pinned in anger against his head.

"Tell Katy to go forward," Ezekiel instructed Nancy.

Nancy squeezed with her calves. As the mare stepped out, Ezekiel gave the colt identical signals. The rope between the two tightened as Leo did not budge. Ezekiel repeated the commands. Leo arched his neck and stepped forward. Ezekiel praised Leo and patted his neck. They practiced many times, halting and starting again, gradually turning to the right and left. The young horse was alert and obedient next to his dam, responding to the solid, firm cues of the man mounted on him, his equine mind schooled but not broken.

They rode like this for an hour, through the fields, past the garden, the orchard, the well, and the brickyard. It seemed that the farm, so busy during spring, summer, and fall, dozed this quiet gray afternoon. As Nancy rode, her heart was full, not only with gratitude to God for the earth and its creatures, but also with admiration and love for her father.

A highly organized man, he had tamed this virgin forest and had built this productive farm out of a wilderness. She knew of his integrity, that his word was his bond, and that he would give his life for those he loved. He had raised his children with the same respect and firmness with which he trained his animals. But added to that wisdom, each child knew that they were more precious to their father than any gem. Unfortunately, things were not perfect. When Ezekiel drank, his personality changed. Though he never became physically violent, he staggered about, laughed loudly, yelled, and wept. To his eldest daughter, this was like a murky disturbance in a clear stream or a scar on the face of a beautiful child. In her mind, such imperfection did not change the core of sterling worth.

"Are you ready to ride him now, my girl?" Ezekiel asked.

"Sure, Pa," Nancy answered.

They stopped their horses, and Ezekiel dismounted. He lengthened the stirrups for Nancy, whose legs were longer than his. Then Ezekiel untied the rope between the two horses. Nancy slid off Katy. Leo stood still and calm as she mounted him. Agile for his age, Ezekiel gripped Katy's mane and swung his leg over the mare's back. They rode toward the creek and wildwood. Leo spooked when a squirrel darted across their path. Nancy responded automatically by sitting deep in the saddle and holding the reins firm and low. The horse calmed and did not bolt.

"The wind's picking up, and it's gonna rain soon," Ezekiel commented. "Let's get back to the barn before this colt gets too antsy. He was a gentleman today, Nancy, but don't forget, he's young and unpredictable."

Nancy laughed. "He's a good boy, Pa. I believe he'll be cantering under saddle and broken to harness before winter's through."

"We'll see," Ezekiel humphed. "Don't go off riding him by yourself. He's too green. If I'm not around, take one of the boys. They can ride Katy unless she's in season. If so, use Cephas."

They returned to the hitching post, and Nancy unsaddled Leo. Ezekiel put Katy in the barn stall. Nancy let the colt loose in the fenced pasture. It started to sprinkle. Leo raced back and forth, bucking in the cold rain, snorting and whinnying.

Nancy stood beside her father. "He only lets us ride him out of the goodness in his heart," she commented.

Ezekiel nodded. He let out a deep breath as he studied the horse. "Be careful, Nancy. This one has a good heart, but he moves quick as a cat, and there's fire in him. He's not steady like Cephas and Katy."

A moment later, Benjamin and Joseph darted toward Ezekiel and Nancy. The milk buckets they carried knocked against their legs as they ran. The boys skidded to a halt near their father. "I wouldn't ride that crazy colt for a hundred dollars," Joseph pronounced as he watched Leo.

"Guess your sister's braver than you," Ezekiel teased as he ruffled Joseph's hair. This twelve-year-old would be as tall as him in a year.

"I'd ride him," Ben announced, his eyes serious.

"Not for a while, son," Ezekiel said. "Your sister's more experienced."

"But Nancy's a girl," Ben said quietly.

"A woman," Nancy corrected her little brother. "And why should that matter, Benjamin? I ride better than most men, anyway."

Ben shrugged. "Ma is watchin' out the window, Nance. She doesn't want you ridin' the colt no more. I heard her tell Delcie and Lyman that Pa shouldn't encourage you. You're a woman, and prayers can't keep you safe if you make foolish decisions and keep ridin' a wild horse."

Ezekiel felt suddenly irritated. Julia was a strong-willed woman. Ezekiel thought about the countless times he gave in to her. He allowed her religiosity and her continual talk about God. She shouldn't be criticizing him in front of the children and Lyman Sherman. These thoughts further triggered his anger.

Ezekiel wasn't about to stop Nancy from riding when the girl loved it so much. "Your Ma doesn't know everything. She just thinks she does," Ezekiel snapped at Benjamin.

Sensitive to her father's discontent, Nancy shivered. Now that she was off the horse, the cold went right through her.

The rain increased. "You three git in the barn," Ezekiel commanded.

Nancy huddled the boys into the barn, and her brothers commenced milking. Outside, Ezekiel looked up. The leaden sky darkened. He shook his head and stalked into the barn. Unable to get his mind off of his wife's criticism, Ezekiel briskly took Katy from her stall and bridled her.

"Where you going, Pa?" Joseph asked.

"To the tavern. Tell your ma I won't be home till late."

"Please stay home for supper, Pa," Ben begged.

"Julianne made apple pie, and she'll be disappointed if you don't try it," Joseph added.

"One thing I don't need is my wife and children tellin' me what to do," Ezekiel stated gruffly as he led Katy out of the barn.

"I'll save a piece for you, Pa," Joe called after him.

After his father was gone, Ben savagely kicked the bucket. The cow skittered. Tears welled in Benjamin's brown eyes.

"It's okay, Benja," Nancy said quietly as she picked up a rag off the barn floor and hung it on a peg.

"I was tryin' to let you and Pa know how Ma felt so maybe there wouldn't be a row at dinner," Ben yelled. "So Pa wouldn't run off to the tavern! I messed it up!"

"It's not your fault, Ben. Not any more than it's mine." Nancy looked out the barn door. It was becoming dark, and the rain was turning to snow. She heard David's voice singing in the distance. Knowing that David and Seth would be home momentarily, Nancy lit the barn lantern before it became too dark to see.

"Pa's not going to heaven, Nancy," Ben blurted. "He's never been baptized, and he gets drunk all the time. I don't hanker for heaven if Pa's not there."

Though Nancy's heart ached, her demeanor remained calm. She took off the wide-brim hat she wore riding and hung it on its peg. Her hair fell to her shoulders. She stood still for a moment, praying silently, thinking of her father and her little brother. Lantern light spilled around her, casting golden light upon her hair and illuminating her high forehead. Her tall, slender shape in men's britches and high riding boots cast a lean shadow on the barn wall. Many a man, if he had seen her at that moment, would have wondered why he had never noticed Nancy Johnson's beauty.

"Pa's good, Ben," Nancy said. "Jesus died for him too. It's not our place to judge others. Just to do the best we can. To work out our own salvation. No matter what any minister says, I can't imagine a loving God condemning our father."

Joseph squirted a stream of warm milk directly into Benjamin's face. Ben sputtered, and Joseph laughed. "Ben, quit worryin' over everything. After dinner, we'll eat pie and play games. Pa will be home later."

Joseph's antics angered rather than cheered Benjamin. He was about to pounce on his brother when he felt Nancy's hand on his shoulder. "Finish the milking, Ben. Josie's just trying to help you feel better. A fight won't help anybody."

"It'd make me feel better," Benjamin growled.

Seth and David opened the barn door. They had heard this last exchange between their siblings. They had also passed their father on his way to the tavern.

Seth stepped forward and laid a hand on Benjamin's other shoulder. "You'd feel worse later, Ben. Like Pa feels the morning after he drinks. All we can do is pray for him."

Benjamin continued milking in silence, unable to squeeze back the tears welling in his eyes. Joseph milked without speaking, his natural cheer doused. After caring for Cephas, David sought to entertain his brothers as they milked by enacting a revolutionary naval battle with piles of manure that he raked hither and thither representing the various ships. Joseph laughed out loud, and Benjamin's brow lightened a little.

During David's antics, Seth and Nancy huddled in a corner, speaking in low voices. Nancy told her brother all that had happened. "My riding triggered it." Nancy took a deep breath. "Otherwise, Pa might have stayed home tonight."

"It wasn't your fault," Seth counseled his sister. "Pa gets restless or discouraged, then he drinks. It's no one's fault. I pray that someday we will find a way to help him. I'm worried about Joel. His creditors are after him. Joel's thinking of moving to the Ohio with his family."

Nancy sighed deeply. "How Mother would miss them! She looks so tired sometimes, Seth. I worry about her surviving this birth. Pa couldn't bear it. And what would happen to the children?"

"They have us, Nancy. We will always be here to comfort and guide them, just as we do now with Father's drunkenness and Mother's burdens."

Nancy looked deeply into Seth's dark eyes. She wondered if he ever wanted more. "If it is God's will," she said quietly, "we will always be here for them."

## 3

Backward turn backward oh time in your flight
Make me a child again just for tonight
Place me again on my dear Mother's breast
Free from the cares of this life let me rest
Let me again see the smile on her face
While she with rapture my form will embrace

The sweetest and best of all dainties on earth
Prepared by our mother in the land of our birth
There in the corner the brick oven stands
Brimfull of dainties prepared by her hand
There are puddings and cakes and bread made of rye
And dearest of all is the old pumpkin pie
Then backward turn backward oh time in your flight
Make me a child again just for to night

—GEORGE W. JOHNSON, FROM "BACKWARD TURN BACKWARD"

*January 1829*

Julia awakened in the darkness of the hour before dawn. Her door lay slightly open. She gazed at the red, pulsing glow at the entrance of her room caused by a dancing fire already blazing in the kitchen hearth. Seth and David had thoughtfully stoked the fire an hour ago before leaving to do chores in the barn. Ezekiel, who had come home late the previous night after spending the week working in Fredonia, lay asleep beside her, breathing heavily.

Julia's face felt parched from cold. The fire in the kitchen slightly took the edge off the permeating chill. She hesitated to arise and leave her husband's warmth. Stretching one leg and changing the angle of her hip, she redistributed the weight of the child. She wondered if the babe would come in the next three days so that Reverend Spencer could baptize the child when he came on Saturday to marry Delcena and Lyman.

Julia thought of how Reverend Spencer strongly believed in infant baptism and would go to great lengths to baptize babies as close to birth as possible. However, Julia couldn't imagine a loving God consigning an innocent to eternal punishment for want of baptism. On the other hand, Julia was always glad to see her own little ones christened as soon as possible. Julia's musings continued. If the babe came today, it would be a singular coincidence. The day was January twelfth and marked Ezekiel's fifty-sixth birthday, Julia and Ezekiel's twenty-eighth wedding anniversary, and Esther's second birthday.

Birthday presents were rare in the Johnson household. However, this birthday was different. A gold watch for Ezekiel lay hidden in Julia's bureau drawer. It was a lovely piece with bold numbers, a fine chain, and her husband's name engraved on the back. The tiny gears, precise and delicate, kept accurate time. Julia had saved a portion of her seamstress income for two years in order to buy this gift. For seven months, the watch had lain silent beneath her clothing. Today she would give it to Ezekiel.

Julia heard Nancy and Julianne in the kitchen beginning breakfast. She rolled on her side in order to arise. Suddenly, Ezekiel reached out and laid a hand on her shoulder.

Julia startled. She hadn't realized that he was awake. "Wait," he mumbled sleepily. He moved his hand to her belly and found the place where the child kicked. "He's a feisty one," Ezekiel commented.

"Or she," Julia said.

Ezekiel shook his head. "No, this one kicks too hard to be a girl."

"Remember my sister Diadamia on our wedding day," Julia smiled, remembering three-year-old Diadamia kicking him so hard that Ezekiel had borne the bruise for a week.

Ezekiel stretched and yawned. "After twenty-eight years, I still feel the smart."

"She was angry because I was moving away," Julia smiled.

"A smart child," Ezekiel humphed, then his voice softened. "Julia, I brought something home for you from Fredonia." Reaching under the bed, he pulled out a box. Julia sat up to open it. Within the box, she discovered a finely made chain. The necklace draped over her fingers like golden yarn. "Zeke, it's lovely!"

Taking the necklace from his wife, he motioned for her to pull up her hair. Tilting her head forward, she lifted her long, gray-streaked tresses. Ezekiel's fingers chilled the back of her neck as he fastened the clasp. When he had finished, she smoothed her hair. Then she turned and kissed his cheek.

"This year, I have a gift for you as well," she commented with a smile. Julia stood up, pulled a shawl around her shoulders, and went to retrieve the watch from the bureau drawer.

After she handed the package to Ezekiel, he carefully opened it. His eyes widened as he handled the watch, but he did not smile.

Julia's eagerness faded. "Doesn't it please you?" she asked.

"Of course. But where did you get the money?" he questioned, shaking his head.

"From my sewing. What's wrong?"

Looking down, he fingered the watch. "The necklace compared to this watch is like the moon in contrast to the sun."

"This necklace is precious to me," Julia said softly as she stroked the chain.

Ezekiel looked at his pregnant wife. He shook his head again. "Julia, you always give more. From the day we married, I was not worthy of you."

"That isn't so," Julia said. Her thoughts turned to that long-ago day. Zeke, so young and handsome, had stared at her in the silk brocade wedding dress, his eyes both joyous and troubled. In that look, she had seen overwhelming admiration, passion, and gratitude. Unabashed tears had softened his ruddy cheeks when the minister blessed their marriage. Although just a lass about to turn seventeen, Julia felt that this man was the fire that lit a hundred candles in her soul.

But so much had happened since that day. They had only been married a short time when Ezekiel had become restless. He had moved his young family from place to place, inexplicable discontent driving him to tame new and wild lands. Finally, they had come to Pomfret with its fertile hills, singing creek, and bounteous fruit trees. The region already boasted three religious societies. Julia, who was desperate for stability, for community, for the opportunity to create a home for their children, begged him to stay. She knew that their staying was his gift to her. In time, his intemperance became the price she paid. Now, when the trigger of discontent and disillusionment shot restlessness through his soul, it drove him to drink rather than to new frontiers.

Looking at her husband on this anniversary, Julia thought of the enigma he was—so gentle in his treatment of her and the children, so honest with his fellowmen, so brutal to his own soul. But Julia was not without hope. The Bible taught that you might know the nature of a thing by its fruits. Her husband's fruits were his children. They were so very sweet.

Julia sat down on the bed next to him and spoke quietly. "You have given me fifteen children, Zeke. We have only lost one to death. They are the most priceless gems."

"They are more yours than mine," Ezekiel returned.

"I recall that it takes two parents to have a child," she remarked, looking at her bulging abdomen.

Ezekiel snorted and smiled. Then he wound the watch and laid it on the nightstand. Their breath steamed in the cold room. He looked up at his wife. "Thank you, Julia," he said. "I wish I could give you a bigger house with a fireplace in every room."

Julia took his hands and held them in hers. She spoke earnestly. "Ezekiel, all I desire is your salvation."

"I haven't faith in God," he muttered, looking away. "You know that."

"But you could, Zeke. God will not give His children a stone when they ask for bread."

"You're wrong. If God truly lives, then I have seen Him hand out stones," Ezekiel said.

"When, Zeke? When did God hand out stones?" Julia implored.

"I'll not speak of it," Ezekiel said shortly.

Julia didn't press the matter. His past was a forbidden topic, and Ezekiel would retreat within himself if she even mildly pursued it. Was his secret a wedge that parsed their happiness and a poison that was at the root of his drinking?

During the early years of their marriage, she had begged him to pray, to attend church, to exercise faith. Only then could the gifts of the Spirit enter his soul. But, for some unfathomed reason, he would not seek God, and he would not confide in her. All he ever told her of his childhood was that he ran away from home at a young age because of his stepfather's harsh treatment. Yet he named their second son after his mother's family, though he had not seen his mother since the day he ran away so long ago.

The smell of eggs, pork, and biscuits wafted in from the kitchen. Ezekiel let go of his wife's hands, stood up, closed the door, and began dressing. From her seat on the bed, Julia watched him, wondering if he would ever come to peace and overcome his intemperance, wondering what the rest of their lives together would be like. Once he turned toward her to ask a question and took stock of the steady contemplative look in her eyes. She possessed such beautiful eyes, dark and penetrating, the light falling on their depths like stars in the night. Before leaving the room, he stroked her hair and thanked her again for the watch. He carefully placed it in his shirt pocket, the ticking near his heart.

When Ezekiel was gone, Julia took off her nightclothes and donned a brown wool dress. After tying up her hair, she pulled the gold chain out from under the dress. Looking in a small mirror, she surveyed a middle-aged and pregnant woman, the gold chain the only thing about her that glistened. Carefully, she lowered her clumsy frame to the floor and said her prayers. She prayed for her relations, for her immediate family, and for her country. She prayed fervently for her husband. And then, consistent with her faith, she asked that God's will be done.

After her prayer, Julia left the room, for there was breakfast to be eaten and work to be done. Additionally, the neighbor ladies were coming later that morning to help finish Delcena's quilt.

When Julia stepped out into the kitchen, little Esther was laughing delightedly, for her papa had given her a birthday present—a box of curly wood shavings and leftover scraps from the carpenter shop.

After the men and school children had breakfasted and left, Julianne and Delcena cleaned up the kitchen. Julia and Nancy went into the sitting room to set up the wedding quilt. As they stretched the quilt onto the frame, Julia was once again struck by the original beauty of the pattern.

Nancy, Julianne, and Delcena had cut the quilt pieces from scraps of varying shades of indigo and brown. They had hand sewn them together into a palm leaf pattern created by Nancy. Nancy had been inspired by Delcena's fiancé. Deeply religious, Lyman had told the family that palm leaves represented protection and an oasis. Jesus Christ's mission was protective, the love of God an oasis, making the palm leaf a powerful symbol.

After the dishes were done, Delcena and Nancy moved the benches from the kitchen table onto either side of the quilt frame. In the corner, near the crackling fire, Julianne placed the box of curly shavings and wood scraps for Esther and any other little ones who might come. Julia put together a platter of bread, honey, and preserves for the ladies to snack on.

Thirty minutes later, Joel's Annie arrived. Her cheeks were pink from the cold, the color contrasting sharply with her vivid hair. Baby Sixtus was bundled in Annie's arms. The neighbor ladies followed: first, cheerful Mrs. Cornwall, then, fluttery Mrs. Risley. The women took their seats and chatted amicably as they quilted. An hour later, stout Mrs. Harriet Bull breezed in with her daughter, Geraldine, who was now married to Sam Granger, the man who had once proposed to Nancy. Mrs. Bull was the local midwife and queen bee of Pomfret. Julia gave her a seat on a comfortable chair at the head of the quilt. Her daughter Geraldine made herself at home in the rocking chair, where she commenced nursing her toddler.

"This pattern rivals the pattern on Geraldine's quilt," Mrs. Bull announced as she surveyed the quilt and lowered her considerable mass into the chair. "As you may recall, Geraldine's quilt has an oak and maple leaf pattern. Julia, our daughters have similar gifts. Everyone speaks of what fine wives your girls will make."

"Thank you, Harriet," Julia said.

"I remember Geraldine's quilt," Nancy spoke. "It was lovely."

Mrs. Bull, who was now threading her needle, looked up at Nancy. Harriet Bull sighed dramatically. "Why, dear Nancy, it breaks my heart that no man has snatched you up. Let's hope and pray that the next quilting bee will be for you. I know that Delcena's luck must be difficult for you and Julianne, her elder sisters."

Julianne, who had been cooing at Sixtus, looked up sharply after hearing Mrs. Bull's comment. She felt the freckles on her turned-up nose grow hot. "Mrs. Bull," Julianne said warmly. "Nancy and I rejoice for Delcie but are not overly concerned about our own prospects."

"And *you* shouldn't be, Miss Julianne Johnson," Mrs. Bull snorted. "You're but twenty years. But Nancy must ask the good Lord's help and keep her mind open to any opportunity for matrimony."

Delcena stood quickly and retrieved the food platter. "Mrs. Bull, would you like something to eat?" she offered, hoping that Harriet Bull would eat rather than talk.

"Why, thank you," Mrs. Bull said as she lowered her needle.

Julia sighed inwardly. She had watched Nancy during the exchange. Her eldest daughter's face had paled at Harriet Bull's comment, yet Nancy's demeanor had remained composed and her needle steady. And so the work continued.

By mid-afternoon the quilt was completed. After the women left, Julia and her daughters took the quilt off the frame. "Tonight, we must get ahead of the weekly work and continue the baking until nightfall," Julia commented as they worked. "Tomorrow is wash day. We will also begin the puddings and pumpkin and nut pies. On Thursday, Nancy and I will fit the wedding dress on Delcena. Julianne must press the men's shirts and suits. Delcena, you must pack as well. On Friday, we will attend to every detail. I plan to bake a large loaf-cake with mounds of frosting, as well as some twisted crullers. Delcena, ask Almera to make evergreen wreaths to use as decorations on the day of the wedding. Nancy and Julianne, the children should be bathed the evening before. What a blessing it is that no one is currently ill."

"But, Mama," Julianne interrupted, her eyes smiling. "You have forgotten to schedule in the birth of your baby."

Nancy looked up with her eyes demure. "Details, details," she said.

Julianne laughed out loud, and Delcena smiled. Little Esther looked up with wood shavings in her hair and joined in, laughing heartily, though she did not know what she was laughing about. Though Julia's back and legs ached from her pregnancy, she chuckled, glad on this wedding anniversary, thankful to God and to Ezekiel for these daughters who graced her life.

Julia's water broke shortly before ten on Friday night. Her first thought was a prayer of gratitude that Delcena's dress was finished and the loaf-cake and crullers had turned out well. She wakened Ezekiel. He lit a candle and quickly dressed.

"I'll be back in an hour with Harriet Bull," he said. Julia nodded. Despite Harriet's unbridled tongue, she was the best midwife in Pomfret Township. When she delivered a baby, the mother and child nearly always lived. For that reason, Julia had endured her participating in the quilting bee. A contraction gripped Julia, radiating through her back. She set her teeth against it. Her breath escaped in short gasps. Time seemed to stand still until the pain passed. Moments later, Nancy entered the room, already dressed and a candle in her hand.

"Papa told me it's time," Nancy said simply as she laid a soft hand on her mother's brow.

"I'll have the babe tonight and be ready to greet the minister in the morning," Julia said with a worn smile.

"I know you will, Mama," Nancy said softly. "Rest now while I stoke the fire and start the water boiling. Your babes come fast."

By the time Mrs. Bull arrived, Julia's contractions were ten minutes apart. Ezekiel went outside and watched the snow fall, bits of white floating downward in the dark night.

Inside, Julia breathed heavily, the pains fast and hard. "I'm too old for this," Julia said to Harriet.

"You'd best tell that to Mr. Johnson. He might not be willing to leave you alone," Mrs. Bull retorted.

Julia chuckled. Delcena's eyes widened; her pious mother's reaction surprised her.

"Birth isn't the time for modesty," good-natured Julianne whispered to her sister.

"Mrs. Bull is never modest, but mother usually is," Delcena whispered back.

Harriet Bull eyed the whispering young women and ordered them to help their mother walk about the room while she and Nancy readied the utensils and bed for delivery.

Within an hour, Julia lay on the bed, the labor bearing down upon her. Yet she trod on familiar ground, having been down this path fifteen times before. It was different each time, much as a scene changes from year to year and season to season. But the pain was always there. Now she entered that tunnel of agony where nothing existed but muscle and searing pressure, her body and soul in partnership with that wet, precious life demanding existence and breath.

When her mother's labor became intense, Delcena threw a cloak over her shoulders and joined her father outside. The snow fell heavily now. With Delcena's own life on the brink of change, a sense of foreboding filled her. She had become dizzy witnessing her mother's pain. The slap of cold air steadied her tremulous knees.

"Mama's doing fine, Papa," she said when she saw the question in Ezekiel's eyes. "I just need some fresh air."

"You sure you want this, Delcie?" her father asked as he put his arm around her shoulders. "The trials of delivering children, putting up with an ornery man, working and starving?"

"It's all part of the package, isn't it, Pa?" Delcena asked. The hair under her bonnet was tied up in rags in preparation for the wedding tomorrow.

Ezekiel nodded. They heard Julia scream. Ezekiel moaned, his arm tightening around his Delcena. "Sometimes it's a bitter package," he muttered. Many a woman died in childbirth. This fear haunted Ezekiel.

Inside, Julia screamed once more as the child blossomed from her body. Harriet Bull gripped the small slick head and drew it out. "It's a boy," she announced. With a steady hand, Nancy tied and cut the cord, separating her mother from her brother. Mrs. Bull held the baby upside down and briskly slapped his backside. Julia drank in the rapture of her son's first cry.

Outside, Ezekiel and Delcena heard the baby's muffled cry. Ezekiel let out his breath. Delcena continued to shake from cold and apprehension. "And sometimes the package ain't too bad, princess," her father said. "Like the day you were born."

Julianne opened the door. "It's a boy. Ma's fine," she declared before ducking back inside.

Ezekiel took his watch out and looked at the time. It was seven minutes before midnight.

After the child and mother were cleaned up, Harriet Bull briskly stepped outside. Snow and wind galloped around her. She eyed Ezekiel and stated, "I don't reckon you should take me home in this weather." Her gaze fell on Delcena, "What are you doing outside, young lady? Your hair will be ruined for tomorrow—and you the bride. I s'pose I'll be stayin' for your wedding. Heaven knows Julia will need my help." She hooked her arm into Delcena's and escorted her into the house. Ezekiel followed.

Once inside, Harriet Bull let go of Delcena and faced Ezekiel squarely. "Mr. Johnson," she announced in a formidable voice, "your wife has safely delivered you a healthy son. Considering her age, she is a lucky woman."

While Ezekiel headed into the bedroom to see his wife and child, Nancy laid a hand on Mrs. Bull's arm to detain her. "Mrs. Bull, you must be exhausted. Would you like to sleep upstairs in my bed?"

"Heavens no! I'll stay down here and clean and furbish the house for the wedding tomorrow. Your poor mother—a new baby and a marriage. Not to mention all these mouths to feed."

"Are you certain, Mrs. Bull? My sisters and I can take care of everything in the morning. I don't mind sleeping on the kitchen floor."

"Off with you Nancy—before the bricks in your bed go cold."

Nancy climbed the steps holding a candle. Delcena and Julianne followed arm in arm.

"Nance," Juli whispered with a giggle when they entered their bedroom. "I'm thankful that Mrs. Bull turned down your offer. I couldn't have borne her a moment longer."

Almera and Susan sat up in their bed. "We heard the baby cry," Almera said. "Is Mother all right?"

"As right as rain," Julianne said as she hugged her sisters. "We have a new brother!" Julianne proceeded to tell them of their mother's fortitude and courage. She finished by screwing up her face and imitating Harriet Bull, "Poor, poor Julia! So many mouths to feed! This house will be properly cleaned and furbished by morning."

"Mrs. Bull grates on me," Almera said. "As if we hadn't already cleaned and readied the house."

"I'm simply glad that Mrs. Bull is downstairs and Nancy is here with us," Susan said. "Imagine her snoring."

At Susan's invitation, Julianne let out an earthshaking snore.

Almera pulled her knees up and hugged them. She laughed and added, "Delce, you're so quiet." Then she giggled. "But I would be too if my wedding guests were Harriet Bull and Philastus Hurlbut!"

"I didn't want any guests—just a quiet family wedding." Delcena shivered with cold. She climbed into bed next to Julianne and pulled the covers up. Her eyes were serious in the candlelight. "Despite Papa's feelings about Dr. Hurlbut, I couldn't deny Lyman his only kin."

Almera threw her head back onto the pillow and giggled. "Harriet Bull will rule the roost while Dr. Hurlbut struts about praying and preaching! Hopefully Papa will behave."

Delcena's brow furrowed. She sighed worriedly. Nancy put her hand on Delcena's shoulder. "Delcie, your wedding will be lovely. Sleep now; tomorrow is your day." Delcena lay down, and Nancy blew out the candle and slipped into bed. In the dark, the Johnson sisters heard Harriet Bull bustling in the kitchen.

"What on earth is she doing?" Almera asked.

Delcena moaned.

Julianne's voice penetrated the darkness. "Don't worry, Delce. I'll lure Mrs. Bull and Dr. Hurlbut into the barn on the task of retrieving Almera's evergreen wreaths. Then, I'll bolt the door."

"The wreaths will be a small sacrifice," Almera giggled. "But Harriet Bull's cries will raise the dead."

"Perhaps David will gag them for us," Susan whispered.

"But sweet Seth will save them," Nancy added with a mock sigh.

Delcena wanted to smile, but she couldn't escape the feeling of unease inside. When she spoke, there was a catch in her voice. "How I will miss this room and this bed and all of you!"

"But Delce, you will have your own man, your own cabin, peace and quiet," Julianne comforted. "You shan't be lonely with so many blessings."

"I will be," Delcena spoke with tears in her voice. It was incomprehensible that tomorrow night she would not be here in this bed, with her sisters.

"One of us shall visit you every day." Julianne rolled over and took Delcena's hand. "Poor, handsome Lyman will grow so weary of us," Julianne added.

The other sisters added their promises. Then nothing more was said. Delcena's breathing became slow and even. After a time, only Nancy remained awake.

For over an hour, Nancy listened to Harriet Bull's heavy footsteps. Finally they quieted. Was the woman asleep in the rocker, her head lolling? Still, Nancy could not sleep. Her thoughts relived the miracle of her tiny brother's birth. Yet her mind refused to rest. She thought of tomorrow and of the loving look and touch Lyman reserved for only Delcena. A tear escaped Nancy's eye, trickled down her temple, and was lost in her hair. Would she live forever under her father's roof? Would she share a room with her sisters until each was married? Then, after caring for her aged parents, would she be alone in this house, solitary as the flame of a single candle?

In the downstairs bedroom, Ezekiel stroked his wife's hair as the brand-new babe lay bundled between them.

Julia spoke softly, exhausted but joyful as she felt her baby against her body. "Zeke, Reverend Spencer will christen him after the wedding. What will his name be?"

"What suits your fancy?" Ezekiel questioned.

"I feel this is our last child, Zeke. I would have one son named after his father."

Ezekiel's hand froze on her head. This was an old bone of contention, something she had not brought up since David's birth over eighteen years ago.

"I thought perhaps your feelings had changed," Julia ventured.

"My feelings have not changed," Ezekiel stated.

Julia remembered clearly that day eighteen years ago when she had suggested they name their third son after his father. How short-tempered Zeke had become at the mere suggestion! Julia's mother, Esther, had been visiting and had suggested the name David for the princely babe. Julia had balked. David was the name of a fallen king; it was not fit for her son. Esther had gently chided her daughter, "It is the name of the man who slew Goliath, the king who united Israel, the man who wrote the psalms, the name from which the mortal line of the Son of God was born." Then Ezekiel had taken a stand, "No son will be named after me. My name shall die with me. This child's name is David." Julia's heart had ached that day. It still ached now eighteen years later. Why? Why did her husband want his name to die?

"Shall we name him Amos Partridge, after my uncle?" Julia asked quietly.

"Amos Partridge Johnson," Ezekiel repeated. His work-worn hands touched the babe's cheek. Even through thick calluses, his fingertips felt the softness of infant skin. "It suits him."

Julia sighed. "Then Amos he shall be." Ezekiel took a drink from the flask on the night table. Then he blew out the candle and nestled near his wife and babe.

The next morning dawned bright and cold. Lyman Sherman and Philastus Hurlbut arrived shortly after breakfast, their horses leaving deep tracks in the new snow. The Johnson household was bustling with activity. Joe and Ben interrupted their snowball fight to take the horses. Nancy greeted the men at the door with the glad news of Amos's birth. Lyman's cheeks were rosy against his fair skin, and his glasses clouded in the indoor warmth. He cleaned them with his pocket-handkerchief.

Nancy ushered Lyman and Philastus into the small parlor where the chairs were arranged in rows. These chairs were of oak and sturdily built by Ezekiel's hand. He had made them over time, adding each additional chair as his family increased. Nancy suggested the groom and best man take a seat and wait patiently, for neither the reverend nor Joel and his family had yet arrived.

The fire crackled in the parlor hearth to the side of the row of chairs. Mrs. Bull, who had not yet awakened that morning, snored in the rocking chair, oblivious to the bustling activity. Almera stood on tiptoe, hanging evergreen bows on the wooden structure that David had built for the wedding couple to stand in front of. Hurlbut's look riveted to Almera's shapely form as she worked. To the side of the structure stood the narrow polished stand that held the family Bible.

After Nancy excused herself from the room, Hurlbut stood up from his chair and strode over to Almera. "Can I be of assistance?"

Almera stopped working and turned to answer him. Uncomfortable with the intense and haughty look in the man's eye, her color heightened. "No, thank you, Dr. Hurlbut. I'm nearly finished. Just one more wreath to get from the barn and everything will be ready."

Then Lyman was on his feet and next to them. He took Almera's hands in his and asked. "Mera, how is Delcena? Is she ready?"

Almera smiled warmly at Lyman. "Nancy and Julianne are dressing Delcie. Mama remade her own wedding dress to fit her. Delcie looks beautiful!"

"I can scarcely wait to see her," Lyman said. "I can't believe this day is here."

"Well, believe it!" Almera laughed at the happy, anxious look in the groom's eyes. She gaily kissed Lyman on the cheek. Then she glanced at Philastus Hurlbut. His eyes drank in the shape of her mouth, the softness of her skin. Almera's smile dimmed. "If you two will excuse me," she said as she left the room.

Hurlbut turned to Lyman. "Cousin," he said gallantly. "I must help your pretty sister-in-law. Remain calm. Tonight will be the night of all nights. For now, Mrs. Bull will keep you company."

Mrs. Bull snored. Lyman turned to his cousin and grinned. "It is difficult to remain calm when I am about to receive such a choice bride. Philastus, I pray I will bless Delcena's life as Christ blessed the Church."

"A worthy prayer," Hurlbut said as he patted Lyman's shoulder. "I have business to attend to."

In the barn, Almera stretched up to take the wreath off of the peg. She had heard footsteps outside but had assumed it was Ben or Joe, who were on duty watching for Joel's family and the minister. Hurlbut was almost six feet tall, quick, and powerfully built. In an instant, he was behind her, his chest against her shoulders, his arms on each side of her.

"Let me help you," he said as he put his hands on the wreath over her hands. Astounded, she felt his soft, manicured fingers—so different from her father's and brothers'. "The wreath is too heavy for such a pretty thing," Hurlbut uttered.

Almera twisted her head around and stared at him. "Sir! I can do it myself!"

His mouth was loose and his breathing hot against her neck. He pressed his body closer. "Move, sir!" Almera cried. "Please."

Hurlbut put one hand over her mouth and wrapped the other around her so tightly that she could scarcely breathe. His voice sounded like a silken razor in her ear. "Cease your trembling, Almera. I am a kind and handsome man. I will not choose evil. I will not injure nor defile you. I am a seventh son, destined for healing and greatness. I am a scholar of God's word, and you are His sweetest creation. Listen to the Song of Solomon! How fair and how pleasant art thou, O love, for delights! This thy stature is like to a palm tree. And the roof of thy mouth like the best wine for my beloved, that goeth down sweetly, causing the lips of those that are asleep to speak."

Hurlbut took his hand from Almera's mouth. Before she could scream, he kissed her with such force that she staggered back, crushing the wreath. As soon as he finished kissing her, he pressed his hand over her mouth once more. "I'll let go of you now, but don't cry out," he whispered. "It would ruin your sister's wedding. Remember, I've not hurt you nor defiled you. I've only opened your eyes—given you a taste of the forbidden fruit."

As Hurlbut loosened his grip, Almera bolted. She ran from the barn, not stopping until she reached the house. She did not notice Seth and Lyman greeting the minister. Squeezing into the door, Almera stood for a moment, catching her breath. In the noise and confusion, no one noticed her there, red-faced and panting. Joel and Annie had arrived. Almera's little brothers raced through the house in their best clothes. David was throwing baby Sixtus in the air. Her sisters were putting food on the table under the direction of Harriet Bull. Only Susan noticed the strange way Almera fled to the cellar. She followed her sister.

"Mera, what's wrong?" Susan asked.

Almera's fear and anger burst from her. In tears she told Susan all that had happened in the barn. Susan wrapped her arms around Almera.

"We should tell Papa," Susan suggested. "He will horsewhip Hurlbut."

Tears crept down Almera's cheeks. "Hurlbut would lie. Delcie would cry, and Lyman wouldn't know who to believe. I would be shamed."

"Not in our family," Susan whispered. "We would know you told the truth."

"I can't tell," Almera gasped. "I can't."

There were heavy footsteps on the stairs. The girls looked up, wide-eyed. Harriet Bull stood in front them, the pupils of her eyes adjusting to the dim light. "I wondered where you two ran off to. Come upstairs with me. There is work to be done."

They trailed behind the powerful woman. When they were upstairs, Harriet Bull looked Almera and Susan full in the face, a lecture about to come forth. Then she hesitated. "Why Almera," she gasped loudly. "You've been crying. What's the matter, lass?"

Almera didn't answer. Philastus Hurlbut had his back to them and was talking to Seth about some point of doctrine. He stopped speaking midsentence. Susan, knowing he was listening, answered for Almera, her usually quiet voice clear and carrying. "Someone has cruelly crushed Almera's wreath. The one that was to hang above the hearth."

"Tut, tut, such things happen," Mrs. Bull clucked. "How girls carry on. Come now. We must all find our seats." Harriet Bull hustled the family into the sitting room.

Five minutes later, Ezekiel took Delcena's arm as she came down the stairs, and together they walked into the crowded parlor. All eyes were on them, the father in his only suit, the daughter in the gorgeous silk brocade with newly puffed sleeves and lace about the neck. Ezekiel's eyes locked onto the groom, who stood straight and handsome, his integrity and kind heart apparent in every word and movement. Lyman's eyes filled with tears as he watched his beloved Delcena. Her smile was warm and her step sure. The hesitancy and fear of last night had evaporated with the dawn of her wedding day. Ezekiel placed his daughter's hand in Lyman's.

The minister's wedding prayer rang long and drawn out, swelling and receding like an oration. Will and George squirmed and made faces at each other, knowing that their father's wrath was sure if they uttered a sound. Julianne held Esther and drew patterns with her finger on the little girl's back to keep her quiet. Julia cradled her new babe against her heart and thought of the blessing of a new son-in-law who had such faith in God. Joel cradled Sixtus in his arms. Annie cried and blew her nose as she thought of her own wedding day and the joy and pain that followed.

Hurlbut, standing next to the groom as best man, opened his eyes once during the prayer in order to glance at Almera. However, he was unable to enjoy her beauty, for although Almera's eyes were shut, Susan, who sat next to her, glared at him sharply. He wondered how long the girl had been staring at him as if he were some base creature. What had Almera told her? His eyes narrowed slightly, and he frowned at Susan. On the other hand, why should he worry? Susan Johnson was a child of fourteen and as thin and shapeless as a stick. She had no power over him.

Susan did not look away, hoping that the force of her glare would repel Dr. Hurlbut from her sister. Philastus Hurlbut smoothed his own features into a slight tutorial smile before piously closing his eyes. Susan, whose mind was much older than her years, felt suddenly ashamed—ashamed for the countless times she had envied Almera's loveliness. She realized that beauty was like the sharpest of kitchen knives, lending both power and danger to the hand wielding it. Maybe a duller knife was a blessing.

Then the wedding prayer ended. Reverend Spencer pronounced Lyman Sherman and Delcena Johnson man and wife, legally and lawfully wed. Their kiss in that small brown house in the dead of winter held the gentle promise of a spring morning.

That evening, after the baby had been christened and the guests had departed, Ezekiel sat near the parlor fire. He took count of each of his children. Seth was reading the Bible in the same room. Benjamin watched David and Joseph play a game of checkers in the corner. Mary cuddled on Ezekiel's lap. Nancy, Julianne, and Susan sat near him darning socks. Will, George, and Esther slept upstairs in their trundle beds. Almera and tiny Amos were in the bedroom with Julia. Joel had left for his own cabin earlier in the evening. Delcena was gone.

"I win!" Joseph triumphed. "Pay up, big brother."

David stood up, laughing. "What do you want, Joe? My shirt or my trousers?"

"Your socks. You might catch cold without your shirt."

David shucked off his boots, then peeled off his socks and handed them to Joseph. David slapped Joseph affectionately on the back and called out to Benjamin. "Bennie, don't feel bad when Josie beats you. I swear he cheats."

Joseph laughed delightedly. "Come on, Ben. I'll teach you the tricks so you can beat the britches off of David."

David moaned and moved his chair next to his father, where he could stretch his bare feet toward the fire. Ben and Joe huddled around the checkerboard.

"Talking about tricks," David addressed Ezekiel, "what is Hurlbut up to giving Lyman and Delcie a gift like that?" David whistled. "Two hundred dollars. Enough money for a down payment on land outside of Jamestown."

Ezekiel frowned. "I've known men like him before. He wants Lyman in his debt. I don't like it. Delcena's still part of this family."

Seth looked up from his reading. "Perhaps we should give Philastus the benefit of the doubt. He seemed truly humble when he gave the gift. It could prove a great blessing to Lyman and Delcena."

Ezekiel remained unconvinced. "I don't trust that man."

Nancy spoke. "But, Pa, Dr. Hurlbut was a gentleman today. He gave a generous gift. Perhaps we were wrong about him. He was strangely quiet after the wedding. He left before the christening and looked lonesome riding away."

"As lonesome as a rattlesnake before it strikes," Susan said.

Ezekiel eyed his fifth daughter. "Out of the mouth of maids," he chuckled. "My black-eyed Susan, you are a wise young lass."

In the bedroom, Almera lay on the bed beside her mother and the baby. She had stayed close to Julia following the wedding ceremony. The sixteen-year-old's eyes were closed and her cheeks pale, her characteristic vibrancy drained. Julia wondered if her daughter were ill. She took a hand off the babe who lay on her chest and laid it on Almera's forehead. At her mother's touch, Almera opened her eyes.

Julia smiled at her. "No fever. Do you feel well?" she questioned.

Almera nodded and turned on her side to face Julia. The girl's lovely brown eyes shone luminous and troubled in the candlelight. She was so beautiful.

"What's wrong?" Julia asked.

"Mama," Almera ventured, "what does the Bible say about the forbidden fruit? The serpent tells Eve it will make her wise. But how?"

"It is the fruit of the tree of knowledge of good and evil," Julia explained. "Before eating of it, Adam and Eve were innocent like children. After they partook, they knew the nature of their bodies, of mortality, and they had to leave the Garden of Eden. It was the way they became human and had children of their own."

"But why did God forbid it?" Almera asked.

"I don't know," Julia said. "Perhaps because it also brought death and pain. My mother used to say that the Garden of Eden represents childhood, that joyous time when we are innocent, protected, and guided by our parents."

"Then the forbidden fruit represents marriage," Almera said, "or the intimacy between a man and a woman. Tonight, Delcie eats the forbidden fruit."

Julia smiled inwardly. Almera was direct, not a child to mince words. She laid Amos down and hugged Almera. "But Child, God also commanded Adam and Eve to multiply and replenish the earth. After marriage, a man and woman's relationship is no longer forbidden. It can bring great joy and the incomparable blessing of children. And Delcena will not leave our family as Adam and Eve left Eden. She will always be a part of us. Now our family is enlarged, linked to Lyman and his kin."

At these words, Almera trembled. Julia stroked Almera's hair. She knew instinctively that tonight her lovely Almera, a budding woman, needed to be a child again, safe in her mother's arms.

*As shades of eve are softly stealing,*
*O'er the flowery landscape bright;*
*Glittering diamond orbs revealing,*
*Smiling goddess, Queen of Night.*

*So, from darkest clouds of sorrow,*
*Gleams anon Hope's brilliant star,*
*Promise of a bright to-morrow,*
*Doubling joys for every care.*

*From the mines most deep and fearful,*
*Diamonds rich, and ores are found,*
*From the eyes most sad and tearful,*
*Loving treasures oft abound.*

—JOSEPH E. JOHNSON, FROM "STAR OF HOPE"

*February 1830*

Annie was dozing when she felt Joel's hand on her shoulder. "Annie, we need to move to the Ohio."

Annie's eyes opened. "What?"

"I had the dream again. We would be happy there."

Annie snuggled against him. "Joel, we can't run away from our problems. Our families are here. Our little girl is buried here."

"In my dream, I see the sun shining on the Ohio River," Joel said as he stroked her hair. "Everything is dark here. I have to leave, Annie."

Annie moved away from Joel and sat up in bed. "Joel, would you leave without me?" she demanded, her spirit balking at her role of obedient wife. "My family needs me. How can we move after all Father has done for us?"

"Your first duty is to me as your husband," Joel snapped.

"And what of your duty to me, Joel?"

"That's why we must move. I can't provide for you here."

Annie felt hot, frustrated tears pool in her eyes. "Please, Joel," she begged. "It was only a dream. With the Lord's help, things will get better."

"Unless it's the Lord's will that we move to Ohio," Joel said shortly.

Months passed, and spring came. Joel did not speak again of moving. Annie knew he was brooding, but she tried to ignore it and live as cheerfully as she could. Annie prayed and hoped for doors to open, for their creditors' hearts to soften. But their financial situation remained bleak. She watched Joel work in the fields and at other men's mills until he was bone tired, only to remain dependent on her father for house and property.

Then, one night, when Joel was gone visiting at his parents' home, Annie said her prayers and retired early with Sixtus. She dreamed of her little girl, Julianne, named after Joel's dear sister. Little Julianne had died on a summer's day.

In the dream, the red-haired child laughed and ran toward a sunlit river on whose banks grew golden trees. She beckoned Annie to follow. Annie tried to call her back, but Julianne kept running. Attempting to follow, Annie discovered that her legs were as frozen as Lot's wife's when she had turned into a pillar of salt. Julianne disappeared around the river's bend. Panicking, Annie fell down, and with her final shreds of strength, dragged herself toward the river, toward her baby girl. She rounded the bend. Tears streaming down her face, she looked up. In the distance, she saw Joel throwing Sixtus in the air. Julianne played at his feet. Beyond Joel, Annie beheld a sawmill where her husband had fashioned shingles of pure gold. Joel turned to her, smiling. "See, Annie, how the sun shines in Ohio." Then Annie awakened. When Joel returned home the next day, she told him that her heart had changed—he must go to Ohio and find a place in the sunlight for them.

*August 1830*

It rained on the warm morning when Delcena began a long and arduous labor. Harriet Bull, Julia, and Nancy attended to Delcena. Nancy wiped her sister's brow, gave her water to drink, and prayed constantly that her sister's life be spared. Julia sat next to Delcena and told her stories of labor and children. Harriet Bull massaged Delcena's stomach and moved her alternately from the birthing stool to the bed.

At one point, Delcena, weakened and paled, uttered, "I can't do it. I will die."

Mrs. Bull slapped the young woman. "Work, work, work," the midwife bellowed. "Of course you will die, but not today, not in childbirth." The stout woman labored feverishly with her heavy face bright red, determined not to give up until the infant was loosed from its mother's body.

As the heavy labor continued for seemingly endless hours, Delcena's loved ones pushed back their growing fears. Nancy's chemise was saturated with sweat. Would her faith sustain her if she lost her sister? Julia strove to keep a positive and collected appearance for Delcena's sake. She stroked her daughter's arm. She prayed that she wouldn't panic, but the emotional remembrance of her eighteen-month-old Elmer's death seven years ago encroached upon her. How was it that human emotions traveled through time, a new situation triggering the same helpless and debilitating fear? Shaking, Julia stood up to get herself and Delcena a drink of water. For a brief, exhausted instant, Julia envied Ezekiel, who was at the tavern drinking away his worry.

After twelve hours of heavy labor, the infant entered the birth canal. It came breech. With her hands, Mrs. Bull angled the legs to make delivery possible. A baby girl emerged. Mrs. Bull slapped the tiny backside, and the baby cried. Julia tied the cord and slipped the infant into Nancy's anxious arms. The child screamed as Nancy cleaned her.

Mrs. Bull kissed Delcena. "You have a little girl, dear. Now all you must do is deliver the afterbirth." Delcena's need to push had not lessened. Intense pain gripped her. Delcena moaned. Mrs. Bull examined her.

"It isn't the afterbirth! It's another child!" Harriet Bull shouted. "Twins!" When the infant boy was delivered, he was at first too weak to take a breath. Mrs. Bull worked feverishly, clearing the child's mouth with her finger, slapping him, and rubbing his chest. When his cry came, Julia's whole soul breathed a thank you to her God. Tears streamed down Nancy's face. "I want Lyman," Delcena whispered.

"As soon as you're cleaned up." Mrs. Bull grinned, her mouth full of stumpy gray teeth.

As soon as Delcena was ready, Nancy went into the kitchen. In the candlelight, she saw Lyman on his knees praying. He had been in that position off and on for nearly twelve hours. He did not know Nancy was there, he was so intent on speaking to his God. At the moment, he was thanking his Father in Heaven, for he had heard a baby's cry. Then he begged once more that Delcena's life be spared. He closed his prayer in Jesus' name.

"Lyman," Nancy said quietly.

Lyman startled and jumped to his feet. "Delcena?" he asked.

Nancy smiled. "Exhausted. But Mrs. Bull assures us she will be fine. Lyman, you are doubly blessed tonight. You have twins. A daughter and a son."

A look of rapture crossed Lyman's face. He hugged Nancy and bounded toward the kitchen. *And Delcena is triply blessed,* Nancy thought, *to have such a husband.*

When Lyman entered the room, Delcena lay in bed with a bundled infant sleeping on each side of her. Her brown hair was wet from sweat, and she looked utterly spent. Still she found the strength to smile up at her husband. "Are you satisfied with your children, Mr. Sherman?" she whispered.

"Yes! Oh yes!" Lyman exclaimed. He laid a gentle finger on the cheek of each babe. "How tiny they are. How exquisite and miraculous." His eyes shone as he looked at his wife. He stroked Delcena's hair and kissed her. "And there are no words to describe the depth of my love and gratitude for their mother."

"I'm so tired." Delcena's voice was barely audible.

"Then sleep, my darling."

Delcena's eyes closed. Her body relaxed as she gave way to a deep and deserved rest. When Lyman took Mrs. Bull home in his wagon, he told her that they would name the babies Alvira and

Lyman Ezekiel. Afterward, he stopped at the tavern to tell Ezekiel about his grandchildren.

Nancy and Julia spent the night at the Shermans'. The next morning, Nancy arose before dawn to bake bread for Delcena. While Nancy worked in the outdoor kitchen, the morning lengthened, growing bright, still, and humid. As she pulled out the final loaves from the brick oven, Ezekiel arrived on the young horse, Leo.

"Hello, Nancy," Ezekiel greeted. "I hear I have some grandchildren."

"Yes, Pa," Nancy answered.

"How is Delcena?"

"Fine, Pa."

Ezekiel tied the horse to the hitching post. Then he helped Nancy carry the bread into the log house.

After placing the bread on the table, Nancy and Ezekiel entered Delcena's bedroom. Nancy noticed her father's pride as Ezekiel hugged Delcena and then, moist-eyed, picked up each of the infants. Julia was near, beaming at her grandchildren. "Did you ever imagine such a blessing, Father?" She smiled at her husband.

Lyman came in. He cradled his little son in his arms and grinned at his wife and daughter. He turned to his father-in-law. "So Father Johnson, what do you think of all this? Look what Delcena has brought into the world."

Ezekiel affectionately slapped Lyman's back. "I couldn't be prouder of the both of you."

Nancy stood in the corner. It felt as if a cocoon separated her from the rest of the family. She felt so alone. Finally Nancy approached her father. "Papa, is it all right if I ride Leo home? You can bring Mama in the wagon."

Julia, who now cradled the baby girl in her arms, glanced over at Nancy. "I'd rather you stay, Nancy. We'll go together later in the wagon."

Nancy shook her head. "With Seth and David burning bricks today, and the girls and Joe in summer school, Julianne will need help with the work and the little ones."

Ezekiel nodded to Nancy, granting her permission. Nancy bent down and kissed Delcena's cheek. Delcena noticed that her sister's lips were cool.

Outside in the humid air, Nancy mounted the horse. Leo pranced in the sun. As she started for home, the road was quiet. Nancy urged the horse into a brisk trot, her loose skirts draped around her as she posted with his rhythm.

As she rode, Nancy's thoughts roamed. She thought of how Delcena and the babies had been spared. Her prayers had been answered. Yet this morning Nancy's heart ached, and she felt to weep when she ought to rejoice. Oh, she wished she did not desire her sister's blessings! She loved Delcena and Lyman. Yet, without meaning to, she coveted their love and the babies sent to them. To escape her thoughts, Nancy moved her right leg behind the horse's girth and pressed it into Leo's side as she lifted her hip forward, giving the signal for Leo to canter.

At this cue, the spirited horse broke into a full gallop, causing Nancy to lose her stirrups. She still could have pulled him back to a trot if a bird had not winged from the trees at the same instant. In fear, Leo threw a tremendous buck. The horse bolted forward as Nancy flew in the air, her slender body twisting, her legs tangling in her skirts as she fell.

From the brickyard, David saw Leo, lathered and blowing, at the entrance of the barn with an empty saddle and the reins hanging. Fearing that his father might be hurt, David shouted for Seth to get Benjamin and follow with a wooden plank in case their father needed to be carried home. Without waiting for a reply, David swung up onto the horse and galloped down the road.

Halfway to the Shermans', David glimpsed the crumpled figure lying by the side of the road. From a distance, the draping white skirt made Nancy look like a broken angel fallen from heaven. Digging his heels into Leo as his heart pounded with fear, the young man traversed the distance. He leapt from the horse and ran to his sister.

"Nancy," he gasped.

Her eyes were closed. Nancy moaned. David noticed that her leg was twisted at an odd angle.

"Talk to me, Nancy," David commanded, his heart throbbing. He called on the heavens. "Please, God, help her."

Nancy, whose pain had been so intense a moment ago that she had prayed for release, heard her brother as if from a great distance.

"Nancy, beloved Nancy," David begged as he sat down and cradled her head in his lap. "Help is coming. Promise me you won't leave us. Promise me!"

As if in a dream, Nancy remembered the toddling, curly-haired David. When nine years old, it had been her job to watch him. "Promise not to play in the fire, David," she had said. "Promise not to stand behind the horses."

"I promise," the little boy had said, laughing, then promptly done whatever he had promised not to do.

Nancy opened her eyes. "You never kept your promises, David," she whispered.

"But you always kept yours," he said as he stroked her hair.

The doctor from Fredonia shook his head as he spoke to Julia and Ezekiel in hushed tones. "Nancy's thigh bone is broken near the hip socket. She will not walk again. Keep her as comfortable as possible. I can't do anything else."

"And you call yourself a healer?" Ezekiel shouted bitterly as the doctor rode away in the twilight. He stalked into the house.

Distraught, Julia followed him. "Zeke, it's not the good doctor's fault."

Ezekiel wheeled around to face his wife, his eyes blazing. Julia must blame him! How could she not? She had never wanted him to allow Nancy to ride.

"Trust in Christ," Julia said as she met his gaze. "Only He can comfort us and help our Nancy."

Ezekiel's voice shook with anger. "Woman, don't tell me of trust in Christ when my girl lays in the other room moaning! God hands out stones, Julia, not bread!"

At the sound of his rage, Julia's strength failed. She covered her face with her hands. Ezekiel took his gun from the mantel and left the house.

Joseph, thirteen now, was outside searching for herbs. The boy knew the medicinal use for each plant in the Pomfret woods. He had read books. He had also learned from the midwife, Harriet Bull, and the old Indian, Jason Goldfinger, who lived in a shack near the tavern. Joe planned to find some hepatica for Nancy's liver, some ginseng to help her grow strong, and most important, some podophyllum. He knew that podophyllum was good for bones and he wanted desperately for his sister's bones to mend. He planned to make her a tea, every single day until she could walk again. Joseph gathered the plants, tucked them safely in the bag, and headed back toward the house.

Joseph was nearly to the house when he saw his father coming out with his gun.

"Pa," Joe asked carefully. "Where you going?"

"I got a job to do in the barn. Git in the house!"

"I found leaves, Pa, to make a tea for Nancy. To help her bones mend and make her strong again."

Rage clouded Ezekiel's eyes. Bitterness and pain pressed in upon him. "Git in the house, Joe!"

Worried now, Joseph shuffled his feet. "Why don't I help you with your job first, Pa?"

Ezekiel exploded. "Git! Before I horsewhip you!"

Joseph obeyed and hurried into the house. He had never been afraid of his father before that moment. He ran to Seth, whispering brokenly. "Seth, Pa's going to do something terrible! He's going to the barn with his gun." Seth put a hand on Joseph's shoulder, then ran from the house.

In a few strides, Seth was to his father. "Pa, what are you doing?"

Ezekiel stopped and let his breath out slowly, his eyes gray coals. "I'm going to shoot Leo so this never happens again."

"No, Pa. I won't let you do it." Seth's voice was firm.

"You want to see it, Seth?" Ezekiel snarled. "It ain't goin' to be pretty!"

"It was an accident, Pa. Killing the horse won't make Nancy better. You know that."

"The horse is crazy. It could happen again! It could be you, or David, or Bennie!"

"Pa, you told me since I was a child that Old Bess is only for hunting game or for self-defense."

Ezekiel's voice was as cold as ice. "I won't let it happen again. I won't be responsible."

Seth continued talking. "You always taught us not to beat or kill something for just being what they are. That's why you always hated the doctrine of the elect, the idea that people go to hell just for being who they are. Leo can't pay for what he did. He's just a horse, a scared animal. You'd never forgive yourself, Pa."

With that comment, something inside Ezekiel broke, and he let out a cry of such agony and rage that Seth felt his heart would break. "But I'm a man, Seth! I taught Nancy to ride that horse against your mother's wishes." Ezekiel pushed his son aside and ran toward the barn.

Inside the barn, Leo calmly ate the hay in the manger. His ears pricked forward when he saw Ezekiel walking toward him.

"Killing Leo will hurt Nancy so much more," Seth said from the barn door.

In agony, Ezekiel dropped the gun and pressed both hands to the sides of his head. He cursed, then he picked the gun back up. But instead of shooting Leo, the man leapt on the animal bareback, sped out of the barn, and galloped down the road. Seth bridled the mare and followed his father.

At a lone table at the back of the dark tavern, Seth watched as Ezekiel, in another corner, drank until he was senseless. Old Bess lay at Ezekiel's side. Seth's goal was simple—to make sure his father and the horse returned home safely that evening. Seth endured the stench of the tavern, the odor of the men's boots, the scent of alcohol and smoke, the filth on the floor where men chewed and spit out tobacco. He hardly heard the gambling and lewd talk around him. At his lonely table, he prayed for Nancy and for his father.

Late that night, after Seth had seen his father safely home and in bed, he went into the sitting room where they had moved Nancy's bed. There was a fire in the hearth to keep Nancy warm. Julianne was bedded on the floor next to Nancy. In the firelight, Seth saw that Nancy's eyes were open.

"Do you hurt too much to sleep?" Seth asked.

"It isn't just the pain," Nancy's voice was low and halting. "I fear this happened because of my sin."

"Nancy," Seth said quietly as he sat on a chair on the other side of her bed. "There is no sin in you. You strive with all your soul to live righteously."

Nancy's eyes filled with tears. "This morning, I coveted Delcena's husband and children. And now Papa blames himself."

"Do you remember," Seth said as he took her hand, "the story of the blind man in Saint John, chapter nine? The man was blind from his birth, and the disciples asked Jesus who sinned, the blind man or his parents."

Nancy nodded. She felt too weak to speak.

Seth continued, "The Master said that neither the man nor his parents had sinned but that the man was blind that the works of God might be made manifest. Nancy, God's works will be manifested in your goodness."

Julianne had awakened. She sat up and took Nancy's other hand. "Nance," she said quietly. "Could we sing to you? Perhaps 'I Know That My Redeemer Lives'?"

Nancy nodded.

Together, Seth and Julianne sang to the sister they loved, comforting her as well as themselves.

*He lives to silence all my fears,*
*He lives to stop and wipe my tears,*
*He lives to calm my troubled heart,*
*He lives all blessings to impart:*
*He lives my kind, wise, heav'nly friend,*
*He lives and loves me to the end,*
*He lives, and while he lives I'll sing,*
*He lives my Prophet, Priest, and King.*

*September 1830*

Joel studied Annie's features as they stood outside their cabin. Her thick, auburn hair hung loose and full down her back, her green eyes flecked with gold, her nose freckled, her skin fair, her cheeks full and dimpled when she smiled. He had already taken leave of Sixtus, who was now playing with Annie's ten-year-old sister, Sarah, up at his in-law's house. Sixtus was dark-eyed and dark-haired, his looks favoring the Johnsons. But little Julianne, the babe they had lost, she would have grown up to look like Annie.

"Be safe, Joel," Annie said, continuing to smile so that she could avoid bursting into tears, "and find us the brightest spot in the Ohio to build our cottage."

"I'll send word as soon as I can," Joel promised, still hesitant to mount his horse. "David or I will come back for you when I have work and a place."

Annie mustered up her gumption and grinned brightly. She was determined to be cheerful and hopeful. If anything happened, she wanted Joel to remember her that way. Joel touched her freckles with his finger. Then he took his wife in his arms and kissed her forehead. Annie, whose full height equaled the top of her husband's shoulders, laid her head on his chest and wrapped her arms around him. She felt her husband's ribs and thought of how he wasn't quite as gaunt as a year ago. She listened to him breathe and was glad that she heard no wheeze or squeak from his lungs. Though he had been fairly sturdy the past four months, she knew how quickly his cough might come. Then Joel bent his shoulders, and she stood on her tiptoes as they kissed good-bye.

Joel mounted his horse and rode away. When he came to the bend in the road that would take him from Annie's sight, he looked back and waved. She enthusiastically swept her white handkerchief into the air, waving it over and over again. As soon as he was gone, she blew her nose into it and used it to wipe her tears. He was on his way to his parents' home to pick up David. Then the two brothers would be off on this journey that would change her life.

As she stood at the roadside, Annie gathered her courage. She would treasure her last days in Pomfret with her family and Joel's family. She thought of her sister-in-law Nancy, who was now crippled. How life could change in a heartbeat! Annie looked at the leaves. Some were still bright green while others sported their full fall colors. All the trees would be barren by January, the trunks and branches hoarding life internally like marrow in the bone, waiting until new buds grew in the spring. Annie shivered and walked back toward the cabin.

After leaving New York, Joel and David traversed much of Ohio. They traveled past Fairport and Cleveland, then southwest through Columbus and down toward Cincinnati. Joel searched earnestly for the best place to bring his family, while David enjoyed the adventure. They rode through lovely country, but Joel kept moving on, searching for something he couldn't put his finger on.

When in Cincinnati, they visited their mother's siblings, Joel Hills and Nancy Hills Taft. These relatives were strangers to David, but Joel remembered them well. Joel had been eleven when his uncle had visited the Johnson's Vermont home. Julia had convinced Ezekiel to let her brother take his namesake, young Joel, with him to Cincinnati for a time. This visit extended to around eighteen months. During this time period, Ezekiel had moved the rest of his family from Vermont to western New York. After Julia and the other children were settled in a rented house in Pomfret, Ezekiel had walked the five hundred miles to Cincinnati to pick up his son.

Now, seventeen years later, Mr. Joel Hills, a country gentleman, warmly welcomed his beloved sister's grown sons into his spacious frame home. The brothers spent their first evening as honored guests at a family gathering. Aunt Nancy insisted they describe in detail each of Julia's children. David charmed the entire family with his vivid descriptions, his voice only halting when he told of Nancy's accident.

The next morning, Joel and David toured the surrounding countryside and spoke with their uncle and his associates about local opportunities. Late that day, following supper, the three retired to the study where Mr. Hills told his nephews stories of their mother as a girl and reminisced with Joel about the time he lived with him.

"Joel," his uncle chuckled, "have you ever told David about the day you nearly drowned? When I found you sprawled out over that knoll, my first thought was that Julia would murder me."

"I remember well," Joel answered seriously. "It was providence that saved me."

"I'd like to hear about it," David encouraged with a twinkle in his eye.

Joel stretched his angular legs toward the fire and began. "One day, I was walking along the bank of the Ohio River when I saw some boys bathing. I wanted to join them, but the boys were strangers, so I decided to bathe alone. I watched them wade out a considerable distance and figured I could safely wade out as well. However, before I waded very far, I stepped off a steep bank and fell into water over my head.

"Not able to swim, I struggled and sank to the bottom. I lay there perfectly helpless, supposing that my time had come to leave this world. Suddenly a strange power came over me. Something said, 'Turn over on your face, and crawl on the ground.' I made the effort without knowing which way I was going. In a moment, I was out of the water. The same power told me to crawl to that knoll Uncle mentioned and get my stomach on it with my head down. After doing so, I became unconscious. When I came to my senses again, water had run out of my mouth, and Uncle was shouting and running toward me."

David smiled warmly at his brother. "Joel, old boy, God has a work for you to do before He calls you home. If you could just hurry and find the place where He wants you to settle, you just might get to it."

Joel shrugged his long frame and looked intently at his uncle. "That's why I'm here, Uncle. I feel the Lord has guided me to the Ohio. But I haven't found the place or opportunity that seems right. At present, God appears to be leaving me in the dark."

Mr. Hills attended carefully to his nephew's words. The older man's hair was completely gray, and time had filled out his once slender physique and given him a distinguished look that had been absent in his youth. He saw Julia and Ezekiel in these young men. After a moment, he spoke. "Your grandmother and mother are the only people I've known whom God never leaves in the dark, His influence invariably whispering thoughts to their hearts." Mr. Hills stroked his gray mustache with a thumb and finger. "God doesn't speak to me, young Joel. I don't know the best place for you. I picture you building a sawmill in an area where new settlers are moving, capitalizing on your shingle-cutter invention, and doing very well for yourself and your family.

"On the other hand, I would be delighted if you stayed here. We could use a teacher at the schoolhouse this winter, but Cincinnati has little use for another sawmill."

"And I have no capital to build." Joel sighed. Discouraged, he wondered if he had been mistaken and if this trip would prove fruitless.

During a moment of quiet, Mr. Hills lit his pipe. After a few relaxed puffs, he spoke once more. "When I look at the two of you, I see my family. Joel, you are built like the Hills clan—tall and slender. In temperament, you are prone to religiosity like your mother. Yet, as a child, I remember that you did not possess her stable nature but had quick mood changes and intense emotions like your good father.

"David, you are as cheerful as the Ellises and as passionate as Ezekiel. In looks, you've acquired the best features of both your father and mother. They were quite handsome in their youth. But you, David, you look like some stripling Greek god."

"Would that the ladies thought so." David laughed. "Uncle, Mother tells us that our brother Joseph is like you, bookish and happy. He is her favorite child."

Mr. Hills laughed out loud and replied warmly. "Is this Joseph lazy as well? Does he torment his younger sisters? How I would like to see Julia again."

David grinned. "I have assumed the role of tormentor. Joseph is more inclined to entertain. Mother would love to see you as well. Perhaps Joel will settle here, and she will come to visit."

Joel shook his head. "Uncle, Cincinnati isn't the right place. I must move on tomorrow. David and I are grateful for your hospitality."

"Uncle Joel, I fear your namesake is looking for paradise. Tell him it only exists in the next life," David said, slapping his brother's thigh. He'd grown restless of Joel's fruitless search and was concerned about Joel's growing discouragement.

Mr. Hills chewed on the end of his pipe. An idea had just occurred to him. "Joel, have you visited Lorain County in north-western Ohio? A town called Amherst?"

Joel shook his head.

Mr. Hills continued. "John Clay moved there a couple of years ago, and we've heard good reports from his parents. I recall them mentioning that he is contemplating expanding his business and building some kind of mill."

Uncle Joel's wife, Mrs. Rhoda Hills, entered the room and served the men pieces of apple pie. Having listened to the last comment, she added. "Be careful if you go there. Our minister warned the Clays of the false beliefs of Shakers in the area."

David grinned engagingly at his aunt as he took the pie. "That reminds me of Mother's last comment as we went out the door. 'Sons, Sidney Rigdon and the Campbellites are active in the Ohio. Beware of their false doctrines.'"

Mr. Hills chuckled. "That sounds like bossy Julia."

Joel's eyes were serious as he contemplated. "I remember John Clay. We were friends as children. We'll head that way in the morning."

Aunt Rhoda eyed bonny David. "I heard in church that John's sister Kathryn is currently living with John and his wife. She's a pretty young lady."

David laughed and took a bite of pie. "Aunt, that idea is as tempting as this pie. Joel came to the Ohio to find a home. I came to find a girl."

"Don't get your hopes up, little brother." Joel broke into a rare grin. "There's no accounting for a woman's taste."

"Truer words were never spoken," David answered. "Take Annie for example."

Then David heard the sound he had heard too little of in the past three years—the wide, full sound of Joel's laughter.

*October 1830*

David teased Kathryn Clay on an overcast day as he drove the team and wagon to the town square in Amherst, Lorain County, Ohio, to obtain supplies for his trip back to New York. "That hat makes you the prettiest peacock." David grinned as he shook the reins and hawed to the mules.

Kathryn was nineteen years old, blonde, blue-eyed, and pretty. Today, she was dressed in bows, gloves, and frills—like she was going to a party rather than into town.

"I'd rather look like a pretty peacock than an old hen," she returned.

David laughed. He found Kathryn both attractive and spirited.

"I don't see why you have to go all the way back to New York to get your sister-in-law," Kathryn pouted. "Why can't Joel do it? She's his wife."

David turned pensive for a moment. "Joel and your brother John need to get busy building the sawmill. They'd best get as much done as they can before the snow comes. The weather permitting, I'll have Annie back here by January. I'll stay until Joel's crops are planted and his house built."

"I was hoping you were planning on settling here, not just staying for the season," Kathryn said with a glint in her eye.

David chuckled. She was forward. Gorgeous, but forward. "Depends on the motivation," he said.

The young woman raised her eyebrows and smiled coyly at David's comment, but she held her peace. For a time they rode in silence as David thought of how the town of Amherst had answered Joel's search. The swift Black River brought new settlers and provided an ideal setting for a sawmill. The soil was black and sandy, the flat land profuse with a variety of trees, the timber on the ridges of white chestnut. In addition, John Clay had jumped at the opportunity to go into business with Joel. The shingle-cutter invention intrigued John, and he saw the opportunity to make money. To facilitate the venture, John invited Joel and his family to live with him in his frame house until they built their own cabin.

For David, the icing on the cake had been the lovely Kathryn. He hadn't really expected that his joke would become reality, that he would become enthralled with a girl from Ohio.

As they passed the courthouse, Kathryn sat up straight and tall, her blue eyes flashing with excitement. She pointed to the adjoining public house, then put her head near David's and whispered confidentially, "Late last night, after you and Joel retired, Almon Babbitt stopped by and told John and me that one of the Mormonite missionaries is being held there. He's a big, talkative fellow by the name of Pratt who was taken prisoner yesterday."

David noted that she smelled nice—like soap and lemon. "Almon Babbitt? Is he that young fellow who dotes on you?"

Kathryn giggled. "He's a lad, barely seventeen. Not at all like you. But he's smart and jaunty; I'll give that to Almon. He aspires to be a lawyer. He came to town yesterday evening to watch court proceedings and see what the judge decided to do with the Mormonite."

"Tell me of this Mormonite," David encouraged.

"Almon says the Mormons have some crazy prophet named Joe Smith who sees angels and wrote a new Bible from some golden plates he dug up. Almon says there's a group of them over in a town called Kirtland in Geauga County. Almon says more are getting baptized every day. They left one of their books with Simeon Carter. That's when Officer Peabody came and arrested Pratt."

"I've heard of the gold plates," David mused. "Didn't Joe Smith come from a New York village? Palmyra, I think."

Kathryn shrugged. "Almon says Smith organized his church in April."

David interrupted in a sing-song voice, "Almon says, Almon says, Almon says. Almon sure says a lot of things to you."

Kathryn dismissed David's comment with the wave of a slender, gloved hand.

"Did Almon say why they arrested Pratt?" David asked as he raised his eyebrows.

Kathryn giggled as she emphasized the first two words. "*Almon says* Pratt lived here a few years ago. Yesterday, the local preachers paid some old settlers to file some trumped-up charges."

In an instant, David's teasing smile evaporated. *Preachers paying people to persecute someone because of their religion.* The taste was bitter in David's mouth. He had seen Joel persecuted by those who claimed to believe in Christ. "You mean Pratt didn't break any laws?"

"None to speak of," Kathryn replied lightly.

David studied the reins. "In this country, no man should be arrested for his choice of religion."

Kathryn laid a gloved hand on David's arm. "You're right, David. But this is different." Then Kathryn paused and gripped David's elbow. "Stop the wagon! That might be Pratt coming out of the public house now. Almon says that Pratt is smart and bold. That Mormonite made a joke of the whole court. For his defense, he and one of his friends sang a hymn, 'O How Happy Are They.' Then Pratt suggested that the witnesses repent of their false swearing and that the magistrate repent of his abuse and blackguardism. If they did that, Pratt said he would kneel down and pray with them. Almon could hardly keep from laughing at the Mormonite's spunk."

David pulled the team to a halt, his interest piqued. Two men were walking out of the public house toward the Town Square.

"The one with the big bulldog is Officer Peabody," Kathryn whispered. "The other must be Pratt. He's a big fellow, isn't he? But not fat like the officer. Come David, let's get closer and maybe we can hear what they're saying." With that, Kathryn's dainty hands took the reins from David and quickly slapped the mules on their rumps.

Both interested and embarrassed at the same time, David pulled his wide-brimmed hat down near his eyes to shadow his face. Kathryn inched the wagon closer to the two men. A moment later, they had no trouble hearing the robust voices.

"Well, Mr. Pratt, it's off to prison with you," Officer Peabody poked fun at his prisoner. "Like the judge said, prison will test your apostleship."

"But I'm only an elder," Pratt returned good-naturedly. Then a thought occurred to the missionary. "Mr. Peabody," Pratt challenged with a grin. "Are you good at a footrace?"

"No," the officer frowned. "But my big bulldog is, and he has been trained to assist me in my office these several years. He will take any man down at my bidding."

"Well, Mr. Peabody, you have compelled me to go a mile, I have gone with you two miles. You have given me an opportunity to preach, sing, and have also entertained me with lodging and breakfast. I must now go on my journey. If you are good at a race, you can accompany me. I thank you for all your kindness. Good day, sir."

David and Kathryn watched in amazement as the prisoner began running away. Officer Peabody stood stock still, as if in shock. After sprinting about fifty yards, the Mormon turned around and shouted another invitation for the officer to join him in a race. Mr. Pratt doffed his hat as he passed David and

Kathryn, then he leapt a fence and ran through a field toward a forest.

"David," Kathryn urged whispering delightedly. "You're quick. Go catch the Mormon for Officer Peabody."

David shook his head. "He runs like a deer. Besides, I want Mr. Pratt to win this race."

At that instant, the officer regained his senses and chased after the missionary, clapping his hands, pointing toward Pratt and bellowing at his bulldog to seize him. "Stu-boy, Stu-boy—take him—lay hold of him! I say—down with him!"

David's heart sank as the huge dog sped away. The man had no chance. David tensed and readied himself to jump from the wagon. He couldn't stop the dog from catching the Mormon, but he would do everything in his power to keep the dog from mauling him. Just as the animal was about to leap on the man, Mr. Pratt stopped dead in his tracks. He clapped his hands and shouted an imitation of the officer while pointing beyond himself toward the forest. "Stu-boy, Stu-boy—go, take him—down with him!" The dog redoubled his speed and ran with all fury past the Mormon missionary and on into the forest. Mr. Pratt then sprinted down an opposite path in the same woodland.

David threw his head back and laughed until tears rolled down his cheeks.

"You better be quiet." Kathryn elbowed David with her own eyes twinkling. "Or Officer Peabody just might send Stu-boy after you."

As soon as David controlled his laughter, he turned to Kathryn, took her in his arms and kissed her on the lips. A thought ran through his mind. Ohio was a singular place, and he definitely wanted to spend more time here.

## 5

*Until the Prophet Joseph came;*
*"Repent," to me he said,*
*"And be baptized in Jesus' name*
*With hands laid on your head."*

*No wish had I, nor could refuse*
*The power that on me fell;*
*Light filled my soul, my tongue was loosed,*
*The glorious news to tell.*

*God then to me this truth revealed:*
*That he had Joseph sent;*
*And on his head the Priesthood sealed*
*To call men to repent.*

—Joel H. Johnson

*October 1830*

David traveled home on horseback, staying in taverns some nights and with hospitable farm families others. During the nine-day journey, he thought a great deal of Kathryn Clay and the possibility of spending the rest of his life with her. He liked her brother, John Clay, well enough, but he wasn't very fond of John's wife, Margaret. She was a shrewd, sanctimonious woman who was quick tongued and suspicious. David was glad to be away from her house.

He looked forward to going home and embracing his family once more. The night before arriving in Pomfret, he dreamt of his sister Nancy. In the dream, she ran to him exclaiming, "Look, David! I'm strong! I can walk again!"

David rode into Pomfret in the afternoon, and Julianne greeted him at the door. Wiping her hands on her apron, she cried with joy at seeing him. She hugged David warmly. After Julianne's embrace, David hurried into the sitting room where Nancy's bed was set up near the hearth. Nancy's eyes were closed. She looked so thin and pale—a shadow of her former self. David's gladness dissipated like dew in midmorning sun.

Nancy's eyes opened, and she turned her head on hearing someone in the room.

David sat down by her. "Hello, Nancy."

"David," she said. On seeing this younger brother, a light came into her eyes. She managed a smile. "I'm glad you're back."

"For a few weeks," David said as he took off his hat. "Then I'll take Annie and Sixtus to the Ohio. Joel's found a good situation, Nancy. He has a partner and is building a sawmill. And I've found a girl. Her name's Kathryn Clay. She's as beautiful and as spunky as a young filly."

"She's a lucky girl if you love her," Nancy said softly. "David, if you settle in Ohio, Joel and Annie will be glad to have family near."

*But I shall miss you terribly,* she thought. She remembered how David had sat at her side for two weeks following her accident, reading the Old Testament to her like it was a glorious adventure, distracting her from her pain. He was a ray of life and light.

"What's wrong, Nancy?" David noticed the shadow that had crossed her wan face. "Are you hurting?"

"No, David, not anymore." It touched her that he worried over her even when he was full of energy and plans. "I'm just frozen in this body." She attempted a joke, "But sometimes I get a fever, and it thaws me."

David felt like tearing his hat to shreds. "I hate that this happened to you."

"The Lord comforts me, David. Someday I will be free of all this."

"I want you to be whole, Nancy, not dead," David cried out. When David was with this eldest sister, there was no façade or pretended courage. Tears burned his eyes.

Nancy looked steadily at her brother. He was a man now, but the boy in him still lingered not far below the surface. Did he know that he was one of the brightest parts of her life? "I'm here, David," she said, "like I promised you. I'll stay as long as God wills it."

As two weeks passed, David saw how things at home had worsened. His father's drinking had increased tenfold. His mother had visibly aged, her features lined with exhaustion and tension. Each night, Seth went to the tavern in order to accompany Ezekiel home. Seth's was a lonely task—ensuring his father's safety while at the same time shielding his mother and siblings from his father's drunken outbursts. Yet despite Seth's efforts, Almera and

Susan were no longer cheery, their personal charms marred by worry. Benjamin was moody and short-fused. Joseph avoided home, spending hours calling on friends, some of whom were of questionable influence. Julianne held up a brave front as she cared for the little ones and waited on Nancy. One young suitor grew tired of calling on Julianne, telling her that she gave away all parts of herself to her family, leaving nothing for him. Juli tossed the incident aside as if it didn't matter, saying, "If he doesn't care enough to understand, then he isn't for me." But Nancy was haunted by the fact that her accident had increased her father's drunkenness and her family's troubles. Each day, she grew weaker rather than stronger.

At first, David tried to cheer them all. But his natural cheer sloughed away as his father staggered home each night, sometimes laughing with false hilarity, sometimes bitterly cursing and weeping. His mother's love for her husband was understandably growing dim and cold. Seth's life was a prison. David feared that Nancy would die. His frustration fused into anger toward his father, anger that he tried to muffle even as it cankered his soul.

Then, on Friday night, Seth brought Ezekiel home long past midnight. As Seth set the lantern on the table and lit a candle, Ezekiel staggered into the parlor where Nancy slept. In the dark, the man tripped over the wooden crutches leaning next to Nancy's bed. As the crutches clattered to the floor, Ezekiel fell, his torso falling onto Nancy's arm and shoulder. Ezekiel staggered to his feet, violently cursing.

"Papa, Papa," Nancy cried out in confusion. Reeking of brandy, Ezekiel incoherently clutched at her arms. He tried to drag Nancy from her bed as he begged her to get up and ride around the farm with him.

Awakened by the noise, David bounded downstairs and into the parlor. Seth was already there. Together, the brothers pulled

Ezekiel away from Nancy. They forced their father into the kitchen where Ezekiel collapsed on the floor and began to weep like a child.

Filled with sick disgust, David stared at his father. David's body shook with rage as he fought down the terrible urge to kick Ezekiel. Seth took hold of David's shoulders and turned him toward him. "David," Seth ordered, his dark eyes penetrating, "leave Pa to me. Take the candle and make sure Nancy isn't hurt."

Shaking with emotion, David obeyed. He went to his sister. "Nancy," he uttered as he approached her. "Are you hurt?" She looked up at David and shook her head. He saw tears on her cheeks, though she didn't make a sound. Her eyes looked cavernous in the candlelight.

The candle trembled in David's hands. In his mind's eye, he saw a black pine box bearing Nancy's body. He placed the candle on the stand next to the family Bible. Kneeling down beside her bed, he buried his head in the quilt and cried out, "I can't stand what Pa's doing to you, to us!"

Nancy reached out a weak hand and stroked David's hair as he kneeled beside her bed. When Nancy spoke, her voice was steady, though tears crept out of her eyes. "David, I dreamed of a tree planted in a dark, barren field. Against all odds, it grew and bore fruit. But when the wind and storms came, it lost its leaves and became dry and hollow, without the strength to stand. We worked desperately to anchor the tree with ropes, but the wind blew too strong. Then, when our will was spent and the tree was about to fall, the wind ceased. The sun came out, and the tree remained. A forest grew up around it. There in the center of this living forest, it stood tall and scarred, its very form telling the story of sacrifice and weakness, of pain, love, and majesty. The tree is like our father, David. Pray with me. What else can we do?"

David covered her hand with both of his. His emotions trembled too near the surface to speak.

"Heavenly Father," Nancy's voice rose softly in the darkness, "forgive us of our sins. May we live worthy of that mansion prepared for us on high. Sin and sorrow encompass our family and threaten to destroy our loving home. Grant us great faith like those in the ancient Church. Shorten this time of sorrow and pain. Forgive our father and bless this family. We cast our burdens into Thy keeping. Thy will be done. In Jesus' blessed name. Amen."

After the prayer, David held Nancy's hand for a time. Then he kissed her slender fingers and went upstairs. He lay down on his bed but could not sleep. After lying awake for hours, David rose before dawn and went into the kitchen, where his father slept on the floor. David saw that Seth had covered Ezekiel with a quilt and tucked a pillow under his head. Love, pity, and confusion rose in David like mountainous waves. He did not have Nancy's peace or her faith. He was more like his father.

Helpless to escape the intensity of these emotions, David pulled on a coat and left the house. The snow had stopped. He walked to the woodpile and began chopping. After an hour, Seth joined David. The two labored in silence as the sun rose and painted the chill sky with brilliant pink. When full morning broke, Lyman Sherman rode up on horseback.

"You're about early today," Seth commented as he stopped chopping. Squinting in the cold sunlight, he looked up at his brother-in-law.

"Seth and David," Lyman said as he jumped off his mount. He approached David and Seth with a sure step and a steady and earnest look. Lyman was a man inclined to action and problem-solving. "Delcena fears that your father's intemperance is weakening Nancy's will to live. We prayed earnestly last night and feel sure that your father must leave at once. His drunkenness is undoing your family."

Seth gazed out at the farm. David remembered the words of Nancy's prayers. *Shorten this time of sorrow and pain.* Delcena and Lyman were praying last night as well.

Seth's voice was solemn and heavy as he gripped the handle of his ax. "Lyman, are you suggesting that we turn our father out of the house he built and away from the farm he cleared? We will never do that."

"You misunderstand me," Lyman said, with a quick shake of his head. "I don't want you to turn your father out. I want you to take him somewhere for the winter. He needs a change of climate, an escape through something other than drink. Nancy needs time to strengthen."

David swung his ax. A thick log let out a crack as it split down the center at his blow. Lyman grinned at David. "You are the handiest fellow with an ax," he admired.

"I could take Pa back to Amherst," David let out a short spurt of breath. "Annie said she will be ready to leave next week."

Seth shook his head. "But you will be staying with the Clays. They are strangers, and it wouldn't be right to force father's intemperance on them."

Lyman noticed the deep shadows under Seth's eyes. "This might be an opportune time for you to leave too, Seth," Lyman suggested. "Especially with Joel's creditors threatening to sue you. What of your uncle in Cincinnati? Delcena told me that he and your father were close friends."

"Uncle would welcome you, Seth," David commented. "When Joel and I were in Cincinnati, he mentioned that they need a teacher this winter. Uncle Joel and Aunt Rhoda have good hearts. They would try to help Pa."

"Nancy is ill. I fear leaving mother and the children," Seth sighed.

David was quiet for a moment. Then he spoke. "I can stay. Annie will be fine traveling alone by steamboat." He thought of

Nancy, his mother, and his other brothers and sisters. He saw the image of his drunken father. He felt as if the lovely Kathryn were receding far from him.

Seth looked at his younger brother. Last night he had seen the rage in David's eyes. For the sake of David's soul, this younger brother needed to be far away. Seth spoke with authority, "David, Joel isn't strong enough for the heavy work of building a sawmill, a home, and planting crops. You will go to Amherst. I'll stay and care for Mother and Father. Besides, I have a commitment to the Pomfret School. Things might change by spring."

Lyman clapped Seth and David on the backs. He stomped his feet to warm them. "Brothers, obstacles arise in your minds like weeds! Mow them down! Seth, take your father to Cincinnati. Alex Cheney could teach the winter school. David, go to Joel and your sweetheart. God will watch over Nancy. I will watch over your mother, though I doubt she will need me. Benjamin and Joseph can now shoulder men's work. Without the strain of your father's intemperance, Mother Julia will have renewed energy, and she doesn't lack for capability."

David watched the smoke from their chimney curl upward into the sky. He turned to Seth. "I think we should consider Lyman's advice," he said slowly. "Last night, Nancy prayed that this time of sorrow would be shortened. Perhaps this is the answer."

Seth searched his brother's eyes. He turned Lyman's words over in his mind. He picked up his ax, his eyes on the blade, a silent prayer in his heart. Finally, Seth spoke. "I'll talk to Pa about it."

Late that afternoon, Seth stood at the door of the tavern, his eyes adjusting to the dim interior as he looked for his father.

Abe Miller's voice rose over the din of noise. "Zeke," Abe shouted, "there's your gentleman son! What a dandy he is!" At that, Ezekiel glimpsed the image of Seth silhouetted against the bright, open door. Ezekiel motioned for Seth to join him and Abe. Seth entered the dim tavern, waded across the tobacco-strewn floor, and pulled up a chair.

Seth delayed speaking his mind until Abe left the table to retrieve another bottle. Then he looked across the table and said, "Pa, I'm thinking on spending the winter in Cincinnati. Joel's creditors are threatening to sue me."

"Curse them," Ezekiel said as he put his glass down.

"Come with me, Pa. Get away from here."

"Aren't you s'posed to teach school this winter?" Ezekiel slurred. "I didn't raise you to be the kind of man who doesn't keep his word."

"Alexander Cheney's been wanting the job for some time," Seth said truthfully.

"What about Nancy?" Ezekiel asked as he wiped his face on his sleeve.

"Mother and the girls will look after her." Seth knew he wasn't answering his father's question. Ezekiel was asking what would happen if Nancy died while they were gone. The same question hung in Seth's mind. "We aren't much help with her, Pa," Seth added quietly.

Ezekiel studied his glass, nodding slowly. Then he closed his eyes. The man was silent for a time, and Seth wondered if the drink had caused him to fall asleep, yet his father's head wasn't lolling. Finally, Ezekiel spoke, and he sounded more sober than he had for weeks. "I'll go with you. But I need a few days. I've got some unfinished work at the carpenter shop in Fredonia."

Ezekiel went home with Seth that afternoon. On the Sabbath, instead of worshipping, Ezekiel took the wagon to Fredonia.

Three days later, he came home with the item he had been working on. It was a cherry-wood chair, ingeniously fashioned to recline to a position that took the weight off of Nancy's hip and thigh. That next day, Julianne, Almera, and Susan sewed pillows for it.

The following morning, Seth and Ezekiel prepared to leave. David helped Nancy into her new chair. "The tides are turning. The time of pain and sorrow shortens," David whispered as he kissed her cheek and tucked the quilt around her. "Would that God listened to my prayers as well as He listens to yours."

"Perhaps God would if you prayed more," Nancy teased.

Ezekiel and Seth approached Nancy to bid her farewell. The two planned to take a steamboat to Toledo and then travel by canal to Cincinnati. Ezekiel took Nancy's hand. "Girl, I'll have you stronger when I come back."

"I promise, Pa," Nancy returned.

Seth took Nancy's other hand. "God be with you," he said as his dark eyes burned with emotion.

"And you, dear brother," Nancy returned. After embracing Nancy, Seth went outside to help David ready the wagon. David would drive Seth and Ezekiel to Dunkirk to see them off on the boat.

In the house, Ezekiel bid his younger children farewell. When he came to his wife, she did not meet his eyes but turned from him and walked out the front door. Ezekiel trailed behind her. Once outside, Ezekiel touched Julia's elbow. She stopped and turned to face him. They stood for a moment, staring at each other. The pain of the past three months towered like a wall between them.

Julia spoke first. "Things will be different here when you come home. I hope and pray that you are changed as well."

"A man can't change his nature," Ezekiel returned as he looked at his wife.

"But he can change his habits," Julia said steadily.

Ezekiel felt a knot harden within him. This woman did not understand. There was a bitter edge in his voice when he spoke. "You are my wife, not my taskmaster."

"Yes, Ezekiel," Julia said, unconsciously fingering the gold chain around her neck. "And I'm in great need of a husband."

Ezekiel felt the weight of the watch in his pocket. He realized that he had never seen Julia without that chain since the day he had given it to her. He nodded shortly at her. "I'll do what I can," he said before climbing into the wagon. David touched the whips to the horses' broad backs, and they were off.

On a chill morning, amid stiff wind and under an overcast sky, the steamboat carrying David and Annie chugged through the icy, rolling waters of Lake Erie as it neared the mouth of the Black River. Relieved that the trip was nearly over, Annie quickly cleaned Sixtus's face and hands with a damp rag. Sixtus squealed in protest. "Hush now," Annie proclaimed. "Your papa will hardly know you; you've grown so big since he left."

Without further ado, Annie hoisted her son to her hip and stepped quickly to join David on deck. She hoped that Joel had received her letter and would be at the port to meet them. The boat slowed and turned. Annie's heart beat quickly with excitement as she caught her first glimpse of Lorain County, Ohio.

"Want down, Mama." Sixtus wiggled in her arms.

"No, baby. It's not safe," Annie said. The little boy kicked his legs and struggled for freedom.

"Ho, Sixtus! Settle down there," David said as he took the child from Annie, swung him in the air, and hefted him to his shoulders.

At that moment, Annie could have kissed her brother-in-law's cheek. Keeping her active child safe and entertained on the boat had proved a mammoth task. She would have been at her wit's end without David. The child immediately quieted on his uncle's shoulders.

Hardly noticing the child's weight, David gazed toward the banks of Ohio. The cold wind blew in his face as the mouth of the Black River loomed before him. Branches of barren trees stretched over the banks, darkening the gray winter shadows in the water below. David, Annie, and Sixtus's breath steamed in the air, and their chapped hands and faces were red from the cold.

Annie tapped her foot up and down, her vision strained toward the distant shore. A few moments later, her round face broke into a rosy smile. She waved her arms high over her head, unable to keep still for the surge of joy coursing through her. In the distance, she glimpsed a tall, thin figure with sloping shoulders.

David smiled at his sister-in-law's gladness. But a moment later, a more pensive look entered his gold-brown eyes. There was a woman standing next to Joel. He knew it was Kathryn. He was glad to see her, but would she understand when his laugh did not come so easily? Would she perceive that his heart now bore the imprint of sorrow?

Three months later, on a windy March night, Annie awakened when Sixtus cried out in his sleep. She lifted the sobbing child from his trundle bed and brought him in bed with her and Joel. Annie patted his back and comforted him. Soon the little boy quieted. However, Sixtus did not fall back to sleep, but began climbing all over his parents in an effort to get them to play with him. Joel moaned in frustration. He was exhausted from hard physical labor. Annie whispered that she would take Sixtus into the study and get him back to sleep there. Before leaving the bedroom, Annie reached for a book she had placed under the bed.

With a quilt over her arm, one hand holding Sixtus and the other the book, Annie felt her way into the chill study. Once inside the room, she placed the book down on a side table and lit a candle. Annie sighed as she put a log on the smoldering fire. She sat down in the rocking chair. The Clays had a comfortable home, but Annie was tired of living under another woman's roof.

Margaret Clay was an able woman, but Annie knew that the two of them were cut out of different cloth. For example, two weeks ago when the precocious seventeen-year-old Almon Babbitt had joined the Mormon Church, Mrs. Clay had told him to never set foot in their house again. If Margaret knew that Almon had lent Annie his Book of Mormon, she would be livid. Now, Annie was about to read it.

Annie sat down in the rocking chair, gathered Sixtus in her arms, and covered them both with the quilt. As Annie hummed and rocked, Sixtus slowly relaxed and slept. Annie reached for the book. Fascinated by the title page, Annie opened it. She read into the wee hours of the morning with her toddler sleeping in her lap. When it was almost dawn, Annie set the book down. The thought that it might be a testament of Christ touched her heart. She closed her eyes with visions of a people never before imagined in her mind.

When Joel awakened at dawn, he was alone in bed. He went into the study and found Annie and Sixtus cuddled together, fast asleep in the study chair. He gently carried his sleeping child into the bedroom. Annie continued to slumber, her head at an odd angle. Joel came back into the study, picked up his wife as if she were a second child, and carried her into bed. Her eyes fluttered open for a moment and Joel told her to go back to sleep. She sighed happily. Joel went to breakfast and explained to Margaret that Annie had been in the study most of the night caring for Sixtus and was now resting. Margaret's jaw tensed. She wanted to tell Joel that Annie should be up fixing her own husband breakfast, but she bit her tongue.

Later in the morning, after the men had left, Margaret burst into Joel and Annie's room. Annie startled and sat up in bed, her wild red hair framing her face. Sixtus whimpered beside her.

"This was in the study! What in heaven?" Margaret shouted as she waved the Book of Mormon at Annie. Sixtus began to cry.

"It's the Book of Mormon," Annie said as she gathered her son into her lap.

"I know that. How did it get into my house? This—this instrument of the devil!"

"Almon Babbitt lent it to Joel and me. I was reading it last night while I was up with Sixtus."

Margaret pursed her lips. "How could you, Annie Johnson? And you a good Methodist?"

"It's just a book, Margaret. There is good in it," Annie said as she sat Sixtus down and took the book from Margaret.

"It's the devil's book! I forbid it in my home! Do not defy me on this!"

Defensively Annie glared at Margaret and declared, "I will respect your wishes in your home. But when I am in my own house, Margaret Clay, I will finish this book. I will find out for myself about Mormonism, rather than trust in idle gossip."

Kathryn Clay ran to the door of the log house David was building. She burst inside and found David setting the bricks in the hearth. "David, you have to tell Joel to give that Mormon book back to Almon Babbitt," Kathryn cried out, her cheeks red from dismay.

David put his trowel down. He felt both confused at the intrusion and very glad to see her. She continued vehemently, "I'd throw the devilish book at Almon myself if Margaret hadn't told him never to show his face around our place again. Why did that stupid boy have to go and join the Mormonites?"

"Perhaps Almon took a liking to Mr. Pratt," David grinned, remembering the footrace with old Stu-boy. David wiped his hands on his trousers, stood, and walked over to Kathryn. He explained that the log house he was building for Joel and Annie would be finished within the week. Then he chuckled and added, "Annie thanks me every day. She's so tired of living under your sister-in-law's thumb."

"Annie's the problem," Kathryn stomped her foot. She did not like David changing the subject. "Margaret found out this morning that she has that Mormon book."

"Settle down, Katie," David responded in a soothing voice. Sometimes she acted like a child. At times he found it charming; at other times he didn't. David continued, "It isn't easy for Annie living in another woman's house. Joel told me he's going to give the Book of Mormon back to Almon tomorrow. Joel believes the evil reports about the Mormons. He read a chapter of the book but isn't interested in reading anymore."

"Are you sure?" Kathryn asked earnestly, the storm in her eyes beginning to calm.

"Absolutely," David said. "The book will be gone soon."

Kathryn let out a deep breath. Taking Kathryn's hand, David noticed how soft it felt. He invited her to walk with him outside.

As they walked around the lot, David sensed spring in the air. He was in a wonderful mood, for he had recently received a letter from his mother telling him that Nancy was up and around on her crutches. She could also sit in her chair for long stretches of time to sew and paint. But that wasn't the only good news. In the letter, Julia said that she had received word from Seth saying that their father was improved and that the two would be home in Pomfret for spring planting. Nancy's prayer was answered.

"I don't see why Joel didn't just burn the book in the fire a week ago." Kathryn said, but she was smiling now.

David stretched his arm around her shapely waist. "Because it's not Joel's book."

"You Johnsons are so blasted polite." She laughed as she leaned into her handsome beau.

David smiled. He loved the way she softened when he touched her. Yet he didn't touch her nearly as much as he would like to. Margaret watched David's every move around Kathryn like a hawk about to strike. But Margaret Clay wasn't here right now. David pulled Kathryn close and ran his fingers through the soft blonde hair that hung past her shoulders to the middle of her back.

Kathryn smiled inwardly as she felt David's hands in her hair. She thought about how she usually wore her hair properly tied up before going out in public. But this morning, things had gone awry. After the men had left, Kathryn had bathed and left her hair down to dry. Then she had overheard Margaret confront Annie about the Book of Mormon. Enraged at Annie's response, Margaret had stormed out of the house intent on immediately going to the sawmill and reporting the incident to her husband.

Dismayed, Kathryn had neglected fixing her hair in her haste to speak with David. But she needn't have worried, for Joel would rein Annie in. All would be well, despite the troublesome Mormons. She knew David adored how her blue eyes flashed and shone. She knew he was enchanted with the flush of her cheeks and the way her lovely blonde hair blew around her face. Kathryn put her arms around David's neck. He bent his head down and kissed her.

After the kiss, Kathryn laid her head on David's chest. "Ah, David," she sighed. "Everything is going to be all right. I was so worried. I should have known Joel wouldn't let Annie be sucked in by the Mormon lies. But Almon's conversion shocked me so. I was nearly as upset as Margaret when I heard that Annie was up reading that Mormon book last night."

David paused. "She was?"

Kathryn nodded and chuckled. "They had such a row. Annie told Margaret that she was going to finish the book when she had her own house. I guess Joel will put a stop to that. Annie has some gall."

David's brow creased, and he whistled softly. "Almost as much gall as you."

Kathryn laughed, enjoying the warmth of David's arms around her. Even with his thick shirt on, she could feel the hard muscles of his back. For a moment, she traced them with her fingers. Then her hands stilled. When she spoke, there were tears in her voice. "David, I was so frightened. I couldn't bear the thought of losing you. If my parents ever thought your family was interested in the Mormons, they'd have John send me home on the next steamboat. All I want is for you to love me forevermore."

David heard the earnestness in Kathryn's voice. He held her tightly but did not express the thoughts in his heart. She was correct when she said that he loved her. He had never felt such delight in a woman before. Yet he knew Kathryn was incorrect on another point. Joel would not stop Annie from studying the Mormon religion. Annie had always been a strong Methodist and Joel a Baptist. From the day of their marriage, Joel had promised never to abridge Annie's or anyone else's liberty in religious matters. David knew without doubt that Joel would not break that promise. Furthermore, David knew that Annie was no simpleton. There must be something to this Book of Mormon, or she would have set it aside without a thought.

On a clear evening three weeks later, after Joel and Annie were comfortably settled in their log home, Annie readied herself to attend the nightly Mormon meeting at Simeon Carter's. Joel, who suffered from a cold, sat near the fire sipping a cup of tea.

"Joel," Annie said with a sparkle, "I wish you could come tonight. Joseph Smith's brother, Samuel, has come into town and will be speaking with us."

Joel shrugged and coughed. His mind had been so troubled about the Mormon religion that he had lost a great deal of sleep during the past two weeks. He knew that this unease had contributed to his illness. Annie put a freckled hand on her husband's shoulder.

"Do you really think Mormonism is of God?" Joel asked.

"I do, Joel," Annie said simply. "But I'm not certain. I hope Almon is there with his Book of Mormon. The lad promised to lend it to me again. Perhaps I'll be able to discern the truth or falsehood of Samuel Smith's testimony."

Joel sighed deeply. There were dark circles under his brown eyes, and his thin lips pulled back in a frown. "This religion is compelling," Joel said honestly. "When we went to the first meeting and Mr. Whitlock spoke about the first principles of the gospel, I was filled with astonishment. To think that he mentioned faith, repentance, baptism for the remission of sins, and the laying on of hands for the gift of the Holy Ghost with signs following the believers. This was the first discourse I ever heard that corresponds with the New Testament."

"Their teachings explain the New Testament," Annie said simply.

At that moment, David came into the house with Sixtus on his back. He had just taken Kathryn home after the two had spent the day with little Sixtus on an outing to town.

Annie smiled at David and gathered him into the conversation. "Joel was just saying that it is astonishing how the Mormon teachings correspond to the gospel in the New Testament."

"Hmm," David responded as he lowered Sixtus to the floor. David's thoughts centered on the fact that he had not told Kathryn that Joel had attended two Mormon meetings a week and a half ago. Annie continued to go every evening. Sixtus ran to his mother and hid behind her skirts, instigating a peek-a-boo game with David.

Joel coughed and continued. "But I wasn't finished, Annie. In the next meeting, when Edson Fuller spoke of the Book of Mormon being equal to the Bible, I could not tolerate that teaching. His testimony seemed full of pride. That's why I haven't gone back. Annie, you may continue to attend as long as you wish. But beware of false doctrine."

"I will heed Paul's advice," Annie said with a smile. "To prove all things and hold fast to the good."

Suddenly a fit of coughing entangled Joel. Annie's face shadowed with concern. Joel planned on walking her to and from the meeting. He did not like her going out alone at night with such vicious prejudice against the Mormons. She placed her hand on her husband's forehead.

"Joel, you're a bit feverish. David, would you walk me to the meeting tonight?" she asked tentatively. "I dislike the idea of Joel going out in the cold."

David hesitated a moment, thinking of Kathryn. He knew how rumors circulated, and he feared to put their courtship at risk. Joel noted the hesitation and looked carefully at his brother.

"This is an important meeting," Joel commented. "Joseph Smith's brother Samuel is in Amherst. He will speak tonight. Perhaps Annie will find out once and for all if this work rings true. If it is false, then we can all put it behind us."

Annie's lively, sweet eyes met David's, and he saw in them how much she desired to go. David nodded slowly. If Kathryn and her family found out, he would explain. It wasn't as if he were going to the meeting. "Come on, Annie," he said, and he smiled at his sister-in-law. "Let's see what you think of this Samuel Smith. You've always had the knack of smelling a skunk a long way off."

Annie elbowed David. "I can smell roses from afar as well," she returned.

When David and Annie arrived at the Carter's home, Almon Babbitt met them at the front door. "Ho, David Johnson," Almon exclaimed in surprise. "Fancy seeing you here. Come in, I have someone for you to meet. I just now said to this fellow, Carlos, you must meet my friend David Johnson."

"I'll not be staying," David replied hurriedly. "Just Annie."

"Ahh," Almon said slowly as he rubbed his chin, raised his eyebrows, and studied David's expression. David, who was usually so good-natured, found this highly irritating. Almon was three years younger than David and five inches shorter. David wished he could wipe that annoying, jaunty look off of Almon Babbitt's rectangular face.

"Goodnight, Almon," David said decisively. "Annie, I'll be back for you at nine,"

"Hang on a minute," Almon took hold of David's arm. "I won't let you go so easily." Almon called into the house, "Don Carlos, my friend David Johnson is here. You must come quickly before he leaves."

A moment later, a young man joined them. Annie did a double take when she saw him. He was over six feet tall, stood straight, and was handsomely built. He reminded her so much of David that it was uncanny. He had a similar high forehead and a full, youthful mouth. His nose was longer than David's and his cheekbones less pronounced. He was blond and blue-eyed, where David possessed brown hair and eyes. Don Carlos was also a bit more long-legged. Annie thought that this young fellow might have some growing to do and could well surpass David's six feet three inches someday. Still, there was something so alike about them.

Almon clapped the young man on the shoulder. "Carlos, let me introduce you to my friend, David Johnson, and his sister-in-law, Mrs. Annie Johnson. Mrs. Johnson has attended our meetings for the past two weeks. David has no desire to attend and has simply escorted Mrs. Johnson here tonight. This is Don Carlos Smith, the youngest brother of the Prophet. Carlos's deportment is so much like David's that I felt they must meet."

Don Carlos grinned and shook David's hand, "Are we really so much alike as old Almon supposes? It is a pleasure meeting you, David Johnson." Then, like a true gentleman, Don Carlos took Annie's hand and helped her up the steps as he warmly welcomed her to the meeting. Lydia Carter, Simeon's wife, glimpsed Annie from the hallway. Hurrying over and linking arms with Annie, Lydia led her into the parlor where the guests gathered.

With Annie taken care of, Don Carlos stepped outside with David and Almon. "David," he offered, "are you certain you won't join us?"

David shook his head, "No, thank you."

To David's dismay, Almon took the liberty to explain, "David is courting a lass named Kathryn Clay. Her family adamantly opposes the Mormons."

David smarted under Almon's explanation.

Don Carlos grinned at David. "Is she pretty?"

David found himself returning the smile. "She is."

"She's beautiful," Almon cut in. "I once had eyes for the lass."

"Woman," David looked sideways at Almon. "She's a bit old for you, Almon Babbitt."

Almon laughed at this. "David Johnson, I am old and wise for my years. So is my friend Carlos. How old do you think Carlos is?"

David studied the young man in front of him. Though Don Carlos looked very young, there was depth and wisdom in his expression. "Eighteen perhaps," David ventured.

"You are off by three years." Almon chuckled. "Carlos is fifteen years old and already ordained to the ministry."

Don Carlos smiled sheepishly at David, clearly ill at ease when his age was mentioned. He shrugged. "The lines of age are rather blurry in my family."

David nodded and chuckled. "I know what you mean. I'm from a family of fifteen children. My younger brother Joe has more scholarly knowledge than the rest of us put together. And I have a younger sister, Susan, who has been a wise sage since she was a wee lass."

"The meeting will begin momentarily," Almon said as he peered into the house and saw the guests in the parlor taking their seats. "Unfortunately, we must bid David good night."

Don Carlos looked carefully at David. "Almon, I think I would rather walk with David if he'll have me." Then, he added with a grin, "I'm in need of stretching my legs, and I've heard brother Samuel preach on many occasions."

"I'll have you," David responded instinctively. There was something about this young man that reminded him of his own siblings. A moment later, the two were walking under a starry, windswept sky, talking amicably.

Yet after a few moments, David fell silent. What was he doing? Don Carlos was a member of the Smith family. Kathryn had told him they were money diggers and fanatics. On the way to the meeting, David had silently prayed that Annie would see through Samuel Smith's façade. Yet, now he was foolishly being taken in by this clear-eyed youth who had the bearing of goodness. David wondered if Don Carlos Smith was an innocent victim of a deluded or dishonest family. If that was the case, the boy was in need of a friend.

"David," Don Carlos broke the silence, "you mentioned that you are staying with your brother and sister-in-law here in Amherst. Tell me about the rest of your family."

As David spoke, Don Carlos listened attentively and compassionately. David found himself opening up and describing the brothers and sisters whom he dearly loved. He told Don Carlos of his last visit home, of Seth's noble dedication to the family, of Nancy's sweetness and of the sadness her accident caused.

"I am so sorry for Nancy and for your father."

David looked at the boy and saw great tenderness in his eyes.

Don Carlos went on. "Your brother Seth sounds much like my eldest brother, Alvin. Alvin was rather quiet, not inclined to mirth. He built my parents a house, hoping they could spend their later years in comfort. But Alvin died before the house was finished."

"I'm sorry," David said with warmth. "How long ago was this?"

"In the fall of 1823, shortly after the angel came to Joseph and told him of the plates. Joseph thinks that Alvin was the noblest of all our parents' children. He wonders why Alvin was not called to be a prophet of God rather than himself."

David was taken aback by the incidental way Don Carlos spoke of the bizarre happenings in his family. "Carlos, do you truly believe that your brother saw an angel, that he translated gold plates?" David burst out. "Have you not considered that he made up this story or was deluded by Satan?"

"David, I don't blame you for not believing," Don Carlos said, his voice now solemn and thoughtful. "But I have known Joseph since I was born. He is good, David, and honest. As Alvin lay dying, he told Joseph to do all he could to obtain the record. My father and my brothers Hyrum and Samuel handled the golden plates. I bear testimony of this."

David's heart beat within him as he stopped walking. He felt that he could not let this sensitive youth continue down this trail. "I fear that your family has deluded you, Don Carlos," he said passionately. "You told me that in your early years, your family was poor and not well thought of. Perhaps there was a desperate need for attention and money."

"No, David," Don Carlos said quickly and intensely. "You don't know my family. You don't know what they . . . what we have been through. Our friends turned on us after Joseph's vision of the Almighty when he was just fourteen. We've been called money diggers, hobgoblins, and believers in witchcraft. After Alvin died of bilious colic, rumors circulated that we insanely dug up his body and dissected it. Father was forced to help our neighbors take Alvin's body from the grave to prove that this had not happened. Can you imagine what that was like?"

"No, Carlos," David uttered. "I can't." Regardless of what Joseph Smith claimed, David felt shame that any man could treat a family so abominably after they had lost a loved one. David did not want to add to this family's sorrow.

Don Carlos continued. "David, I had no friends as a child. Neighbors wouldn't let their children play with me. But I knew my family. We worked, laughed, and prayed together. We know Joseph, and we know that he tells the truth. We will give up everything to help Joseph fulfill his mission, to help bring about the kingdom of God on earth. My family is pure, David, regardless of what the world thinks of us. Joseph did see an angel. He did translate the golden plates by the gift and power of God. Read the Book of Mormon, David. Pray about its truthfulness. Then come to me and tell me which of us is deluded. Please read it, David. I would have you for a friend."

David stood silent for a moment, moved by Don Carlos's words. This boy needed a friend. Finally, David spoke. "Don Carlos, I will be your friend, whether or not I find the Book of Mormon true."

David walked silently on the way home with Annie. The wind whistled through the trees and grass. Annie could guess what was in David's heart as he gripped the Book of Mormon that young Don Carlos had given him. David now knew firsthand that the vicious rumors about the Smiths were false. Yet he loved Kathryn Clay.

When they arrived home, Joel was awake, sitting near the fire reading his Bible. Annie ran to her husband, no longer able to contain her joy. "Joel, I am nearly convinced that Mormonism is the pure religion we have longed for." Standing before him, she spoke of the power of Samuel Smith's testimony and of the witness of light and joy that filled her soul.

Joel's heart beat quickly. He looked at the sweet, soft form of his wife, knowing that he both loved and admired her. Could she be correct? He put his Bible down. Forgetting for a moment that they were not alone, he pulled Annie onto his lap and wrapped his arms around her. "Then I will take my Bible in hand, and we will attend all their meetings. Annie, my darling, I promise that I will investigate this subject thoroughly, and together we will pray for divine direction."

David remained standing, the weight of the Book of Mormon in his hands as he watched the tenderness between Joel and Annie.

He felt very much alone. Annie looked into her young brother-in-law's troubled eyes.

"David," she said softly, "are you all right?"

David's shoulders bowed. "I have promised my new friend that I will read the Book of Mormon," he said quietly. "If I keep this promise, I will hurt Kathryn and perhaps lose her."

"My brother," Joel said, "if Kathryn cannot respect your liberty to act and think for yourself, then perhaps she was never yours to keep."

"Yet I love her," David said dismally.

Annie was the first in the household to be fully converted to the Church of Jesus Christ of Latter-day Saints. The day following Samuel Smith's preaching, she read the remainder of the Book of Mormon. When she read the account of the Savior blessing the children and the angels ministering to these little ones, she wept. It was as if a conduit of light went from the pages of the book into her very soul, as if an earthly veil was lifted from her mind and heart and she knew of a surety of eternal light and love. Beyond doubt and question, God spoke to her through these pages. She knew that somewhere, the Savior blessed her baby girl, somewhere angels surrounded her Julianne. Annie felt the Nephites' unspeakable joy, the love and light that words and tongue could not describe.

Joel's conversion came more analytically than Annie's did. He attended the meetings for the next two weeks, comparing the preaching of the elders with the words of his own Bible and the teachings in the Book of Mormon. As he studied and prayed, he came to four conclusions. First, that as all protestant churches had sprung up from the Church of Rome, they had no more authority to administer in the ordinances of the Church of Christ than the

Church of Rome had. Second, that a supernatural power did attend the Mormon Church. It had risen independently of all denominations. Therefore, its origin must be of heaven or the devil. Third, it seemed unreasonable to Joel that God would suffer the devil to bring forth a work with the gifts and blessings of the ancient Church of Christ, corresponding to that which He promised to bring forth in the last days for the gathering of the House of Israel. Fourth, the principles taught in the Book of Mormon corresponded with the Bible, and the doctrines of the Church were the same as those taught by Christ and his apostles, with signs following the believers. As Joel voiced these conclusions and recorded them on paper and in his heart, great peace filled him. He embraced the work of God with his whole soul.

David's conversion came at greater cost. Don Carlos stayed with the Simeon Carter family the week following his introduction to David. In the evenings, David did not attend the meetings with Annie and Joel. Instead, he stayed home and read the Book of Mormon.

Yet early each morning when the sun rose, Don Carlos appeared on the Johnson doorstep to help David plow the fields and plant Joel's crops. As the two men sowed seeds in the spring sunlight, Don Carlos related to David the details of the restoration of the gospel. David listened attentively to his friend as they worked, surrounded by the fresh smell of dark, fertile earth.

On the third morning that Don Carlos worked with David, Kathryn rode up on horseback at about ten o'clock. It had been four days since she had seen her beau, and her thought was to tease him while he labored. Her long hair was braided and wound on the top of her head. She sat sidesaddle on her mount and looked regal and lovely.

Don Carlos whistled softly as she approached from a distance. "Kathryn Clay?" he whispered under his breath.

David nodded slightly as he waved a greeting to Kathryn.

"I'll go," Don Carlos suggested.

"No," David said as he put a hand on his friend's shoulder. "I'll introduce you."

"But I'm a Mormon," Don Carlos warned.

David smiled slightly and forced his voice to sound light as if he were joking. "Carlos, it's high time Kathryn found out I've a hobgoblin for my friend."

Kathryn smiled warmly when David introduced her to his new friend. She found the young man handsome and attractive, a fitting companion for her David. "Don Carlos, where are you from and what brings you to Amherst?" she asked with a flirtatious lilt to her voice as she wound her arm through David's.

"I'm from Kirtland," Don Carlos said, clearly hesitant to explain further for his friend's sake.

David, however, plunged in. "Don Carlos is the brother of Joseph Smith. He and his brother Samuel are in Amherst as missionaries. Annie and Joel have been attending the Mormon meetings of late. Carlos was kind enough to befriend me."

Kathryn's smile evaporated, and her arm stiffened in David's. Thick silence surrounded the three. The sun shone brightly and warmed the air and earth about them. Don Carlos excused himself and walked toward the house.

"David, how could you?" Kathryn demanded as a torrent of frustration burst from her. She pulled away from him and stared at him, her slender hands clenched into fists. "How could you spend time with this Mormon? This Smith? How could Joel and Annie be so stupid? The Mormons . . . the Mormons are a bunch of deluded reprobates!"

"You don't know them, Kathryn," David said as he reached out his hand to touch hers. "You don't know what you are saying. I know Don Carlos to be honest. I am reading the Book of Mormon, Kathryn. I am considering what they teach."

Kathryn pulled away from his touch as if he were diseased. Hot tears filled her eyes. "You would not do this if you cared for me, David," she cried. "If you loved me, you would run from this religion as fast and furiously as you could."

"I love you, Katie, but I'm a man," David said in agony. "I must do what seems best. Can't you even consider that Mormonism might be true?"

"What will John and Margaret do when they find out?" Kathryn asked as she looked down at her hands.

"John will probably do nothing. Joel's sawmill and shingle cutter are about to make your brother a good deal of money. If your parents won't accept me, we could marry in secret, Kathryn. Joseph and Emma Smith did the same."

"No," Kathryn shouted, and when she looked at David, her eyes were stormy with fierce emotion. "I will never marry a Mormon! The husband of Kathryn Clay will never be known as a delusional maniac, a hobgoblin, a bugbear!" With that, Kathryn Clay mounted her horse. Her proud shoulders shook with sobs as she rode away.

That evening, after David finished working in the fields, he did not go home for supper. Instead, he walked the streets and fields far into the night. The stars came out, first as pinpricks, then as pulsing spheres, three dimensional in the sky, each with its own place in the heavens. At the thought of Kathryn, tears coursed down David's sunburned cheeks. Yet, he remembered the man Enos, whom he read of in the Book of Mormon. David kneeled down in a field and prayed long and fervently. As David prayed, it seemed that time stopped in reverence to the Almighty. The stars and moon wrapped their light around David. The damp earth cradled his knees. The words of Nancy's prayer came into his mind, each word as bright and pulsating as the nearest stars in the blackest sky. *Grant us the faith of Thy ancient Church.* David wept, knowing that the God of Heaven had answered his prayer. He knew now that the Savior of the world bled and died for the Jews, Gentiles, Nephites, and Lamanites. And for David Johnson.

*Oh, thou mighty God of Jacob*
*Listen to my humble prayer,*
*As I bow the knee before Thee,*
*Wilt thou take me in thy care.*

*I will ask Thee not for power,*
*I will ask Thee not for might,*
*But instead, oh give me wisdom,*
*To direct me in the right.*

*This I ask through Christ our Saviour,*
*Who our sins and sorrows bore,*
*And I'll give to Thee the honor*
*And the glory evermore.*

—JOEL H. JOHNSON, FROM "SUPPLICATION"

*May 1831*

During the last week in May, Sylvester Smith baptized Annie in the cold waters of the Black River. The trees along the banks bore leaves of new green. A light wind blew, and the air smelled of mud and emerging life. After the baptism, sparkling water streamed from Annie's auburn hair. Her freckled face shone a translucent pink. She smiled at Joel, and her eyes were alight with glimmering thoughts—love for Joel, her children's births, the words of God, and the thrill of opened heavens and answered prayers. Joel held out his arms to her, thinking that he had never beheld a more beautiful sight. He stooped and gathered the soaking Annie in while she stood on tiptoe and kissed his cheek.

Joel and David were baptized a few days later with eight other converts. The group gathered at the river at dusk. Their conversation blended with the chorus of frogs and crickets. Elder Sylvester Smith announced that he would baptize the first five converts, and Edson Fuller the remaining. Joel's was the fifth baptism. When Joel came forth from the water, his commitment to serve Christ beat in his heart. Smith clapped Joel on the back, and the two gripped hands in brotherhood. Next, David shook Joel's hand, noting the look of inner strength in his brother's eyes.

Once on the bank, Brother Sylvester wiped his face with a towel and nodded to David and Edson Fuller. It was their turn. David eagerly stepped into the chest-high water, feeling the soft mud of the river bottom squeeze between his toes. As Edson Fuller followed, his eyes darted back and forth from the river to the woods in a strangely distracted manner. Brother Fuller frowned. He gruffly took David's arm with one hand and raised the other arm to a square as he muttered the words of the baptismal prayer. He quickly immersed David and then moved away from him.

"Brother Edson, are you well?" David asked.

"What am I doin' here? What am I doin' here?" Fuller muttered. Then he stalked out of the water, mounted his horse, and galloped away, dripping wet.

Dismayed and confused, a chill ran through David. Had he done something to anger Brother Fuller? Was his baptism valid? Sylvester Smith watched after Edson quizzically. Then he turned to the others and commented, "Brother Edson has been strangely different of late. We must all remember him in our prayers. Brother David is now baptized, and I will continue with the rest."

As David walked toward the bank, he wished that Brother Edson had not been strangely different during *his* baptism. David exhaled a quick breath of air, fighting his disappointment. As he neared the shoreline, Joel reached out and grasped David's arm, pulling David out of the river and into a warm embrace. "Little brother, we are members of Christ's Church! Baptized by those having authority through the laying on of hands. Nothing else matters."

"Except what your mother will think when she finds out." Annie smiled with a wink at David.

Joel and Annie's warm words thawed the chill left by Edson Fuller. David smiled back at Annie. "Poor Mother warned us about the Campbellites. But we have done something far worse—we have joined the Mormonites!"

"You will have to do some quick talking when you go home this fall," Almon Babbitt whispered to David as Sylvester Smith and the next convert stepped into the water. "I'll go to Pomfret with you. Lend you a hand—I mean a tongue. Teach your pretty sisters the gospel."

"You don't come near my sisters," David said with a quick elbow in Almon's ribs.

Annie stepped over to the young men. "Mother Julia will recognize the truth," she whispered. Then she briefly squeezed David's hand. "Oh, David, God be praised! I'm so happy for you."

As weeks passed, the summer days dawned humid and hot, the afternoons often punctuated by cloudbursts. It was haying season. This meant little time for anything else. The Mormons' daily religious gatherings became weekly Sabbath meetings. The farmers of Lorain County approached the haying with the energy and determination of combat. Men battled heat, rain, and exhaustion in order to get their hay in on time. It was the most stressful and demanding labor of the growing season.

Still, David enjoyed the haying. In the first place, it meant constant employment and the opportunity to earn feed for Joel's animals and cash for himself. Second, he reveled in the physical challenge and the glory of recognition. Nine times out of ten, David was chosen to lead the hands across the field. This was a sought-after distinction given the finest mower. Local farmers ignored the fact that David was Mormon when they noted his strength, his skill with a scythe, and the knack he had of setting a brisk rhythm that challenged other men to follow. Despite the unpopularity of his newfound religion, David had earned a grudging respect from other men in the community.

One morning in mid-July, David arose an hour before dawn and gulped down cheese, bread, and cider. Almon would arrive momentarily, and they would be off. Uncharacteristically nervous before a haying, David's foot tapped up and down as he chewed a crust of brown bread. It was John Clay's field he would be working on today, and David wondered if he would see Kathryn.

She had been in his mind for three days straight ever since Clay had stopped by to ask David if he would help mow the remaining hay. Almon Babbitt, who had been at the Johnson's at the time, had offered his services as well. John accepted Almon's offer under the duress of polite behavior. It was customary for the women of the household to feed the hands lunch, hence David's anxiety and his hope.

David hoped for a chance to talk with Kathryn alone. The two had not spoken since that day in the field with Don Carlos. Following his baptism, David had sent Kathryn a note explaining his testimony. It had been returned to the Johnson doorstep unopened with a scrawled message on the envelope stating that he was no longer welcome at the Clays' residence. Still, David longed to hold Kathryn one more time, to know for certain that there would never be hope for the two of them, to tell her that he was sorry he had hurt her and that he would never forget her.

David sighed as he waited for Almon. Could John Clay's offer of work mean the family was softening toward Mormonism, toward David? Almon's sharp tap at the door interrupted his thoughts.

A moment later, Almon and David strode toward the Clay fields, carrying their scythes in their hands. In the waning moonlight, there was a bounce to Almon's step and an ambitious glint in his eye. Almon chattered about his plans to be a great attorney someday, to brilliantly defend Joseph Smith against spurious lawsuits. Almon figured he'd speak so cunningly that the whole court would end up dumbfounded. When Joseph no longer needed him, he'd run for political office.

David listened politely, at times biting back a chuckle. It was good to have Almon with him to get his mind off of Kathryn. David had to admit that he was growing fond of the lad. Despite Almon's high-faluting dreams, he had an open spirit about him and a busy, observant mind. And who could tell what Almon would make of himself someday? Action followed Almon's words, and one couldn't predict what he would say next.

"So, Almon," David ventured, "why do you think John Clay invited us to work today—two men who have been told to never set foot on his land again?"

"For the same reason he's still partners with your brother at the sawmill. Money. John Clay wants to get his hay in. He figures you'll do the work of two men, so it'll cost him less. Why do you think I offered to help anyway? I figure I'll do the work of half a man so you don't get cheated." Almon clapped David on the back. "Us Mormon boys have to stick together."

David laughed out loud. But a second later, he was quiet, introspective.

Almon eyed him shrewdly. "Are you holding on to hope for Kathryn's hand?" Almon's words triggered a quick glance from David.

David noticed that the boy's eyes were open and honest. Almon wasn't poking fun. David shrugged.

"I've known Kathryn Clay for some time," Almon said seriously. "She's a lot like me—always thinking about what she wants for herself. Marrying a Mormon will never figure into her plans."

"Then how did joining the Church figure into your plans, Almon?" David asked. "You say you are always looking out for yourself. But Don Carlos taught me that Mormonism, true Christianity, means giving up things, loving God more than you care about yourself. It means preaching the gospel, maybe giving up your money, your home, and your reputation, perhaps even the person you love. It takes all you have to give, and yet your own sacrifice pales in comparison to Jesus' love and sacrifice. That's what keeps you going. I'm thinking the gospel has changed you, Almon. I'm hoping it could change Kathryn too."

Almon grinned at David. "That's one way of looking at it. But there's another side. I read the Book of Mormon out of curiosity. The strange thing was that it seemed wholly true to me—like putting pieces of a broken eggshell back together. I figured that belonging to the true religion is an asset. Sure it's a sacrifice too, but God is one powerful ally."

David smiled and shook his head at Almon's audacity.

Almon laughed and thumped David on the back once more. "Stick by me, David. I mean to be president one day—or at least a rich man!"

David punched Almon playfully in the arm. "I plan on it, Almon Babbitt. Like you said, us Mormon boys have to stick together."

Ten minutes later, David and Almon gathered with the other hands as the dark eastern sky lightened. The door to the frame farmhouse opened, and John Clay stepped out. David noticed that the curtains were drawn back in Kathryn's window. Was she watching them? John Clay strode over.

A blond, burly young man named Samuel Jones eyed David and snorted. He called to Clay, "I heard tell that your pretty sister, Katie, has a kiss for the best mower."

"I don't know about a kiss," John said, "but Katie and my wife, Margaret, are fixing you fellows a nice lunch."

David looked from Kathryn's window toward the sunrise. As it edged into the sky and teetered on the horizon, it seemed to him like a fiery, living dragon dwelling just beyond the eastern edge of the world.

"David Johnson," John Clay shouted with such force that it startled David. David glanced over, and Clay's eyes were not friendly. A stranger would never have guessed that David had lived in Clay's home for much of the winter, that four months ago they had presumed they would soon be brothers-in-law. "Johnson, you will lead this gang of hands through the field!"

David met Clay's eyes and nodded slowly. He pushed the image of Kathryn from his mind. He touched the edge of his scythe with his forefinger. Then, he whet the blade on the grindstone. David swung the scythe effortlessly from right to left. "Come, friends," he shouted, "let's mow this grass while the dew is still on!" With David leading, the men moved through the field like a swarming battalion, their blades sweeping with each step, leaving broad swaths of grass in their wake.

Six hours later, it was noon, and the mowing was done. After lunch, the men would work until dark, raking and turning the cut grass so that it would cure into hay. The door to the farmhouse swung open. Kathryn and Margaret emerged in starched bonnets, carrying trays of fruit, bread, honey, and cheese. John Clay brought the men brandy and rum.

As the women neared the hands, Kathryn could not stop herself from staring at David—his deeply tanned face, his tow-cloth shirt drenched with sweat, his arms muscular and glistening in the sunlight. Kathryn steadied herself and went to serve him. But before Kathryn reached David, Margaret briskly marched between the two and handed David his food. Almon, sitting beside David, elbowed his friend and began talking to him. Kathryn felt hot anger rise in her. Almon and the Mormons had ruined everything. Everything. Masking her feelings, she turned and smiled at the other men as she offered them lunch.

"Well, Miss Katie." Samuel grinned as he took a peach from Kathryn's tray. "We hear the best mower will get a kiss. I did one fine job out there." Men chuckled and a few eyed David. They all knew that Samuel was not the best mower.

"The best mower would get a kiss," Kathryn replied coyly, "if he were not a Mormon."

Laughter erupted as David reddened and studied the blade of his scythe. Almon Babbitt jumped to his feet and exclaimed merrily. "Then it is your loss, Miss Kathryn, for though I am an excellent mower, I am even better at kissing!"

Kathryn's face turned red, and she glared at Almon. "You, boy, ought to be thrashed for your impertinence!"

"We'll thrash both these Mormon boys for you, Ma'am," Samuel offered, his smile lined with malice.

David looked up. The brown of his eyes mixed with molten gold as they flashed from Kathryn to Samuel. His thoughts spun. Kathryn had ridiculed him. Samuel had voiced a threat. David was sick and tired of blind prejudice. No men would attempt a thrashing and come away unscathed. At David's fierce look, Kathryn's blue eyes filled with angry tears. "Not during the haying! The Mormons are too useful during the haying," she cried. Then she put her tray on the ground, gathered her skirts, and ran toward the house.

"Then we'll wait till after the hay is in," one of the men called after her.

John Clay stood up. He wasn't about to let his men get out of hand. He felt a grudging pity toward David. He blamed Joel for the young man's troubles. Why had his old friend been so stupid as to listen to the Mormon lies? John Clay hoped to make enough money on the haying to buy out Joel's interest in the sawmill.

Clay pointed to the clouds gathering in the distance. "If my hay is ruined by the rain, no man will be paid for today's labor," he called out. Lunch was cut short, and the men resumed their work, toiling as quickly as strength allowed. Some raked and covered the new hay. David and Almon rolled the old hay into cocks to protect it from rot.

As the afternoon shadows lengthened and the work continued, David noticed that Almon grew weak and short of breath. He whispered for Almon to take it as easy as possible without drawing notice. The men worked until their hands burned and their arms ached. When the work was done, it was nearly dusk. The sky loomed thick with dark clouds, but it had not yet rained. John Clay made sure that David and Almon were the first to receive their wages and be sent on their way. He didn't want any hands lying in wait for the Mormon boys and causing trouble.

The thunderstorm broke loose as David and Almon walked home. Lightning riddled the sky, and the rain was cool and fierce. The bounce was gone from Almon's step and his face was flushed.

At first, the noise of the storm covered the sound of footsteps behind Almon and David. When David finally realized someone was following them, he turned around quickly, scythe in hand, his posture defensive. Yet it was a woman standing there, soaked and crying. Upon seeing Kathryn, David felt utterly defenseless. Her bonnet hung off her shoulders, and her long hair was matted and sopping. Mud splatters dotted her skirt. Tears mingled with the rain on her cheeks.

"Don't you see, David," she cried as she faced him. "Don't you see that you have ruined my life? Now I must marry someone I don't love. I beg you. I beg you to stop this Mormon foolishness."

"Katie," David whispered in painful frustration, "it is not foolishness. It is who I am. It is what I believe. I must be true to God. Why can't you love me as I am and allow me my faith?"

"No, David, no!" she sobbed. David put one arm awkwardly around her as she wept. Almon gazed down the road and saw a group of five hands in the distance moving determinedly toward them. Samuel was among them. Almon shook with fever in the downpour. He reached out and touched David's shoulder. "Time to go."

At Almon's words, Katie swung fiercely from David and slapped Almon across the face with all the force she could muster. "I hate you, Almon Babbitt!" she screamed as her tearful face twisted in rage. Almon stepped back as a welt appeared on his cheek. The men began running toward them.

David turned to Kathryn. "You are unfair to Almon, Kathryn. May God forgive you."

"You've hurt me, David Johnson! You've used me wrongly!" Kathryn screamed. David stared at her dumbfounded.

"Don't you worry, miss, we'll take care of these Mormon boys for you," Samuel shouted.

David turned to Almon. In seconds, the men would be upon them. Almon's cheeks were fiery red, and there was fear in his eyes. "Can you run?" David asked

Almon shook his head. He could barely stand. "Don't leave me to those jackals," he begged.

David's heart pounded in anger. Any love he had felt for Kathryn turned to fury directed toward the approaching men. "We Mormon boys stick together," he whispered fiercely in Almon's ear.

The gang divided and surrounded David and Almon. David swung his scythe in a wide circle. "If any man comes near us, I will mow him down," he shouted.

"Drop your scythe and fight like a man," Samuel said with narrow eyes. "If we all use our scythes, you might survive, but your friend won't."

David ignored Samuel and yelled ferociously at the other men. "Is it worth your arm, your eye, your hand? Not one of you will leave here whole!"

"Behind you!" Almon gasped.

David swung round, his scythe whistling. A man jumped back, the blade cut his shirt and scratched his chest.

"Stop it, David!" Kathryn screamed. "Stop it!"

"It ain't worth it," another man called out. "This Mormon's crazy. I'm goin' home."

Most of the other men snorted in agreement. Samuel eyed David maliciously. He knew he had lost this battle. But when he turned to Kathryn, he figured he had won the war. "Of course we'll stop, Miss Katie. We only wanted to protect you. The Mormon nearly murdered Henry. He'll get his due. Let me help you home."

As Samuel put his arm around Kathryn, David slowly lowered his scythe, breathing hard. The thought that he had almost killed a man stunned him. He looked at Almon. The youth could hardly stand. David huddled Almon against him, half carrying the young man. Without looking back, David and Almon left the road and cut through the dark, rainy woodland.

By the time they reached the Babbitt doorstep, it was night, and the rain had moved on. This was the first time David had been to Almon's home. Even in the scarce moonlight, David was astounded by the rundown appearance of the farmstead. Pigs and dogs snored in the slovenly yard. The house was ramshackle with shingles falling from the roof and windows broken. The door hung ajar with the hinge bent. In the dim interior candlelight, David noticed that there were coarse benches instead of chairs, and a black, sooty hole where the hearth should have been. Somewhere inside, an adult voice laughed harshly. Another cursed. Within seconds, a group of filthy, curious children surrounded David and Almon.

"Ira, Bill, help me get in bed," Almon muttered feverishly to two unruly-looking boys.

"Get yourself in bed, Almon," one of the boys retorted.

"Don't you see, he can't stand up?" the other boy said as he waved David aside. "Go home, Mister. We'll take him."

Almon looked at David as his younger brothers roughly propped Almon up with their shoulders. Almon spoke. "If I'm not at meeting tomorrow, bring Jared Carter." At this thought, David nodded. He had heard that Simeon Carter's brother, Jared, an elder who had recently moved to Amherst, had great faith and the gift of healing.

Suddenly Almon reached out and gripped David's arm, his hands shaking. His face was flushed with fever and his eyes were watery with tears. "If you'd been sick, I would have run off. I wouldn't have risked a beating."

"The rum and fever have addled your brain, my friend," David responded gently. "You wouldn't have left me. Us Mormon boys stick together." Almon managed a smile.

"Quit jawin', Almon, or I'm done helping," one of the brothers complained.

The other exclaimed, "By Jove, he's hot."

David stood by the door and watched the boys half drag Almon to a filthy straw mattress. Melancholy filled David. If he were home sick, his mother and sisters would have kept constant, loving watch over his bedside. Joe would have made him herbal remedies. Ben would have checked on him every hour with that furrowed brow. Seth would have read the Bible to him to pass the time. Nancy would have prayed for him.

A few moments later, David walked toward Joel's home with the images of his family still in his mind. He took the road this time, too exhausted to care if a gang lay in wait. A thought rose like a dark phantom. He had almost killed a man. What would his family think of him if they knew? All his life, his mother had taught him to turn the other cheek, to love his enemies.

He was a Mormon. He knew the story of the righteous Lamanites who laid down their weapons of war. Yet, he had nearly killed a man with his own scythe. The man's blood would have been on David's hands forever. Rage had consumed him. David stumbled to the side of the road and retched.

An hour later, David entered Joel and Annie's orderly, candlelit log house. Joel sat at the table writing a letter. Annie was settled in the rocking chair sewing. Joel looked up briefly, his forehead creased in concentration. "I'm trying to write to Seth and Mother about the gospel. But it's difficult putting my thoughts into words." He looked back down at the paper.

"There's cooked squash. And bread and milk," Annie commented as she continued to sew. "And strawberries with cream."

Utterly spent, David felt as if his knees would buckle. His scythe clattered to the floor, the sound startling Joel and Annie. They both looked up from their work.

"David, you're tired," Annie said as she put her sewing down. "I'll help you to the table and bring you dinner."

"How'd the haying go?" Joel asked as he watched Annie guide David to the table. Sitting across from David, he looked at his younger brother closely.

Tears filled David's brown, gold eyes. "Almon is ill," he moaned, "and I am no longer worthy of the sacrament." Around the small oak table, Joel and Annie listened as David's story spilled forth. "I almost killed a man," David finished painfully.

"But it was self-defense. Self-defense is not a sin." Annie said.

"The man who came up behind me didn't have a weapon," David said dismally. "He had dropped his scythe and only meant to tackle me."

"So that others could come and knock you senseless." Annie stomped her foot. "And with poor Almon sick. They should all be thrashed. I'd like to give Kathryn a piece of my mind. David, please eat."

But David could not eat. He turned to his sister-in-law, his fists clenched, his voice pained. "Annie, I could have killed that man in his sins. His name is Henry O'Leary. I've worked with him on a dozen fields. I've never had trouble with him before. He's a quiet sort."

"With a dark heart," Annie insisted vehemently, her instincts protective as a mother bear's. "David, the prophet Ammon cut off a lot of arms when he saved Lamoni's servants by protecting his flocks."

"But Ammon didn't do that in anger," David cried. "There was rage in my heart."

"Of course there was. Righteous anger," Annie countered.

"I fear such anger is not righteous. I fear it will destroy me." David recalled the sickening fury he had once felt toward his own father.

Thus far, Joel had listened without comment, but finally he spoke. "The spirit of those who persecute us is the same spirit that persecuted the members of the ancient Church. David, whether you sinned or not balances on this question. Did you act to protect Almon or to injure another? You are the only man who knows whether you are worthy of the sacrament."

Annie humphed indignantly at her husband. "I'm a woman, and the only one who seems to know anything. Of course David is worthy of the sacrament! Joel, you Johnsons sometimes look at things so deeply that you don't see what's plain as the noses on your faces."

Joel eyed his wife with an exasperated look. Although David thought Joel correct, Annie's insistence comforted him. Joel was about to give Annie a piece of his mind when David smiled slightly and said, "Our Johnson noses are plain, Joel. And rather large for our faces."

Annie giggled. Joel exhaled sharply and reached for the bowl of strawberries. Annie tapped his knuckles with the serving spoon. "No! You already ate your share. I saved those for your brother."

David looked at his brother and sister-in-law. "Joel, your wife is miraculous—sweet as a strawberry and fierce as a feral cat."

Annie rubbed Joel's neck. "He loves me still, David. That is the real miracle. If you want, you can share the strawberries with Joel."

"Eat half of them," David said handing the strawberry bowl to Joel. David tore off a piece of bread and dipped it in milk. He found he could eat now.

"How my heart aches for poor Almon," Annie said pensively. "I wish I could cool his fever and feed him strawberries tonight." She continued to rub Joel's shoulders and watch David eat, though another thought lay tucked away in her mind. Annie had a precious secret, one she had not even told her husband yet— Annie suspected she was with child.

The next morning, the Sabbath dawned bright with puffy, white cumulus clouds. After donning their Sunday best, the Johnsons piled in the wagon with Joel and Annie in the front and David holding Sixtus in the back. Joel hawed to the horses.

When they arrived at Brother Barney's, about twenty Saints were already gathered. Joel and David helped the other brethren move chairs and benches into the spacious barn where the meeting would be held. The women chatted sociably among themselves. Brother John Whitmer, one of the eight witnesses to the Book of Mormon, had come to preach.

David scanned the group for Almon but did not find him. After the chairs were in place, he took a seat next to Jared Carter and his family. While Joel waved Annie and Sixtus over, David told Elder Carter about Almon's fever.

"Brother Stone was laid up with the fever yesterday," Brother Carter commented. "Elder Smith and I administered to him, and he's here today, fit as a fiddle."

"I hope it works for Brother Almon," David ventured.

"It will according to his faith and the Lord's will," Brother Carter stated simply.

As the meeting commenced, Sixtus became restless. Annie tried playing silent finger games with him but to no avail. During the invocation, Sixtus whined, and David saw that Joel was feeling tense with his child's misbehavior. David took the child from Joel and carried him out.

Once outside, David put Sixtus down and looked up at the clouds, which had traded their bright white for the dark thickness of an imminent squall. Yet David breathed relief. He still doubted his worthiness to partake of the sacrament and felt it was just as well if he missed this portion of the meeting. David loosened his stock tie and watched Sixtus play. Five minutes later, lightning sliced the sky. It began to sprinkle.

David grinned at Sixtus, who was now racing in circles around him. Thunder clapped, and a horse whinnied. "You're in luck, Sixtus," David said as he picked up the little boy. "That barn roof is only half shingled and this meeting's about to end." As the sprinkle turned into a downpour, David ran with Sixtus back to the barn, thinking that the congregation would be dispersing and running for cover. However, as they neared the entrance to the barn, the meeting was still in full swing. Intent faces listened to John Whitmer, who stood on a small platform and told of how he had held the golden plates in his hands, how he had hefted them and seen the engravings.

David looked up to the unshingled portion of the barn roof. It seemed it was raining all around the barn, with the only bit of blue sky directly over the barn. David and Sixtus quietly went back to their seats. They were the only members of the congregation dripping wet.

Brother Carter tapped David's shoulder and whispered in his ear. "The Lord has answered my prayers, and the meeting is uninterrupted." David's body tingled as a surge of faith coursed through him. He took off his soaking stock tie and gave it to Sixtus to play with.

The rain stopped before the meeting ended. Afterward, David accompanied Jared Carter and Sylvester Smith to the Babbitt residence. Mrs. Babbitt frowned as she opened the door. She was a thin, bedraggled, hard-looking woman. Her eye twitched. After the elders explained who they were, she pointed to the filthy straw mattress in the corner, where Almon writhed, his fever raging. "I don't believe a lick of Mormonism," she said sternly. "But my boy does." With that, she wiped her hands on a grimy apron and left the room. Two little girls played in the corner. The rest of his family was nowhere to be seen.

"Almon, I brought the elders," David said. Almon opened his bloodshot eyes and grinned. No matter how sick he was, Almon was still himself—ambitious and precocious, self-serving and big-hearted, full of faith.

David watched silently as the elders laid their hands on Almon's head and blessed him to be healed by the power of the holy priesthood, according to his faith in Jesus Christ. After the prayer, Jared Carter bade Almon to arise. A moment passed. Then to David's amazement, Jared Carter bade Almon to arise in the name of Jesus Christ. As Almon stood up, he shed both the bedclothes and his fever. His body and mind were cool and clear.

After embracing Almon, Sylvester Smith left for home—his duty done. David and Jared Carter went outside and waited for Almon to dress. After a short time, Almon joined them, dapper and grinning. David wondered how Almon's clothes could be so clean when his home was so dirty.

"David," Almon said cheerfully. "Didn't I tell you the Lord was a powerful ally? Let's walk to your house and see if Sister Annie has enough food for a man with an appetite."

Joyously, David embraced Almon. He invited Brother Jared to join them. Jared Carter said he would be pleased, for he'd heard of Sister Annie's culinary skills.

As the men walked the three miles to Joel's house, Almon and Jared Carter talked animatedly about the restoration of the gospel. Yet David was quiet, lost in his own thoughts. Walking beneath a sky of intermittent sunshine and windswept clouds, David's thoughts traveled through time and distance back to Nancy's bedside in Pomfret. He pictured her high cheekbones and steady gray eyes. He imagined two elders blessing her. In his imagination, Nancy stood tall once again, leaving her crutches behind as Almon had left his fever, healed by the Lord, whole forevermore.

Seth chewed his lower lip. It was late afternoon, and he had spent most of the day working in the fields. He lifted the Book of Mormon from the mantel and stared at it. It had arrived yesterday with a letter from Joel about his and David's conversion. Seth had not been able to sleep last night. He had been agitated, fearful for his brothers' souls.

With the Book of Mormon in his hand, Seth left the house. He carried the book to a shack in the wildwood—a place where he had gone many times in prayerful solitude. Seth knelt down, the book at his side, and began to pour out his heart to his Heavenly Father. The crash of a nearby tree startled him. He opened his eyes and looked around the shack. Outside, a wild animal shrieked. Trying to ignore these distractions, Seth closed his eyes and attempted once more to pray. However, the creature's horrifying wails drew nearer until they became deafening. It sounded as if the animal were within a few feet of the shack. Every nerve on edge, Seth held absolutely still with a prayer for safety in his heart. He wished he had brought a gun with him.

Then the sound ceased. Seth waited and listened. A strange thought passed through his mind. Could this incident be his answer—a sign that the Book of Mormon was of the devil? Moments passed. The noise did not begin again, nor did he hear the animal running away. Finally, Seth opened the door and peered out. He saw nothing but trees, brush, and the shadows of twilight. It would be dark within the hour. If the creature was earthly, Seth figured it was somewhere in the wood. There was no safety in the woodland that night. Tentacles of apprehension spread through him. Seth picked up the Book of Mormon and hurried home along the well-worn path. As darkness fell, bringing with it the mystery of night, Seth wondered what might have happened had he the faith to stay in the shack praying. Would he now have the answer? Would he know for sure if the book in his hand were of God or of Satan?

The next day, as Seth labored in the wheat field, Judge Houghton's son dropped off a court summons. At lunchtime, Seth opened and read it silently. It concerned Mr. Barrett's freight wagons that had been destroyed several years ago when a deluge broke the dam of Joel's sawmill, causing flooding. The note claimed that with Joel gone, Seth, as his partner, was responsible. The wagons were extremely expensive and far beyond Seth's ability to redeem. Seth thought about how ironic it would be if he went to jail, for there he'd have plenty of time to read the Book of Mormon.

That evening, Seth went to seek advice from Esquire Timothy Johnson, Annie's father. Esquire Johnson knew the details of Joel's business better than any other man. When Seth arrived, Esquire Johnson welcomed him with a warm handshake.

He was a well-to-do landowner in the community, a portly gentleman with a mass of fine white hair. His small, watery-blue eyes lay amidst a web of deep wrinkles. He leaned on a beautiful mahogany cane and wore a vest and cravat.

"I've a mind of what brings you here, young Seth," Esquire Johnson said as he invited Seth to sit with him in the parlor. It was well furnished with a fine-woven carpet and an astral light on the tea table.

Seth's eyes widened at the man's comment. "Then you know of Barrett's wagon concern?"

A short laugh escaped the gentleman. "So Old Houghton's sued the note. No, I wasn't thinking of that. My concern is of greater import. Have you heard from Joel lately? He and Annie have joined the Mormons."

Seth sighed deeply. "I ought to have come seeking your advice on *that* matter rather than on my own selfish business. Joel sent me a letter and a Book of Mormon this week. It has troubled me greatly. Though I've only read a small portion of the book, I fear they have been deceived."

Esquire Johnson raised his eyebrows and spoke matter-of-factly. "My Annie's never been an easy one to deceive. I've seen some strange things in my day, and this is one of the strangest. Young Seth, bring me that Book of Mormon when you've finished with it. I'm inclined to read it for myself."

Seth nodded and added a bit ruefully, "I will, sir, if I'm not in jail."

At this, Esquire Johnson laughed. Then he advised Seth to answer the court summons and take with him a schedule requesting they allow him to make affordable monthly payments. Then, the old gentleman went into the pantry to get Seth a cup of milk and a piece of pie.

Esquire Johnson smiled secretly as he put the snack on a platter. He had a plan of his own. Tomorrow, he would secretly pay for the wagons and end this case. He liked Seth Johnson. He was a sensitive young scholar and had helped Annie and Joel a great deal. It would be a pleasure to return the favor. What good was money anyway, Esquire Johnson wondered, if not to help out the young?

The Sabbath dawned bright and warm. Seth offered to take Susan and Nancy to their Baptist meeting while Julia and the rest of the children attended the Presbyterian service. Julia asked if she could take Joel's letter and share it with Reverend Spencer. Seth agreed with a sigh, knowing it couldn't hurt Joel's reputation, for his name was already ruined with the Presbyterians.

Later that morning, following the meeting in Reverend Spencer's yard, Julia sent the children home. She approached the good minister and requested a private conference with him. The reverend escorted her to a glade in the woods behind his home where there were two wooden benches. Julia handed Joel's letter to the minister after briefly explaining its contents.

As he read, the bald Reverend Spencer's face reddened, and beads of sweat trickled down his temple. The disease of Mormonism had spread to a family in his own congregation! Young David Johnson had been a member of his church. He knew that it would be difficult keeping his voice calm with the fury that coursed through him. He could hardly believe that he had once offered Joel Johnson a college education if he accepted the Presbyterian faith and agreed to become a preacher.

Reverend Spencer spoke bluntly as he blotted his brow with a handkerchief. "You must sever your relationship with Joel and David before their delusion poisons your entire family and infiltrates the community. This will be difficult, as these men are your own flesh and blood. Remember that the Savior himself said that it is better to cut off a limb from the body than to allow the soul to be thrust into purgatory. Sister Johnson, acknowledge the falsehood of Mormonism before the church. Tell them the devil has sway over the hearts of your sons. You must be vigilant in your opposition. Unless they repent, it is as if Joel and David are dead."

Julia stared dumbfounded at the minister. Tears clouded in her eyes, and her voice shook slightly, but she held her head high as she spoke. "Though my sons err, it is only in looking beyond the mark as they seek true religion. They are not dead to me." At that, she stood, turned, and walked away. Reverend Spencer called after her, adamantly warning Julia Johnson of her pride.

As Julia walked home, the sun blazed overhead. Her chemise damp from sweat, she pushed Reverend Spencer's words from her mind. The man didn't know everything. Instead, she thought of how each family member had reacted differently to Joel's eloquent letter describing his belief in a restored gospel. Julianne did not struggle emotionally as Seth did. She simply suggested giving Joel, Annie, and David time. She felt they would try this new religion, find it false, and come to their senses. Julia thought her daughter's advice much wiser than Reverend Spencer's. She prayed that would be the case.

Her mind then turned to Ezekiel. After finding out about his sons' conversion to Mormonism, Ezekiel refused to have it discussed in his presence. The very thought infuriated him. Julia knew that her husband blamed her for nurturing the religious fervor that caused his sons' delusion. Yet she also knew that he loved Joel and David and would not break that kinship. Julia's heart continued to ache when she thought of her husband. Though he did not drink as heavily as the previous fall, he spent little time around his hearth, choosing the fields, the carpenter shop, or the tavern instead.

Only Nancy seemed at peace—dear Nancy with those calm gray eyes. A year had passed since her accident. Now she spent her days painting and sewing. On reading Joel's letter, Nancy suggested the family read and study the Book of Mormon together before rendering judgment. Even if the book were false, Nancy explained that she felt strangely thankful that David had found increased faith in God.

Julia decided that she must shield her younger children from talk of Mormonism. She had seen the worry and hope in Benjamin's eyes when he overheard her speaking with Seth on the subject of God raising up a prophet. She would bide her time until her own thoughts were clear on the subject and she knew how to counsel them.

When Julia arrived at home, Julianne and Susan bustled to prepare the meal. Seth was at the table adding a postscript to a letter he had written to Joel the day before. Almera waited near him with a hand on her hip, impatient to set out the dishes.

Seth finished writing and looked up at his mother, his brown eyes sober and thoughtful. He spoke in that careful, quiet way of his. "At meeting, Mr. Town's folks said they would pick up the letter this afternoon. They leave tomorrow for Toledo. They'll see it gets to Amherst. Would you like to read it or add a note?"

"Both," Julia said with a smile. Seth handed her the letter. As little Amos tugged on her skirts, she hoisted her youngest onto her hip and sat down in the rocking chair. She read the letter. Julia was touched by Seth's words for they echoed the feelings of her own heart.

*Pomfret, Chautauqua County, New York, August 22, 1831*

*Dear Brother Joel,*

*How shall I address myself to you? In what language shall I attempt to answer your letter? My feelings are truly inde-scribable, and an unaccountable sensation pervades my frame. Oh, for some angel, no, for the Holy Spirit to guide my pen while I attempt to address a few lines to you.*

*I have read and reread your letter. When I have been reading, I have sometimes said in my heart, "This is directed by the Holy Spirit." But when I have read the Book of Mormon (I have read it some), I have said, "Alas! The time has surely come foretold by the blessed Savior that the devil has so much power on earth."*

*It is true that I know not but the Lord has raised up a prophet, but I have fears lest this one is one of those false prophets spoken of and warned against by the Savior and His apostles and that the right way of the Lord has been perverted by him through the influence of the devil. I have read the book a little and find no evidence of its being a revelation of God; neither do I find any reason to look for a revelation from heaven of this nature. The manner of your being convinced of this doctrine and book I am not prepared to condemn, but since Satan will, if possible, deceive the very elect, I fear that you might have been deceived.*

*The style, popularity of the book, and doctrine I would not object to did it bring sufficient evidence to me of its divine origin. Its statement that the Indians are the seed of Joseph, I might easily conceive to be correct, should I once believe the work to be a revelation from God. Men's not believing it would be no evidence of its not being true to me.*

*Oh, how careful we should be to embrace nothing but the truth as it is in Jesus. You express your fears for the professing Christians that they possess the same spirit that crucified the Lord Jesus Christ. I fear you are too quick to judge. You exclaim, "Oh, when will mankind be rational?" I ask the same question. You say, "Had I the pen of an*

*angel, I could not paint my feelings." I think it would take
an angel's pen to describe mine.*

*Your injunction to search the scriptures and to pray to
God for direction, I acknowledge to be good. Perhaps no
better could have been given by an angel. I do not feel
disposed to trifle with these things and confess that profes-
sors of religion do not treat the subject as they ought. You
say that you pray to God that I might come to a full knowledge of the truth, to which I say "Amen."*

*Farewell,
Seth Johnson*

*Postscript: Although I might submit anything of a worthy
nature to you, dear brother, I cannot submit what pertains
to my everlasting welfare to any being whose life may be
deceived. I have often said that this earth is not my home.
My treasure is laid up in heaven, and I am required to live
faithful and contend earnestly for the faith once delivered
the saints.*

As Julia read, there was a knock at the door. It was Mr. and
Mrs. Town. Julianne invited them in for supper. They declined,
saying that they must be on their way. They would wait outside so
as not to disturb the dinner. Seth retrieved the envelope, and Julia
wrote a hasty note on the back to her sons in Ohio. As she wrote,
she said a prayer in her heart for them.

*My dear children,*

*I want to address you but know not how. It is impossible to
describe my feelings. I was truly glad to hear from you.*

*When I heard that you were well in soul and body, my soul
rejoiced. I long to see all my children enjoy pure and unde-
filed religion. But when I understood that you had
embraced new doctrine, I feared lest you have been
deceived. I hope you will all strive for the truth. They hurry
me so that I can write no more.*

*Your affectionate mother,*
*Julia Johnson*

As Julia handed the letter back to Seth to seal, a chorus of
siblings asked if he had remembered to send Joel, Annie, David,
and Sixtus their love and concern. Seth quickly penned a few
more lines.

*The others would write but can't. They send their love and
say they fear for you, but if you enjoy your religion, go on.
Father came home last Wednesday but is gone to Fredonia
again. Forgive my harshness if I have been too harsh and
my brevity if I have been too short. Farewell my dear
brothers.*

When Seth went to court two days later with his proposed
payment schedule for the Barrett's wagons, he was surprised to
find that the case had been settled. Judge Houghton refused to tell
Seth any of the details. He simply bid Seth a good day and gruffly
ordered him on his way.

*"The Lord bless you!" Long years ago,*
*When as a Saint I was a child,*
*Those words of love, did thrill me through,*
*As Joseph took my hand and smiled.*

*Oh! when will come the long sought day,*
*When all, with love and friendship true,*
*Can meet, and take the hand and say,*
*"My brother, dear, the Lord bless you!"*

—JOEL H. JOHNSON, FROM "THE LORD BLESS YOU!"

*October 1831*

Rain soaked Annie's cloak on a gray Monday morning in late October. Her shoulders bowed as she packed salt pork and bread in the wagon for the journey to the Church's general conference in Orange, Ohio. They would leave before noon and travel thirty-five miles over bumpy, muddy roads. As she loaded, she dreaded the long trip ahead but at the same time was buoyed by her excitement to attend. After tightening the canvas over the wagon, Annie tramped back to the cabin. Once under roof, she scraped the mud from her shoes, hung her dripping cloak near the hearth to dry, and warmed her hands by the fire.

Her chapped, freckled hands limbered, and Annie stepped to the table where she had left a kettle of husked corn that she would boil for a quick meal. The cabin was unusually quiet—Joel had left earlier in the afternoon to meet with some of the members. David was in the barn with Sixtus doing a final check on the stock.

Unusually tired this morning, Annie sat down at the table, wishing that she had time to rest. She noticed that Joel had left out a piece of paper. It was the license Joel had received when ordained an elder. This ordination had clinched Joel's decision to sell his interest in the sawmill and to await whatever calling came. Annie sighed and recalled how proud she felt at his ordination and yet how relieved she was when Joel was called to preside over the congregation in Amherst and to preach in the surrounding vicinity. She had feared he might be called as a traveling missionary.

As winter approached, her pregnancy caused her to feel vulnerable and apprehensive about the future. It triggered memories of the months preceding Sixtus's birth—that time when Julianne had died in spite of her prayers. Lately, Annie worried about dying in childbirth, she feared losing Sixtus or the babe within, and she feared Joel's recurring cough that might take his life and leave her to raise her little ones alone. Each day, Annie forced these thoughts to the back of her mind, reminding herself of God's goodness and the joy of the restored gospel. Last summer, the Lord's perfect love had cast out all fear. Annie wondered why these frightening thoughts lingered hauntingly on the edges of her mind.

Annie shook her head, longing for more faith. With an elbow on the table, she rested her cheek in her hand. Her unruly auburn hair lay tamed under a white, knitted scarf. In her mind, she pictured her lanky husband with his square jaw, long, thin mouth, and dark, intense eyes, so unwavering in his determination to serve the Lord. He had received the Melchizedek priesthood on September twentieth. Annie picked up the piece of paper and read it.

*A license, liberty, and authority given to Joel H. Johnson, certifying and proving that he is an Elder of this Church of Christ, established and regularly organized in these last days A.D. 1830, on the 6th day of April. All of which has been done by the will of God the Father, according to His holy calling and the gift and the power of the Holy Ghost, agreeable to the revelations of Jesus Christ given to Joseph Smith, Jr., the first Elder of the Church, signifying that he has been baptized and received into the Church, according to the articles and covenants of the Church. Done on the 20th day of September, in Amherst, Loraine County, and State of Ohio, in the year of our Lord one thousand eight hundred and thirty one.*

*Signed and sealed by Elders Jared Carter and Sylvester Smith*

A shiver crept through Annie as tears rushed to her eyes. She did have faith. This was the same priesthood, the same power of God to act in His name, which Jesus had given Peter, James, and John. Those three personages had laid their hands on the head of Joseph the Prophet and given him the keys of the kingdom. Her Joel held this same priesthood. The thought was glorious beyond belief. It was a blessing to live in these latter days! Soon she would meet the Prophet Joseph for the first time. If only the rain would stop.

Annie set the paper down and wiped her eyes. This was no time for tears. She stood up, took a deep breath, and hefted the heavy kettle. Stepping over to the hearth, she hooked the kettle to the iron bar and swung it over the fire. She breathed heavily after this job was done. It felt as if increased gravity tugged at her limbs. She sat down on a stool near the hearth and hugged her knees, watching the orange and crimson flames lick the blackened bottom of the kettle. Rain pounded the roof, and wind gusts buffeted the walls of the cabin.

As Annie breathed in the familiar smell of burning wood, she wondered once more if she should have submitted to Joel when he suggested she stay home from the conference. A week ago this very day, Joel had told her that he worried she might catch a chill camping at night. Yet Annie had been insistent, arguing that her time of sickness had passed and in a few months she would be too uncomfortable to travel. Now was the time to go and meet with the Saints. Joel had respected her opinion and consented. As Annie sat by the fire, listening to the whistle of the wind and the crackling of the flames, she hoped that Joel's argument that she should stay home would not be proven wise.

Ninety minutes later, the wagon wheels slogged in heavy mud as the mule team plodded through rain. David and Joel sat in the wagon seats, fully exposed to the wind and chill. Almon rode an old horse alongside. Annie cuddled with Sixtus in the wagon bed surrounded by blankets, clothing, and food, the canvas cover keeping the two relatively dry. They slept periodically, their bodies cushioned by a thin, straw-tick mattress.

The storm partially gave way as evening approached. Blue-gray clouds wove around the descending sun, blending with the first pink of sunset. It was breezy with intermittent showers. During the final hour of their journey, Sixtus rode on the horse with Almon. Annie perched in the front of the wagon bed near Joel and David. To pass the time and to take their minds from the chill gusts that breached their wet clothing, they sang. Neither Joel nor Annie had strong voices, but David and Almon carried the melody. They began with one of Annie's favorite hymns.

*Earth with her ten thousand flowers,*
*Air, with all its beams and showers,*
*Heaven's infinite expanse;*
*Ocean's resplendent countenance—*
*All around, and all above,*
*Hath this record—God is love.*

It was dark when they arrived at Irenus Burnett's farm in Orange, Ohio. Brother Burnett greeted them and directed them to a campsite. A short time later, Annie and Joel bedded down in the wagon with Sixtus between them. David and Almon spread a tarp over the wet ground, laid their bedrolls out beneath the wagon, and slumbered there.

The next morning, Joel arose silently and readied himself for the priesthood meeting. It was cold, and he encouraged his sleepy wife to stay warm under the covers and to go back to sleep. Annie didn't protest. Almon and David required no encouragement to remain in their bedrolls, as they did not stir. Joel dressed, fed the animals, and breakfasted on cold biscuits.

Minutes later, Joel approached a group of about thirty-five men gathered outside the Burnett's frame house.

Simeon Carter hurried over, warmly clasping Joel's hand. "Brother Joel, welcome."

Joel had seen little of this friend since Simeon's recent trip to Independence, Missouri, the land promised by the Lord as the new Zion.

Joel's heart beat in anticipation as he and Simeon walked toward the house. He would meet the Prophet momentarily. Joel looked around. A few men wore fine, stovetop hats and full broadcloth suits, but most dressed like him—in a farmer's best coat, a homespun wool shirt, a stock tie, trousers, and boots.

In the center of this group of priesthood holders, one man, attired much like Joel, gestured with his hands as he explained a point of doctrine. His cheeks were reddened from the weather. He was in his mid-twenties, with a tall, broad, muscular frame. He had light brown hair that the wind swept back, revealing a high forehead. Beardless and smooth-skinned, his features were finely molded, his lips full, and his demeanor confident and pleasant. On spying Joel, the man turned and called out a cheerful, "Good morning."

"President Joseph Smith," Simeon whispered with a smile.

Joel's heart jumped at this. The Prophet Joseph left the group and walked toward Joel.

"Brother Joseph," Simeon introduced. "Here is Elder Joel Johnson, who presides over the Amherst Branch. Brother Joel, meet the Prophet of God."

"I know I don't look much like a prophet," Joseph said with a chuckle. He put both his hands on Joel's shoulders. "Brother Simeon has read me some of your verses. Brother Joel, you write with the pen of an angel. I suppose that you think I am a great, green, lubberly fellow."

Tears gathered in Joel's eyes at this warm welcome. "Brother Joseph, no angel's pen could describe my feelings right now. I behold the man whose mission it is to bring forth Christ's ancient Church."

"The Lord bless you. Come, Brother Joel, there is a little time before the meeting starts. Let us get to know each other and converse about my calling and yours."

As they walked and talked together, the Prophet asked Joel about his family and upbringing. When Joel described those living in Pomfret, Joseph counseled him to visit them and bear testimony of the gospel. Joel agreed to go as soon as time and circumstances permitted. He told the Prophet that his deepest wish was to see his family embrace the truth. As they continued to talk, Joel noticed that the other brethren were filing into the farmhouse.

"I suppose we must be getting back," Joel said with a wistfulness that he could not hide.

"Do you have any questions first?" Joseph queried with a smile. "I don't suppose they will start the meeting without us."

Joel was silent for an instant, then he asked the question in his heart, "What of your trip to the land of Zion? What is it like there?" Joel had heard about Zion in recent Sabbath meetings. He knew it was a promised place for the gathering of the Saints in the last days. He knew that a temple would be built there and that the Prophet and other elders had recently journeyed to Jackson County, Missouri, the Lord's designated Promised Land.

Joseph's blue eyes were bright with life as he spoke. "Brother Joel, Zion is on the edge of the United States and looks into a vast wilderness. When we were there, we could not help but think of our highly cultivated society in the east, of how the people inhabiting the land of Zion are nearly a century behind the times. Most of them live without the benefit of civilization, refinement, or religion. There is great darkness there. We prayed, wondering when Zion will be built up in her glory, when the wilderness will blossom as a rose, when the temple will stand, unto which all nations shall come in the last days."

Then Joseph smiled softly in memory as he often did when recalling past experiences with revealed truth. The Prophet lifted his hands as he spoke, his enthusiasm increasing with each sentence. "Our prayers were answered, Brother Joel. Our anxiety was relieved with a revelation that we were truly in the land of promise, that the place now called Independence is the center place. It is wilderness, Brother Joel, so unlike the timbered states of the East. As far as the eye can reach, the beautiful rolling prairies lie spread out like a sea of meadows and are decorated with a growth of flowers so gorgeous and grand as to exceed description. And nothing is a richer stockholder in the blooming prairie than the honeybee! Thick forest grows on the watercourses, but only there. Buffalo, elk, deer, bear, wolves, beaver, and many smaller animals roam at pleasure. There is a rich abundance of the feathered tribe—turkeys, geese, swans, and ducks. After we left Independence Landing, we had the most excellent meal of wild turkey!

"In my mind, I see this place built up in the last days. Out of Zion, God shall shine. On the third of August, I dedicated the site for the temple—it lies westward on a spot not far from the courthouse."

A shiver spread through Joel at Joseph's description. "Our prophet has the tongue of an angel," Joel proclaimed. "All will desire to go to Zion."

Joseph's eyes twinkled as he laid a hand on Joel's shoulder. "For at least five years, we are commanded to build up Kirtland as well. I don't know when we will all gather to Zion. And my wife, Emma, thinks my tongue is more like a stream—always flowing.

Come, Brother Joel, now we must get back to our brethren, or I will be sorely chastised by Oliver and Hyrum."

"Mama, where's Papa?" Sixtus demanded on awakening inside the covered wagon.

"Papa's gone to meet the Prophet," Annie explained as she sat up. She reached out her hand and moved her little boy's bangs out of his eyes with her finger. Sixtus tossed his head and crawled over to the edge of the wagon. He peered out of the opening in the canvas. Annie followed on all fours, her head just above her son's. The morning was cloudy, but it wasn't raining.

"Where's Uncle and Almie?" Sixtus questioned.

"Guess!" David called. The bed of the wagon jiggled under Annie and Sixtus as David and Almon rattled it with their feet.

Sixtus shrieked with delight. "Under! Under!" he shouted.

"Stop," Annie exclaimed. In her pregnant state, she was not enjoying the ride. "It seems I have three children to tend, not one." This comment brought both chuckles and apologies from David and Almon.

When they were all up and dressed, Almon swung Sixtus onto his shoulders and announced that they would go for a walk to discover the lay of the land. David gathered and chopped wood. Annie went to fetch water. David started the cook fire in an area surrounded by three tree stumps and a thick log that they would use to sit on.

A short time later, Annie walked back carrying a heavy kettle of water in each arm. She saw the fire blazing warmly. David noticed that his sister-in-law's usually straight shoulders curved with the weight of the load. He hurried to her and took the water kettles from her. "You look tired, Annie. Sit while I make tea."

"David, your future wife will be the luckiest woman," Annie commented with gratitude as she sat down on the shortest stump and looked into the flames. She rested her elbows on her knees and cupped her chin between both hands.

"If I ever find such a wife," David retorted. Soon he had the tea boiler steaming over the blaze. He poured cups of tea for Annie and himself. After serving Annie, David took a seat near her, stretched out his legs and crossed his ankles. "Let's make up a rhyme to pass the time," he suggested with a grin.

Annie giggled, enlivened by the tea and her brother-in-law's good nature. Making up rhymes was something she never did when Joel was around. He was much too good at it for it to be fun for her.

"You start." David grinned at his sister-in-law.

"All right," Annie said. "Promise you won't tell it to Joel."

"Not on my deathbed." David chuckled.

"Here we sit," Annie began.

"By the fire pit," David added.

"Having a lazy day."

"'Tis preferred to cutting hay," David said, then he changed his mind. "I think I shall always stay."

"This poem is quite inane." Annie giggled.

"Brother Joel would call it a bane!"

Annie doubled over in mirth. David chuckled. Then he saw Almon approaching with Sixtus on his back. The little boy's legs dangled, and he was laughing. They were accompanied by a tall youth carrying an infant. Two women were with them. One was a stately woman with dark ringlets and a starched bonnet. A second infant was in her arms. The second woman was small and elderly with stooped shoulders and a firm, spry walk. David recognized the youth.

"Don Carlos," David cried out. Annie, caught in the middle of a giggle, looked up, turned her head, and immediately quieted.

On seeing the lovely woman in the prim bonnet, she strove to appear more dignified by smoothing down her unruly hair. In a single bound, David was next to Don Carlos. The two embraced. Almon winked at Annie as he unloaded Sixtus.

A moment later, Don Carlos introduced the group, "David, Sister Annie, this is my mother, Lucy Smith, and Emma, my brother Joseph's wife."

The Smith women greeted Annie with warm smiles and nods. Annie smiled back but trembled inwardly. Here were the mother and wife of the Prophet. Did they think her terribly silly? Mother Smith had bright eyes and webs of wrinkles. Emma in contrast stood tall, elegant, and straight-backed. Her large, brown, almond-shaped eyes were alive with intelligence. Her hair shone dark and comely.

"Please have a seat and let me get you both a cup of tea," Annie offered.

"Thank you, Sister Annie," Emma replied as she sat gracefully down with the child in her arms.

Mother Smith patted Annie's hand. "None for me, dear. While you and Emma visit I'm going to take the babies back to the house to nap and get them out of the wind. I came because I couldn't pass up the opportunity to meet the young man Don Carlos has mentioned with such fondness."

"Ah, but you already knew me," Almon joked.

Mother Smith chuckled. "Of course I remembered you fondly, Almon Babbitt. But I was thinking of the other young man, Brother David Johnson."

David grinned. "Mother Smith, meeting you and Sister Emma is my pleasure," he said, bowing his head charmingly.

While Annie made Emma a cup of tea, David held out his hands to take the baby girl so that Emma could sip her tea more comfortably. However, the child did not comply but buried her face in Emma's dress. The baby disengaged only when tempted by Mother Smith's open arms.

Almon laughed. "Here is the only female able to resist Brother David's charms."

A slight shadow fell over David's features, and Annie could tell that he did not find Almon's comment humorous.

Annie changed the subject. "Emma, your children are beautiful. What are their names?"

"Julia and Joseph," Emma responded.

"Those are fine names. My mother's and brother's names," David commented. As Annie handed Emma the cup of tea, David addressed his friend, "Carlos, I thought you would be at the priesthood meeting this morning."

"I'm occupied today," Don Carlos replied with a smile as Baby Joseph reached up and touched his face, "looking after Mother and Sister Emma."

Mother Smith glanced sideways at Don Carlos. Despite her humph, the light in her eyes made it clear that she adored this youngest son. "Don't believe him, David. Emma and I look after each other. The truth is that last evening Carlos complained about the age of the priesthood brethren compared to him. Joseph let him off the hook."

Don Carlos shook a long finger at his mother. "Joseph gave me a different assignment," he corrected. "He didn't let me off the hook."

"And what is this assignment?" David asked curiously.

Mother Smith sighed dramatically. "To rustle up a couple of young fellows and hunt some wild turkey for dinner."

"An inspired task!" Almon slapped his thighs. "I knew Joseph was a prophet!"

David laughed out loud. Mother Smith twinkled at the young men. "I must warn you. The turkeys are sly in these parts, and Don Carlos had no luck finding them earlier this morning."

Almon threw his hands in the air dramatically. "Fear not! Don Carlos was alone this morning. Now his brethren come to his aid! The trick is to sound like a hen." Almon demonstrated by cupping his hands to his mouth and clucking loudly.

"No, no," David interrupted. "You challenge them like another tom." With that, David let out a superb and deafening imitation of a turkey gobble. At the sound, Baby Joseph laughed, but Baby Julia stared accusingly at David. Then, her round little face crumpled and she let out a tremulous wail. David immediately stopped gobbling while Mother Smith soothed the infant. Sixtus ran about clucking.

"And I thought you just banged rocks together to startle the birds out of the brush." Don Carlos shrugged. Then he added, "Get your guns, boys. We'll escort Mother and the little ones to the house on our way."

After the others had left the campsite, Emma remained. Annie wondered why this lovely, articulate lady had sought her out. Was it because Joel was a new elder and the Prophet wanted to find out more about the family? Or could it be that Emma was in need of the companionship of another young mother?

"Your children are as beautiful as their names," Annie commented. She glanced over at Sixtus who was lining small rocks into a row.

"They are a great blessing to Joseph and me," Emma replied.

"I once had a little girl. Your Julia reminds me of her," Annie added softly.

"What happened to her?" Emma asked. Her dark brown eyes looked steadily into Annie's green.

"She passed away when but a small child," Annie stated simply. "Whooping cough." Then Annie looked down and studied her hands. She felt exposed, too quick to lay her heart open to this woman whom she didn't know. Annie did not want

Emma to think she pitied herself. Many women lost little ones. "But after this trial, the Lord has blessed me, Sister Emma," Annie added quickly as she looked up at Emma with a small smile. "I have a hearty son and a knowledge of the true gospel. My husband is a good man, and I am with child once more."

Emma sighed deeply as she spoke of her own memories. "I too have been blessed after the trial of my faith. Three summers ago, my first son died shortly after birth. I was desperately ill. Then Martin Harris lost the first one hundred sixteen pages of the Book of Mormon. Because Joseph was chosen to protect the record, the blame fell on his shoulders. The spirit of the Lord withdrew, and all was enshrouded with darkness. Months passed. Joseph repented, and I recovered. The Book of Mormon came forth with the glory of God within its pages. It brought undeniable truth and light. Even though I was an active participant in the scenes that transpired and was present during the translation of the plates, it is still marvelous to me. I strive to recall this miracle whenever my faith is tried. Then I feel confidence and hope."

In the wake of Emma's openness, Annie spoke from her heart. "When I first read the Book of Mormon, I was filled with faith and joy. But other times, I'm weak, Sister Emma. And afraid. I fear to lose another child. I fear losing Joel. I fear to trust in God's will. How I envy your strength and confidence."

Emma shook her head and looked at Annie with great kindness. "Sister Annie, you mustn't envy me. Earthly life has been a hard schoolmaster. I bore twins on April 30 of this year, but not the little Joseph and Julia you met today. Joseph and I named our twins Thaddeus and Louisa. They died the day of their birth. The next day, Sister Julia Murdock passed away while giving birth to her own twins. Their father, John Murdock, asked if we would adopt the babes. Our baby boy, Joseph, is named after my husband, and my little girl, Julia, after the mother who bore her."

Emma saw the tears gathering in Annie's eyes. Her almond eyes were soft and lovely, full of compassion. She reached out and laid her hand on Annie's. "Don't shed tears for me, Sister Annie. I am blessed as well. When I grow weary from the task of tending two infants, I think of the great blessings that little Joseph and Julia are. They fill my arms and heart with life and love. Would I have such patience had I not suffered such grief?"

Annie could not stop the rush of tears as she felt the touch of Emma's hand. She had heard other sisters whisper that the Prophet's wife was a brilliant conversationalist, very proper and a bit proud. But Annie found her wise and beautiful, patient and compassionate. Were such qualities the gifts of suffering endured and overcome? The thought that such pain might be an ingredient for such wisdom and goodness made Annie weep.

Emma was instantly next to Annie with an arm around her shoulders. "Dear Sister, I didn't know my words would move you so. I don't want to grieve you. Forgive me."

Annie pulled a used handkerchief out of her dress pocket and wiped her eyes in an effort to stop crying. However, when pregnant, her emotions overtook her and required time to calm. She turned to Emma with red eyes and a blotchy face. "Dear lady," she gulped, " I hate to think of how you have suffered when you are so very good."

At this, a soft, ironic laugh escaped Emma. "Oh, I am not so very good. Just last night I told Joseph that I dislike living in others' homes. First we lived with the Whitneys and now we are in Hiram with the John Johnson family. I long for my own hearth. But it is difficult for Joseph to tend to our needs when he must tend to the Church. Sometimes I am a great trial."

At these words, Annie shook her head. "No, Sister Emma, you are not a great trial, but a great blessing."

It was early afternoon when the meeting ended. By this time, Emma had joined her mother-in-law and twins in the Burnett house. Emma greeted Joel as he left the meeting. "You must be Elder Johnson. I'm Emma Smith. I greatly enjoyed meeting Annie and Sixtus."

"Thank you," Joel said with a small bow. "One of my life's greatest blessings was meeting your husband this morning."

A moment later, Joel blinked as he stepped outside into the daylight. The earlier clouds had given way to sunshine. Shadows of crimson-leafed trees spread across Joel's path as he walked across the property. Joel felt almost as if he were moving through a wondrous dream. When he arrived at the campsite, he found Annie teaching Sixtus his letters by writing in the dirt with a stick. The squatting child spied his father, jumped up, and darted toward him, his little legs churning under his soiled wool gown. Joel tossed his little boy into the air and embraced him. "Papa, Papa, I smart now," Sixtus squealed.

Joel and Annie walked together while Sixtus ran with them, jumping and throwing fall leaves into the air. With Annie's small hand in his large one, Joel told his wife the details of the meeting. "Simeon said the opening prayer. The opening hymn was about Zion. Elder Rigdon told us that when God works, He makes His children one. God binds their hearts from earth to heaven and teaches them about the Zion of which David spoke. Elder Rigdon counseled us to assemble in perfect faith and humble ourselves before the Lord, seeking for our will to be swallowed up in the will of God."

"It is a hard thing, isn't it, Joel?" Annie commented. "Allowing our will to be swallowed up in the will of God. Sister Emma and I spoke about the same thing today."

Annie would have told Joel more about her conversation with Emma had Joel not continued speaking with intense enthusiasm. "Joseph said that if we will but cleanse ourselves and covenant before God to serve Him, it is our privilege to have an assurance that God will protect us at all times. He also spoke of the work in which he is presently engaged—a translation of the fullness of the Bible. He counseled that the Saints must beware of covetousness lest the heavens be sealed. Each elder spoke and made a covenant to the Lord."

"And what did you covenant, Joel?" Annie asked.

"I said that although I had professed religion for a number of years, I now bear testimony of the goodness of God and consecrate all to the Lord."

"That is the weighty promise of a good man," Annie said as she put an arm around Joel and gave him a hug. "I wonder when I will see the Prophet," Annie mused. "His wife is extraordinary."

"I'll introduce you as soon as there's an opportunity. The brethren have another session in an hour and one tomorrow morning. Then there will be a meeting for the general congregation tomorrow afternoon. You'll likely hear the Prophet preach then."

Joel's stomach growled, and Annie laughed. "You're so excited, you'll forget to eat. Let's get back to the camp and I'll feed you, my own beanpole."

While Joel attended the second session of conference, Annie napped with Sixtus in the wagon. They awakened at dusk, and Annie rekindled the fire. Afterward, she sat on the stump with a blanket wrapped about her for warmth. Sixtus threw small sticks into the dancing flames. Clouds extended like stretched cotton beneath the blackening sky. Annie sat very still, not thinking or worrying as she listened to the prattle of her little boy. She simply felt the cool wind and breathed in the crisp air, conscious of how good it was to be alive. Then she heard laughter as Almon and David tramped back to camp carrying two turkeys.

As they plucked the turkeys in the firelight, Almon animatedly described their adventure. To Sixtus's delight, his Uncle David added sound effects. "We neared a thicket of young oak trees when David here let out a ferocious gobble."

David gobbled.

Almon continued, "A turkey returned the gobble. We quietly sneaked toward the sound. Out strutted Old Tom Turkey—three feet tall, his tail fanned, his long crop dragging from his head to the ground."

David threw his chest out and strutted a few steps.

"At the sight of us, he jumped from the ground and flew toward the nearest tree. Crack went Don Carlos's gun. There were some jakes, hens, and chicks with Old Tom. Boom! Boom! David and I shot. Carlos got the tom and David and I two jakes."

David gave a weak gobble and collapsed on the ground.

Sixtus laughed in glee. Catching the spirit of the hunt, the little boy strutted around the fire, periodically pointing a stick at David and Almon while shouting "boom." The young men obliged by clutching their chests and collapsing each time the little boy pretended to shoot them. Annie sighed and helped with the plucking. At the rate Almon and David were going, it would likely never be done.

Later, Joel returned from the second conference session. As they waited for the turkey to finish roasting they talked about the day's events. Annie, David, and Almon listened attentively as Joel described the meeting. Orson Hyde had sung the opening prayer. Thirteen elders had been ordained high priests. Joel tried to name them all from memory and came up with eleven out of the thirteen. Then he described two of the new high priests whom he felt an immediate affinity toward. Their names were Joseph

Brackenbury and Edmund Durfee. They were both middle-aged men who were spiritually seasoned and humble. They had conversed with Joel after the meeting. Brother Brackenbury had a deep spiritual nature and a brilliant understanding of the scriptures.

After supper, Sixtus fell asleep on Annie's lap. Annie suggested they sing a hymn and say a prayer before she carried Sixtus to bed and retired herself. Following the prayer, Joel walked with his wife and son to the wagon. He bid them good night and tucked heavy blankets around them to ward off the cold.

"Are you warm enough?" Joel asked.

"All but my nose," Annie responded.

In the darkness, Joel felt for Annie's upturned nose with his forefinger. He found it. It *was* cold. He rubbed it until it was warm. Annie laughed. She felt sleepy and happy.

Joel kissed her. "I'll come to bed shortly," he said quietly. Before returning to the campfire to talk with David and Almon, Joel found a clean shirt. He folded it neatly and placed it in the corner of the wagon to don first thing in the morning.

Annie was nearly asleep when she was awakened by cheerful voices outside the wagon. "Good evening, Brother Joel. You know my friends Edmund Durfee and Joseph Brackenbury. Hello, Brother Almon. And you, sir, must be David Johnson. Don Carlos has spoken a great deal of you."

"Brother Joseph, we are at your service," Joel said.

At these words, Annie was fully awake. She scrambled to the edge of the wagon and peeked beneath the canvas covering. The Prophet's form was illuminated by lantern light as he shook hands with David. Annie saw that he was large-boned and strong with a noble look and bearing. She thought of what a striking couple he and Emma must make. Three other men were with him. Annie recognized one as Don Carlos.

Joseph continued, "Elders Durfee and Brackenbury have discovered that our host, Brother Burnett, has a quantity of corn that has not yet been husked. We three gentlemen invite Brother Joel to join us as we challenge these three young fellows to a husking match."

"The experience of age versus the strength of youth," Elder Brackenbury said with a chuckle as he put a hand on Joel's shoulder. Joseph Brackenbury was a man of average height with intelligent, bright eyes. He had a distinguished look, and his receding dark hair was edged with gray. In the meeting, Brother Brackenbury had spoken eloquently as he consecrated all to the Lord, saying that he felt blessed that he could bear testimony of the Book of Mormon, which he was determined to do until the end of his life. Edmund Durfee stood about the same height and sported a full head of gray hair and a short gray beard, which he wore proudly, even though facial hair was not in fashion. He was the quieter of the two.

"What say you, my friends?" Don Carlos grinned at David and Almon.

"I think we can humble these fellows," Almon said. "Though there are four of them and only three of us."

David, who had never met the Prophet, nodded with a smile. He hadn't imagined that this man of God was such a jolly fellow.

Joseph looked at David and spoke as if he were reading the young man's thoughts. "Dear Brother David, I have a boyish nature and cheery temperament. Some Saints have been offended by this, feeling that it is not worthy of a prophet of God. And yet, a friendly stick pull and corn husking does me good." The Prophet Joseph glanced at his brother with a smile and added,

"Don Carlos has not yet been able to beat me in a wrestling match, though he thinks his friend David Johnson could do so."

David's face broke into a grin. "Brother Joseph, I am not up to wrestling a prophet."

Joseph laughed and clapped David on the back. "Perhaps someday, when we know each other better."

Once in the barn, the men divided the ears of corn into two equal piles. At the sound of Elder Durfee's whistle the men on both teams began ferociously husking the corn. The older men would have won had not Almon periodically kicked ears over into their pile when he thought no one was looking. When Elder Brackenbury noticed Almon cheating, he informed Joseph with a chuckle. At that, the Prophet merrily chastised young Brother Babbitt.

When the corn was husked, the men went back to camp and drank their fill of cider. Their breath steamed in the cold night, but their bodies were warm from the work. The windswept sky was filled with a thousand stars.

"When old Brother Burnett goes into his barn tomorrow," Almon commented with a laugh, "he will think it another latter-day miracle. Angels came and husked his corn."

The men chuckled. When they were quiet, the Prophet Joseph looked up at the heavens and then back at his companions. "Brethren," he said softly, his eyes dark and thoughtful in the moonlight. "It has been my experience that angels only come and perform the work of God when mortal men cannot. I pray each day for the strength to finish the work God has given me."

David's heart filled as he realized the import of Joseph's words. Here was the man who communed with Jehovah, who spoke with angels. Joel seemed to be experiencing a similar thought, for he suddenly spoke, his voice strong with emotion as he repeated a verse that had been forming in his mind throughout the day:

*Thou servant of the living God,*
*Like thee I've sought among the sects,*
*To find a few that have not trod*
*The path His holy law rejects.*

*With thee, His Seer, I've found at last,*
*The keeper of my Father's house.*
*My lot, and all, with thee I cast,*
*To solemnize my youthful vows.*

*For thou art chosen of the Lord,*
*To gather up the pure and wise;*
*With Priesthood power as thy reward,*
*His Church again to organize.*

*Alone no longer can I roam;*
*My heart is with the pure and brave;*
*With thee and thine I'll find my home,*
*Myself and all my kin to save.*

*Thy holy cause I will defend,*
*While all thy sorrows, joys, and care,*
*Shall be my own, till life shall end,*
*With Thee eternal life to share.*

David looked at the Prophet and saw the emotion in his eyes as Joel finished speaking.

Elder Brackenbury spoke. "Brother Joel has voiced my feelings."

"And mine," Elder Durfee added.

"And mine," David whispered.

The Prophet Joseph gripped the hand of each friend. "God bless you, dear brothers."

The next morning during the general priesthood session, Joel listened intently as Sidney Rigdon spoke about the privileges of the Saints in the last days. He told those who were ordained high priests the previous evening that the Lord was not well pleased with some of them because of their indifference to being ordained to that office. He exhorted them to faith and obedience in order to set forth the power of that priesthood. Orson Hyde, Joseph Brackenbury, and three other brethren immediately said that they received the rebuke in meekness. Joel wondered how he would have reacted personally, knowing that he tended to be highly sensitive to criticism. Would he have been humble like these five brethren? As the meeting progressed, the brethren also discussed ways to financially support President Joseph Smith and others engaged in the translation of the Holy Bible.

After the meeting adjourned, Joel found Elder Brackenbury outside on a log, reading the Book of Mormon. Joel approached. He had been moved by Brother Brackenbury's humility and wanted to tell him so. Joseph Brackenbury looked up and smiled at Joel. Wrinkles flared out from the corners of his eyes. "It's a wonderful conference," he commented.

Joel nodded. "You accepted Elder Rigdon's rebuke in the spirit of meekness. That would have been difficult for me," Joel admitted quietly.

"Have a seat." Joseph Brackenbury patted the portion of the log next to him. "I have found that I learn a great deal from rebukes and that I usually deserve them more than 'tis easy to admit. Let me read something to you." Joel noticed the trace of English accent in his new friend's voice. It was strange that he hadn't noticed it before. Perhaps it was only apparent when the man was at ease.

"In the Book of Mormon, Alma teaches the people of Ammonihah about the high priesthood. I've read this before, but it has such new meaning now that I am a high priest. I might not have studied and understood this passage had not Elder Rigdon rebuked me. It has deepened my love for the Lord and my understanding of my calling and purpose. Listen: And this is the manner after which they were ordained—being called and prepared from the foundation of the world according to the foreknowledge of God, on account of their exceeding faith and good works; . . . And thus, being called by this holy calling, and ordained unto the high priesthood of the holy order of God, to teach his commandments unto the children of men, that they also might enter into his rest. . . . Yea, humble yourselves even as the people in the days of Melchizedek, who was also a high priest after this same order which I have spoken, who also took upon him the high priesthood forever. . . . Now these ordinances were given after this manner, that thereby the people might look forward on the Son of God, it being a type of his order, . . . and this that they might look forward to him for a remission of their sins, that they might enter into the rest of the Lord."

Joseph Brackenbury closed his Book of Mormon. "This is why I was born, Brother Joel, to teach of the Son of God, to help bring peace and repentance into the world that God's children might find rest."

During the final, general session of the conference, Annie had difficulty hiding her disappointment when the speakers were announced following the opening hymn. Sidney Rigdon, Oliver Cowdery, Hyrum Smith, and Orson Hyde would address the congregation. She had greatly hoped to hear the Prophet himself. But as the meeting commenced, she was not disappointed. Sidney Rigdon gave a powerful discourse on the Zion of Enoch and on the establishment of Zion in the last days. Oliver Cowdery spoke about the restoration of the priesthood and bore his testimony of the Book of Mormon. Hyrum Smith bore witness of his brother's calling. Hyrum's gentle, compassionate nature touched Annie deeply. This was a man in whom there was no guile or false pride. The Prophet himself gave the closing prayer. As Joseph offered this prayer, Annie sensed the intimacy between this man and God. When Joseph pled for the well-being of each Saint and for the growth of Zion, Annie felt that if she opened her eyes, she would behold Jehovah standing near His faithful servant, with outstretched hands, listening to every word.

The next morning, Joseph, Emma, and Don Carlos came to the Johnson campsite when the wagon was loaded and the family about to leave. The Prophet shook each individual's hand, even that of little Sixtus. This was the first time Annie had personally met the Prophet. It was a moment she would never forget.

"God be with you, Brother Joel, until we meet again," the Prophet said. Then he turned to Annie. "Sister Annie, I feel that Brothers Joel and David should go to Pomfret, New York, as soon as circumstances permit and bear testimony to their family. I promise that the Lord will bless you while they are gone. You will bear this child in health, and your husband will return to you."

Tears gathered in Annie's eyes as the Prophet gripped her hand. She felt as if his faith coursed into her. "Thank you," she whispered.

The Prophet turned to shake hands with David and Almon. His blue eyes twinkled. "Brother David, next time we meet, we must wrestle. Brother Almon, I counsel you to be honest in matters other than corn husking."

Don Carlos embraced Almon and David. "We will see each other soon," he said. "Until then, stay well, my friends, and strong in the faith."

Emma hugged Annie. "You will be in my prayers," Emma said softly.

"And you in mine," Annie returned.

*Hail! Book of Mormon! for thy rays*
*Dispel the shades of night,*
*Diffusing in these latter days,*
*Most glorious beams of light.*

*We hail it, Lord, for this great cause:*
*It guides our wandering feet,*
*Renews our knowledge of Thy laws,*
*And makes our faith complete.*

—JOEL H. JOHNSON, FROM "THE BOOK OF MORMON"

*October 1831*

The Johnson family began studying the Book of Mormon on a crisp October evening while Ezekiel was away in Fredonia. After the younger children were in bed, Julia, Seth, and Nancy sat together around the hearth. A few moments later, Lyman Sherman arrived and joined them, explaining that Delcena had stayed home with their six-week-old infant, Mary, who was coughing. After their little son, Lyman Ezekiel, had passed away the previous spring, Delcena wouldn't risk taking little Mary out in the cold. As they began reading the book aloud, Julia was skeptical and a bit fearful. She sought to discover the power it held over Joel and David to thus know how to counteract it.

Susan and Benjamin begged to join them, but Julia would not allow it. She did not want her spiritually vulnerable children to be caught in the web of Mormonism. As the evening progressed, the group was surprised at the purity and simplicity of the text. They decided to continue reading every possible evening until they finished the book.

Three days later, as Seth read aloud page twenty-five in the third chapter of the first book of Nephi, a great change occurred within Julia. As she listened to Seth's voice and gazed at the log smoldering in the hearth, warmth and peace encompassed her. Although she didn't know if this young Nephi were real or just a creation of Joseph Smith's dangerous and overactive imagination, his words touched a chord of Julia's heart so deeply that she could not deny the sweetness of the melody.

In the account, Nephi pondered a vision of his prophet-father, Lehi. The vision included an iron rod leading to a tree of delicious fruit. As Nephi prayed, his eyes were opened and he beheld a fair and lovely virgin bearing a child in her arms. This child was the Lamb of God. Julia listened as Seth read that love was the fruit of the Lord's condescension to earth, the fruit of the tree of life, the most joyous thing to the soul. Tears filled Julia's eyes. She knew this love of God. She felt it when she read the Bible, when her countless prayers were answered, when she beheld tenderness in her children's eyes, when she recalled her mother's touch. She felt this love again in the pages of the Book of Mormon.

Seth continued to read. "And I looked, and I beheld the Son of God going forth among the children of men; and I saw many fall down at his feet and worship him. And it came to pass that I beheld that the rod of iron which my father had seen, was the word of God, which led to the fountain of living waters, or to the tree of life."

The word of God was an iron rod. Julia knew this. She had gripped it tightly when her mother passed away, when Nancy was injured, and when her body and soul ached from disappointment and exhaustion. She would hold to the word of God when all else failed. It was her guide and sustenance.

Seth continued reading of how Nephi beheld the baptism of the Redeemer of the world. Nephi saw the Lamb of God going forth and healing the children of men. Julia no longer heard the wind outside or the crackling of the fire, nor even the noise of the children upstairs. She only heard Seth's voice as he read on. "And I looked and beheld the Lamb of God, that he was taken by the people; yea, the Everlasting God, was judged of the world; and I saw and bear record. And I, Nephi, saw that he was lifted up upon the cross, and slain for the sins of the world."

Seth stopped reading. He looked up from the text and looked into the eyes of Julia, Nancy, and Lyman. Nancy's gray eyes were soft with wonder. Julia's cheeks were wet with tears. Lyman's features shone with great joy.

"I feel these are the words of God," Lyman uttered. "I feel it in my heart."

"But Lyman, even the very elect can be deceived by false prophets," Seth said shakily.

"These words move you, Seth," Nancy said. "I heard it in your voice."

Seth nodded and studied his hands. "That is what troubles me."

"Mother," Nancy interrupted and nodded toward the stairs. "Look."

Ben stood at the top of the stairs, his slender, five-feet-eleven frame leaning on the rail, his brown eyes moist and serious. Susan sat on the first step, clasping her ankles, resting her chin on her knees. Both had stayed home from the apple-paring bee, which the more social Almera and Joseph had attended, to eavesdrop and to hear the words of the Book of Mormon for themselves.

Julia broke the rule she had set. She dabbed her eyes and smiled at Ben and Sue. "Come down here, my errant ones. We are finished for tonight, but whatever we learn from this book, you shall know as well."

"Thank you, Mother," Benjamin said with emotion. "I want to hear more."

"Me too," Susan added.

"Ben and Susie," Seth spoke, his voice calm and instructive as he counseled his younger siblings. "You must remember that even Satan can appear as an angel of light. We must be cautious and yet open minded, not overcome with emotion. And most of all, we must continue to pray for the Lord's guidance as we study. He will not lead us astray."

Seth's cautious words did not dampen Lyman's enthusiasm. "Seth, a bright hope arises in my heart. To think that there might be a prophet on the earth again! To think that there may be answers to the many questions we have raised as we have discussed the scriptures!"

Seth turned to his brother-in-law and best friend. "But Lyman, it is truly frightening to think that such moving words could be of the devil, that Satan could be so deceptive. Could the man who penned this wondrous vision be deceived? It may be that these words came from Joseph Smith's mind and heart and he is deluded into thinking they are true revelation. But even if that is the case, their pure teachings about the Lord make it clear that Smith's soul harbors in its depths a love for God. It terrifies me to think that Satan might have the power to fool a man with such gifts."

"Dear Seth, I do not think that possible," Nancy said quietly. "If we lack wisdom, God has promised to answer our prayers. I think we must finish the book with open, honest hearts and faith in God."

Seth nodded at his sister, though his mind was still troubled. He carefully placed the orange and red maple leaf, which Nancy had pressed to be used as a bookmark, on the page and closed the book.

During the weeks that followed, Julia often pondered Seth's words. She was inclined to believe the book true, yet she was wise enough to know that she was fallible, that the possibility existed that she could be wrong. As the group continued, Julia felt humble joy as she read of the mothers and fathers of the young stripling warriors. These parents had covenanted to forever lay down their swords. She experienced sorrow as she studied how the Nephite people became proud and lost their faith. She rejoiced in the coming of the Lord, Jesus Christ, to ancient America.

In the depths of her soul, she did not feel that the young Joseph Smith was deceived. She could not imagine Satan as the

author of such sweet and joyous truths. Therein lay her new and
wondrous hope: Perhaps God had brought forth a new record of
scripture through a living prophet. But what if she were wrong? If
so, wherein did faith lie?

Seven weeks passed. December came to western New York
with overcast skies, brisk winds, and snow flurries. The family had
nearly finished reading the Book of Mormon. Esquire Timothy
Johnson, Annie's father, had joined the study sessions. Esquire
Johnson habitually brought his costly astral lamp that enabled the
group to pass the book to different readers without repositioning a
candlestick. With its ring-shaped reservoir, the astral lamp cast a
warm, bright light with no shadow below the flame. During one
meeting, Lyman earnestly commented that this oil lamp was
fitting illumination for their study. No other work dispelled spiritual darkness like the Book of Mormon.

On the first Thursday of that month, an hour before the
family gathered, Julia inspected a cake that she had just pulled
from the oven. Lightly browned on each side, its warmth radiated
into her hands, warming her cold-stiffened fingers. After setting
the cake on the table, Julia closed the cast-iron oven door. Ezekiel
had designed and built this oven for her. It had two chambers and
an ingenious pipe system to facilitate heating evenly.

To Julia, it seemed strange that such a common thing as an
oven could turn her thoughts toward her husband. Once again he
was in Fredonia. She thought back on Ezekiel's return from
Cincinnati the prior spring. The anger and hurt on both their
parts had burned out, leaving something like a crystal behind.
This crystallized marriage was both brittle and hard—but with a
shape and value that had formed over time. She and Zeke became

quiet around each other, respectful but not intimate. They carefully hid their resentments. She knew that Ezekiel still frequented the tavern. But at night, rather than coming home drunk, he stayed in a room until he sobered. She never mentioned the meetings she hosted when he was away. How would he feel when he found out that his own wife believed the Book of Mormon to be the word of God?

Julia fingered the gold chain around her neck. Could love slip away like the change of seasons? She did not know how to find the man who once moved her with each look and touch. His soul was hidden somewhere beneath the crusty surface of an aging farmer stooped under the weight of continuous work, haunted by the power of sorrow, seeking illusory weightlessness when summoned by the demon of drink.

Alone in the kitchen, Julia sighed. Upstairs, she heard Julianne singing to the little ones as she put them to bed. Julia moved to the window and peered outside. Gray snow spotted the ground. The night would be cold and dark with an overcast sky obstructing the starlight. She saw Esquire Johnson's coach approaching. As expected, he had picked up the Shermans on his way.

A short time later, a group of people brightened Julia's sitting room: Lyman held little Alvira on his lap, and Delcena nestled the baby in her arms. Nancy lay on the parlor cot, her gray eyes alert and ready to learn. Julianne sat on the floor beside Nancy, with her skirt tucked about her legs. Ben and Joe sat next to each other on a bench. Both boys' hands were red and clean from scrubbing in the limestone sink. Ben's hands lay folded in his lap, while Joe gestured as he teased Almera about the reverend's son. Almera threatened to push Joe off the bench. Susan sat silently knitting, the needles' clicking softly harmonizing with the background music of the crackling fire. Twelve-year-old Mary perched on a stool near the fire, drawing pictures on a slate when she became bored, yet determined to remain awake for the cake at the end.

Seth handed the Book of Mormon to Joe and asked him to be the first to read aloud. Joe read with great expression—his intonation the same as when quoting Shakespeare. When it was Seth's turn to read, each phrase was absorbed and measured, his voice lined with thought. Esquire Johnson sat next to Seth, wearing spectacles, clad in his vest and cravat, studying his fingernails, sometimes asking questions, rarely disclosing his own thoughts.

Julia prayed as she heard the words of this amazing book. She prayed in her heart as she pondered the dear faces around her, their features illuminated by the central light of the astral lamp, softening or furrowing as thoughts played across their eyes. They listened to the words of the last prophet to record his testimony in the Book of Mormon.

"Behold, I would exhort you that when ye shall read these things, if it be wisdom in God that ye should read them, that ye would remember how merciful the Lord hath been unto the children of men, from the creation of Adam, even down until the time that ye shall receive these things, and ponder it in your hearts. And when ye shall receive these things, I would exhort you that ye would ask God, the Eternal Father, in the name of Christ, if these things are not true; and if ye shall ask with a sincere heart, with real intent, having faith in Christ, and he will manifest the truth of it unto you, by the power of the Holy Ghost; and by the power of the Holy Ghost, ye may know the truth of all things."

Seth paused.

"Amen," Lyman said, agreeing with each word in the passage.

Seth handed the book to Lyman and looked down at his hands. As Lyman continued reading, Seth struggled to make some sense of his thoughts and emotions.

Since the coming of the Book of Mormon, Seth had prayed to understand the mind and will of God concerning it. Regardless of how moving the words of the book, he could not escape his suspicions at its claims. He knew that Lyman Sherman, his closest friend and brother-in-law, read the book with great faith. His mother embraced it. But to Seth, it was like a puzzle he could not solve. There was a missing piece. He could not determine whether or not Mormonism was of God. He did not know which way to go, nor which direction to lead his younger brothers and sisters.

As Lyman read, Julia glanced at Seth. His forehead was furrowed. A surge of gratitude for this son engulfed Julia. Seth was her strength and support. She relied on his wisdom and work ethic. His younger siblings leaned on him almost as if he were their father, constantly coming to him for advice and counsel. He was their firm and fair disciplinarian. Julia longed to lay a hand on his brow and smooth the furrow. Since a little boy, he had had that look when knowledge eluded him. She prayed silently that he too would come to know the truth within the pages of the Book of Mormon.

Two weeks before Christmas, in the early afternoon, a knock sounded on the Johnson front door. Esther, who was nearly five, ran to open it. Three men with bristly, unshaven faces stood before her. Each had snow on his hat and carried a knapsack. Two were tall and one of average height. The tallest was very thin and had dark shadows under his eyes. He looked weary from the journey. In contrast, the shortest had sharp green eyes and a thin-lipped smile. He tapped his foot nervously. However, it was the third who interested Esther. He was tall and straight and very familiar. He grinned at Esther and called her name as he elbowed past the other two. Bending down on one knee, he stretched out his arms. Esther backed up a step, smiled with a tease in her eyes, and haughtily asked, "Who are you?"

"Your own brother. Guess which one?" the man answered, the gold in his brown eyes twinkling.

"David, David, David," she squealed as she leapt into his arms. David picked her up and swung her around. Esther buried her head in his shoulder and locked her arms around his neck. From this position, she heard many things: the squeals of little Amos, Almera's cry of delight, the sound of Nancy approaching on crutches, and the rapturous exclamation of her mother as she joined the embrace, "Joel! David! My sons! My sons!"

After Joel warmly hugged his mother, he turned to the third man. "Mother, sisters, this is Almon Babbitt."

Julia shook Almon's hand. "Any friend of my sons is a welcome guest."

David grinned at his sisters. "Almon did not come solely out of friendship. He heard rumors I have beautiful sisters," David's eyes met Nancy's, "whom I am so happy to see again."

Almon's wind-burned face colored a deeper shade of red. David had certainly gotten even for the many times Almon had teased him about women.

Yet Almon was up to the challenge. He smiled at the Johnson ladies. "And they are even more lovely than their descriptions. You must be Nancy," he said as he held out his hand.

"My brothers did not mention such a kind friend in their letters," Nancy said as she leaned on one crutch and allowed Almon to take her hand. Like a prince, Almon kissed her fingers.

Almera lightly nudged Susan and rolled her eyes. Then she tugged on little Esther's leg and asked, "When are you going to get down and allow Susie and me to hug David?"

Esther possessively kissed David's scratchy cheek. "Not never," she stated as she locked her arms more tightly around David's neck and buried her face in his shoulder. David, instead of prying her loose, laughed out loud and returned the hug.

A few moments later, Almon trailed behind the family as Julia ushered them into the sitting room and insisted they eat and rest. Surprisingly, Almon's eyes did not fasten on Almera like other men's, but instead drank in the feel of the room—the clean-swept floor, the Dutch clock on the wall, the crackling fire, the painted pictures on the mantelpiece, the curtains at the frosty windows.

"Joel, old man, you look bushwhacked," David said merrily as he sank down into a chair with Esther fastened to him. He felt a great burst of energy in the joy of being home.

Joel smiled, stretched his legs toward the fire, and closed his eyes.

"Where are the others?" David asked as Susan and Almera handed out bowls of applesauce.

Nancy answered. "Father is in Fredonia. Joe, Ben, Mary, and the little boys are in school. Seth, of course, is teaching. Julianne is staying with Delcena because Lyman is in Jamestown with Philastus Hurlbut. Lyman is due back tonight."

Joel opened his eyes and commented, "Lyman wrote that Doctor Hurlbut is now a Methodist preacher in Jamestown. I would like to give Philastus a copy of the Book of Mormon. In some areas, entire congregations have joined the Church of Christ."

Nancy continued, "Joel, things have changed since you last heard from Lyman. Sad news reached us a week ago. There has been an uprising in Jamestown, and Doctor Hurlbut has been excommunicated from his church."

"What are the charges against him?" Joel questioned.

Almera let out a sharp breath of air and was about to speak when Julia interrupted. "We must refrain from speculation. Lyman has gone to Jamestown to find the truth and, if possible, to protect his cousin's good name."

David raised an eyebrow. "That is assuming Doctor Hurlbut was worthy of a good name to begin with."

Julia looked at David closely. He looked well, but older. How she had missed this son! She spoke with a bit of a tease in her voice. "We must not put our trust in evil reports. There are also ugly rumors circulating about my own sons who have embraced Mormonism." Julia looked from David to Joel. "Yet I have found the teachings of the Book of Mormon to be the pure and simple words of Christ."

Joel's color heightened. He stood and moved quickly to his mother and took her hands in his. The exertion caused him to cough. His face became very red, and Susan brought Joel a drink of water. After a gulp, Joel spoke. "Mother, my prayers are answered. How does Father feel? And Seth?"

Julia looked up into Joel's eyes. "I fear to discuss it with your father. As for Seth, the Book of Mormon moves him deeply, but he is still troubled on some points of doctrine. Lyman is greatly excited about this work and will be overjoyed to see you. I desire to know more about Joseph Smith before I commit myself to baptism. But I believe the Book of Mormon to be of God."

"And you, Nancy, what do you think?" David interrupted. He felt great joy in finding Nancy in better health, and he could not stop thinking of the chance that she might be healed by the power of the priesthood.

"David, you have found God, and my prayers have been answered."

"But do you believe it, Nancy?"

Nancy nodded, her eyes shining. "With every portion of my heart."

"Hallelujah," David exclaimed with such force that little Esther startled on his lap.

"Almera and Susan?" Joel asked as he sat back down in his chair.

Almera sighed, her color high and her lovely eyes deeply serious. Joel saw that she was a beautiful woman now, not the pretty baby sister who had cuddled on his lap as Esther now cuddled on David's. Almera spoke. "When I read of Christ's coming to the Nephites, it was like experiencing my deepest hope. Yet Reverend Handy's son and I have been courting. When I told Elijah of the Book of Mormon, he spoke of the power of deception and forbade me to continue with it. I don't know what to do."

Joel looked at Almera earnestly. "Mera, David wanted to marry a woman named Kathryn Clay. But she could not accept his testimony. He had to make a choice."

Almera nodded, but the joy had fled from her eyes. Elijah was handsome and unerringly honest. He had a frame house of his own and planned to follow his father as the minister of the Fredonia Baptist Church. Out of many suitors, Almera had grown to care for him.

Joel continued, "At first, I believed the evil reports I had heard of Mormonism. But Annie thought it might be true, and I would not abridge her right to study the sect. That freedom is a privilege our fathers died for. Elijah should not forbid you. He is not worthy of you if he does so."

Almera shook her head. "I know, Joel. I know. But a Baptist minister cannot be married to a Mormon."

"But a minister's son can study Mormonism," Joel countered. "I should like to talk with Reverend Handy. I was a member of his congregation for many years."

Almera shook her head. "Neither Elijah nor Reverend Handy will open their minds to it."

David looked at his sister and spoke without the trace of teasing in his voice. "Mera, there are other fish in the sea. Though I haven't had the heart yet to cast out my line, perhaps we can help each other do so."

"Why should David and Almera use fishing line," Susan questioned dryly, "when the creatures jump out of the water and land at their feet?"

David chuckled and turned to Susan. "And what of you, Sly Susie? What do you think of the Book of Mormon?"

"I would be baptized today if I dared ask Father," Susan answered.

"Susan is like Mary of Bethany," Julia added, "longing to hear each word of the Book of Mormon. Benjamin is the same."

"And Joe and Delcie?" David asked.

"Joseph reads it much as you read the Bible as a boy," Julia smiled at David, "as if it is a great adventure. But he does not feel the doctrine like Susan and Benjamin. Delcena believes it to be the word of God, as does her husband."

As the family's discussion continued, Almon experienced a strange phenomenon—his tongue was tied. To Almon, it felt as if he observed a faraway scene, a moment frozen in time. A haunting loneliness crept through him. He watched little Amos crawl up on Julia's lap. There was grace in how the child rested in her arms, in how he wound his small hands in his mother's long, gray-black hair, in the way the rocking chair moved gently back and forth like a rhythmic song. And although Mother Julia discussed the scriptures as if she hardly noticed the babe, Almon knew that she was simultaneously nurturing her small son and that the child felt it. This fascinated Almon, for he had no memory of a single moment like this. He only remembered shouts and disorder, a frenzy to eat before someone else ate his share. He wondered what his younger siblings with their runny noses and raucous squeals would be like had they a mother like this.

"Mr. Babbitt, would you like more applesauce?" Susan asked as she gathered the dishes.

"No, thank you, Miss Johnson. Call me Almon," the young man returned as he handed her his bowl.

Susan nodded politely. "And me, Susan," she said as her face grew hot. But Almon paid no mind to her shy embarrassment. He was thinking that, if raised here, his brothers might have gained the integrity of men like Joel and David. His sisters might have had the polite gentleness of the girl before him, or the sweet openness of the chair-bound, gray-eyed Nancy, or the intriguing beauty of the modest Almera.

Almon sighed, realizing that he was cast from a different mold—the Johnsons would not be tempted to stretch the truth in their own self-interest or to cheat at a game in order to win. The better part of Almon longed for a home like this. He determined to win this family's esteem and be part of it forever. He wanted his future children to have a mother like Julia Johnson.

As the day lengthened, Almon enjoyed being treated like an honored guest when introduced to Seth and the younger members of the Johnson clan. To show his appreciation, he helped young Ben and Joe with chores, but all the while his mind tarried elsewhere. At suppertime, he began a disciplined study of Almera and Susan, for he intended to court and marry one of them. He keenly observed how they moved, spoke, and interacted with each family member.

That evening, Julia suggested the family retire early so the guests might rest from their journey. They gathered in the sitting room, where Nancy read a chapter from the gospel of John. After singing a hymn, all knelt, except for Nancy, who remained in her chair with her head bowed. Seth prayed, thanking the Lord for the safe arrival of David, Joel, and Almon. He asked the Lord to protect their father in Fredonia and Annie and Sixtus in Ohio. He asked God to bless and keep safe Almon's family. Then, Seth prayed for guidance and discernment in their study of Mormonism.

After the prayer, Julia directed George and William to sleep in her room. In addition, she requested that Joe and Ben retire on the kitchen floor. This would leave the upstairs boys' room for Seth, Joel, David, and Almon.

After good night wishes, the men filed upstairs. Though weary from their journey, Joel did not forget his reason for coming. He bore his testimony once more and then asked Seth what troubled him about the Book of Mormon.

"I have found the simplicity of Christ's gospel within its pages," Seth answered carefully as he pulled off his boots. Then he looked up at Joel. "I understand why you are converted. Yet, I cannot fully banish from my mind the warning in Second Corinthians. 'For such are false apostles, deceitful workers, transforming themselves into the apostles of Christ. And no marvel; for Satan himself is transformed into an angel of light. Therefore it is no great thing if his ministers also be transformed as the ministers of righteousness; whose end shall be according to their works.'"

David stretched out on his bed. He grinned and spoke before Joel had a chance. "You know the Bible, Seth. But I know Joseph Smith. He is as far from a deceitful worker as a worm is from an elephant. We've husked corn with the Prophet. Almon here was the only deceitful worker at that affair."

Almon cuffed David in the shoulder. "A wise man leaves husking out of his conversation when describing a prophet to an unbeliever," he chided.

"I'm far from wise, and I reckon Seth is far from an unbeliever," David retorted.

"You are right on one of those counts, my brother." Seth grinned. "The riddle is which one."

David laughed, and Seth chuckled. David's presence lifted a load from Seth's shoulders.

Joel cleared his throat and spoke earnestly. "Seth, consider in Matthew. 'Beware of false prophets, which come to you in sheep's clothing, but inwardly they are ravening wolves. Ye shall know them by their fruits. A good tree cannot bring forth evil fruit, neither can a corrupt tree bring forth good fruit.' Joseph Smith has brought forth good fruit. He has passed that scriptural test."

Seth's brow furrowed. "This church is so young. It is the time of planting, not harvest. It is too early to talk of fruit."

"The Book of Mormon is a fruit," Joel stated.

Seth looked at Joel intently. "You may be right, Joel. But the Book of Mormon may be just a blossom. Blossoms can be deceptive. They don't always endure to a harvest."

"The Church of Christ will endure," Joel said simply.

Seth nodded. "Joel, I pray to find peace, to know if this is Christ's Church. If so, it would bring me unspeakable joy."

"Do you pray with faith, with confidence, believing you will receive an answer?" Joel asked.

Seth sighed deeply. "I have faith in Christ. But do I have confidence enough to find the answer?" He shrugged. "What if I embraced this gospel and turned my life and the lives of our young brothers and sisters toward it. What if then I found my faith was built on illusion? How could a man bear that?"

"The book you hold in your hand is not an illusion," Joel said simply.

That night as the Johnson brothers slept, Almon tossed and turned on the straw-tick mattress. He could not make up his mind on which of the sisters to pursue. Almera was clearly the loveliest, but there was something intense about her—Almon preferred a lighter maple syrup. He found Susan intriguing—her spare comments denoted that there was a great deal beneath her shyness. But Almon was given to impatience and did not like to dig deeply. Still, he reasoned, no woman was perfect. He had found Susan looking his way on numerous occasions during supper. He remembered how her cheeks had turned crimson when he smiled back at her. Perhaps she was the one.

On the other hand, he reasoned, Almera was caught in the clutches of the Baptist minister's son. It could be God's purpose for Almon to rescue her. Perplexed, Almon pictured little twelve-year-old Mary with her blonde hair and brown eyes. The child was a healthy combination of spunk and sweetness. If only she were seven or eight years older. Perhaps he should wait for her to grow up. Almon groaned. Seven years was far too long of a wait. He hadn't the fortitude of the Old Testament prophet Jacob who worked long years for Rachel. Almon turned over on his back and stared at the dark ceiling. He couldn't remember ever having so difficult a decision to make in his life.

The next morning, on the Sherman farm, Joel and David walked with Lyman. The day was bright and the air cold enough to see their breath. The crisp, dry snow squeaked under their boots, and remnants of the last storm clung to the skeletal branches of the trees. Smoke wound upward from the chimney of the cottage. The women and young children visited inside around the warmth of the hearth.

As the three men walked, Lyman voiced his thoughts. "I should like to have read the first one hundred and sixteen pages of the Book of Lehi, which the preface says were stolen," Lyman commented, his eyes peering out through the lens of his glasses. "What exactly happened to those pages?"

Joel answered. "Martin Harris, one of the three witnesses to the Book of Mormon, borrowed them to convince his wife of the book's truthfulness."

"I've heard of Martin Harris," Lyman commented. "The newspaper described him as an honest, wealthy farmer whom the illiterate scoundrel, Joseph Smith, hoodwinked."

Joel nodded and smiled. "At least they admit Martin is honest. Anyway, Martin lost the manuscript. Most think his wife stole it. Joseph didn't realize it was missing for many weeks because Emma bore their first child. But the child died. Sister Emma was gravely ill and the Prophet unable to leave her side."

Lyman remained quiet for a few minutes as his mind tarried on his own grief following the death of his infant son. The explanation in the Book of Mormon that young children were pure and needed no baptism had comforted Lyman. Yet he could still feel and taste the tears he had shed when he buried his child. Lyman spoke somberly. "It seems that the Lord does not protect his own Prophet from the sorrows of life."

"Nor did our Father in Heaven protect His own Son from death," Joel said quietly, "but instead gave Him as a sacrifice for each of us."

David spoke. "In the Church of Christ, we call each other brother and sister. Brother Joseph does not put himself above others because he is God's prophet, neither does he believe that the Lord esteems him of more worth than other men. He endures the trials of life like the rest of us. He is the most humble of men, but lively and energetic as well."

"I should like to meet him," Lyman mused. "To look into his eyes and see for myself if there is truth in them."

"There is," Joel said. "I've seen and felt it."

"And I," David added as he clapped Lyman on the back.

Lyman nodded and repeated. "I should like to meet the man."

The men walked in silence for a time, then David changed the subject. "Lyman, what of your cousin? Why was Hurlbut chased out of his own congregation?"

"Due to a rumor that he had an illicit affair with a maid," Lyman stated as they climbed a small hill. His glasses clouded with steam. He felt ashamed of these charges against his cousin. "Philastus swears that the woman made unjust claims, like Potiphar's wife against Joseph of Egypt."

"Do you believe him?" David asked.

Lyman nodded slowly. "My cousin is a handsome man, and women have always been drawn to him. But Philastus has been more than kind to me. Though some people think him pompous, I cannot imagine him committing such an act. I believe that he did not return this woman's love, and she sought revenge. Philastus won't speak much of it in order to protect the maid. Joel, my cousin is interested in the Book of Mormon. He plans to visit here in a few weeks after he has done his best to clear his name."

Joel spoke. "This woman's false accusations may lead your cousin to the true church."

"I hope so," Lyman said.

David looked into the winter sun while keeping his thoughts to himself. He knew that his sisters, especially Almera and Susan, intensely mistrusted Doctor Hurlbut. David was not one to cast stones, nor was he one to cast aside his sisters' judgment of character.

When Almon awoke, the sun was high in the sky. Light pooled in the window. Momentarily confused, he blinked his eyes and sat up. David's mattress was a jumble of clothes and bedding. Seth's and Joel's were neatly straightened. The room was silent. Almon smiled as memory splashed into his mind. He recalled that a few hours ago, in a drowsy, dreamlike state, David had threatened to drag him out of bed by his heels. Seth and Joel had told David to leave the poor fellow alone lest they combine forces and thrash him. Then Almon had fallen back asleep. He yawned. He was in Seth and Joel's debt. The house was so quiet. Was he alone? If so, he hoped they had left a plate of breakfast for him.

When Almon opened the door of the room, he realized he was mistaken. He was not alone in the house. A woman's singing voice wafted up to him, sweet and melodic.

> *The moving moon went up the sky,*
> *And nowhere did abide;*
> *Softly she was going up,*
> *And a star or two beside.*

Almon couldn't figure out which female Johnson the sound belonged to. He moved stealthily to the stairs and peered down while trying to stay hidden behind the bedroom wall. There was a young woman in the kitchen whom he did not recognize. She sat in a chair and was clad in a blue dress and white apron. Her hair hung down her back in a long, dark braid. Her profile was neat and pretty with a straight nose and upturned lips. She sang as she dressed a line of flax.

Almon watched, admiring the movement of her fingers as they worked the flax fibers into a fan on her lap, the top of the hank secured with a ribbon around her waist. On completing the fan, she nimbly twisted the fibers onto a notched distaff, singing all the while.

> *O happy living things! no tongue*
> *Their beauty might declare:*
> *A spring of love gushed from my heart,*
> *And I blessed them unaware.*

At that moment, Almon realized that she was nearly done dressing the hank of flax and would shortly stand up and put it on the spinning wheel. That would cause her to face the stairs and perhaps see him. He stepped backward, thinking he would quickly go back to his room and wash and comb his hair before making her acquaintance. A loose board let out a loud creak.

At the sound, Julianne stopped singing and looked up. "Good morning, Mr. Babbitt," she called out. "Pa leaves that board loose on purpose. It gives away George and William when they try to sneak downstairs after bedtime. Mary has learned to walk around it."

Almon laughed. "Good morning," he said as he stepped into view. He ran his fingers through his hair, hoping to tame it.

Her smile was very friendly. "There is breakfast waiting for you in the kitchen."

"I-I don't believe we've met," Almon stuttered.

"I'm Julianne. Two years older than David and two years younger than Delcena."

"Delcena?" Almon couldn't seem to remember anything at the moment.

"Delcena is the sister who married Lyman Sherman." Julianne laughed at Almon's embarrassed look. "There are so many of us. We don't expect you to learn all of our names in one day."

"I think I have it now," Almon said.

"Really?" Julianne questioned brightly.

Almon puffed his chest out like an orator. "I'll name the Johnson siblings in order. Joel, Seth, Nancy—"

"Nancy comes before Seth."

Almon began again, reciting slowly this time as he counted on his fingers, "Joel, Nancy, Seth, Delcena, Julianne, David, Almera, Susan." He tapped his temple with his finger. "Is Ben next or Joe?"

"Joe."

Almon snapped his fingers and said the rest of the names in a rush, "JoeBenMaryWilliamGeorgeEsther."

Julianne laughed and corrected, "GeorgeWilliamEsther. And you forgot Amos."

"Oh, yes. How could I have forgotten Amos?" Almon chided himself with a shake of his head. "And where are the bunch of them anyway?"

Julianne smiled. "JoeBenMaryWilliamGeorge are at school with their schoolmaster Seth. The rest went to the Shermans' right after I came home from there. My brother-in-law, Lyman, arrived home last night."

"And they left me here."

"You were deeply asleep. Come eat breakfast now. Then I'll give you directions."

"But first I must comb my hair, and you must continue your song," Almon implored. "I shall die if I don't hear the end."

Julianne laughed. "My brothers would not forgive me for your demise," she replied as she fit the distaff into the hole in her wheel. As she spun, she finished the song.

> *I pass, like night, from land to land;*
> *I have strange power of speech;*
> *That moment that his face I see,*
> *I know the man that must hear me:*
> *To him my tale I teach.*
>
> *He prayeth best who loveth best*
> *All things both great and small;*
> *For the dear God who loveth us,*
> *He made and loveth all.*

Fifteen minutes later, Almon finished eating. Julianne stopped her spinning and gave him directions. "I wish we had a horse left at home to offer you," she added.

Almon grinned. "I don't mind walking. Especially if I have a lovely lady like you to accompany me."

"But I must stay home and spin." Julianne let out an exaggerated sigh.

Almon snapped his fingers in real disappointment and took his coat off a peg. While he put it on, Julianne went back to her spinning. But Almon did not give up so easily.

Almon opened the front door and noticed the ice on the step. He raised his eyebrows, thrust his foot out, and slipped. Hearing his yell, Julianne left her spinning and rushed to the door. Almon sat on the ice rubbing his knee.

"Are you all right?" Julianne asked with genuine concern.

"Yes, I think so," Almon said.

"Those steps are treacherous. I ought to have warned you." Julianne offered her hand to help him up. Almon looked up at her with twinkling eyes. He took her hand. When he was on his feet, he did not let go. Then he went down on one knee and recited the rhyme:

> *The needle's eye that doth supply*
> *The thread that runs so true;*
> *I stump my toe, and down I go,*
> *All for the wanting of you.*

Julianne smiled and gently removed her hand.

Almon stood up and grinned at her. "How can I convince you to walk with me that we might get to know each other better?"

Julianne couldn't tell if he were serious or not. Earlier that morning, Susan, who was usually so quiet, had spoken a great deal of Almon Babbitt. "You are an eighteen-year-old lad, and I am five years your senior," she said with a wink, "too old of a maid for you to court."

"Then promise to wait for me to grow up." Almon winked back at her, then turned quickly and started down the path.

Julianne sighed and shrugged. She loved the bright colorful things in life, and Almon was colorful. Julianne admired his jaunty walk for a moment before going into the house and returning to her spinning.

*We praise Thee, O God, for the joy and the song*
*Which unto us this beautiful season belong;*
*We love and adore Thee, for light and for love,*
*And for all the rich blessings that come from above.*

—JULIA HILLS JOHNSON, FROM "THE JOY AND THE SONG"

*December 1831*

"Go on now. Make your ruckus in the snow," Betsy Brackenbury ordered as she shooed her four young sons outside. Her husband, Joseph, was in the sitting room giving her eldest, Gilbert, instructions for running the farm while he was away. Elder Joseph Brackenbury would depart on a mission within the hour.

Betsy took a slab of pork from the larder, cut off a generous hunk, and carefully wrapped it. She had preserved the meat two months prior using her own recipe of salt, sugar, and herbs. Her pork was spicier than most. She packed the meat in her husband's knapsack opposite his Book of Mormon and Bible. Her husband would think of her each time he took a bite, and this gave her satisfaction.

As she worked, Betsy's gray hair framed a pleasant face tanned and weathered from countless times working outside without a bonnet. Efficient and practical, she rarely gave way to emotional displays. Yet as Betsy closed the knapsack, her eyes pricked. Joseph did not know that each time she bid him farewell, she wondered if she would see him again.

Betsy heard Baby John's cries from the yard. She went quickly into the sitting room, where her husband and eldest son were talking. From the window, she could see that John was angry but not injured.

Joseph spoke to his wife. "We're finished now. Gilbert understands the accounts and will plant in the spring if I'm not back."

"Gilbert, go outside and give your brothers a tongue lashing. I think the bigger boys caused Johnny's crying. I want to tell Father farewell."

"Yes, Mum," Gilbert said with a smile. He donned his coat and headed for the door.

Joseph looked out the window. "Johnny's all right. Charlie is brushing him off. What a good brother Charlie is."

Betsy turned around and gazed at her husband with her hands on her hips. There was a slightly amused look in her eyes. Joseph wasn't home enough to know that Charlie comforted John only after driving him to tears.

"When do you suppose you'll be at the Johnsons?" Betsy asked matter-of-factly. She had a thirst for detail and wanted to know the specifics of his travel plans. Joseph explained that he would travel by foot to Amherst, where he would pick up a letter from Annie Johnson—then on to Kirtland to join Edmund Durfee, his companion. From there, they would embark on a steamboat, departing from Fairport Harbor to disembark in Dunkirk, New York. If all went as planned, they would arrive at the Johnson home in Pomfret, Chautauqua County, about two weeks before Christmas.

"When you are in Amherst, tell Sister Annie I'll come and stay with her when her time comes, if she wants me. Gilbert can look after the boys." Betsy sighed, knowing that Annie Johnson could well have her babe before Brother Joel came home. That was a hard lot for a young mother.

"She'll appreciate that." Joseph smiled into his wife's hazel eyes, feeling pride in her independence, charity, and midwifery skills. Betsy Brackenbury was an amazing woman.

"Does Brother Joel know you are coming?" Betsy inquired as Joseph put his arms around her waist.

Joseph chuckled. "No. He will be pleasantly surprised. The Prophet called us to this mission after Brother Joel had left."

"When I prayed last night, I was comforted by the Holy Spirit. There is a great work for you to do in New York," Betsy commented. "An extraordinary work."

"Nothing other than the work of the Lord could take me from you."

These words touched Betsy. She laid her head on his shoulder. He stroked her gray hair. She drew her finger across the wrinkle lines on his brow as she spoke. "And only the Lord's work allows me to gladly let you go. What a happy day it will be when you return."

Ezekiel Johnson was busily shaping a curved chair comb with his bow saw when the door of the shop opened and a gust of cold air struck his ruddy face. He looked up. Philastus Hurlbut stood in the threshold, dressed in a well-tailored overcoat. Although he was a customer, Ezekiel felt immediately annoyed by the arrogant curve of Hurlbut's upper lip. Ezekiel grunted a greeting, inwardly wishing that Fred Styles, the shop owner, were back from his errand. Addressing distasteful customers was not Ezekiel's forte.

"Good day, Mr. Johnson." Hurlbut closed the door and walked over to Ezekiel. He held out his hand.

Ezekiel nodded but kept his hand on the bow saw. "Afternoon, Philastus. What do you want?"

Hurlbut lowered his hand. "I'm staying in Pomfret, visiting Lyman and Delcena. I head home to Jamestown in ten days. Thought I'd stop and order some chairs from the finest shop in Chautauqua County." Hurlbut ran his hand along the grain of the chair Ezekiel was working on. Hurlbut continued, "It is interesting to me that the pieces of these chairs are held together by tension."

Ezekiel eyed Hurlbut. "The tension makes them strong," he said shortly.

"Yes," Hurlbut raised his eyebrows. "if the tension is too weak, the pieces won't hold together; if it is too great, the wood cracks."

"These chairs won't crack," Ezekiel growled.

Hurlbut smiled. "Of course not. You are a fine carpenter. But enough of chairs for the moment. Did you know that Joel and David are preaching Mormonism door to door? They've set the ministers howling. Delusion! Prophets! Where are the signs?"

Ezekiel felt his face grow hot. "I saw them last Sabbath. Their religion is their business. Not yours or mine."

"Well said, my friend. But this religion is spreading like wildfire. Lyman is nearly converted, as well as some of your family and a good deal of the neighborhood. Two additional elders arrived at your home two days ago. Their names are Brackenbury and Durfee. Did Mother Julia send you word?"

Ezekiel's eyes darted to Hurlbut's. "No one's told me."

"They are teaching your wife and Seth," Hurlbut added. "And your younger children."

Ezekiel looked down. Would he lose all of his children to this religious fervor, this hogwash about angels and golden plates? "My wife does not have my permission to join with them," Ezekiel growled. Then he asked, "Is Seth a Mormon too?"

"Seth is listening to the Brackenbury fellow. He is not yet fully converted, but nearly so." Philastus Hurlbut saw anger and hurt in the icy gray depths of Ezekiel Johnson's eyes. "Didn't your wife ask your permission for the young ones to be taught?" Hurlbut questioned innocently.

Ezekiel's face was stony as a sickening chill ran through him. Hurlbut put his hand on Ezekiel's back as if he were comforting him. Ezekiel instinctively jerked away from the touch, his tension palpable. Philastus Hurlbut rubbed his hands together to warm them. "Mr. Johnson, you misunderstand me. I am your friend. I came to Pomfret to discover the root of this nonsense. My cousin is kind-hearted, vulnerable, and easily deceived. So is your wife. I'll find the Mormons' weakness. I'll discover who believes what. Would you like me to keep you informed?"

Ezekiel knew that Mormonism had the power to widen the trench separating him from his family into a chasm so wide that no bridge could span it. He feared losing them all. The door to the shop opened. Fred Styles entered. Thoughts whirled in Ezekiel's mind. Two men had invaded his home without his permission. He could not trust Julia to protect his young children from religious fanaticism. Ezekiel glanced at Hurlbut and nodded curtly. Hurlbut smiled and raised his eyebrows. "I won't disappoint you," he whispered.

Philastus Hurlbut turned to the shop owner and shook his hand. "Mr. Styles, I need four chairs like the one Mr. Johnson is working on. I'll be back for them in ten days." After agreeing on a price, Hurlbut pulled his coat tightly around himself, waved to Ezekiel, and left the shop.

Ezekiel slowly let out his breath. It would take continuous work to complete Hurlbut's order. That would not allow him time to travel home this Sabbath. Confused and angry, Ezekiel reached for the flask of peach brandy under his bench and took a long, slow drink.

Joel, David, and Elder Brackenbury walked home together as darkness approached. They had just left the Bull's farm, where they had been preaching. Under a gray sky, bare trees cast long, dim shadows on the bleak winter ground. However, the chill weather did not dampen the men's spirits. Mrs. Bull had invited them back.

As they walked, David laughed and clapped Joel on the back. "I thought all was lost when Harriet Bull shook her finger at you and asked how you dared take the devil's message to the woman who delivered your own sweet babes."

Joel smiled as David continued. "Then, when you tried to bear testimony, she let out that wail and turned to me. 'David, I love you like my own and want to thrash you within an inch of your life!'"

Elder Brackenbury glanced at David with a twinkle in his eye. "I cannot decide whether your response was proper for a missionary of the restored gospel."

David chuckled as he thought about what he had said. *Feel free to thrash me, Mrs. Bull. They whipped the Lord's disciples for their testimonies. Now that I'm a member of Christ's Church, I consider a thrashing a sign that follows the believers.*

"My jest just made her wail all the louder," David remarked with a shrug. "I don't suppose it was in line with the Holy Spirit. But Elder Brackenbury, when you spoke, she hushed up and listened. You are a marvel. I've never seen Harriet Bull quiet before. When you preach it is as if a light shines in the room. I was dumbfounded when Mrs. Bull invited you back to preach next week when her husband is home."

Elder Brackenbury turned to David and sighed wearily. "She did not interrupt, David, but did she listen? Did she understand? Was her heart open to the truth? I did not feel that confirming whisper of the Holy Spirit nor see the light of Christ in her eyes. I fear that as she stood there with her lips pursed, she was holding her tongue and biding her time. I wonder what we are in for when we return."

"A thrashing perhaps," Joel commented wryly as he lit the lantern.

David chuckled. The three walked in silence as darkness thickened around them.

"Let's sing," Elder Brackenbury suggested. "Christmas draws nigh, and my thoughts linger on my wife and children."

"Mine too," Joel admitted. Elder Brackenbury raised his voice to the Lord as Joel and David joined in.

*Joy to the world! the Lord will come!*
*And earth receive her King;*
*Let ev'ry heart prepare him room,*
*And heav'n and nature sing.*

*Rejoice! rejoice! in the Most High,*
*While Israel spreads abroad,*
*Like stars that glitter in the sky,*
*And ever worship God.*

The next afternoon, Julia asked Joel, Seth, David, and Julianne to take a walk outside with her. She donned a hooded wool cape and opened the door. The sky was overcast, causing the weather to be less frigid. Once outside, Julia spoke her mind. "I've decided to be baptized."

"Annie was certain you would accept the gospel," Joel mused. His voice sounded satisfied.

"Have you told Papa?" Julianne questioned.

Julia shook her head. "Not yet."

David whistled softly. "And what if Father refuses to give permission?" he asked.

"I plan to be baptized tomorrow night, the same as Lyman," Julia explained. "The elders will perform the ordinances quickly and quietly so that the neighbors do not protest or heckle."

"Then Father won't know about this," Seth stated. "Are you certain that is the right thing to do?"

"What choice does Mother have?" David interjected. "Pa won't give his blessing. Seth, you know that."

"The Bible teaches that a wife ought to submit to her husband, but it also teaches that we must repent and be baptized. What is a woman's duty in this situation?" Joel wondered aloud.

Julia spoke steadily. "I have a duty to my husband, but I also have a duty to my Savior, myself, and my children. I *will* be baptized into Christ's Church. I have decided it is best that I go ahead without your father's knowledge. I do not know for certain if he would grant me permission or not. I don't want to risk openly defying him. He may be angry after it is done. But I will be baptized. I will have made those sacred covenants and will be a member of Christ's Church."

"Are you certain that this is the right path?" Seth asked again, his dark eyes deeply troubled.

Joel interrupted before Julia answered. "Seth, doesn't Mother have the right to choose her own religion as much as any individual?"

Seth nodded quickly. He could see that Joel didn't understand his concern. "Yes. But every action has a consequence. If Mother joins this religion, the consequences for the entire family will be enormous."

Julia stopped walking. She took Seth's hands in hers and looked into his eyes. "Son, I am certain. I've prayed and fasted and have been filled with unspeakable light and peace. You are right in knowing that this choice *will* change our lives. It will make all the difference."

Julianne smiled. "And your choices, Mother, tend to change lives for the better."

Early the next morning, with a cloak over her housedress, Almera went outside to empty a chamber pot. She was surprised to find a note with her name on it on the doorstep. She picked it up and opened it. It was from Elijah Handy, the reverend's son.

*Almera, my darling, meet me behind the gristmill. I must speak with you alone. I will wait there until you come, no matter how long it takes. Elijah.*

Shivering, she nearly ran the mile to the gristmill. With so many people in her family, she wouldn't be missed until breakfast. She found Elijah sitting on a rock behind the mill, his breath steaming in the cold air as he stared at the frozen creek. When he heard Almera's footsteps, he ran to her, took her hands in his, and kissed her. He was a black-haired, blue-eyed, solidly built young man.

Almera pulled her head back and looked into his eyes. They were troubled and angry. "What is it, Elijah?" she asked, still shaking from the cold.

"I have heard a rumor that Lyman Sherman is to be baptized."

"That's true," Almera said, her cheeks red and her teeth chattering. She tried to find the courage to tell him that her mother was going to be baptized as well.

Elijah kicked the frozen ground. He didn't seem to notice that she was freezing. "Lyman is a Freewill Baptist, a member of my father's congregation!"

"Lyman has changed his mind. My mother is considering joining the Mormons as well," Almera blurted. She shuffled her numb feet to gain feeling in them.

Elijah gripped Almera's hands. It hurt to have her fingers held so tightly when they were so chilled. "Almera, we love each other. We have planned our lives together. You must stop this insanity within your family! If your mother is baptized, she joins a church founded by the devil. It is a mockery of true religion. Her soul will be lost. You must convince her if you can!"

"It's hard for me, Elijah," Almera began, wanting to explain that her belief in Mormonism and her love for him were tearing her in two.

"I know," Elijah said. "She is your mother. God will help you save her. How I love you!" He kissed her again. But though she cared for him, Almera was too cold that morning to return the affection.

That night, the Johnsons ate a quick dinner and prepared for the baptisms. Earlier in the day, the men had built a dam near a bend in Canadaway Creek in order to form a pool. They had broken up the thin sheet of ice on the top of the water. Shortly after supper, the Sherman family arrived with Philastus Hurlbut.

Laden with young children, lanterns, blankets, and winter clothing, the family trekked through the woods toward the creek. Lantern light illuminated the ghostly shadows cast by thick, bare trees. David supported Nancy down the icy path so that she too could witness the ordinances. When the path narrowed, he carried her. Though her health had improved, he was surprised at how light she felt under his arm and at the sharpness of the angles of her bones.

Ahead of them, Almera reached an arm around her mother's waist. "Mama, I wish we didn't have to sneak to your baptism like thieves in the night. It's so cold."

Mother Julia gave Almera a quick hug. "I don't mind the night baptism, nor the cold. What a joy it is to be joining Christ's Church. I only wish that your father could rejoice with me. My sins will be erased, and I will make a new covenant with Heavenly Father. Oh, Almera, how wonderful it is that the gospel has been restored in our lifetime!"

Almera remembered the account in the book of Mosiah describing the baptisms at the Waters of Mormon. Like those ancient people, Almera's mother was willing to mourn with those who mourned, to comfort those who stood in need of comfort. She was a witness of God at all times and in all places. As Almera walked with her mother through the black winter woods to an icy pool, warmth filled her. "You are a heroine, Mama," she whispered, "like Ruth and Esther."

"Thank you, my dear," Julia whispered back as she squeezed Almera's hand.

When Julia stepped into the water, the cold stunned her for a moment. She paused and caught her breath. Elder Brackenbury smiled and took her hand as he led her deeper into the frigid creek. The fire of Julia's testimony was stronger than the feel of the icy water. Joseph Brackenbury said the words of the prayer and immersed her. As she arose from the water, she was shaking, but her face was peaceful in the moonlight. Elder Brackenbury helped her out of the pool to where Seth waited with blankets. His mother's dress was heavy with water and very cold. He quickly wrapped her in blankets and held her close to him, fearing she might catch a chill. He told the children to huddle around her to block any wind.

Lyman stepped quickly into the pool. Elder Brackenbury baptized him. The ordinances were finished so quickly—a short prayer in the name of the Father, Son, and Holy Spirit, a complete immersion into the water in semblance of Christ's death and resurrection. It was done. So simple. So stunning. Seth whisked his mother home, where dry clothes and warm tea awaited her. Before leaving, he advised Lyman and Elder Brackenbury to hurry before their clothes froze on them.

As Lyman stood dripping and shivering, Philastus Hurlbut stepped up to congratulate his cousin. "Hurrah for your newfound religion," he exclaimed. "May it bring you joy. I am considering joining, myself."

Lyman grinned at his cousin as tears rolled down his cheeks.

"Come, Lyman, let's get you home," Delcena said as she handed him a blanket.

Almon watched while Julianne gave Elder Brackenbury a heavy coat to put over his wet clothes. Then the vibrant young lady whispered something to her brothers Ben and Joe. The boys laughed, hooked arms with their older sister and escorted her down the path. Almon wished that Miss Julianne were on his arm.

Almera watched Philastus Hurlbut as he followed Delcena and Lyman away from the pool. Philastus carried Alvira, Delcena's toddler, in his arms. Almera felt the urge to protect her niece by snatching her from Hurlbut. Although he had left Almera alone for years now—ever since that terrible incident on Delcena's wedding day—she had not forgotten nor forgiven him. She believed every rumor about him. The possibility of his baptism sickened her. How could he accept the restored Church when an honest man like Elijah wouldn't consider it? But her Elijah was proud—too proud to even suppose that Joseph Smith could be a prophet. Tears filled Almera's eyes. Philastus Hurlbut was proud too, and a womanizer. It wasn't fair! Words of scripture ran through Almera's mind. Judge not, that ye be not judged. Almera began to tremble. Could it be that she was the proud one? Too proud to believe that Hurlbut could repent?

"Mera, are you well?" Susan asked when she noticed her sister shaking.

"Just cold," Almera answered.

"Might I escort you ladies home?" Almon stepped between the two sisters and took each by the arm.

All the way home, Susan could not turn her mind from the thrill and warmth of Almon's hand on her arm.

David and Nancy were the last to leave the pool. As they walked, with David's arm bearing Nancy's weight, the young man did not feel the cold of the night. His heart swelled with love and gratitude for the Lord, his family, and the missionaries. He lifted Nancy to help her through a tight spot between two maple trees.

"I'm sorry I'm such a burden," Nancy sighed.

David grinned and teased. "I'm paying back a debt. You lugged me around enough as a child."

David put her down, keeping one arm around her to support her down the path.

"You were the wiggliest boy. I never imagined you would grow up to be my own human crutch." A moment later, Nancy spoke seriously. "David, do you think I should wait until warm weather to be baptized? Mother worries about the effects of the cold on my crippled condition."

In the calm of the winter woods, with lantern light teasing the darkness, David voiced the secret hope he had harbored since Almon's healing. "Nancy, I don't think you will be crippled much longer. I saw Almon healed by the power of the priesthood. He had a high fever one moment, and the next it was gone. I think we should ask the elders to lay their hands on your head and bless you. Imagine walking again."

Tears filled Nancy's eyes. "David, it might not be God's will that I walk again."

David grinned. "How could it not be God's will? A loving heavenly father would rejoice to see you walk again. Perhaps even Pa will be converted after such a miracle."

"Oh, David," Nancy whispered with a quiet sob. "Imagine walking again. Is it truly possible?"

"You must have faith." David said as he held her more tightly to stop her trembling.

"The thought is more than I can bear," she whispered. "First, I must be baptized."

Hours later, in the upstairs bedroom while the other men slept, Seth and Elder Brackenbury talked until late in the night. They sat at a small table in the corner with a single lit candle. They discussed Christianity before and after Constantine, the loss of spiritual gifts, the paganization of Christian doctrine, and the displacement of the ancient Church of Christ with the churches of men. Then Elder Brackenbury spoke in great detail about the need for a restoration and the mission of the Prophet Joseph Smith. Seth's mind moved in cadence with the elder's, understanding and agreeing with each premise. In the candlelight, Elder Brackenbury saw that Seth's eyes were moist and tinged with sadness.

"I see your reason," Seth commented. "The pattern is apparent, and it seems this is Christ's Church. Yet . . ."

"Yet you fear I may be wrong," Elder Brackenbury suggested.

Seth nodded and looked down at his long fingers folded together on the table. "I must know that it is God who speaks through Joseph Smith. I don't know why the heavens remain closed to me."

"I have something for you to read." Joseph Brackenbury reached for his satchel and took out a number of sheets of paper fastened together. "Joseph Smith asked God about the prophecy of Enoch mentioned in the book of Jude in the New Testament. The Lord revealed the doings of olden time to His Prophet. It is sacred text, Seth. The Prophet allowed me to copy it and bring it with me."

After handing the papers to Seth, the elder ran a hand through his receding gray hair. "I'm very weary."

"Go to bed, my friend," Seth said. The men prayed together. Joseph Brackenbury slept within moments of closing his eyes. Seth sat at the table with the papers in his hands and began reading.

*And it came to pass that the God of heaven looked upon the residue of the people, and he wept; and Enoch bore record of it, saying: How is it that the heavens weep, and shed forth their tears as the rain upon the mountains? And Enoch said unto the Lord: How is it that thou canst weep, seeing thou art holy, and from all eternity to all eternity? . .*

*The Lord said unto Enoch: Behold these thy brethren; they are the workmanship of mine own hands, and I gave unto them their knowledge, in the day I created them; and in the Garden of Eden, gave I unto man his agency; And unto thy brethren have I said, and also given command- ment, that they should love one another, and that they should choose me, their Father; but behold, they are without affection, and they hate their own blood . . .*

*Wherefore, for this shall the heavens weep . . .*

*And it came to pass that the Lord spake unto Enoch, and told Enoch all the doings of the children of men; wherefore Enoch knew . . . and stretched forth his arms, and his heart swelled wide as eternity . . .*

*And behold, Enoch saw the day of the coming of the Son of Man, even in the flesh; and his soul rejoiced, saying: The Righteous is lifted up, and the Lamb is slain from the foundation of the world; and through faith I am in the bosom of the Father, and behold, Zion is with me.*

Seth finished the passage. His heart pounded in his chest. He closed his eyes and found that he was weeping. A tingling spread through him, warm and comforting as sunlight and powerful as a flaming sword. The heavens opened for Seth Johnson that night. Like Enoch, Seth's heart swelled with a portion of that love that is bound- less enough to encompass creation and personal enough to change a man. The words of scripture entered his soul as water from heaven. As he wept, fear and doubt evaporated like night mist at dawn.

The next morning, Philastus Hurlbut rode to Fredonia on the

pretense of checking on his order of chairs. He waited in the shadows across the street from the carpenter shop until he saw Mrs. Styles bring her husband lunch. When she was settled inside the shop, Hurlbut strode quickly across the street and burst through the door. "Mr. Johnson," he exclaimed loudly, "I am in distress! Your mother and Lyman have become Mormonites!" Mrs. Styles gasped, and her gloved hand flew to her mouth.

"What?" Ezekiel blurted gruffly.

"They were baptized by Brackenbury in the middle of the night."

"Why didn't you bring me word?" Ezekiel accused.

Hurlbut threw his hands into the air. "There was nothing anyone could do. They kept it secret—waited until darkness."

"The devil has great power! Dark deeds done in the black of night!" Mrs. Styles exclaimed as she blew her nose. "Reverend Handy warned us of Mormonites who claim to be apostles. They are beguiling and can easily fool the simple-minded and the proud. I can understand it happening to Mrs. Johnson, being a Presbyterian, but Mr. Sherman was a member of our church—a Freewill Baptist!"

"Hush, woman," Mr. Styles interjected. "It's Zeke's wife you are talking of."

Dorcas Styles sniffed. "It is not my fault that Mrs. Johnson has been deceived."

Hurlbut's voice was smooth and seemingly compassionate. "Dear Mrs. Styles, we must all beware. The devil can appear as an angel of light and deceive the very elect. We must find a way to help Mr. Johnson's family before they are beyond salvation."

Ezekiel stared at his hands. It felt as if the world had gone mad. Questions spun in his mind. The voices of conflicting thoughts bore down on him. Julia, the choice of his heart and mother of his children, had been baptized into a strange and delusional sect without his knowledge or permission. The hogwash that his sons brought from Ohio had spun this evil web. But his sons were not evil. They had a right to their own opinions. Julia was bound to him as wife. She knew better. She had deceived him.

Mrs. Styles did not know what to make of Mr. Johnson's speechlessness. She had never been without words. "Mr. Johnson, are you well?" she asked.

Ezekiel did not answer.

Hurlbut whispered to the lady. "The poor man is in shock."

Mrs. Styles nodded and laid a gloved hand on Ezekiel's arm. "Dear Mr. Johnson, you must ride home quickly. Reclaim your authority. Insist that your wife recant her baptism. Safeguard your children. The Lord will bless your efforts."

Ezekiel angrily shook off Dorcas Styles's gloved hand. In an instant, he was up from the carpenter bench. Ezekiel jerked on his coat.

"You're going home then?" Hurlbut questioned.

Ezekiel curtly nodded. "This will make your order late."

"I care a great deal more about your family than an order of chairs," Hurlbut said.

"Zeke, come back as soon as you can," Mr. Styles offered. "Your bench will be waiting." Ezekiel grunted a thank you to the shop owner and was gone.

After Ezekiel Johnson had left, Dorcas Styles faced the two men. "Why is Mr. Johnson angry with me?"

Hurlbut patted her hand. "Don't concern yourself with an old man's moods. Mr. Johnson is a surly fellow, but his heart is in the right place. Perhaps he is angry because he supposed God would single-handedly protect his family from Mormons. Go tell Reverend Handy and his son Elijah what has happened. Perhaps they can help Mr. Johnson."

Mr. Styles spoke up. "Zeke don't care much for Reverend

Handy."

Philastus Hurlbut smiled charmingly at Mr. and Mrs. Styles. "Common enemies make strange bedfellows. Reverend Handy and Ezekiel Johnson are both engaged in a desperate fight against Mormonism. Hurry, Mrs. Styles. Secure the good reverend's aid."

After the two-hour journey to Pomfret, Ezekiel stopped at the tavern to fortify himself with drink before the painful task of confronting his wife. Because of this stop, Elijah Handy was the first of the two to reach the Johnson farm. After hearing Dorcas Styles's report to his father, Elijah was determined to rescue Almera, even if he had to physically drag her away from the clutches of sin.

Elijah banged on the door. David opened it and stared levelly at the blue-eyed, black-haired young man.

"I want a word with Mr. Johnson," Elijah said.

David sensed Elijah's mood. Though David was the taller man, Elijah was strong. "He's not here. Try the carpenter shop in Fredonia," David said.

"No matter. Where's Almera?" Elijah glared at David with distaste and distrust.

"She's not in the house," David said shortly.

"Where is she?"

David didn't answer.

"What have you Mormons done to her?" Elijah shouted. "It's no secret that your mother was baptized. In the darkness! Into the devil's church! Those so-called missionaries are ravening wolves dressed in sheep's clothing, preying on the emotional weakness of women! And you, David, you are idiotic enough to believe them!"

"You are as ignorant as the Romans who crucified Christ," David said shortly, his voice loud, his own anger rising to meet

Elijah's.

Seth joined David at the door. He put one hand on David's elbow and held the other out to Elijah who shook it grudgingly.

"Elijah, come in," Seth said. "David, why don't you go out to the barn and ask Almera if she would consent to speak with Mr. Handy in the sitting room."

"I'll go to the barn myself."

"No," Seth said sternly in a schoolmaster's voice. "You may speak to Almera in our sitting room if she chooses."

Elijah's eyes flashed past Seth. Almon, Ben, and Joe stood in the doorway to the kitchen, their eyes not moving from Elijah's form. Elijah knew he was outnumbered. Inwardly he cursed the brothers of the woman he loved and wanted. Seething, Elijah stalked into the sitting room. Joe came in and cheerfully asked Elijah if he would like to play a game of checkers while he waited. Elijah stared at the youth incredulously and shook his head.

A few minutes later, Almera came into the house with David. She wore a brown wool dress and an apron. Her dark hair was twisted becomingly around her face and knotted at the base of her neck. Her lips were full and her brown anxious eyes luminous in contrast with her pale features. Upon seeing her, passion rushed into Elijah. He ran to her and took both of her hands in his. "Almera dearest, I love you. Come away with me. My father will marry us tonight. Your hands are shaking. Come with me. I know your good father would grant permission if he were here. There is no time."

"Permission for what?" a voice snarled from the entrance of the room. All eyes turned to Ezekiel, who stood with wild gray hair, red eyes, and a bottle of drink in his hand.

"Mr. Johnson, thank goodness you are here." Elijah turned to Ezekiel. He kissed one of Almera's hands and continued to hold the other in a tight grip. "I've asked Almera to marry me. I'll take her away now. I'll protect her. With your permission."

"With my permission." Ezekiel snorted sarcastically. "Asking a father's permission! Ha! Something unheard of in this family. What a nice change. And what, pray tell, will you protect her from?"

The fact that Ezekiel was drunk registered with Elijah. He pitied Almera—a drunken father and a deluded mother. "I'll protect her from the men who baptized your wife a Mormon. I'll make sure that doesn't happen to her."

Ezekiel laughed without mirth. "Boy, sometimes a wife is harder to control than you might suppose."

"Not Almera. Almera will honor me and obey me."

"Then take her," Ezekiel shouted. He turned to Almera, ready to tell her to flee from this home, which tore people apart. She was sobbing, her lovely features crimson and twisted in emotional agony. She was beautiful even as she was torn apart. Ezekiel was not so drunk that his love for her was completely erased. "I cannot force her," he roared. "Let her answer for herself!"

For an instant, the men all stared at Almera. Her vision was misted and blurred by tears. There they stood—her drunken father, her protective brothers, and the young, angry man who wished to be her husband.

When Almera spoke, her voice was fragile and halting, broken by the weight of emotion. "I cannot, Elijah, I cannot."

"Almera, you can. You will!"

"I believe it, Elijah," Almera whispered. "I believe in Mormonism. I honor my mother. There would be no happiness for us."

"Is this delusion stronger than your love for me?"

"Yes," Almera cried as she took her hands from his and covered her face.

Elijah looked down at his own empty hands. Seth moved to Almera's side and put his arm around his sister's shoulders. David stood opposite Elijah.

"Go, Elijah," David said. "Almera has spoken."

"Almera is deluded," he gasped. "You will pay for this!"

"Please, Elijah," Almera begged. "Go."

With that, Elijah Handy turned on his heel and left the house, mourning for the woman he loved and cursing this delusional family of a drunken man.

"Julia!" Ezekiel thundered from the bottom of the stairs. "Julia!"

"She isn't here, Pa," Seth spoke as if he were addressing a child. "She's at the Shermans. She'll be back by dark. I'll get you something to eat, and you can rest."

Ezekiel spun around to face this son. "Are you Mormon too?" he demanded.

"I haven't been baptized, but I will be," Seth said.

The drink caused Ezekiel's mood to turn in a split second. Tears filled Ezekiel's eyes. Crying, he bowed his head like a child full of shame. "My sons dishonor me," he sobbed.

"No, Pa," Seth said evenly, and he took his father into his arms and held him tightly. "We honor you. We honor you by following God."

# 10

*The gates are wide open, and they beckon us all.*
*Each to follow and serve at the sound of Thy call;*
*Thro' portals of praise, and thro' Zion's fair gates,*
*We will pass on with songs to the work that awaits.*

—JULIA HILLS JOHNSON, FROM "THE JOY AND THE SONG"

Julia sat by Ezekiel as he slept. Thin red streaks coursed her eyes—evidence of the stress of a restless night. With the house closed up for the winter, she heard no outside noises, just the muffled sounds of her daughters preparing breakfast in the kitchen. She had not yet faced Ezekiel's anger. Last night, he had fallen into a drunken sleep before she had returned from Delcena's. He remained asleep.

Ezekiel stirred. The morning sun struck the window, the light forming a rainbow of prisms on the opposite wall. Julia stared at it as she waited. There was no escaping the conversation that she must endure when he awakened. She would rather have it in here, away from the children and the guests. Julia closed her eyes and prayed. *Heavenly Father, give me wisdom and patience. Help me know the right course.*

Julia turned to look at Ezekiel as he slumbered, his gray hair awry, his beard stubbled. He snored unevenly, and his body jerked in response. His worn features were not softened by sleep but formed so that each wrinkle looked cut out of earth's granite rather than molded of its clay. His soul felt so foreign. Then, as she studied him more deeply, she glimpsed a shadow of the young man he had been—fine looking and passionate, gazing out at the world with piercing blue eyes, building farms from virgin forests, and loving her with every breath he took. With her fingertips, she lightly touched his wiry gray hair.

Ezekiel startled awake. His head pounded as he realized that he was home, that his wife sat on the bed next to him. The morning sunlight lanced his eyes. His hands jerked to his aching head.

"Dear Zeke," Julia said.

To Ezekiel, her voice was soothing—like cool water. Then, the memory of yesterday struck him like a blow to his stomach.

"You deceived me, woman," he muttered bitterly. "You were baptized Mormon in the dead of night without my permission."

"It was done at night because we feared heckling and opposition." Julia's shoulders were straight and her voice steady.

Ezekiel's muscled torso hardened as his gray eyes narrowed. "The Bible says the wife submits to the husband. I never lied to you, never raised my hand against you."

"I was afraid you would deny me permission. It's the Church of Christ. I could not bear the thought of not joining."

Ezekiel cursed under his breath.

Julia ventured forward as if she hadn't heard him. "We could read the Book of Mormon together. You could see for yourself that it is true."

"No!" Ezekiel spat, his voice as sharp as the crack of a dry branch. "I won't be deceived by its magic. This religion could destroy us."

"Christ's gospel unites, not destroys," Julia pled.

"Enough," Ezekiel shouted.

There was a knock at the door. Joel opened it without being invited in. Joel stood straight and tall, looking gauntly noble with the morning light behind him. Stubble shadowed his thin face. His square jaw was set. Julia looked at her eldest son who had been easily frustrated as a little boy, who always tried to work harder and smarter than the next man, from whom verses flowed as easily as a meandering stream.

Joel addressed his father, "I've met Joseph Smith. He is a prophet of God. I've read the Book of Mormon. It is the word of Jehovah. I thank Heaven I put aside my blind prejudice and gave Annie permission to study Mormonism. You must not abridge Mother's right to worship God. You taught me respect and freedom! If you must be angry, rail at me, not her."

Ezekiel straightened and met his son's eyes. "You're a man, Joel. Your life is your business. Your wife asked your permission. Mine tricked me. I can't trust her now."

"Not trust Mother?" Joel said incredulously.

Before he could speak further, Julianne came to the door of the bedroom, shot a look of warning to Joel and spoke directly to her father. "Good morning, Papa. Breakfast is ready, and everyone is at the table waiting for you."

Ezekiel focused on Julianne. She'd always been a brave, pert little thing. Here she was standing up to his fury with a smile and welcome to breakfast. "Take your places at the table," Ezekiel ordered gruffly. "Have 'em wait while I wash up. I've some words for those Mormon elders and for my children."

Five minutes later, when Ezekiel strode into the kitchen, he was clean shaven and neatly dressed. Elders Brackenbury and Durfee stood up to greet him. Ezekiel's family, seated on the long benches flanking the sides of the table, waited tensely. Even William and George knew better than to poke or kick each other under the table.

Ezekiel saw the dishes and food before him. The silverware shone bright as new coins, his daughters having polished it with ashes the night before. The food was inviting—eggs, ham, brown bread, preserves, honey, cider, milk, and coffee. His children's faces were pink-cheeked and smooth. All but Nancy had brown eyes like their mother. The young ones looked his way warily, like he was a stranger they must approach cautiously. More pain shot through Ezekiel's head as he recognized their expression—the same feeling he had experienced as a child in fear of his stepfather. When had he betrayed his own?

Joel stood up. He spoke clearly, like the man he was. "Father, this is Joseph Brackenbury and Edmond Durfee, elders in the Church of Christ. Elders, meet my father, Mr. Ezekiel Johnson."

"Mr. Johnson." Elder Brackenbury stood and stepped forward, quick to shake Ezekiel's hand. Elder Durfee followed. Elder Brackenbury spoke. "We deeply appreciate your family's hospitality. We have anxiously looked forward to meeting you."

"It's a pleasure, sir," Elder Durfee added.

Ezekiel looked into the men's eyes. If there were lies there, they were well hidden. Perhaps they came by their delusion honestly, like his own sons. Ezekiel determined not to vent his anger on these two men, sensing he must be careful now. If only his head would cease pounding.

After shaking the Mormons' hands, Ezekiel sat down heavily in his chair. The elders followed suit. With a grim look, Ezekiel spoke, his words measured. "As my sons' friends, you are welcome in my home. As Mormon missionaries, you are not. You can sleep in my house and eat my food, but I won't have you indoctrinating my children. I don't appreciate you baptizing my wife without my permission, though the blame is on her shoulders, not yours."

"Sir, we never meant offense," Elder Brackenbury said. "Nor did she."

"None is taken if you heed my words from this day forward," Ezekiel said shortly. "My wife's actions are between her and me."

Julia stared straight ahead. At the moment, Ezekiel did not act the part of the drunken farmer. He appeared forthright and fair, showing respect to his guests. She was the only one who had lost his respect. She had not realized that his disapproval would pain her so deeply.

Ezekiel surveyed his children. He took a long breath before he spoke. "I know how Joel, David, and Seth feel. How many of the rest of you believe in this Mormon religion?"

One by one, Ezekiel's children raised their hands. He saw that they were wary, but not so wary that they would not stand next to their mother, opposing him. Even baby Amos followed suit, stretching his chubby arm up as high as he could.

Ezekiel gritted his teeth in an effort to push aside the pain in his head. He glanced at Julia. She sat up arrow straight—a proud,

proud woman. His children's hands hung in the air like flags signaling his ineptness.

"Put your hands down," he ordered gruffly. "This religion is based on lies. Your mother as good as lied when she broke my trust by being baptized behind my back. The Bible teaches that a woman obeys her husband. Your mother's hypocrisy doesn't sit well with me. If you are honest, it shouldn't sit well with you either. If you are under age, I forbid you to be baptized into the Mormon faith."

Beneath the table, Nancy took her mother's hand.

Susan stared at her father. He had never criticized their mother publicly before—not when he was dead sober like he was today. He had never before hindered his children's freedom in religious matters. "No, Papa," she burst with a shout. "Almera and I, Ben and Joe—we're old enough to think for ourselves!"

Ezekiel glared at Susan as his temper rose. He had worked extra days this month to buy her a lace collar for her seventeenth birthday. His shy, black-eyed Susan now challenged his authority. Ezekiel's composure broke. "You will obey me," he roared.

With scarlet cheeks, Susan lowered her eyes, unable to blink back her tears.

Almera stared straight ahead. Her ache was too deep for words or tears. She was not yet of age. She had lost Elijah because of her testimony. And now she could not be baptized. She felt cold and defeated. She had given up so much.

Benjamin breathed raggedly as he struggled to control his emotions. He desperately wanted to join the Church of Christ. But this was his father—the man he loved and was bound to obey. Amiable, kind-hearted Joe put his hand on Ben's shoulder to steady him.

Ezekiel asked Nancy to bless the food. After the blessing, David ate quickly. His eyes were dark and furious. He hated his father's bullheadedness. He knew that his mother was hurting. Tears were on his sisters' cheeks. He hated them being hurt like this. If only Nancy were healed! Then his father would know that this wasn't a crock full of lies, that this was the gospel of Jesus Christ.

Almon Babbitt glanced at his friend. He could tell David was spitting mad. Almon thought Mr. Johnson crazy. Didn't the man know how lucky he was? He had the nicest wife and children on earth. He ought to revel in it, not push them away by making a mountain out of a molehill. Almon stole a quick glance at Julianne as she commenced pouring the younger children milk. He was taken by the turn of her wrist. Almon grimaced. She infiltrated his mind like a fog, but she hardly noticed him. He was weary of paying attention to Susan and Almera—however affable they were. It certainly hadn't made Julianne jealous.

Ezekiel ate quickly, then stood up. "I gotta get back to Fredonia to finish an order so I can feed this family." He pushed his chair away from the table. The elders bid him good-bye. Ezekiel left, knowing that his family did not fathom the sheer will it took to move and speak this morning with his head pounding so fiercely that he thought it might explode. Only brandy could take away pain like this.

By the New Year, a small branch had been established in the Pomfret-Fredonia area. Lyman Sherman, who had been ordained an elder, was called to lead the branch. Ezekiel continued to spend weekdays in Fredonia at the shop. The elders informed the Johnson family that the branch was ready to stand on its own, and they must soon move on. Seth, Nancy, and Julianne asked that Elder Brackenbury baptize them before leaving.

The day before the scheduled baptism, Nancy woke with a rasping cough. The fear of deadly consumption was in everyone's mind. Joe stayed home from school to help doctor his sister.

Joe was thoughtful as he pressed together a warm poultice for Nancy. He hoped he could help her. He thought back on the day when, as a young lad, he had overheard his mother speak to his father of his weak constitution, of how she feared her Joseph would die of consumption. Joe had felt terror that day. As the years passed, this fear turned into determination—determination to study herbs and learn how to doctor himself and others. Joe had spent countless hours with Injun Goldfinger and Harriet Bull, learning everything they knew. Whenever the doctor visited, Joe asked incessant questions. His mother had encouraged his study, providing a corner of her kitchen for him to dry and pound the herbs he gathered near the lush Canadaway Creek. Joe would do everything he could to strengthen his sister.

However, as the day went by, Joe's best efforts did not help Nancy. When the men came home in the evening after prose-lyting, David went in the sitting room to check on her. Nancy's cheeks were flushed and her eyes red and dull from the fever. She asked David to bring the elders in to bless her after supper. The meal ended, and Joe took the younger children upstairs with Julianne to help them wash up for bed. Ben and Almon went to the barn to feed the animals.

As the dishes were cleared away, David approached Elder Brackenbury. "I must speak with you alone." Elder Brackenbury nodded, and the men donned coats and went outside into the bitter cold. David's color was high, and he tapped his foot with nervous energy.

"What is it, Brother David?" Joseph Brackenbury questioned.

David spoke quickly, his eyes flashing sparks of gold. "When you bless Nancy, could you command her in Jesus' name to walk again?"

Elder Brackenbury looked down for a moment. Then he looked up and met David's questioning eyes. He took his fists from his coat pockets and opened his wide, graceful hands in an appealing gesture. "Though I know the restored gospel is true, I don't know if Nancy will be healed. I don't know the Lord's will."

"But I do," David said quickly. "Nancy is destined to be whole again! This is Christ's ancient Church, and you said yourself that it is a day of miracles. You are an instrument in God's hands. You must do this and end her suffering!"

Elder Brackenbury pushed his hands back into his pockets. He spoke slowly. "I will do what I can. But remember, David, I only say the words the Holy Spirit puts into my mind—the words I am guided to say. We must strive to understand God's will."

"This is God's will! I know it!" David said fervently as he clapped Elder Brackenbury on the back.

The men went back into the house. A few moments later, the missionaries, David, Julia, Seth, and Joel stood around Nancy's bedside. David's heart pounded so violently, he wondered if it could be seen through his shirt.

Elder Brackenbury gently inquired, "Sister Nancy, do you have the faith to be healed?"

"I have faith in God's will," Nancy said quietly with her gray eyes focused on the missionary's face, "whether it be health or sickness, life or death."

The sturdy Elder Durfee swallowed, his visible Adam's apple moving in and out. "Such faith is remarkable. A gift from God," he commented.

The elders placed their hands on Nancy's head. "Sister Nancy Johnson," Elder Brackenbury began. His wide hands moved gently as if searching for something. Then they stilled as if they had found what they were looking for. "Your spirit is elect, pure, and intelligent, bright as a jewel in God's crown. Through the power of God, I bless you with strength and wisdom. This fever shall leave your body and you will be baptized into Heavenly Father's kingdom. The Redeemer of Israel has heard your prayers. Future generations will call you blessed, and your name will live on, even when your mortal life is over. Wait patiently upon God and be at peace. I say these things in the name of the Lord, Jesus Christ. Amen."

After he finished speaking, all was quiet for a moment. "Thank you," Nancy whispered, her voice fragile with emotion. The promise that future generations would remember her touched her deeply. Perhaps she would have a family someday. Perhaps the candle of her life would not always burn alone. The elders took their hands from her head. Julia, Joel, and Seth bent down to kiss her forehead. Nancy smiled up at them, her gray eyes brimmed with tears. Only David stood unmoving. He waited—waited for the words that would not be spoken, for the miracle that would not occur, his fists clenching in and out like beating hearts.

As if the others could read his thoughts, they turned toward him almost in a single movement. "David?" Seth asked. "Are you ill?"

David's chest heaved. He could not speak. He could not explain the weight of disappointment bearing down on him. David hurried from the room. Blindly grabbing his coat from a peg, he found refuge outside in the winter night. David stared up at the sky which was thick with stars—each as frozen and burning as the searing pain inside of him.

A few moments later, Elder Brackenbury joined David. "Forgive me, David," he said. "I could not command Nancy to rise from her bed. I don't know if it was my own lack of faith or the Spirit constraining me."

David spun toward the elder. The tears in the missionary's eyes shone in the moonlight. Brackenbury's compassion and humility doused the bitter words David almost spoke. He turned back to stare at the sky.

"Brother David, can I help?" Elder Brackenbury questioned.

After long moments, David spoke. "I wanted it so much. To see Nancy walk again, her suffering to end. When Nancy broke her hip, it was like Pa became diseased—all swallowed up with bitterness and drink. I thought if she were healed, he'd be humble and believing. Ma would be happy. The hate would stop."

"Your parents don't hate each other, David."

David turned toward Elder Brackenbury. For an instant, his look was wild. The black and white moonlight hid the gold in his eyes. David's voice broke. "It's me! I'm the one who hates! I hate my own father!"

Elder Brackenbury put his hand on David's shoulder as the young man sobbed, his warm tears hardening into crystals in the freezing night.

Before dawn, Nancy was up on her crutches. Her fever was gone, and she felt well and strong. Seth, David, and Julianne were also awake, stoking the fire and getting ready to chop wood and make bread.

"I'm well and can be baptized," Nancy announced as she entered the room on her crutches. "Today—as we planned."

"Are you sure?" Seth questioned.

"Yes." Nancy smiled.

A grin sprang from Seth as he noted Nancy's spry voice and healthy complexion. "Would you mind if Juli and I joined you in the freezing water?" Seth asked.

Nancy's gray eyes filled with joy. "I can scarcely wait."

"Oh, Nancy!" Julianne jumped in the air for joy.

Seth scratched his chin as he teased, "Juli's physically of age to be baptized, so Father won't stop her, but mentally?"

Julianne laughed, "You, Seth Johnson, behave like such an old man that I fear you will need a cane to walk to the lake this afternoon."

David watched the three with folded arms and troubled eyes. Nancy pivoted on her crutches and turned to him. Her gray eyes shone with love and concern as she spoke to her younger brother. "David, thank you for coming home from Ohio and bringing me the gospel. Every day, your strength and love lightens my burden. There is wholeness beyond the physical. Today I am strong and well. My soul has never felt so complete. That is our miracle."

David looked into Nancy's gray eyes. "I just wanted more," he said quietly.

"I know, David," Nancy whispered.

David unfolded his arms and embraced Nancy. Seth and Julianne put their arms around Nancy and David. The kitchen window filled with the rosy light of daybreak. Almon Babbitt watched the four siblings from the top of the stairs and yearned to be part of them. But he dared not take a step forward, for a floorboard might creak and betray his eavesdropping.

In early afternoon, Seth dismissed his scholars so that the baptismal ordinances could be performed before sunset. Canadaway Creek was too frozen for immersion, so the family traveled by sleigh the six miles to Lake Cassadaga. When they arrived, the men hacked away the ice. Joe and Ben built a shallow pit of rocks in the snow in which they built a fire. The women whispered prayers of thanksgiving. No hecklers marred the service.

Seth was the first baptized, then Julianne. Nancy was the last to be immersed. Nancy and Julianne changed into dry clothing under a makeshift canvas tent. They were then wrapped in blankets. When they were sitting around the fire, Julia served her daughters warm tea. Shivering and smiling, they thanked her. Seth and Elder Brackenbury changed clothes and joined them. The adults sipped hot tea while the young people played in the snow and slid on the ice.

"We'd best head home soon," Seth said as the sun set, spreading its amber light on the frozen lake. Julianne left the group and twirled around under the crimson sky with her arms outstretched. The children joined her laughing. "This is the most wondrous day!" Juli sang out as she fell in the snow.

"Juli, you are young at heart," Seth called to her and laughed.

*And you are the most wondrous creature on earth,* Almon thought as he slid toward them on the frozen lake with his arm hooked in Susan's.

When the family arrived home, there was a note under the door. Seth picked it up and read it silently. "It's from Mrs. Bull," he announced to the group. "Inviting the Johnson family and the Mormon elders to her home this Sabbath for preaching."

"Let's take wagers on who will do most of the preaching," David commented. "Mrs. Bull or Elder Brackenbury?"

Elder Brackenbury chuckled.

"I'll put my money on Elder Durfee here." Almon grinned as he put his arm around the quiet man's shoulders.

"Not I, Brother Almon," Elder Durfee said good-naturedly. "I'm slow of speech like Moses."

"Come now," Almon said. "It's a time of miracles."

David let out a quick burst of air. Nancy's miracle hadn't occurred—at least in the way David had hoped.

He felt Elder Brackenbury's hand on his shoulder. "The restored gospel, 'tis a priceless miracle."

Sunday arrived with gray skies and wind. Julia asked Susan and Almera to stay home with the younger children, who were coughing. Nancy was bundled and situated on a small sleigh. David and Seth walked on each side of the sleigh. The rest of the household, including the missionaries, followed after them as the family made their way to the Bull farm. Joe and Ben trailed behind, throwing snowballs at each other.

On the way, Almon stepped to Julianne's side. He chatted with her of life in Ohio, animatedly describing Elder Pratt's escape from Stu-boy and the haughtiness of Kathryn Clay. He told her of turkey hunting with Don Carlos Smith and husking corn with the Prophet. He spoke of Sixtus, Annie, and the coming baby. Captivated by her alert carriage, her cheerful, attentive eyes, and the way she cocked her head, Almon was in heaven.

"Will your family gather to Ohio with the Saints?" he asked.

Julianne's eyes became thoughtful. "Mother wants so much to join the Saints. We all do. But Father won't go. Not ever."

A lead weight entered Almon. For a moment, the two walked next to each other in silence. Julianne was the first to speak. "We must make the best of it. The Chautauqua hills have their own wild charm."

Almon kept his eyes on the ground ahead. "But Ohio will have no charm for me without the Johnson family."

Julianne swallowed as she thought of the way her sister Susan's eyes lighted each time Almon was near.

When they arrived at the neighbor's home, Mrs. Bull ushered the Johnsons into her sitting room. Reverend Handy, the leader of Fredonia's Baptist church, stood with a hand on the mantel. He was a broad, energetic white-haired man and a passionate preacher. Near Reverend Handy sat his son, Elijah, whose scowling eyes swept the group, looking for Almera.

In another corner of the room sat Reverend Spencer. The Presbyterian minister had baptized nine of the Johnson children. His face was solemn and his bald scalp red and speckled. He met Julia's eyes and shook his head sadly to show his disappointment. On the far side of the room, Sam Granger, who had once wooed Nancy, sat with his wife, Geraldine, a Bull daughter. Near them, wiry, sharp-nosed Zedekiah Bull sat between two of his grown sons, like a slice of jerky between two great slabs of beef.

As they entered the room, Almon sidled up to David and whispered that he felt more the victim than the guest. David took a mental count of the men. They weren't outnumbered. "Us Mormon boys stick together," David whispered loud enough for Ben and Joe to hear. Almon raised his eyebrows and grinned.

Mrs. Bull invited her guests to find seats. With open, friendly smiles, Elder Durfee and Elder Brackenbury canvassed the room, introducing themselves and shaking hands. When all were seated, Harriet Bull, the supreme matriarch, puffed herself up and announced candidly, "Julia Johnson and I have been friends for many a year. After hearing this Brackenbury fellow speak, I saw how easy it is to get fooled. I've invited you all here in hopes that you will start thinking straight again. Since this is a friendly visit, let's eat together before the preaching starts. Geraldine, you serve Mr. Brackenbury first to show our Christian goodwill. Julia, do you have anything to say before we start?"

Julia sat up straight and met Harriet's eyes. She was not pleased with Harriet for tricking her family into coming this morning. Yet Harriet had delivered her babies and very probably saved Delcena's life in childbirth. Julia spoke. "I, too, have only goodwill toward you. I pray that the light of truth will be with us this Sabbath."

"Amen to that," Harriet exclaimed as she slapped her thigh. "Julia, you always did have a way with words." With a false smile, Mrs. Bull's daughter served Elder Brackenbury the first slice of cake and cup of tea.

After all were served, Mrs. Bull gave the floor to Reverend Handy. He preached a scathing sermon about the rising of false prophets in the last days. He then turned the time over to Reverend Spencer who spoke of future punishment and the literal hellfire and brimstone that would follow all those who were deceived.

Elder Brackenbury asked permission to speak. Harriet Bull gave a curt shake of her head. "No, sir. Today you listen for the good of your poor, lost soul."

Joel was about to make a rebuttal when Mr. Bull surprisingly spoke up. "Harriet, it's a free country. I want to hear what the man has to say."

Harriet Bull let out a sharp breath. "What?"

"No, Pa," his daughter exclaimed. But it was too late. Joseph Brackenbury had seized the moment of opportunity and was on his feet. He opened his Bible and explained point by point the need for a restoration and the evidence that God, through Joseph Smith, had restored the ancient Church that Christ had organized upon the earth. He listed the signs of Christ's Church and the signs that followed the true believers.

As Brackenbury spoke, Reverend Handy became increasingly agitated. His thoughts reeled. It sickened him the way this Mormon twisted the truth. What power the man had over people's souls! Reverend Handy struck the mantel with his fist.

"These are all lies," he shouted. "No signs have followed these peoples' conversion."

Nancy's quiet voice filled the room. "I had a fever and was ill a few days ago. The elders laid their hands on me, and I was completely well the next morning and able to be baptized. Is not that a sign following a believer?"

Reverend Handy derisively shook his finger at her. "If you walked again, that would be a sign. Fevers break daily. Miss Johnson, you used to be a true believer. You have taught in our schools. You have more intellect than this!"

"Sir, there is a spiritual sensibility that exceeds intellect," Nancy countered.

Sam Granger surveyed the woman who had spurned him. "Nancy, don't you think it would be a simple thing for God to make you whole when He sends down angels with golden plates? Unless you think the Almighty too busy speaking to Joe Smith."

"Come, Sam," Geraldine cut in with a warm smile at her husband. "I too would believe in Mormonism if dear Nancy were healed."

"Amen," Mrs. Bull exclaimed.

Reverend Spencer stood, thinking that Reverend Handy was too angry, too passionate. Reverend Spencer transformed his expression into a mask of compassion. "We would all be asking for baptism if our beloved Nancy could walk again. But she is not whole."

"My soul is whole," Nancy cried, "healed and strengthened by the glorious message of this restored gospel."

Reverend Spencer went on as if she had not spoken. He walked over to Joe and Ben and laid a friendly hand on each of their shoulders. "Joseph Ellis Johnson, you are one of the finest scholars in Chautauqua County. At your young age, you have already earned the respect of your peers and elders. Benjamin Franklin Johnson, you once came to me in tears, asking me how you could escape that awful pit prepared for the wicked. Before Mormonism reared its ugly head, you were one of my best Sunday School boys. My young friends, I implore you to hear me. Why is your sister still a cripple when Christ's ancient apostles made the lame walk and the blind see? She would be healed if this were Christ's ancient Church. But it is not. These teachings are ashes, whited sepulchres, pillars of salt that shall crumble like Lot's wife. If you follow this course, your souls will burn eternally. I beg you not to let this be your future."

David looked at his hands, trying to control his fury. Reverend Spencer turned to David and reached out to put his hand on his shoulder. David's head jerked up. Seeing the fire in David's eyes, Spencer pulled his hand back, as if he had been burned. "David Johnson, you must repent before it is too late. Satan has great sway over your heart."

"You whited sepulchre. All is clear to me now," David muttered between clenched teeth.

Instead of responding angrily, Reverend Spencer shook his head sadly and turned to Julia. "Sister Johnson, you must reconsider. Look at David. His soul is lost. Think of your young children. How I fear for them."

"I think of them with every breath I take," Julia said. "The Book of Mormon teaches that God is love, not fear."

Reverend Spencer's eyes narrowed. "You are deluded beyond hope."

Elder Brackenbury stood on his feet. "Sister Nancy cannot walk. At least not yet. Sometimes we must wait on God's wisdom, trust in the timing of His seasons. The scriptures teach that it is a wicked generation that seeks a sign. Nevertheless, Sister Nancy will walk again—whether in this life or the next, I do not know. In the gospel of John, the man born blind had many years behind him before the Savior put clay upon his eyes."

"You are the blind man!" Reverend Handy stood up, shouting and shaking his fist at Elder Brackenbury. "And you too, Joel Johnson! It sickens me that you were once a member of my congregation. You shall pay dearly for the false doctrine you have preached to these people. Your body shall rot and your soul burn. Mark my words."

Seth stood up. He had had enough. He saw the tightness in Joel's jaw, David's clenched fists, and the pain in Nancy's eyes. He looked around the room and spoke with quiet authority. "It is time for my family and friends to leave. Gentlemen, though you claim to be men of God, today I cannot comprehend how you imagine yourselves Christians."

"Seth Johnson, as a deluded Mormon, you are no longer fit to teach our children," Reverend Spencer said vehemently. Seth ignored the comment and led his family from the room.

Reverend Handy turned to Mrs. Bull, breathing hard. "You did your best, good lady. They are hardened past redemption."

David, Joel, Almon, the missionaries, and Benjamin spent Tuesday morning sawing blocks of ice from Lake Cassadaga and hauling them home to a deep pit lined with straw and sawdust. David and Joel climbed down into the pit while the others unloaded the ice and handed it to them. Uncharacteristically tired, Elder Brackenbury was winded by the exertion. As he bent to lift another block of ice, he suddenly placed his hand over his abdomen and rocked slightly forward. "Brethren, I am ill," he gasped.

"Benjamin," Joel instructed from inside the pit, "help Elder Brackenbury to the house."

"No need," the elder said. "I can walk." But as he turned, he fell on one knee and doubled over. Elder Durfee sprang to his side, and David leapt from the pit. Together, they formed a chair with their arms and carried Joseph Brackenbury to the house. Joel instructed Ben and Almon to finish packing the ice. He followed the men.

Benjamin and Almon watched the men walk away. Ben was the first to speak. "I'll get in the pit." Almon pushed the blocks to Ben, who eased them into place. After they had maneuvered the rest of the day's load, Almon shoveled in straw and sawdust. Ben spread it evenly over the ice with a rake. When they were finished, Benjamin leaned on the rake and looked up out of the pit at Almon. "Do you think he'll be all right?" Ben asked.

"Sure, he'll be all right," Almon responded. "My pa used to get sick like that every Wednesday."

Ben's brow furrowed. Almon went on, "Don't worry about a storm when there's just one cloud in the sky. God will protect him." With that, Almon grinned and kicked stray sawdust and snow into the pit, and onto Ben's black hair. "Now your hair's gray, like an old man's." Almon laughed.

Defensive and annoyed, Ben clamored out of the pit, slipping with each step. Almon laughed harder. Benjamin pushed Almon down into the snow. Ben was about to jump on him when Almon stuck out his hand. "Come on, Ben. We're friends."

Benjamin reconsidered and helped Almon up. When they neared the house, it was getting dark. Through one of the windows, Almon glimpsed a number of the Johnson women sitting together talking and sewing. While Almon focused on the scene, Benjamin picked up a load of snow and dumped it on Almon's head. Almon gasped in surprise and shook like a dog. Benjamin backed up and waited for Almon's reaction.

But instead of continuing the horseplay, Almon just turned to the youth and pronounced, "Benjamin Franklin Johnson, I think you have the most beautiful mother and sisters on earth."

This comment took Benjamin by surprise. He cocked his head at Almon. "You learn somethin' new every day," Ben replied. "Almon Babbitt, you're smarter than you look."

The next day, Elder Brackenbury became increasingly ill. While Julia, Joel, and Seth waited on the sick man, Julianne decided it would be fitting to distract and entertain her younger siblings. She went into the cellar and brought up apples, onions, potatoes, and popcorn. She gathered her siblings around the roaring fire in the sitting room hearth, where the group roasted their delicacies. They played charades and Blind Man's Bluff. Julianne led them in ballads, and little Esther pulled David's boots off and pretended his feet were twin babies. She wrapped them in rags and rocked them to sleep.

Later in the afternoon, Julia interrupted the children's play. "Joseph, Elder Brackenbury is in severe distress. I don't know what else to do."

Joe stood up and pulled his boots on. "Mother, I'll make a tea of chamomile and mandrake. It's a stomachic and purgative. Mandrake deadens pain as well."

"Please, Joseph," she implored. "As soon as you can."

But despite Joe's tea and the family's prayers and blessings, Elder Brackenbury's condition deteriorated throughout the night. In the morning, Julia sent Benjamin to get Dr. Adams in Fredonia. Benjamin went to the carpenter shop first. He burst in and tearfully told his father of Elder Brackenbury's condition. At the sight of his distraught son, Ezekiel immediately left his workbench and went with Benjamin to fetch the doctor.

When they arrived at Dr. Adams's office, the tall, aging, distinguished doctor was conferencing with three medical students.

Benjamin recognized one, a man in his late twenties who had grown up on a nearby farm. His name was Hans Wilson. Wilson advised Dr. Adams to refuse to help, reminding him that Brackenbury was one of the cursed Mormon missionaries and that this was God's vengeance. Ezekiel's face hardened with anger at the prejudice. Tears of frustration filled Benjamin's eyes.

Dr. Adams glanced quickly at the father and son. Then he turned to his students. "I'm a scientific, not a religious man," he stated. "I don't think a Mormon's any more deluded than a Baptist. You wouldn't want me to stop serving all of the Baptists in the neighborhood, now would you?"

"Amen," Ezekiel muttered. Together, Ezekiel, Ben, and Dr. Adams traveled the seven miles to the Johnson home. The household waited quietly, as if holding a collective breath, while Dr. Adams examined the sick man. Afterward, he spoke to Ezekiel, Julia, Elder Durfee, and Joel in the hallway. "This is bilious colic. I'm sorry. But I see no hope for survival."

Tears crept down Julia's cheek. Ezekiel studied his wife and saw that she was exhausted. Doubtless she had spent the night at the sick elder's bedside. Compassion for his wife and for the dying man pushed away the anger he had harbored. The group heard Elder Brackenbury groan. Elder Durfee, Joel, and Julia went into the room.

The doctor spoke to Ezekiel. "At times like this, I wish I could believe in God." Ezekiel nodded and kindly offered the good doctor a drink of brandy.

Thirty minutes later, while the suffering missionary briefly slept, Ezekiel grimly measured the width and breadth of Joseph Brackenbury. When the sick man writhed in pain, Ezekiel shook his head in thick sorrow. How could his wife still believe in Mormonism when their strongest man lay in the throes of death?

Two hours later, after a brief meal, Ezekiel and Dr. Adams prepared to return to Fredonia. Before leaving, Ezekiel spoke briefly to Julia. "Spare nothing for his comfort. I'm taking the sleigh with me. I'll be back Saturday morning with the coffin."

"Zeke, we pray for a miracle," Julia said with red eyes.

Ezekiel nodded and looked directly into her eyes. "Prepare yourself and the children," he said simply.

On Saturday, January 7, 1832, Joseph Blanchette Brackenbury awakened. His pain had eased somewhat, and his mind was clear. He knew without doubt that he would die that day. He bore his testimony for the last time to the Johnson family, and he asked Elder Durfee to take the news of his death to his beloved wife, Elizabeth, and his five sons. "I long to see them once more in the flesh," the good man said weakly. "Tell them I died strong in the faith. Tell them that I rest in the arms of Jesus." Two hours later, with Julia and Edmond Durfee clasping his hands, Joseph Brackenbury died.

Outside, the cold wind howled. The sky was thick with clouds. In mid-afternoon, Ezekiel traveled the road from Fredonia to Pomfret with a pine coffin, painted black, tied to the sleigh. On the way, he encountered Joel and Edmond Durfee. Joel briefly told his father the circumstances of Elder Brackenbury's passing and explained that he and Elder Durfee were taking the news to members of the little branch that Elder Brackenbury had organized.

A short time later, Ezekiel arrived at home. Although the household mourned, the work continued. Julianne and Nancy wept silently as they sewed a white shroud for the body. Julia and her other daughters cooked, though their eyes were red from tears.

They knew that guests would come to pay their final respects on the Sabbath. Lyman and Delcena had arrived. Their faces were lined with sorrow. Joseph and Mary mechanically played with the youngest children in the sitting room. Benjamin was in the barn crying.

Ezekiel walked up the stairs. He stood in the doorway and watched as Lyman, Seth, and David washed the cold flesh of the man they had loved. They closed his eyes, shaved his face, and combed his hair. Julianne brought up the completed shroud. Together, the three men lifted the stiff limbs that felt so heavy and cold in death and began dressing the body.

Ezekiel went downstairs and asked Almon to help him remove the coffin from the sleigh and place it in the sitting room. David and Seth bore the body downstairs and placed it in the open coffin. The children looked on curiously. George and Will dared each other to touch the hand of the dead man. They were silenced when their mother bent down and kissed the cold cheek, the string of her white scarf falling onto the still fingers.

After supper, Julia hardly had the strength to walk. With great effort, she retained her erect composure until she was in her bedroom and had closed the door. Then, she crumpled onto the bed and sobbed. Ezekiel, who had watched his wife from the kitchen, followed her into the bedroom. He closed the door behind him. Without a word he sat down on the bed beside her and placed his hand on her shoulder. Gently, he untied her scarf and unloosed her hair. He moved her head into his lap and stroked her long gray tresses. He grieved for her, knowing what it was like to be abandoned by God. "In the midst of life, there is death. It is a cruel truth," he said when she had quieted.

She looked up at him with red eyes and wet cheeks. "He died so far away from his wife and children," Julia choked. "Zeke, we are also so far away from each other."

Ezekiel bent his head with pain in his eyes. He did not stop stroking her hair.

"Yet you love me," Julia gasped and began weeping again.

"Aye," Ezekiel whispered. "Forevermore." That night Ezekiel went to sleep without a drink of brandy, and Julia found solace in the arms of her husband rather than in the arms of her God.

The Sabbath brought both mourners and hecklers to the Johnson home. Ezekiel stood outside the door with his gun Betsy in hand. He questioned anyone who came near, determined that no one would upbraid the dead or injure his family. Only friends of Joseph Brackenbury were allowed in his home that day.

During late afternoon, a feathery snow fell. Sam Granger rode up on a gray gelding. "Git off my property," Ezekiel yelled.

"Give your family my condolences." Sam's mouth twisted as he spoke. "It's too bad a Mormon high priest hasn't the faith to withstand poison like the ancient apostles."

"Are you sayin' you poisoned this man?" Ezekiel growled as he moved Betsy to his shoulder and pointed the gun at Granger's chest. Ezekiel kicked his foot backward, banging it against the front door. It was the signal that he needed another man. David came outside and stood near his father. Snow stuck to his long eyelashes.

"I'm not saying anything," Granger said with an eye on both the gun and David. "Brackenbury had a lot of enemies. The most powerful one being God."

"Who poisoned Mr. Brackenbury?" Ezekiel shouted as he cocked the gun.

"No one needed to poison him. God took care of it. I told Reverend Handy I'd deliver this." Granger threw an envelope at David's feet. Snow flurried. Granger whirled his horse around and left.

David picked up the envelope. "Read it to me," Ezekiel ordered, his eyes icy slits as he kept the gun pointed in Granger's direction. David tore open the envelope.

David read the letter through clenched teeth. "To the Johnson family. Though I fear many of you are beyond reason and hope, caught up in your own pride, perhaps one of you may have ears to hear. The cause of your strongest man's death is explained in the book of Deuteronomy: *But the prophet, which shall presume to speak a word in my name, which I have not commanded him to speak, even that prophet shall die.*"

"The devil take Joy Handy and Sam Granger," Ezekiel muttered as he took the paper from David and tore it into a thousand pieces. He flung the pieces into the wind. "Don't tell your Ma of this. It would pain her more."

Grief stricken and emotionally exhausted, David stared at his father, an old and angry man, a man with stunning courage and tragic weakness, a man as loyal as the air he breathed. David looked away and watched the fat flakes of snow floating down as if they had some purpose. A screen of love and grief at Joseph Brackenbury's passing both shielded David and softened his vision. He stood absolutely still as scars of hate in his soul broke open, leaving an exposed and beating heart—the knowledge that he was much like his father in love and passion, pride and shame.

Ezekiel watched his son. He saw David's stoic tears as the young man looked at the falling snow, his gaze beyond time and grief. For some strange reason, Ezekiel remembered the moment Isaac Chapel gave him the gun he held now. Ezekiel had bound himself with an oath to protect his children, not to see them suffer like he had as a youth. But he had failed. Ezekiel knew one truth plain as day: pain was universal. Ezekiel shouldered the gun on one arm and put the other around David. "Son, go on inside where it's warm. Betsy and I'll take care of things out here."

Late Monday afternoon, the Ezekiel Johnson family and a handful of other mourners trekked the mile from the Johnson home to the Pomfret Township graveyard. It was located on a rise near the central corner of town, opposite the tavern, post office, and gristmill. Earlier that morning, while Ezekiel's sons dug the grave in the frozen ground, Ezekiel had warned the men at each of those locations that he wouldn't put up with any hecklers. Because of this, the afternoon was quiet. The men of Pomfret knew both Ezekiel Johnson's temper and his gun Betsy.

Elder Durfee, Joel, Lyman, Seth, David, and Almon each carried a portion of the coffin's weight. Nancy rode on the sleigh. The others walked. Ezekiel trailed behind them, pushing a wheelbarrow full of sawdust and straw. As he walked, Ezekiel knew that it would be his boys' final task to bury the casket. Ezekiel had heard before the ugly echo of dirt clods hitting coffins. His load would go in first and muffle the sound.

When they arrived at the gravesite, Elder Durfee opened the service with a simple prayer thanking the Lord for the restored gospel and beseeching the God of Heaven to protect Brackenbury's body until the day of resurrection. Julianne then sang a hymn.

> *Why do we mourn for dying friends,*
> *Or shake at death's alarms?*
> *'Tis but the voice that Jesus sends,*
> *To call them to his arms.*

> *Are we not tending upward too,*
> *As fast as time can move?*
> *Nor should we wish the hours more slow,*
> *To keep us from our love.*

After the song, Lyman delivered a short sermon. He talked of the resurrection of the just and the reward of the servants of the Lamb. He told of the elder's strength and commitment. "Elder Joseph Brackenbury has given his life in the service of his God. We are the fruits of his labor. May the strength of our testimonies equal his sacrifice! May the God of Heaven look down on us as shining examples of Joseph Brackenbury's love, of the worth of his life. Elder Brackenbury's death so far away from home and family will not be in vain. We will stand true to the gospel of Jesus Christ. We will not forget this man who gave all to bring us truth. On some final day, we will join him as links in an unbroken chain of faith and loyalty extending from Elder Joseph Brackenbury to our children's children until the day of the Lord."

Seth offered a final prayer. Most of the men were beyond tears, their grief an aching weight they bore within. In silence, they buried the casket. The women in the group could not hold back their sorrow. Benjamin did not help shovel the earth and snow into the grave. Instead, he looked down with hot tears scorching his cheeks, even though he knew Elder Brackenbury was with God. Joseph wept openly with Julia's arm around him. Julianne could not stop thinking that the fences along the borders of the graveyard would be wreathed in grapevines during the summer and fall, yet Elder Brackenbury wouldn't be alive to see them.

Later that night, after all had retired, David couldn't sleep. Outside, a heavy snow fell. He climbed out of bed and paced.

"David, are you well?" Joel's voice arose out of the darkness.

"My mind is troubled. I keep thinking of Alvin Smith. Don Carlos told me that after Alvin died of bilious colic, neighbors cruelly dug up the remains. I fear for Elder Brackenbury's body."

"David, no sane man would venture out on a night like this," Joel said.

David nodded as he stared at the window white with wind and snow.

"But the world is not sane," Seth said with grief in his voice. David and Joel startled, for they thought Seth was asleep.

Joel spoke. "We can only pray and trust in the Lord."

*Three men with shovels stood in the shadows of the graves. One was larger than the others. Snow swirled around them. They had no difficulty finding the fresh grave with the loose dirt forming a lump in the snow. Their shovels flew as they began their task.*

Joel jerked awake. "Seth! David!"

The brothers sat straight up in bed.

"A dream," Joel panted. "I saw them about to dig up his body!"

"Do you think we should go to the graveyard and check?" Seth asked.

David had already begun to put his boots on.

In minutes, all of the men in the household, including Lyman Sherman, who had stayed the night, were up and dressed. Lanterns were lit. Seth had awakened Ezekiel and told his father of their task. Ezekiel thought his sons insane from grief, but he dressed nonetheless and took Betsy from the mantel.

David outran the rest as he blindly raced through the snowstorm in the direction of the graveyard, a lantern swinging at his side. If all was well, he would know soon enough. If not, he didn't want to be too late. When he neared the cemetery, he glimpsed lantern lights winking in the snowy night like a handful of lightning bugs. With a fierce shout, he dropped his lantern and streaked toward the grave.

The largest man looked up as he and two others were about to lift the coffin from the ground. He heard the dark figure racing toward him before he saw it. In panic, he perceived other lanterns a short distance away, countless men's footfalls muffled by the storm.

"Flee!" Hans Wilson screamed. "The devil told the Mormons we're here!"

The three medical students ran for their lives. David leapt into the air. Wilson threw his shovel, grazing David's jaw. David tasted blood as he grabbed the big man's legs. Hans Wilson fell with a thud. David was on him in an instant. The two rolled over and over in the snow as they struggled. Finally, David twisted the man's arms behind him and dug his knee into the small of his back. With one hand, he pushed Wilson's face into the snow. A moment later, he allowed the man a breath. "We meant no harm," Wilson begged.

"No harm?" David shouted, all rage, muscle, and vengeance. He pushed the man's face into the snow once more.

Then there was a hand on David's shoulder. David did not look up, did not loosen his grip. He heard his father. "We're here, son."

Lyman Sherman's voice, "Let him up, David."

"Us Mormon boys stick together," Almon growled.

David loosened his grip. Hans Wilson threw David off and sprung to his feet, only to feel the barrel of a silver trimmed gun in his chest.

"Meet Betsy, son," Ezekiel Johnson said grimly. "Looks like you'll be spending the night with my boys and having breakfast with the constable in the morning."

"He'll have trouble drinking his coffee without fingers," Almon glared at the prisoner sinisterly. "Did you know Mormons cut off their enemies' digits one by one and burn them like incense to atone for their sins?"

Ezekiel smiled grimly at Almon's threat. But Lyman Sherman was not pleased. He felt Hans Wilson's fear. "Brother Almon isn't serious," Lyman said. "We belong to the Church of Christ. Although you attempted to desecrate our friend's body, we will treat you fairly until you are turned over to the constable."

"I'm a medical student. I meant no harm," Hans Wilson said to Lyman.

Ezekiel snorted and kept his gun trained on Wilson. Almon turned to talk to David, but David was already gone, back at Elder Brackenbury's grave, helping Joel, Seth, and Elder Durfee bury the beloved man's body for the second time.

# 11

*How sweet the lingering dreams of olden time*
*Of childhood's spring in far-off native clime,*
*'Mid wild Chatauqua's hills we used to stray,*
*Where wood-nymph fairies held a magic sway.*

*The village bell, though full three miles away,*
*We heard distinctly on each new-born day;*
*Its peal, more solemn on the Sabbath air,*
*Marked time for school, for service and for prayer.*

*The school-house! ah! the red one on the hill,*
*Full two miles South, Laona's noisy mill;*
*Midway between the two we met our birth,*
*Our boyhood thought the brightest spot on earth.*

—JOSEPH E. JOHNSON, FROM "THE OLD SCHOOL HOUSE"

*January 1832*

In the early morning, a week following Elder Brackenbury's funeral, Seth was the first in the schoolhouse. Stiff from the bitter cold, he squatted down and opened the stove door. Blowing on the coals to ignite them, he watched the sparks dance. The schoolhouse door banged open. Joe entered with an armload of wood.

"Let's get this old place warmed up," Joseph called out as he dropped his load of wood and rubbed his hands together. He stomped his feet to gain feeling in them. Despite the cold, Joe felt happier than he had in a long time. He was glad to be back to this place where he felt great success, where he could lose his thoughts in literature, ciphering, and poetry.

The door banged open again. "Old Joe! You're back!" Morris Cook, a bright-eyed fifteen year old with a quick mind, quick feet, and straggly platinum hair nearly tackled Joe in a bear hug.

Joe laughed his soft, happy laugh, which Seth had not heard since Elder Brackenbury became ill. "Morris, it's good to see you."

Morris grinned at Joe. "I didn't know if you'd ever come back. Rachel's outside with the tadpoles."

Morris referred to the younger Johnsons as the tadpoles. Joe thought of Rachel Risley, with her blue eyes, long light brown braids, rosy cheeks, and slightly prominent nose. She and Morris were his best friends.

Morris helped Joe load the wood into the stove. "Come outside, Joe," Morris said under his breath, "where the master won't be looking down his long nose at us. We must talk."

"Long nose, eh, Mr. Cook?" Seth, who was reading, raised his eyes.

"Our schoolmaster is eavesdropping," Joe whispered with a grin.

"Sorry, sir," Morris mumbled quickly.

"Apology accepted," Seth replied. He knew that Morris's parents had been part of a group who had cried for Seth's resignation when the Mormon missionaries first arrived. Surely the Cooks had hoped they had seen the last of Master Johnson when he was absent due to Elder Brackenbury's death. Seth sighed. He had taught Morris Cook for years and found great reward in nourishing his young, bright mind. Since Seth's conversion, school attendance had declined substantially. Seth wondered how long the Cooks would allow Morris to continue.

"Mr. Joseph Johnson." Seth turned to Joe. He always referred to his siblings formally when teaching. "A word with you privately. Then you are free to join Mr. Cook and the *tadpoles* outside."

Morris cuffed Joe on the shoulder before leaving the schoolhouse. Joe turned to Seth and shuffled his feet. Outside, the chatter in the yard had increased, and Joseph was anxious to join his schoolmates. He had not seen his friends for nearly three weeks. Joe thought of how Ben, Sue, and Almera had stayed home. They had feared unbearable jibes in the aftermath of Elder Brackenbury's death. But Joseph had known that his friends would greet him with open arms. Morris's reception had proved he was right.

"Joe," Seth said as he looked at his brother intently, "there is deep prejudice against us. I don't know what this day will bring."

"Not here, Seth," Joe said wistfully. "You're the master here."

Seth sighed, and there was sorrow in his eyes. Joe was tall as a man, almost sixteen, but a lad still. Seth dearly loved his friendly, guileless brother who drank in knowledge. He did not want to see him injured. "Go on," Seth said. "Watch out for Mary and the boys."

Joe put his arm around Seth. "Don't worry, big brother. The tadpoles are safe here. We are loved here." At Seth's doubtful look, Joe quoted one of the many phrases Seth had taught his scholars. "Love kindled by virtue always kindles another."

Seth thought of how in Pomfret Township the spark of brotherly love had been consumed by other flames. "Pride, Envy, and Avarice are the three sparks that have set these hearts on fire," Seth quoted.

Joe snapped his fingers and grinned. "Big Brother, a day will come when you cannot out-quote me."

"But that day is not today," Seth said, forcing life into his voice. "Join your friends, Joseph. You were born to be cheerful." *And was I born to be melancholy?* Seth wondered. He could not escape the deep shadows that surrounded him since Elder Brackenbury's death.

When Joe went outside, he found his siblings Mary, George, and Will with his friend Rachel, standing alone on the edge of the schoolyard. Something was wrong. Joe ran to Rachel, who bent over eight-year-old George as she dabbed his swollen, bleeding lip with her handkerchief. Mary had her arm protectively around seven-year-old Will, who was sobbing. The side of Will's cheek was swollen. Mary's blonde braids hung down her back. Her brown eyes blazed across the yard at twelve-year-old Eddy Cornwall. Morris Cook and some of the other older boys were questioning him.

"What happened?" Joe asked as he lifted up William. "Will? George? What happened?" George looked up at Joseph with tear-filled eyes. Will shook his head and couldn't stop crying. Joseph kissed his little brother's bruise.

"Rachel, Mary, what happened?" Joseph repeated.

Rachel was the first to speak. "Eddy Cornwall picked a fight with George. Will joined in before Morris pulled Eddy off."

"Eddy's four years older than George," Joseph exhaled. "He's mouthy but not usually a brute. What set him off?"

Mary spoke between clenched teeth. "Eddy said Elder Brackenbury died 'cause he followed the devil. He said Mama was crazy and buried her Bible to join the Mormons. George got mad and jumped on him. Then Eddy pinned George down and wouldn't quit hitting him."

"I'll take him to Seth. Eddy'll learn to mind his tongue and keep his fists to himself."

"Everybody hates us now," Mary cried. "Kenny Risley and Ben Wilson aren't allowed to play with George and Will anymore."

"Rache, is that true?" Joe looked levelly at his friend. Kenny was Rachel's younger brother.

Rachel's blue eyes filled with tears. "Joe, we've been best friends since we were five. I'll keep meeting you in the old lonesome gulf to pick wintergreen and gather chestnuts, no matter what."

Joseph stared at Rachel.

Mary began crying. Then her tears turned to fury. She stomped her foot. "I'm taking Will and George home."

"You can't go," Joseph hissed. "We just came back. Everything is going to be all right."

Joe put Will down. Mary gritted her teeth and watched her big brother walk over to the group of boys. "For somebody so smart, he doesn't know much," she tearfully whispered to Rachel.

Joseph strode across the yard, his features uncharacteristically stern. His friends, Morris Cook, Willard Lewis, and Blanchard Darby flanked each side of Eddy Cornwall like they were protecting him.

"Edward Cornwall, I've got business with you," Joe challenged.

"We've taken care of him, Joe," Morris said. "He won't bother the tadpoles no more."

Joseph looked at Morris, then narrowed his eyes at Eddy. "Go tell my little brothers you're sorry."

Eddy smirked at Joe. "George hit me first. You Johnsons think you're high and mighty because your brother is schoolmaster. All that's changed now that you're dirty Mormons."

"Eddy, shut your stupid trap," Morris said.

Joseph lunged forward and grabbed Eddy's ear. "I'm taking you to Master."

"Let him go, Joe." Blanchard stepped up and stared at Joseph grimly. Blanchard was shorter than Joe with a head of thick, curly brown hair. Willard stood next to Blanchard and nodded in agreement. "Let him go."

Joe looked at Morris. "They're right," Morris said. "You gotta let him go."

Eddy savagely kicked Joe's shin. Unconsciously reacting to his smarting leg, Joe's grip on Eddy's ear loosened. Eddy pulled away, yelled an expletive at Joseph, and ran off.

"Eddy, I told you to shut up," Morris yelled after him.

"I thought you boys were my friends," Joseph said thickly. He knew that if his brother Ben were here, Eddy would be eating dirt right now.

"We are," Morris assured. "We ain't mad at you. It just won't help to hurt Eddy. We all know none of this is your fault."

"None of what?" Joe demanded.

"You know what," Willard said. At the moment Willard's large teeth reminded Joseph of a rodent.

"Do I?" Joseph's fists were clenched.

Blanchard narrowed his eyes. "Come off it, Joe! This cursed Mormon stuff."

"You don't know anything about that." Joseph was breathing hard.

Morris stepped between Joe and Blanchard. "We're friends," Morris begged. "It's a free country, and Joe can believe whatever he wants. Blanchard, you leave Joe alone about his family's religion.

What we have to remember is that we're friends. Think of all the things we've done together. How we've stuck up for each other all these years. How we never told on each other."

Willard's shoulders relaxed. "Morris is right."

"You fellows let Eddy beat up my little brothers," Joe growled.

"No, we didn't, Joe," Morris countered. "We stopped Eddy and told him he'd better not touch them again. We jes' don't want you to lose your temper. It would cause more trouble for Master Johnson."

"What kind of trouble?" Joe asked.

"People want him out of the school, Joe," Morris muttered. "They don't think he's fit anymore."

Joseph spun toward Willard and Blanchard. "What about you two? Is that what you want?"

Willard shrugged and shook his head. "No. He's our master."

Blanchard exhaled and looked at his feet. "I don't understand what's goin' on, Joe."

"Well, I know." Morris clapped Joe on the back. "Joe's our friend, and Master Johnson never preaches at school, so I figure he should stay." Morris cupped his hands to his mouth and shouted across the yard to Eddy and a group of eleven-year-old ruffians. "Next time I strangle anyone who touches the Johnson tadpoles!"

"Maybe there won't be a next time," Rachel said, her voice tinged with sadness. Joe turned around. She had walked over without him noticing. Rachel pointed to the path leading down the hill away from the school. Mary, George, and Will were nearly to the bottom of the hill.

Joe would have gone after them if Seth's ruler hadn't struck the clapboard at that moment. Master Johnson stood at the entrance to the schoolhouse. All chatter and motion in the yard instantly halted as the children looked up at their schoolmaster. Joe noticed Seth gazing at Mary, George, and Will heading home. Mary turned briefly and focused on Seth. He nodded slightly. Mary turned back around and continued. Joe closed his eyes and exhaled. His brother was going to let them go without a fight.

Seth turned to his pupils. "Quote of the day," he announced as he motioned for his scholars to file into the schoolhouse. "From *The Divine Comedy* by Dante Alighieri: Consider your origin; you were not born to live like brutes, but to follow virtue and knowledge."

While Seth was teaching science, there was a knock at the schoolhouse door. Stout Judge Houghton was the first to enter, trailed by Mr. Risley, Mr. Cook, and Mr. Cornwall. Last was Alexander Cheney, a young man with dimples who had been one of Seth's first scholars. For the past three years, Mr. Cheney had substituted for Seth. Seth stopped the lesson and greeted the unexpected guests. Alexander Cheney was not smiling today as he focused on the wood floor.

"A word with you, Mr. Johnson," Judge Houghton said.

Seth turned to the children. "Students," Seth instructed. "Take out your quills and write from memory Sir Isaac Newton's Mathematical Principles—the three laws of motion." Most of the students pretended to write while straining to hear the conversation in the corner.

"Mr. Johnson," Judge Houghton spoke briskly, "attendance is declining in this school. Your services are no longer needed, and you are henceforth dismissed. Alexander Cheney will replace you immediately."

"What gives you the right to dismiss me? The students' parents provide my income, not you," Seth said as he squared his shoulders.

"We speak for the parents," Mr. Cook snapped. "No deluded Mormon is going to teach our children." He pulled a newspaper article out of his coat pocket and thrust it at Seth. With a shaky hand, Seth took the article. He scanned the words published in *The Fredonia Censor.*

> **Death of a Mormon Preacher.** — *Died, in Pomfret on Saturday, 7th inst.* Joseph H. Brackenbury, *a 'Mormon Preacher.' He recently came to this town from Ohio, in company with one or two individuals of the same society. — They preached, exhorted, and with great* zeal *and* apparent *humility, attempted to propagate their doctrines. Two or three embraced their sentiments so far as to be baptized — one a Free Will Baptist, the other a Presbyterian.*
>
> *In confirmation of their doctrine and divine mission, they professed to have power to heal the sick, and raise the dead. It is credibly reported that they attempted twice without effect, to heal a Miss Nancy Johnson, made a cripple by falling from a horse. The company of Brackenbury attempted also to heal him, and since his demise, to raise him from the dead.*

The cruelty of the article stunned Seth—to take their deepest pain and mock it. He swallowed back his hurt and anger, struggling to keep his voice calm as he spoke. "I assure you that I do not influence my students toward any sect. I believe that each individual is endowed with freedom of will and conscience."

"We don't want any part of your beliefs. Our children are no longer your students." Mr. Cornwall's face was red.

"I have taught here for nine years," Seth said. "Surely that is worth something." Seth felt as if his throat were constricting, as if it were difficult to breathe.

"Seth Johnson," Judge Houghton warned, "don't fight this. You cannot win."

Mr. Risley spoke up. There was compassion in his eyes as he looked at Seth. "Mr. Johnson, in past years, you have been a model for all young men. You must understand that a schoolmaster's upstanding character is vital in a free republic where young people are educated in order to someday govern themselves. If you denounce this fanatical sect, we will welcome you back as schoolmaster."

"That I cannot do," Seth said quietly. He turned and went to his desk where he began gathering his things and putting them in his satchel. Every quill stilled as twenty pairs of eyes stared up at him.

"Master, are you leaving?" six-year-old Josiah Wilson spoke without raising his hand.

"Yes, Josiah." Seth looked at the child. He strained to keep his voice from breaking. "Mr. Cheney is your schoolmaster now. Work hard for him."

Joe pushed his chair back. He would leave with his brother, though it broke his heart.

"Joe, stay!" Morris burst out.

"He's my brother," Joseph whispered.

"Two wrongs don't make a right," Rachel said stringently out of the corner of her mouth as she glared at Mr. Risley, her father.

Alexander Cheney stepped toward Joe. "J-Joseph Ellis Johnson, I would be honored if you would stay and continue as my scholar."

Joseph shook his head as he fought tears.

Then Seth spoke. "Joseph, as your schoolmaster I have one more request. Continue here, in school. I beg you."

Joe couldn't stop the sob that wrenched from him.

Seth put his hands on Joe's shoulders and whispered gently, "You love this place. 'If thou follow thy star, thou canst not fail of a glorious haven.'" Seth guided Joseph back down into his chair.

Tears streamed down Joseph's face.

Seth straightened and shouldered his satchel. With dignity, he walked toward the door. Alexander Cheney stepped quickly to Seth, detaining him with an outstretched hand. "Only the brave can forgive. Seth Johnson, forgive me."

Seth turned around and clasped Alexander's hand. "Teach them well," he uttered. Seth looked at his scholars for one last time. Rachel stood on her feet. "Consider our origin," she quoted loudly. Morris's voice joined her, "We were not born to live like brutes, but to follow virtue and knowledge."

With those words ringing in his ears, Seth left the Pomfret schoolhouse. He did not go home that day but walked through the snow to the broken-down solitary hut where he had once taken the Book of Mormon. There he sat longing for the wisdom and faith of his mentor Joseph Brackenbury, whose voice he would not hear again on earth. He thought of the dear students whom he had given his best, whom he would never teach again. He thought of his father's intemperance and his mother's pain. He longed for the touch of Sophia, that gentle love that was beyond his grasp. He prayed but could not overcome the weight of his loss. Seth's chin fell to his chest and he wept, cold and alone, sorrow bowing his gentlemanly frame while snow strained the roof of the solitary hut.

After dinner, it was dark. Julianne pulled on gloves and a man's wool coat. Seth had not come home. No one else seemed much concerned. They figured he had a hard day and was at Lyman's or in Fredonia. But Julianne wasn't satisfied. After Elder Brackenbury's death, she worried about things that used to never bother her. She wanted to know where Seth was.

"Juli, where are you going?" Susan asked her.

"I'm going to find Seth if I can," Julianne said. "Maybe he's back at the schoolhouse getting his things or hiding out in Joel and Annie's old cabin."

"There's a hut in the woods," Susan said. "Seth goes there to pray and study. He's never told anybody, because he likes the privacy. Let's look there first."

Julianne nodded, wondering how many other things quiet Susan knew that no one else had noticed. Though Susan was six years younger than Juli, Susan's height, serious nature, and angular features made it difficult for a stranger to tell which sister was the elder. Susan put a cloak on, while Julianne lit a lantern.

As they walked through the woods, the girls stayed close to each other with Julianne carrying the lantern between them. It was eerily quiet, the world black and white in the snow-covered world. When they neared the hut, Julianne noticed footprints.

"It's Seth," Susan said. "You can tell by the size of the boot."

The young women hurried to the hut. It was eerily dark and quiet. There was no lantern light or fire kindled inside. "If he came here, he's gone now," Juli said shivering.

"The footprints only go in, not out," Susan whispered. Juli handed the lantern to Susan and knocked on the door. "Seth," she called. "Are you in there?"

No voice answered them. With a pounding heart, Julianne pushed the door open. Susan stepped in with the lantern.

They gasped as they saw their brother's form in the shadows. He sat on a chair as if he were asleep with his head resting on an old table. His eyes were closed. Juli ran to him. "Seth, Seth! Are you all right?" she cried. He did not respond. She took one of his hands and rubbed it. "Dear Seth, please, please wake up!"

Susan saw Seth's eyelids flutter. She set the lantern down and knelt down by Seth, taking his other hand in hers. Her heart pounded.

Julianne prayed, "Dear Father in Heaven, help Seth to wake up so that we can get him home." Juli stretched up and put her arms around Seth. "Seth. It's me, Juli. Susie's here too. You must wake up!"

Seth opened his eyes and lifted his head as if it took great effort. Juli rubbed his shoulders. Seth looked down into Susan's eyes. He looked so confused. Susan tried to explain, "Seth, you fell asleep in this cold place."

Seth's dark eyes grilled into Susan's. "It's cold and dark on earth," he whispered. "Susan, only death is warm. What am I to do?"

Susan shuddered as tears coursed down her cheek. "We need you. Mama needs you. The little ones need you." Seth looked from Susan to Julianne.

"You're to come home with us, Seth," Julianne begged. "Please. You could freeze to death here all alone."

Seth nodded, and Susan and Julianne helped him stand.

At four the next morning, Almon and Elder Durfee prepared to leave. Julia fed them a cold breakfast and packed food in their knapsacks. Joel and Julianne came downstairs to bid them farewell.

"Give Annie this letter," Joel told Almon as he handed him an envelope. "Tell her I'll come as soon as I've done all I can to forward the work here."

Almon nodded.

Joel embraced the two men. "God be with you," he said.

Julia hugged Almon as if he were her own son. "Dear Brother Almon," she said. "You will always be welcome at my hearth."

When Julia turned to speak quietly to Elder Durfee and Joel, Almon found he was standing opposite Julianne.

"The house will seem empty without you," Julianne said. "You have been such a friend to us all."

Almon swallowed and stared at her. He drank in her expressive eyes. He clasped her hands and kissed her cheek, "And I shall be empty without you," he said in a rush. Then he turned and followed Edmond Durfee out the door.

Julianne stared after him. From the top of the stairs, Susan watched. There were tears in her eyes. She put her hand to her mouth to keep from crying. Her sister had received the kiss and words she had hoped would be hers. As silent as a shadow, she turned and went back into the bedroom before anyone knew she had ever been there.

Eight days later, it was dusk when Almon arrived in Amherst. His legs felt numb and leaden from walking the two hundred and fifty miles from Pomfret. He had been alone for the last day of the journey because Elder Durfee had gone to Huron County to inform Elizabeth Brackenbury of the tragic loss of her husband and to try and find some way to be of comfort to her.

In the shadowy twilight, as darkness descended, Almon walked past the courthouse and down the icy road to the Johnson cabin. It seemed so long ago since he had heard Parley P. Pratt mock the court's trumped-up charges. It felt as if Julianne were a world away. Anything could happen before he saw her again. When he arrived at the cabin, he knocked on the door.

Annie heard the knock and slowly made her way to answer it. Her baby was due within a month, and she felt heavy and clumsy. On seeing Almon, she cried out. She looked behind him for Joel, but her husband wasn't there.

"I came alone," Almon said quickly. "Joel is well but is still in Pomfret preaching."

Annie nodded and motioned Almon inside out of the cold. She blinked her eyes to hide her tears. Then she turned to Almon with a smile, determined to mask her disappointment.

"Have you come to attend the conference?" Annie asked.

At his confused look, Annie explained that there was to be a conference the next day for the elders at the Carters' home. "The Prophet will be anxious to hear news of the Church in Pomfret," she added.

Sixtus ran out of the bedroom, where he had been playing. He caught sight of Almon and leapt forward, his legs long and clumsy like a colt's. "Almy! Almy!" he shouted. Almon hefted Sixtus and hugged him tightly. Putting him down, Almon caught Annie's eyes, but looked quickly away.

"How is everyone in Pomfret?" Annie almost begged. "You must tell me everything."

"I will tomorrow," Almon said quickly. "But I need to get home now." He knew that he should tell her of Joseph Brackenbury's death, but he just couldn't do it. His mind jumped to Edmund Durfee. How could he ever find words to break such news to Mrs. Brackenbury?

Almon put those thoughts aside and refocused on Annie. He took an envelope out of his pocket and handed it to her.

She saw her name printed on the front in Joel's neat hand. Her heart pounded. "Thank you, Almon!"

Almon nodded stiffly, opened the door, and quickly departed, leaving Annie bewildered by his strange behavior but excited at the news from Joel. She hurriedly opened the envelope. As she read, she rested her free hand on her abdomen as if to protect and comfort her unborn child and herself.

*January 16, 1832*

*Dearest Annie,*

*I fervently pray that this letter finds you and Sixtus in good health. Brother Almon may have already told you the sad news concerning our beloved brother Joseph Brackenbury. It is true. He is dead—that bright and valiant soul who bore testimony with his last breath. His efforts have not been in vain. He baptized Mother and Lyman Sherman first. He opened Seth's mind to the truth. All of my brothers and sisters are converted, though Father won't allow those who have not reached their majority to receive baptism. Your father's heart is softened toward the truth, and he meets with us often. How I wish I could say the same for my own father!*

*My thoughts wander back to the joyous day Brothers Brackenbury and Durfee came to assist us. At that time, regardless of prejudice, there was much inquiring among the people. Then our beloved Brother Brackenbury was taken sick with bilious colic and remained in great distress, which he bore with the fortitude of a saint for almost one week. He expired with an unshaken confidence in the fullness of the gospel which he had preached and a firm hope of a glorious resurrection among the just.*

*The sectarian priests, taking advantage of these circumstances and howling like wolves, have slackened the faith of those who were believing, and the work here seems to have stopped. Will my mother and her children be the only ones who remain firm in their faith? I will stay here for a while longer to see if I can be of any assistance in combating the enemy.*

*I am greatly concerned for Seth. Elder Brackenbury's death dealt him a great blow. To add to Seth's melancholy, two days ago, he was dismissed as teacher of the local school due to his conversion. The morning of his dismissal, he did not come home. It was past ten at night when two of my sisters discovered Seth in an old hut in the woods, nearly frozen. I have never before beheld Seth in such a dejected state. Though he seems well in his mind today, I wish he had a wife such as you to cheer and comfort him. The rest of the family is in good health. Your family also. Nancy is much stronger than when you last saw her.*

*I will come home as soon as I am finished here. David has decided to remain in Pomfret with Mother. Benjamin will come with me and help with spring planting. I long to return to you, to Sixtus, and to that dear little stranger who may even now rest in your arms. Trust in the Lord, my dearest. He will bear thee up. Expect me no later than early Spring.*

*Your affectionate husband,*
*Joel Johnson*

The unborn baby kicked as Annie bit her lip and cried. She hugged the letter to her chest. She couldn't pretend to be cheerful anymore. Joseph Brackenbury was dead, and Joel was so far away. She had no family close by to lean on for comfort. She was so large, uncomfortable, alone, and afraid. But most of all, her heart ached for Betsy Brackenbury and her sons. Why had God deserted them and left them to such grief? Shouldn't faith in God make the world a less dark and menacing place?

"Mama, Mama, why crying? Why?" Sixtus pulled at her skirts. She looked down at her gangly child. He looked up at her, his eyes wide and his expression confused by her tears. She strove to gain control.

"I have a letter from Papa, Sixtus," she said. "He misses you and sends his love." Mechanically, Annie readied Sixtus for bed. As Annie lay next to her slumbering son, she listened to the wind howling at the windows and chimney. The darkness seemed suffocating. Her stomach cramped and the baby kicked. Annie prayed for comfort and relief but felt increasingly nauseous. After what felt like hours, she threw up in the chamber pot. The smell in the room was overwhelming. In the darkness, Annie lifted the pot and felt her way through the cabin to the front door. She opened the door and threw the contents of the pot into the snow. Shaking violently, Annie closed the door. The cold from the wood floor penetrated through her stocking feet. She took her cloak from the rack and huddled it around her. Red ashes from the smoldering fire gleamed in the hearth. With her head reeling from sorrow and sickness, Annie managed to take a candle off the table and light it in the coals. She sat again at the table, her freckled hand shaking as she picked up a quill. Haltingly, she scribbled a few lines to Joel.

*January 24, 1832*

*Dear Husband,*

*I am ill tonight and all alone in the cold and darkness. I try to pray, but the heavens are black around me. Can Brother Brackenbury really be gone? Dead so far away from his home and family? My heart weeps for his wife and sons—to have their terrors come true, to be separated from him whom they love. Joel, I beg you to come home quickly. I am sick and alone. It is so cold. Our babe will come soon, and I fear I cannot endure this birth without you. I don't think our Heavenly Father requires you to be so far away right now when I am in such need. I pray to see your dear face again in this life. I will try to bear up until then.*

*Your Annie*

Two days later, Annie felt slightly better when she awakened. After milking the cow, she washed her face and stoked the fire. She and Sixtus ate cold biscuits for breakfast. They were dipping candles when there was a knock at the door. Annie tied a scarf around her hair before answering it.

When she opened the door, the Prophet and Hyrum Smith stood before her. Annie's color rose. Why was this man of God at her threshold? Did he know she had been ill and weeping for the past two days?

"Sister Johnson." The Prophet smiled and took off his hat, his cheeks reddened by the cold. Annie thought of how hearty he looked, so full of life. Joseph Brackenbury was cold and dead.

"Come in," Annie said.

After stomping snow off their boots, Joseph and Hyrum stepped into the cabin and shut the door behind them, but they did not take off their coats. Sixtus ran over. Hyrum picked him up and tossed him into the air. Joseph Smith looked carefully at Annie Johnson. After an instant, Annie looked down. Under his gaze, she felt that she might weep again. Did she have an endless supply of tears?

Joseph spoke. "Before I left, Emma asked me to stop by and see how you fared. Then yesterday, when Brother Almon informed me of Elder Brackenbury's death, my heart turned to Brother Joel and you. Hyrum and I hastened over this morning. We mourn the loss of such a mighty servant of God. We know that he performed a work on his mission that will last through the ages. His efforts shall bring forth a fruitful bough in Zion. If we could perceive the glorious mansion prepared for him, we would find comfort."

At the feeling in the Prophet's voice, Annie could not stop her tears. He took Annie's hands in his. "Sister Johnson, I promise that your husband will return to you. Until then may the Lord bless and keep you."

"What of Sister Brackenbury?" Annie whispered.

"Elder Durfee arrived this morning and told me that she bears her grief with the faith and patience of a true saint. The Lord Jesus Christ will strengthen Sister Elizabeth and her children. He will bear their sorrow upon His mighty shoulders."

Annie swallowed and nodded. She did not want to cry uncontrollably in front of the Prophet and Brother Hyrum. "Give my love and best wishes to Emma," she said quietly as she blinked back tears.

"I will." Joseph gently let go of her hands. He made eye contact with Hyrum, and Annie knew that they must be off.

Hyrum spoke to Annie. "Our brother Samuel has been called to serve a mission in the eastern country. He will likely pass through Pomfret on his way and could deliver a letter to Brother Joel."

"I have one," Annie said. Then she hesitated. "Are you sure it isn't an inconvenience?"

Hyrum smiled slightly. "Sister Johnson, Brother Almon has already written two letters to Brother Joel's family in Pomfret. He instructed Samuel to take one when he and Brother Hyde leave on their mission. He then asked Lyman Johnson and Orson Pratt, who will follow the same route, to deliver the other. Joseph, here, questioned Brother Almon about his motives. Were the letters written for the benefit of the brothers or sisters in the household? Or for one *sister* in particular?"

Joseph smiled at Annie and continued with the story. "Brother Almon blushed and said it was none of my business. I think we have found a soft spot in young Brother Babbitt's armor."

Annie smiled through her tears. She thought of her sisters-in-law and wondered which Almon was interested in. Then she thought about the letter she had written. "I don't know if my letter is fitting to send," she admitted. "I wrote it in my sorrow."

"I think Brother Joel will find it fitting because it is from you," Hyrum said gently. Still doubtful, Annie went to the table and picked up her letter to Joel. After carefully folding and sealing it, she handed it to Hyrum. A moment later, she sighed as she watched Joseph and Hyrum mount their horses and ride away through the thin winter sunlight. She wondered if it were right of her to send this letter which begged her husband-missionary to come home just when so many others were leaving. But she hadn't the fortitude of Emma Smith nor the faith of Elizabeth Brackenbury. She was simply Annie, Joel's Annie.

Benjamin grimaced from the ache in his weak ankle as he walked a stride behind Joel. He thought of how they had been walking for three days and had covered over one hundred miles. It was early March, and they followed the road near Lake Erie, through the Ohio–Pennsylvania borderlands watered by Conneaut Creek. Joel was pushing hard to get home. A week ago, Samuel Smith had given him a letter from Annie. Ever since the letter, Joel had one thing on his mind—his family in Amherst. Annie was sick and needed him.

Ben knew it was vital that Joel return home quickly, and he was doing his best not to slow him down. Yesterday they had walked through drenching rain. Today, the fog coming off Lake Erie was cold and thick and sliced right through Ben's leg. Joel marched steadily onward, unable in the miserable fog to see the grim pain in his brother's features or the tears in his eyes.

"We'll be at the Rudd homestead before dark. We can spend the night there," Joel commented. "Pa and I walked this way from

Cincinnati when I was your age. It was just a woodland trail then. We camped each night, didn't sleep in a bed once. There was scarcely a settler. We passed through a town that had been burned out by Indians a year before. Saw bones left on the ground. Pa was something then, Ben, a true woodsman. I'll not forget that journey. You should have seen the happy look on Ma's face that June day when we breezed into Pomfret. Her hair was dark as ebony then. Pa swung her around. Ma cried and kissed me. I hadn't seen her for more than a year. I hope my Annie's all right."

Ben didn't respond. It was taking all of his strength to keep going.

Joel turned toward his brother. "How you doing, Ben?"

"My ankle's hurting bad. I can't go much farther tonight."

Joel stopped and took Benjamin's bag of clothes from him. "The leg will feel better tomorrow, after you've rested," he assured as he continued to move steadily forward. "We're nearly there."

Ben couldn't understand why his tall, skinny, eldest brother wasn't coughing anymore, why he seemed to have been granted the strength of Hercules on this journey.

Thirty minutes later, they arrived at the Rudd home. After explaining who they were, they were warmly welcomed into the house. They eagerly consumed large bowls of thick bean soup, and Benjamin went to bed where he slept fitfully. Joel remained in the sitting room talking to Erastus Rudd about the growth of the Church in that area.

Brother Erastus was a tall, broad, loosely built man. His light brown hair was thin and receding. His blue eyes were troubled, and he stroked his wrinkled, clean-shaven chin as he spoke. "Five of us were baptized after Elders Smith and Hyde preached in the Conneaut Center School three weeks ago. But already three have fallen away."

"Why?" Joel asked, shaking his head. "Why would they so quickly abandon their faith?"

"On account of prejudice and lies. That and old Solomon Spaulding's romance novel."

"What?"

"Solomon Spaulding was a neighbor of ours who died in 1816. An old timer from these parts by the name of Nehmiah King heard the elders speak. He's telling people that Hyde preached from Spaulding's manuscript."

Joel's eyes widened as he looked at Brother Rudd. "What was the novel about?"

"It was a romance about a group of Romans whose ship blew to the Americas. Up until the elders came, no one listened much to old Nehmiah's stories. Now everyone is listening. Henry Lake is strutting Nehmiah from farm to farm, saying Joe Smith copied Spaulding's work."

"Can't something be done?"

"I've tried talking to people, Brother Joel. When I was a young fellow, Mr. Spaulding read me some passages from his manuscript. It's a love story—to me as different from the Book of Mormon as night is from day. But people believe what they want to believe."

Joel shook his head. "Satan is unrelenting in his opposition to the work of God." For a moment, Joel stared into the fire. Should he remain here two days and preach on the Sabbath? He thought of how Elder Brackenbury had died without seeing his wife or children again. Joel decided not to alter his course. He would return to Annie as quickly as possible. He looked up at Brother Rudd. "I must travel home in all haste to see to my wife's welfare. Hold to your faith. This work is the great stone that shall roll forth and fill the whole earth. I will pray for you."

"And I for you, Brother Joel. Tell me of this wife you must hurry to."

"Her name is Annie. She is small, cheerful, and lively with hair as bright as copper. Last week, I received a letter from her, and she is in great need."

Erastus Rudd looked at the earnest young man before him. He remembered feeling such passion for his wife as a young man.

"God speed, Brother Johnson. Such a wife is a gift and not to be trifled with."

Annie was nursing her month-old baby daughter while Sixtus played outside. Much had changed since she had written Joel. Elizabeth Brackenbury had come in early February to help her with the birth. They had wept together, and this good woman's faith had nourished Annie. She knew again that God had not forsaken His little flock of Saints.

The morning after the baby had been born, Elizabeth had read aloud to Annie the account of Sariah, the Book of Mormon's faithful matriarch, murmuring when her sons tarried too long in Jerusalem. This account comforted Annie as she strove to forgive herself for her own lack of faith. She had called her baby Sariah from that day forward.

Betsy had left as soon as Annie was on her feet. Since that day, the rhythm of new motherhood and the delicate beauty of her babe had consumed Annie. Although the fog and rain had been unrelenting, she felt herself growing strong once more.

Annie felt the gust of cold air on her back when the door opened. She pulled the blanket over Sariah to protect her from the draft. "Close the door, son," Annie instructed Sixtus without looking up.

"Annie."

Annie turned her head and saw her husband stooping to enter the cabin. His trousers were dirty and he was unshaven. A huge lump moved through Annie's chest and settled in her throat. "You are home," she cried out and began sobbing.

Joel was to her in an instant, his long arms wrapping around her. The babe disengaged and let out a shriek of dismay at the change in her mother's attention. Joel's large hands touched the sides of his baby's head, and Annie saw that he also was crying. They kissed and held each other with the baby between them while Sixtus ran around shouting "Papa's home! Papa's home!"

Benjamin remained outside the door, rubbing his sore ankle with one hand while scraping the mud off his boots with the other. He did not look up until he heard Annie's happy voice gathering him in. "Oh, Benjamin, you are so tall now! How will I ever cook enough to feed you?"

# 12

*Spring is coming, bees are humming*
*In the fragrant air;*
*Birds are singing, bells are ringing,*
*All is bright and fare.*

*Flowers are blooming, and perfuming,*
*Nature all is bright;*
*Tendrils twining, bright sun shining,*
*Shedding golden light.*

—GEORGE W. JOHNSON, FROM "SPRING"

*May 1832*

Susan opened the window in the upstairs bedroom. Sunlight touched the fields and seeped through every nook and cranny of the angled roof. Sue was glad for springtime. The fair weather gave her increased privacy inside the house while most of the family labored outside. It wasn't that Susan didn't love her family. Quite the opposite, she cared about each individual in a way that was steady and observant. Though not overly affectionate, she was unwaveringly loyal. However, the incessant noise and the constant needs of each family member taxed her quiet nature. Susan's soul required time to sit and think each day, to study the shape of things, to observe the patterns of people, nature, and God, to comprehend the tempo of her fears, and to hear the music of her own soul when so many saw her as just another Johnson sister—not as good as Nancy, as vivacious as Juli, or as beautiful as Almera.

For four hours every morning, it was Susan's lot to work the wool fibers into thread. In the corner of the girls' room stood the walking wheel. Susan breathed in the fresh air as she lifted a portion of the clean, carded wool out of the basket. A moment later, she was busy at the wheel, skillfully stepping back and forth, her left hand feeding the wool, her right hand controlling the wheel. The wheel hummed loudly, and the work was tedious. Perhaps the very monotony of the work caused Susan's inner world to deepen, for her thoughts roamed free.

Today, Susan thought of the meadow full of wildflowers where Almera wandered. Then there was the shadowy glade where Joseph searched for herbs. She pictured the sunlit fields where her father and brothers labored and the bridge over the creek where the boys would go at sunset. They would sit on the edge of the bridge, their legs dangling as they fished and swatted at mosquitoes. Yet these joys had little to do with Susan and her daily tasks. They were like slivers of brightness winking through the cracks in the house, glimpses into another world.

As she spun, her mind turned to the words of the Book of Mormon and the rich joy the gospel first brought her. Then Elder Brackenbury had died and joy turned to sorrow. Susan thought of how the missionary's death had affected her father. Since that day, her father had been quiet about Mormonism. He hadn't objected when two missionaries, Gideon Carter and Sylvester Smith, had come to lodge with them. But Susan had noticed the hooded look in his eyes whenever the scriptures were read. She knew his long absences in Fredonia were not just for work but for drink as well. Her father's heart was softened toward his family, not their religion.

Susan's intuitive knowledge was both a gift and a burden. Sue watched Seth do all in his power to hide his troubles from the family. Susan knew how he rubbed his forehead and paused between tasks as if he were lost. Sue understood how he felt. She understood Seth because she was a great deal like him.

The wheel hummed, and Susan's mind wandered away from Seth to the day over three months ago when Almon Babbitt left. She would never forget the razor-sharp pain she felt when she watched him tell Julianne good-bye. Susan didn't speak of him anymore. She did not comment on the letters he sent the family. If only she could forget that he was as vibrant and varied as the whole outdoors, as different from herself as night was from day, as alive and free as her dreams.

Downstairs, Julia kneaded bread, enjoying the fresh May morning. She thought of how her children's faces had lost their pale winter hue. Ezekiel and David, with the help of little George and William, planted and plowed this morning. Seth, Joseph, and Julianne labored, boiling the maple sap in the outdoor summer

kitchen. Mary had taken Esther and Amos to the meadow to pick
strawberries and wildflowers. Susan was upstairs spinning wool.
Almera had just come in from outside and was cleaning in preparation for the Sabbath. For the moment, Julia did not think about
the lesion growing between herself and Ezekiel. Instead, she
sensed the cohesive threads of work binding her family together.

After putting the bread in the oven, Julia's thoughts turned to
tomorrow when she would host the Sabbath meeting in her yard.
Two elders from Amherst, Sylvester Smith and Gideon Carter,
had been staying with them for the past two weeks. They had
traveled throughout Chautauqua County teaching. Julia rejoiced
that the gospel seeds planted by Joseph Brackenbury, which had
lain dormant through the winter following his death, now
sprouted. Ten individuals had already been baptized. Annie's
father was among them. In Jamestown, to Lyman's joy, Doctor
Philastus Hurlbut had joined the Church. Julia knew that the
gospel would go forward and fill the entire earth.

The day lengthened as the sun rose in the sky. In the corn-
field, David plowed while Will rode the mare Katy to steady her.

"I'm hungry," Will complained from his position on Katy's
back.

"Mother will ring the dinner bell soon," David assured him as
he continued to labor with the plow.

"David, someday I'll grow up like you and sweat clear through
my shirt," Will remarked. David chuckled.

"David Johnson." The lyrical sound of a woman's shout startled David. Little Will's head jerked around. David stopped
plowing, shaded his eyes, and squinted in the direction of the
voice.

Hope Randall, a nanny in Judge Houghton's house, walked toward David. She had been coming to the Johnsons' a great deal lately, feigning interest in the Church in order to get close to David. Hope's parents had died when she was a toddler, and she had been raised by the charity of a Christian family in Fredonia. Hope's face was wide and not particularly lovely. She possessed thin, uneven lips and washed-out blue eyes that were deeply set for a woman's. With a willowlike form, she had shoulders rounded slightly as she strolled with her hips leading. As she approached David, Hope leaned slightly to the right, a basket dangling from her arm like an ornament.

David unhooked Katy from the plow and lifted William off the horse. He was pleased to see Hope. He encouraged her fondness for him because he found her form attractive. He knew that he would never marry someone like her, but she brightened his life when so many old friends shunned him because of his religion. Hope sidled up to David. "Away with you. I've a picnic for us."

"Can I come?" William questioned.

"It's a lunch for two, Willie, not three," Hope said breathlessly. "You wouldn't get any food."

The dinner bell rang. "Take Katy to the barn before you go into the house to eat," David instructed his younger brother.

Hope put her arm through David's and led him toward the wild wood. "I came across this old hut in your woods when I took a stroll a few evenings ago," she said.

"You shouldn't stroll in our woods at dusk." David bent a branch back from the path so that Hope could easily enter the woodland. "It would be a shame if we mistook you for a deer."

"So I remind you of a deer," Hope replied.

"More of a wood nymph." David cocked an eyebrow and put his arm around her.

When they came to the hut, Hope coyly pulled at the door. It creaked open. The old shack had been swept and aired out. There was a rug on the dirt floor and bouquets of wildflowers in every corner. A bright cloth covered the small table.

"What happened here?"

"I did this late last night while everyone else slept." Hope laughed at David's surprise.

David shook his head and kissed her forehead. "Who would have thought that such an old, run-down place could look so nice?"

"I did it for you, David—to make you happy."

Hope put her arms around his neck and kissed him. She smelled of maple syrup and wildflowers. Physical longing surged through David. He deepened the kiss as he ran his hands down Hope's back. The dress was smooth against her skin. Hope's hands slid under David's shirt, and she began kneading the muscles of his back as she kissed him.

Every nerve of David's body burned with desire. Yet his mother's teachings reverberated in his mind. He had sisters whose virtue he guarded. He had made personal covenants with God. Sweating, David tore himself away from the girl. His face was flushed as he stumbled toward the door where carved sunlight sliced into the hut.

"You want me, David," Hope cried out fiercely, grabbing his hand, trying to pull him back to her. "You love me!"

David jerked his hand away. "You're wrong, Hope."

Hope's pale eyes bored into his, and her mouth was twisted in pain. "You made me believe you loved me. If you won't have me, then all is lost."

"You are never lost if you trust in God and keep His commandments." David's voice sounded strange to himself. He spoke like someone else—like his mother, Joel, or Seth.

Hope was pleading, begging. "I love you, David. It doesn't matter to me that you're Mormon. I'll never leave you. I'm not a wanton woman, David. I only want to give myself to you so that you'll keep me forever."

"I can't," David whispered.

"You love me!" she cried.

"No," David said. "I'm sorry." He dared not touch her again. Physical desire was a searing fire. He turned from Hope. As he left the hut, he heard the girl's lonely cry of rejection. Kathryn Clay's sobs echoed in his mind. Each woman he touched was injured at his hands.

After walking through the thickest portion of the woods, David headed back to the field. He found his father there and George and Will. George dropped corn seeds into furrows while Ezekiel walked along behind the boy and covered the seeds with soil. Will was busy hooking Katy back up to the plow. Ezekiel looked up as David approached. "At lunch, there were two more mouths to feed. Now four Mormon missionaries are eating at my table instead of two. One is the brother of that Carter fellow. Says he knows you from Amherst."

"Jared Carter?" David asked.

Ezekiel cleared his throat and grunted as he stood up. "Yep. Him and a man named Calvin Stoddard."

"Jared Carter is a good man," David commented. He did not tell his father that he knew of Calvin Stoddard as well. Calvin Stoddard was Joseph Smith's brother-in-law. Don Carlos once told David that Stoddard was skeptical about some principles of the restored gospel. Don Carlos did not trust him completely. On the other hand, David knew that Jared Carter was a man of unwavering faith. David remembered the Sabbath in Amherst when Almon was ill with fever and Jared Carter had administered to him. It seemed like a lifetime ago. Yet that event had triggered

David's desire for Nancy to be healed. David thought about how that hope had been an illusion. And now he had deluded Hope Randall into thinking that he loved her.

David's jaw tensed as these thoughts jumbled in his mind. Ezekiel studied his son's expression. He hadn't approved of the way David had gone off into the woods with the girl who worked for Judge Houghton. "You didn't take advantage of that young girl, did you?"

David's eyes shot to his father's face. "No, sir," he ejected.

Ezekiel went back to work. He believed his son. But that did not erase the fact that Ezekiel would never forget the way his mother had been misused by his father. He would not have a son of his ever shame a woman like that.

David looked away from his father and took a deep breath. He hadn't really told his father the truth. He *had* taken advantage of Hope Randall, though not in the sense Ezekiel was thinking. David had encouraged seeds of love to spring forth in her heart for his own pleasure. Tomorrow was the Sabbath, where he was supposed to renew his baptismal covenants by partaking of the Lord's Supper. In the Book of Mormon, King Benjamin taught that the baptismal covenant meant helping others, mourning with those who mourned, and comforting those who stood in need of comfort. But instead of doing these things, David had caused more pain to a young woman. He was unworthy again. Would he ever be able to overcome temptation and become a man of God?

Ezekiel spoke as he continued to plant the corn. "David, finish plowing this field before you go off preaching with your friends. Will's ready to help."

Will, who was busy swirling patterns in the loose soil with his toe, looked up and grinned. "David, the sweat's all dried up on your shirt now. You better git it wet again." As Will and David began to plow, Will chatted merrily. "Ma gave us bread, cheese, and pie for lunch. What did you and Hope have?"

"Nothing much," David said quickly. For the next three hours, David's stomach twisted in hunger as he shouldered the plow and broke the hard earth. As he worked, he thought of the men of God whom he knew. First, there was Joseph Brackenbury, a man with unwavering commitment who gave his life in service. Next was young Don Carlos Smith, the friend whose goodness was deep and sure. Then there was Jared Carter with his boundless faith, and David's brother-in-law, Lyman Sherman, whose cheerful kindness and depth of testimony shone through his every action. There were his brothers, Joel and Seth, fully committed to the truth. At their head stood the Prophet Joseph Smith, whose faith, courage, intelligence, love, and strength made him worthy to commune with Jehovah. David's back and shoulder muscles bulged as he maneuvered the plow through the hard ground. While he labored, David wondered if he could ever overcome his weaknesses enough to hold the priesthood. Or was he like the one barren apple tree in their orchard that appeared healthy and strong, but because of an inner flaw, never bore fruit?

Early the next morning in the bedroom, Ezekiel sat at the desk and cleaned and polished his gun, knowing all the while that it pained Julia to have him break the Sabbath. His head ached slightly from drinking the night before. This flow of Mormon missionaries staying at his home irked him. He thought of how he only allowed it because Seth had asked him if it was all right. Ezekiel figured Seth had the right to invite guests into his home, considering he was an adult and worked so hard for the family. Besides, if Ezekiel had refused, the missionaries would be staying with Delcena and Lyman. Delcena's health had been frail last winter, and Ezekiel knew that extra guests would cause his daughter additional strain.

Seth came in the room and sat down on the bed. "Pa, I want to talk to you about a couple of things."

"Go ahead." Ezekiel set the gun down and looked at Seth. He knew that this son held the family together. He knew that Seth suffered deeply over Joseph Brackenbury's death and his own dismissal as schoolmaster.

"Pa, David's setting up outside for the Sabbath meeting. I was wondering how you would feel about putting your best clothes on and attending with me. I won't push anything on you."

Ezekiel sighed and ran his finger along the gun's silver trim. He knew that it would mean the world to Seth if he converted to Mormonism. Couldn't his son understand that religion was illusive, that it would let you down in the end? He'd go to the meeting for Seth. Afterward, he'd make it clear once more that he didn't believe it, that he'd never accept it. Why couldn't his family accept him the way he was?

Ezekiel nodded shortly. "I'll go this time, since it's in my own yard."

"Another thing, Pa," Seth went on. "Would you think about traveling to Ohio with me after the haying?" Seth's voice was earnest. "We could stop at Kirtland and meet Joseph Smith. Then on to Amherst to visit Joel, Annie, Ben, and the grandchildren. Perhaps we can bring Ben back home with us."

Ezekiel spoke shortly. "I don't know." He went back to cleaning the dark barrel of his gun.

Seth left the room. Ezekiel remembered the black winter after Nancy's accident and how Seth had gone with him to Cincinnati when Ezekiel could not endure being at home. Maybe Seth needed to get out of Pomfret now to escape the shadows of

Brackenbury's death. Yet the last thing Ezekiel wanted to do was to meet this so-called prophet who had turned his family upside-down. Ezekiel set down his gun. He put on his best clothes—the broadcloth suit he hadn't worn since Delcena's wedding.

Julia stared at Ezekiel when he came out of the room. If he weren't so annoyed, he would have chuckled at his wife's expression. "I'm going to the meeting because Seth asked me to," he said shortly.

The family sat together on a front bench. Ezekiel felt restless and uncomfortable. Gideon Carter spoke about the restoration of the gospel of Jesus Christ. Almost against his will, Ezekiel listened. The talk confused him. For an instant, he almost wanted to believe it was true, that there was a benevolent God in heaven who spoke to men on earth. But that was hogwash. If there were a God, He didn't care about individual men. Men were alone on the earth with just their own strength and each other to lean on.

Next, the elders blessed and passed the sacrament. Ezekiel watched Julia, Seth, Nancy, and Julianne partake of the bread and wine. When it was offered to David, his son shook his head and let the sacrament pass by him. Ezekiel's forehead crinkled. What was going on with David? Did it have anything to do with Hope Randall?

Jared Carter stood to speak. "My brothers and sisters," Carter said. "You have heard this day about Joseph Smith and the restoration of the gospel with all of the blessings of the early Saints. The Latter-day Saints are gathering to Kirtland, Ohio. Some are called to build up Zion in Independence, Missouri. We will become a mighty people. Zion will be redeemed! We have read from the scriptures and felt the Spirit of the Lord change our hearts. Remember the words of the Savior: 'Then said Jesus to those Jews which believed on him, If ye continue in my word, then are ye my disciples indeed; and ye shall know the truth, and the truth shall make you free.' The ancient Church of Christ has been restored. Find freedom through faith in the Lord Jesus. Be free to partake of His healing power, both in body and in spirit. Be free from sin. Have courage. Tomorrow we will leave you as we go forward preaching Christ's gospel to all who will listen. I bid you farewell until we meet again, either in this life or to dwell in the heavens with the Saints of God. In Jesus' name. Amen."

Jared Carter turned to go back to his seat. Just as he was about to sit down, he hesitated and faced the audience once again. His eyes shone with tears as he announced in a loud voice, "The Spirit bids me to say one last thing. I am commanded to tell the members of this congregation that they are confined to a choice. There will be a decision wrought with each of you this day that has the power to change the eternal worlds. The largest part of this congregation will resolve to serve the Lord and seek for truth."

Ezekiel glanced at his wife and saw that she was crying. The words Jared Carter said about a choice had gotten to her. A lead weight settled in the pit of Ezekiel's stomach. What was Julia wrestling with? Was she thinking of leaving him and taking the children to Kirtland or to that place in Missouri the Mormons called Zion? There was one decision Ezekiel had made long ago. He would not allow his family to split apart. He would not allow them to leave him.

The next evening after supper, Julia and her older adult children sat at the table together. It was a rare quiet time in which they could meet together for a family counsel. Joe was outside playing games in the yard with the young children. The missionaries were proselyting. Ezekiel was at the tavern.

"Seth," Nancy asked, "did you speak to Father about visiting Kirtland?"

Seth sighed deeply. "Yes. I asked him to go to Ohio with me after we get the hay in. I suggested we stop by Kirtland to meet the Prophet and then go on to Joel's. Pa didn't answer me one way or the other."

"But he didn't refuse," Julianne interjected hopefully. "I think Papa has softened. Think of how he came to the Sabbath meeting. There is hope that he will be redeemed from intemperance and will embrace the gospel. Perhaps we will someday gather with the Saints after all."

Susan shook her head. "Papa hasn't softened enough to consent to my baptism, or Almera's, or Ben's, or Joe's. If he won't let us join the Church, he won't agree to move to Ohio and gather with the Saints."

"We mustn't give up on Father," Juli insisted. "After he meets Joseph Smith, his heart might change."

"If he agrees to meet the Prophet," Susan said doubtfully.

"Oh, I wish we could leave this town now," Almera burst out. "We are so alone."

Julia looked at Almera, her eyes full of concern. Since the breakup with Elijah, Almera seemed nervous and dissatisfied. "The gospel is spreading," Julia encouraged. "The missionaries are teaching some of our neighbors. There is a congregation of Saints in Jamestown now."

"And they shall gather in Kirtland and leave us here alone," Almera exhaled.

Julia felt tears begin to pool in her eyes. Almera's outburst struck home. Julia was deeply worried about raising her children away from the body of the Church. Her daughters had no marriage prospects. Her Joseph already had so many questions. They had all suffered abuse and abandonment at the hands of their neighbors. The thought that they might never gather with the Saints lay heavily on her heart. She knew that Delcena and

Lyman would follow the Prophet, and Joel and Annie as well. Would the rest of them be left behind? Julia prayed constantly that Ezekiel's heart would be softened, that he would stop drinking, that they might gather with the Saints as a family. But what if Ezekiel would not change? Her greatest fear was losing her children from the kingdom of God. This could so easily happen if they were not with the body of Saints. She blinked back the tears and spoke to those around her. "My deepest hope is that someday we will all, as a family, live in Zion together."

David looked away from his mother and stared at his hands. He had washed them before dinner, but the dirt from the fields never came completely off. Would he ever be worthy to walk the streets of Zion? That city was reserved for the pure in heart.

Seth nervously tapped his fingers. If his father refused to move, what would become of his mother, of his younger brothers and sisters? There was such darkness in the world. Hope on earth was so fleeting.

"Seth and David," Julia said as a tear stole down her cheek. "Have you thought of going ahead to Kirtland and obtaining inheritances from the Prophet? Your brothers and sisters could move there with you as they come of age. Julianne might go now and keep house for you."

Seth looked up at his mother and frowned. "But what of you and Nancy?"

Julia did not respond.

Seth looked over at Almera and Susan. There was color in Almera's cheeks. His sister felt hope at the thought of moving to Kirtland. Susan stared at the table, her black eyes unreadable. Seth's eyes met Nancy's and Julianne's. "What do you think?"

Nancy shrugged. "I don't know. We must pray and ask the Lord's guidance. I only know that we cannot leave Father alone. It would break his heart."

Julianne spoke. "Maybe Father's heart will change if he goes with Seth to meet the Prophet."

Seth thought of his young siblings outside. How could he move to Kirtland and leave them without a brother's guidance during these formative years? They might not desire to join him when they came of age. And what of his mother? How could he leave her alone with an intemperate husband? If Seth left, the family that he had held together would be split asunder. But if he did not go to Zion and invite them to follow, what would become of them? Would they become like the seeds tossed to the wayside, which never took root? Seth felt unutterably weary. These decisions meant eternal life or death. He could scarcely bear their weight. He had to take his father to meet the Prophet.

On an evening later in the week, Julianne sought out Susan. Her younger sister had seemed so solitary lately. Julianne found Susan alone in the girls' room, sitting on the floor and brushing out her long, dark hair.

"Let me," Juli said as she took the brush from her sister and sat down on the bed. Susan rested her head on Juli's lap while Julianne brushed her hair. The feel of the brush on her scalp was luxurious. She closed her eyes, deeply relaxed.

Julianne spoke. "Seth told Mother that he has decided to visit Ohio after the haying, whether or not Pa wants to go. Seth is determined to meet the Prophet and seek his counsel for our family."

"Seth shouldn't go alone," Susan said as she opened her eyes.

"He's a grown man, Susie," Juli said.

"But if he travels by foot, it could be dangerous."

"Perhaps Papa will go with him."

"Or Lyman. He is anxious to gather with the Saints."

"Can you imagine meeting Joseph Smith?" Juli mused. "Oh, Sue, I wonder if that day will ever come."

Susan spoke. "I wish I could go to Kirtland with Seth."

Juli smiled whimsically at the thought. "The two of us should accompany Seth. We would have such a jolly time and make our brother smile. That would be a feat these days."

"Juli," Sue stated seriously, feeling as if she were the elder sister, "Mother couldn't get along with both of us gone. Almera hasn't your patience with the little ones."

"Then it is settled. You must go, Susie. You are far too pale, all dark eyes and dark hair. The journey would get you outside and bring some color to your cheeks."

Julianne continued to brush Susan's hair. "But what about Almera?" Susan questioned. "A trip would do her good."

Juli sighed and hugged Sue's shoulders. "Almera pines so much for Elijah Handy. We'll encourage her to go as well. But Sue, you must go. You admire Almon Babbitt, and he is in Amherst."

Susan felt suddenly cold. "He does not admire me," she said simply.

"That's not true, Susie." Julianne began plaiting Susan's hair. "Almon admires all of us. Remember how he told Ben that we are the loveliest sisters in the world."

"Juli," Susan's voice was low and serious. "I saw Almon say good-bye to you. I believe Almon loves you."

Julianne's hands stilled. "I don't think so, Susie. I think he feels the same way about all of us. I am much older than him."

"But when you are sixty and he is fifty-five, no one will know the difference," Susan said seriously.

Juli laughed at the image. "Oh, Susie, let's not talk about Almon Babbitt anymore. I want you to go on this journey. There is laughter and exploration out there of which you need a part.

And it would be good for Seth. He is so turned inside himself, he talks to you and Nancy more than to the rest of us."

Susan turned to look her sister in the eye. "I would go with Seth, Juli. But not to see Almon Babbitt. Could you ever love Almon?"

Julianne looked down at her hands, away from Susan's dark and delving eyes. "I don't know, Susie. I would have to know that you did not love him. He would have to grow up a great deal." Suddenly Juli laughed at herself. "But by the time Almon grew up, I would be a very old maid, and he would no longer want me. That is if he ever wanted me to begin with."

Susan did not laugh. "Juli, I wish that I were more like you. I am so serious and shy. Men don't like that."

Julianne took out a handkerchief and blew her nose. "Don't say that, Susie. You are God's masterpiece."

"No," Susan said, "I am God's handmaid. But I should like very much to journey with Seth and meet the Prophet."

Julianne hugged Susan again. "Then I will do all I can to convince Mother, Father, and Seth that you must go to Ohio. You are wise and realistic, Susie. Someday, a man will love you for that. Just like we do."

The next morning, David watched from the woodpile as the four missionaries bid his mother good-bye and left the house. After they had walked about fifty yards, David dropped the ax and sprinted over to them. The men stopped when David caught up. David faced them with his shirtsleeves rolled up and his hands rested squarely on his hips. David's eyes blazed golden in the early morning sun, and his handsome features bore a look of determination. "Brethren," David said, "I must speak to you before you leave. I am dissatisfied with my former baptism. Brother Sylvester, you remember that when Edson Fuller baptized me, he was strange and angry that day. He didn't have the Holy Spirit with him."

Sylvester Smith nodded. "That's true. A short time later, Edson Fuller was cut off from the Church."

"Then my baptism might not be valid. I must be baptized again."

"But Brother David," Gideon Carter counseled, "that doesn't mean that your baptism was not recorded in heaven. Edson Fuller held the priesthood at the time, and Heavenly Father knows of your faith and of the intents of your heart."

David's hands dropped to his side. "There is another reason as well. I have not lived worthy of the communion of the sacrament. I desire to be baptized again in order to recommit my life to the Lord and to know that my sins are forgiven. I shall do all in my power not to repeat them."

Gideon Carter gazed for a long moment at David. Then he slowly turned to his fellow missionaries. "I have never experienced or heard of a case like this before. Have any of you brethren?"

The three men shook their heads. David's heart beat quickly. He felt uncomfortable and self-conscious.

Jared Carter looked over at David. He put his arm around David's shoulders to reassure him. Then he spoke. "I think we should pray and ask Heavenly Father what we should do. David, why don't you wait here by the woodpile while the four of us retire to the woods to pray?"

David nodded. He sat down on a log and nervously chewed on a piece of grass while he waited for the elders to come back. Last night when he had prayed, he had felt no peace until the thought came to him that he needed to be baptized again. By doing so, he would show his commitment to God and know that his soul was clean and that he could follow his resolve to serve others rather than injure them. After that thought, sleep had come quickly. But had he erred in this desire for rebaptism? Were the heavens closed against him?

Ten minutes later, the missionaries returned to David. Jared Carter smiled at him. "We haven't received the answer that you must be baptized again to belong to the kingdom of God. The only answer we have received is to leave this up to you."

A tremendous sigh escaped David. Then he grinned. "Then let's get on with it. I will be baptized."

The men walked together to the part of Canadaway Creek that had been dammed for baptisms. Jared Carter and David Johnson took off their boots. They walked out into the water, feeling the mud between their toes. Jared Carter raised his hand to the square and spoke to heaven as he said the words of the ordinance. "David Johnson, as an elder in the Church of Christ, I baptize you in the name of the Father, and of the Son, and of the Holy Ghost. Amen."

David Johnson went down into the water as shafts of sunlight beamed through the trees. He rose again with a look of great joy. "I feel like a new man," David proclaimed. "Clean and renewed by my Heavenly Father through the grace of His Son, Jesus Christ."

Jared Carter embraced him. "Young Brother David, your baptism is recorded in Heaven, and the Holy Spirit rests mightily upon you. You shall be a great man in the kingdom of God."

The two men left the creek and joined the other missionaries, who vigorously shook hands with David in congratulations. Jared Carter shook his feet dry and put his boots back on.

David grinned. "Brother Jared, would you like to change into a pair of my dry clothes before you leave on your journey?"

"Certainly not," Jared Carter responded. "The sun is out, and I shall dry soon enough."

With that, the four men picked up their knapsacks and went on their way toward the east. After watching them walk away, David turned and ran joyously toward the house, anxious to tell Nancy about this latter-day miracle. He, David Johnson, was born again and forgiven of his sins.

## 13

Since, Lord, Thou hast the truth restored,
Through Joseph, in my youth,
I've sought to live by every word
Proceeding from Thy mouth.

While sitting by him, day or night,
The words of life to hear,
My heart was filled with love and light,
Devoid of doubt and fear.

I knew that every word was true,
Through Thy sweet voice to me;
To all this fact I'd bring to view,
That dwell on land or sea.

—JOEL H. JOHNSON

*August 1832*

Seth's hands clenched as he surveyed the fields. Yet his tension had nothing to do with the crops. The wheat and corn were coming along nicely. The hay was in. The air was fresh and humid following the afternoon cloudburst. All was in order for the trip to Ohio. Yet this trip was the source of Seth's anxiety. Seth looked up at the sky, at the lowering sun, at the clouds, puffy above him but constricting into tighter shapes at the horizon line. The sky did not feel endless to Seth, but like a dome overhead enclosing his world, a barrier between himself and eternity. All of Seth's dreams were focused into one final hope—that his father's heart would change when he met the Prophet.

Seth thought of how they were to leave for Ohio tomorrow, of how his father had grudgingly agreed to stop by Kirtland on the way to Joel's home in Amherst. Almera and Susan were traveling with them. The dinner horn blew, and Seth turned toward the house.

Inside, Mary, Susan, and Almera busily set the food on the table. The children each found a place along the side benches. Lyman, who had spent the day helping David and Seth rake the remaining hay, was the sole dinner guest. Ezekiel sat at the head of the table with Lyman and Seth flanking each side of him. Julia's place was at the opposite end. As the chicken, squash, and bread were passed around, Lyman addressed Ezekiel, "I'm going to Ohio with you after all."

This statement caught Ezekiel off guard. Delcena was in her third trimester of pregnancy and had not been well. Originally, Lyman had hesitated leaving her. Lyman continued, "My cousin, Philastus Hurlbut, will be here in the morning. We'll travel with you to Kirtland and then head back home on foot through Erie County, where my mother and sisters are staying with some Hurlbut relatives."

Susan glanced at Almera and saw her color rise as she tensed. Would she ever get over her fear of Hurlbut? Julia spoke to Lyman. "Is Delcena feeling well now?"

Lyman shrugged and shook his head. His eyes were worried. "No. Could you look after her while I'm gone?"

Ezekiel interrupted his wife's response. He snapped at Lyman. "Why are you traipsing off to Ohio? My daughter is sick, has two little ones, and is with child."

Lyman looked steadily at his father-in-law. "Father Johnson, Delcena has asked me to go. We hope to move to Kirtland within a year and gather with the Saints. My mother and sisters will come as well. Delcena wants me to go now, before the baby comes, in order to find a home for us. We have prayed a great deal about this and feel it is the right way."

Ezekiel frowned. The thought of Delcena and his granddaughters moving away bothered him. If only the Mormons had never come. He wasn't looking forward to traveling with Philastus Hurlbut either. "Do what you wish, Lyman. You and Seth go meet your prophet. But I won't leave my girl alone in her condition. I'll stay with Delcena and run your farm. David can take over here."

Julia spoke. "Years ago, you traveled to Cincinnati shortly after we moved to Pomfret. You left me in a new place with six young children. I was with child. Susan was born while you were gone. Perhaps you are being too hard on Lyman."

Ezekiel glared at his wife. "You were hearty, not delicate like Delcena. Joel was in Cincinnati and needed to be brought home. You know that."

David entered the conversation. "Pa, we can manage here. Mother, Julianne, and I will help Delcena."

Ezekiel recoiled as he whirled toward David. "You three will have your hands full with Seth, Almera, and Susan gone. I'll stay."

David's facial muscles tensed, but he remained silent.

"Pa," Seth spoke carefully. His hopes for his family were like a piece of glass about to shatter. "It is my deepest wish that you travel with me. Benjamin will be sorely disappointed if you don't visit him."

Ezekiel's eyes focused on Seth, and his brow furrowed. Lyman exhaled a quick breath. "Perhaps I should stay home, like originally planned."

Ezekiel grunted. "Perhaps we shouldn't stop in Kirtland at all, but go straight to Amherst to visit Joel and Ben."

Julia shook her head. "Ezekiel, you promised to visit Kirtland with Seth. Lyman should be allowed to make his own decision."

Ezekiel's face reddened. His wife was always contradicting him! Almera stood up. Her voice was high with emotion. There were circles of red on each cheek. "Stop it, all of you. I beg you. I will stay with Delcena."

"But Almera," Nancy said, "you wanted so to visit Ohio."

Almera shook her head and spoke quickly, her words tumbling out. "I only wanted a change. Staying with Delcie would be that. We will have a quiet time with the little girls. I can easily feed Lyman's stock. If anything goes wrong, I can go get help."

Ezekiel looked at Almera, his beautiful girl whose eyes always told her emotions.

"Please, Papa," Almera begged. "I will be a great help to Delcena."

Ezekiel looked from Almera to Seth.

"Then will you come with me as you promised, Father?" Seth asked. "Can you put your mind at rest concerning Delcena?"

Ezekiel pushed his chair back from the table and stood up. A mirthless laugh escaped him, and his voice was sarcastic. "It doesn't appear I have much choice, as I gave my word. I'm going out for a while. We'll leave tomorrow morning when Hurlbut gets here."

While the dishes were being cleared, Susan pulled Almera aside and whispered, "Why did you offer to stay with Delcena? Pa might have come around. Philastus Hurlbut won't bother you with Pa and Seth near."

Almera's eyes swam with frustrated tears as she gripped Susan's arm. "Susie, I can't bear him. When Hurlbut was here last month, he asked delving questions about my breakup with Elijah. He looked at me so pompously, like he figured he could read my mind. I can't bear him! Perhaps he has repented, but I'm afraid whenever he is near."

Susan nodded at her sister and looked away. Her eyes clouded. She had looked forward to Almera's companionship. Susan headed out of the kitchen and toward the stairs.

"Susan, where are you going?" Julia called from the sink. The dishes weren't finished.

Susan stopped halfway up the stairs and turned around. "To pack for the journey, Mother, if you can spare me?" she answered.

"With Almera staying with Delcena, you will be the only woman traveling with a group of men."

"I know, Mama. I don't mind," Susan lied.

"But I mind, Susan. It isn't proper."

Susan felt as if her throat were constricting. She gulped. "Mama, I must go. I beg you," Susan whispered. Susan had not realized, until she feared it would be taken away from her, how desperately she wanted this trip.

Seth looked up from the small table in the corner where he sat reading a copy of recent revelations that Joel had sent him. "I will watch over her, Mother. Let Susie come."

Susan's eyes met Seth's, and she hoped he saw the gratitude in them. Julia sighed. This daughter was so quiet. Usually, it was difficult knowing what was going on inside of her. She clearly had her heart set on this journey. "Go child, but stay near Seth in

Kirtland," she advised. "When you get to Amherst, I'm sure Annie will be glad to have help with cooking and tending the children."

"Thank you, Mum," Susan whispered. She did not run and hug her mother as Juli or Almera would have. Susan breathed a deep sigh of relief and continued up the stairs. From the top of the stairs, she looked down at Seth. His head was bent over his studies once more. "Thank you, dear brother," she whispered.

In the tavern, Ezekiel sat at a table alone, moodily drinking a glass of brandy. He knew that to unify his family, he must either accept Mormonism or find a way to get his wife and children away from it. Neither seemed possible.

Hope Randall entered the tavern. She wore a cloak around her, even though it was summer. The hood shaded her features. In the dim light, her eyes focused on Ezekiel Johnson. Hoping that no one would recognize her, she quickly slipped to his table.

"Mr. Johnson," she whispered, "meet me in the woods behind the mill in fifteen minutes. I need to speak to you alone about David." Then she was gone. For an instant, Ezekiel wondered whether she had even been there at all.

It was twilight when Ezekiel walked out of the tavern. He glanced at the cemetery on the rise where Joseph Brackenbury was buried. He walked behind the tavern and past the back of the post office. The gristmill loomed before him, the large wheel powered by Canadaway Creek. He heard Hope Randall's voice from within the trees that flanked the waterway, "Follow me, Mr. Johnson."

He followed the girl down a narrow path running parallel along the east bank of the creek. After they had gone nearly a mile, she stopped. They stood near the shore of Canadaway Creek, across from Ezekiel's property. The girl's shoulders were bowed, and she focused on the black water as she spoke. "Mr. Johnson, I am with child."

Ezekiel's heart pounded. He exhaled sharply as his fists clenched. "David will marry you, Miss. I'll see to it."

Hope's head came up swiftly, and she stared at Ezekiel. In the twilight, her face looked gray. The lines of her cheekbones were sharp with anguish and her eyes were destitute. It sickened Ezekiel to think that his son was to blame.

"Don't you know your own son? This is not David's child," she whispered, shrinking back as if she were afraid the man would strike her. Hope's voice crescendoed. "A man used me against my will, Mr. Johnson. When I suspected my condition, I tried to seduce David, knowing that he would marry me if he thought the child were his. But he would not have me. David is too Mormon. Too good."

Relief and bitterness rose in Ezekiel—relief that his son had not used the girl so, bitterness toward an unknown man's cruelty, the woman's weakness, and the unborn child's fate. "Who is this brute? He will pay."

"If I told, it would be so much worse," Hope moaned.

"Does David know you are with child?" Ezekiel questioned.

Hope looked down and shook her head. "No, sir."

As Ezekiel focused on Hope's form in the gathering darkness, images rose before his mind. The angle at which Hope held her head reminded Ezekiel of his Susie, the shape of her arm of Julianne, the sorrow in her voice of Almera, her utter helplessness in the wake of fate of his beloved Nancy. Ezekiel put his hand to his head. He felt very old. This young woman was without a father or brothers to protect her. She was like his mother. Ezekiel shuddered. His voice softened. "Tell my son your situation, that a man has forced you. If David loves you, he will marry you and raise the child."

Hope shook her head. Her voice quavered. "David does not love me. I know that now."

"What can I do for you, child? Do you want money or my protection?"

Hope took a shuddering breath and wiped her eyes with her sleeve. She straightened and once again looked at the man before her. Ezekiel saw strength in her, defiance against the shame that awaited her. "No, thank you, Mr. Johnson. I've taken care of things. I'm going away tonight. A Quaker friend will help me travel east. She has found a place for me to stay until the baby is born. Then I can get a job working in the textile mills. I brought you here because I fear for David. If Judge Houghton hears of my pregnancy, it will go hard for David. There are evil men who would delight in punishing a Mormon for fathering an unholy child. It would justify their cruelty. But David is not the father. That is the truth."

Ezekiel looked at the girl with compassion in his eyes. "What will become of you and your little one?"

"I don't know," Hope whispered.

"Remember the babe's innocence," Ezekiel said with feeling. "Never allow any man to treat this child harshly. Promise me."

Hope was taken back by the intensity of Ezekiel's voice. "Why does my child matter to you, Mr. Johnson?"

Ezekiel did not answer. He took thirty dollars out of his pocket and offered it to Hope. She shook her head and turned away. "I'm not asking for charity."

"It is payment of a debt," Ezekiel said steadily. "A man once helped me when I was young." He gently opened the girl's hand, put the money in, and closed her fingers around it. For an instant, he held the girl's hand tenderly in both of his, as if she were his own daughter. "If you or your child are in need, write to me. You have a friend here in Pomfret."

"Mr. Johnson, why are you so kind to me?"

Ezekiel did not answer. He patted the girl's hand once more.

Hope was dumbfounded. "I told you that I tried to seduce your son to force him to marry me. You offer me your friendship and money. Are you a lunatic or an angel from heaven?"

Ezekiel Johnson laughed mirthlessly at her forthrightness. "Lunatic, Miss Randall. I don't believe in angels or God. I'm no candidate for heaven."

Hope Randall looked directly into Ezekiel Johnson's eyes. "You are wrong, sir. In meeting a man so kind as you, I can imagine for the first time a loving Heavenly Father." With those words, Hope Randall slipped into the woods once more, leaving Ezekiel standing by the creek where his wife had been baptized, haunted by the words of Hope Randall. If this young woman, who had been used so cruelly, could imagine a kind God, why couldn't he?

Susan stood next to Seth on the steamer. She gripped the railing as the vessel chugged through Lake Erie. The sky was a pale summer blue, and she felt sticky from the humidity. The lake was so large that she couldn't see the opposite shoreline. She wondered if this trip on Lake Erie felt much like sailing on the ocean. There was a strange sense of both freedom and vulnerability. She'd wondered if she would ever feel the spray of the salty sea or see those giant waves. Yet Lake Erie's waves were enough for her.

Philastus Hurlbut walked over and joined them. He glanced at Susan. She continued to stare out at the water and sky. Hurlbut slapped Seth on the back. "It is amazing how the steamboat has changed the world. Decades ago, who could have imagined that travel would become so quick and convenient? Lyman tells me this came about to further the spread of the gospel. What do you think, Seth? Is our Heavenly Father so intimately engaged in every part of human affairs? Does He inspire the heathen to invent things for the good of His Saints?"

For Seth, it took a visible effort to take his mind off of his own thoughts and attend to Philastus Hurlbut. Seth begged Hurlbut's pardon and asked him to repeat his question. After Hurlbut did so, Seth spoke. "I confess I haven't thought much on that subject. I suppose any invention by man could be used for either good or evil. Perhaps in the end, God will consecrate all efforts toward His divine will."

"But can he consecrate our prayers for the good of others? If we pray for others, how can our prayers be answered when each man has his own agency? It seems our prayers for people other than ourselves are largely a waste of time. Take your prayers for your father as an example."

Susan turned her head and stared at Philastus Hurlbut. This time he did not look her way. She thought of how arrogant his eyes were.

Seth spoke. "No prayer is wasted. I have prayed long for my father. He has agreed to come and meet the Prophet."

"With all due respect to your family," Hurlbut said, "I cannot imagine that your father will ever change. I have known men like him. Your father is not of the temperament to stop drinking, to believe in God, or to allow his family to gather with the Saints. His heart is set against the gospel. Meeting Joseph Smith won't change that. If you gather with the Saints, he will be left behind. I see no other possibility."

Seth did not answer but simply stared out at the water they passed through. The boat moved steadily forward, leaving empty space and distance behind them, like the onward beat of time.

Hurlbut spoke again, his voice dripping compassion. "Dear fellow, I hope I haven't offended you. Your love for your father does you credit. But my point of view is more realistic and thus enlightening. Joseph Smith is a seer, not a magician."

"No offense taken," Seth said quickly.

Susan spoke, determined to change the topic. "Dr. Hurlbut, you must tell Lyman's sister Electa hello from me when you visit the borderlands on your way home."

"Why Miss Susan, you have a voice! I don't believe I've ever heard it before. To what do I owe this singular pleasure?"

Susan felt her cheeks grow hot and beads of sweat trickle down her temple.

Hurlbut continued, "But let me address your comment. I will be delighted to tell sweet Electa hello from you."

A few moments later, Hurlbut left. Susan was troubled by Seth's look. It was as if his dark eyes burned a hole in the water. "Don't listen to him, Seth," she said quietly.

"If he's right, Susie," Seth's voice was low and flat, "then our hopes are ashes. How will our family survive spiritually if we don't gather with the Saints? It is vital that Father accept the gospel and be redeemed from intemperance."

The next day in Kirtland, Ohio, at the Newel Whitney Store, Joseph Smith's face broke into a broad smile as he shook Ezekiel's hand. "Mr. Johnson, your sons are extraordinary men. David and my youngest brother, Don Carlos, are great friends. Joel Johnson is as hard working, intelligent, and compassionate as any man I have met. And young Almon Babbitt never ceases singing the praises of the entire family. May God bless you for raising such fine children."

"It's my wife's doing, not mine."

Joseph grinned. "Brother Almon tells me that your wife is an extraordinary mother. And I have reason to believe that you are an honest, hard-working father. Your children are doubly blessed."

"Thank you," Ezekiel muttered.

The young prophet turned and introduced himself to Seth, Susan, Lyman, and Philastus. Ezekiel remained quiet and observant. He was taken aback by Joseph Smith. He had expected to find a man as full of himself as Hurlbut and the other preachers he knew. But there was honesty and kindness in Smith's look. He seemed genuinely interested in each individual. His facial expressions were real, not feigned. Furthermore, Ezekiel hadn't realized that Joseph Smith was so young, about the same age as Seth.

Joseph Smith turned back to Ezekiel. His voice was quiet and steady. "Mr. Johnson, I realize that you are not a member of the Church. Do you have any questions that I might answer?"

Ezekiel exhaled a quick breath through his nostrils. "You seem honest enough, Mr. Smith, but I don't believe in angels and visitations from God. Joseph Brackenbury died in my home. It broke my family's heart. I built the man's coffin. Some say he was poisoned. It seems that a real prophet would foresee things like that and stop them from happening."

Seth felt both embarrassed and pained by his father's comment. Ezekiel did not turn his eyes away from Joseph's face. Deep thought replaced the former cheerful, friendly look in the Prophet's eyes. "Mr. Johnson," Joseph said. "I, too, justly mourn the loss of Elder Brackenbury. He was a fine man of talent and wisdom. He was a great strength to the Church. I don't know why God takes some of His valiant servants and leaves other to labor on. When Newel Whitney and I were traveling back from Missouri in June, I was poisoned. Newel laid his hands on my head, and I was well immediately."

Ezekiel stared at the Prophet and asked bluntly, "Do you suppose that your life is more important to God than Joseph Brackenbury's? Is that why you think you were spared?" There was bitterness in Ezekiel's voice. Philastus nudged Seth.

Lyman pushed up his glasses. "Father Johnson, I don't think that such a young church could survive without its Prophet. Though I grieve for Elder Brackenbury, I thank my Heavenly Father that Brother Joseph was spared."

Joseph looked at Lyman, then back at Ezekiel. There was grief in his voice. "I know that I am not individually necessary for God's plan to go forward. He has told me that if I fall, someone will be raised up to take my place. I have been spared from death, but God has not seen fit to spare me from sorrow. A few months ago, a mob, led by apostates, attacked the home I was staying in. They dragged me out of the room where my wife and I were caring for our twin babes who were ill with measles. Out in the yard, Elder Rigdon was beaten senseless. I was stripped, abused, tarred, and feathered. Elder Rigdon's skull was severely injured, and he was out of his mind for some time afterward. As a result of exposure from that night, my little boy contracted a severe cold. I laid my hands on his head, hoping he would be healed, but our small son died a few days later. Out of the five children who have come to my wife and me, only our little girl is left.

"My faith was tried like yours. Why didn't a miracle occur for the babe I love? For my wife whose heart was broken and broken again? I don't know all things. But Mr. Johnson, there are some things I do know. The Church of Christ has been restored to earth. I have been instructed by the Father and the Son to organize it. The Book of Mormon was translated from golden plates by the gift and power of God. The priesthood was restored by John the Baptist and the apostles Peter, James, and John. I felt the hands of those messengers on my head. I know these things to be true. God knows it. And yet the world asks me to deny what I have actually seen and experienced. I cannot do it, even if my family suffers, even if my life is sought on every hand. I cannot do it, neither dare I do it. I can only go on and work to fulfill the mission God has given me."

Ezekiel Johnson gaped at Joseph Smith. If he sensed anything about the measure of this man, he sensed one thing—that Joseph Smith was not a liar. Could this comely young man be mad? He did not seem so. Was it possible that he was telling the truth? "Mr. Smith," Ezekiel said, "I apologize for speaking harshly."

"You were honest, not harsh," the Prophet said with a sad smile. "Mr. Johnson, unbelief is a heavy burden. One I wish I could lift from your shoulders."

Ezekiel and Joseph Smith studied each other. There was no sarcasm or contempt or animosity in either man's eyes, but instead some level of understanding. In their short interchange, a link had been forged. "Mr. Smith," Ezekiel said, "I think your shoulders have enough burdens to carry without me adding another one. May you prosper."

"And may God bless you, Mr. Johnson."

At six o'clock that evening, following an early supper at the inn, the four men gathered in one of the two rooms they had rented. Susan was in the other room resting. Lyman and Philastus sat on the bed with their backs against the wall. Seth stretched out on the floor. Ezekiel sat at the desk, drumming his fingers restlessly. Two small windows were open, allowing a cross breeze to break the heat. A handful of flies buzzed around the room.

The newspaper crinkled aloud as Lyman opened the first issue of the Church's publication, *The Evening and Morning Star.* Earlier that afternoon, while Ezekiel had purchased a few supplies at the Whitney Store, the Prophet had pulled Seth and Lyman aside and given them the paper. "We received the first copy from Independence last month," Joseph had explained with a warm smile. "Oh, my friends, what joy that our little band of brethren has become so large and grown so strong to be able to issue a paper of our own. It contains revelations and information that gratify and enlighten the humble followers of truth. Enjoy."

Philastus Hurlbut yawned, and his eyes were half closed as Lyman began reading out loud. Seth's brow furrowed in concentration as he listened intently to every word. Ezekiel continued to tap his fingers.

Lyman's voice was calm and rich with feeling: "With the help of God, the first number of *The Evening and Morning Star* comes to the world for the objects specified in its prospectus, which was published last winter. That we should now recapitulate some of is leading objects, and briefly add a few remarks, will naturally be expected; and we cheerfully do say that this generation may know—

"That *The Star* comes in these last days as the friend of man, to persuade him to turn to God and live, before the great and terrible day of the Lord sweeps the earth of its wickedness; . . .

"That it comes to declare that goodness consists in doing good, not merely in preaching it;

"That it comes to show that all men's religion is vain without charity;

"That it comes to open the way for Zion to rise and put on her beautiful garments and become the glory of the earth. . . .

"That there may be errors both in us and in the paper, we readily admit, but we mean to grow better, till from little children, we all come into the unity of the faith and of the knowledge of the Son of God, unto a perfect man, unto the measure of the stature of the fullness of Christ, which we pray may be the happy lot of thousands, before He comes with the hundred and forty and four thousand that are without guile."

Ezekiel stood up, and Lyman stopped reading. Ezekiel turned to look at Seth. "I need some air. I'm going on a walk."

"I'll go with you, Pa," Seth offered. He pulled himself up from the floor. Seth moved with the leanness and grace of a gentleman.

Ezekiel shook his head. "I'd rather go alone. Your meeting with Joseph Smith starts in an hour. I'll be back by then to stay with Susan."

Ezekiel was nearly to the door when Seth detained him with the question he had been wanting to ask for hours. "What do you think of Joseph Smith, Pa?"

Ezekiel shrugged. "He has qualities I admire and seems honest enough. I'll see you boys later."

Seth watched Ezekiel go through the door. "Have a nice walk, Pa."

After his father had grunted a good-bye and closed the door behind him, Lyman grinned at Seth. "Your father just said that he thinks Joseph Smith an honest man."

Seth's eyes met Lyman's. Seth's heart pounded. Hurlbut stretched and stood up. His lips turned up in a smile. "The demon of sleep is trying to capture me. I too must walk. Don't wait for me. I'll meet you at the schoolhouse for the brethren's meeting."

After Philastus left, Seth paced the room. Lyman looked up at his friend. "Would you like me to continue reading?"

"Yes." Seth abruptly sat down at the desk chair.

"Moses, while delivering the words of the Lord to the congregation of Israel, that is, to the parents, says, 'And these words which I command thee this day, shall be in thy heart: and thou shalt teach them diligently unto thy children, and shalt talk of them when thou sittest in thy house, and when thou walkest by the way, and when thou liest down, and when thou risest up. And thou shalt bind them for a sign upon thy hand, and they shall be as frontlets between thine eyes.' If it were necessary then to teach their children diligently, how much more necessary is it now, when the Church of Christ is to be an ensign, yea, even an ensample to the world, for good? A word to the wise ought to be sufficient, for children soon become men and women. Yes, they are they that must follow us, and perform the duties which not only appertain to this world, but to the second coming of the Savior, even preparing for the Sabbath of creation, and for eternity."

Seth jumped to his feet. Lyman set the paper on his bed and looked at him. There was a frightened, wild look in Seth's eyes. "Seth, what is it?" Lyman asked. "Are you ill?"

"Do you see how important it is, Lyman, that my family gathers with the Saints? My mother's children must be taught. The words of Christ's restored gospel must be written in their hearts," Seth exclaimed. "Lyman, if Father does not join the Church, my younger brothers and sisters will be lost. I know it. I cannot allow them to burn with the wicked at Christ's coming! And the thought of my father enduring eternal punishment rises before my eyes like an unthinkable horror."

Lyman focused on his friend with concern. "Seth, our God is a loving God. You know that. We have spoken of that many times. You must not succumb to fear but have hope and a strong mind."

Seth was shaking and dripping with sweat. "What is happening to me, Lyman? I burn with anxiety. Is it the adversary torturing me?"

"Dear friend, let's pray. Our God is stronger than all other powers." The two men knelt together. Lyman prayed aloud, asking His Father in Heaven for Seth's internal torment to cease. After the prayer, Seth breathed more evenly. Lyman looked at his pocket watch. "We'd best leave now," he said, "if we are to meet the Prophet and brethren at eight. Seth, this is thrilling to me. Listening to the Prophet is like sitting at the gates of heaven."

Ezekiel Johnson sat on a stump in a nearby field, under the shade of a rambling oak tree. He tried to make some sense of

Joseph Smith. There were qualities he sensed in the young man and admired: fortitude, compassion, forthrightness. Could Mormonism be the truth? The thought teased the corners of Ezekiel's mind. Then he remembered something. He recalled the lonesome journey when he ran away from home over forty years ago. He had slept alone in the woods at night with old Betsy in his arms. On the third night, fear and exhaustion had given way to a deep sleep. He had dreamed he lay with his head in his mother's lap. The dream had been so real that on awakening, he had imagined he saw her face and had reached up to touch her. But she was an illusion. Were Joseph Smith's visions like that? Did the young man live in a waking dream? Ezekiel nodded slowly. There was no other explanation that made any sense at all. He felt deep pity for the young man who imagined he was a prophet. These visions of heaven would lead this boy through torment. Joseph Smith would take Ezekiel's family with him. But Ezekiel could not hate him. He could not hate a boy who believed he was telling the truth.

After Philastus Hurlbut left the inn, he strode quickly down the dusty street in search of Ezekiel Johnson. It was not long before he spied Ezekiel on a stump beneath an oak tree. Hurlbut saw Ezekiel wipe his eyes with his sleeve. Was the old man crying? Philastus Hurlbut rolled his eyes.

"Hello, Mr. Johnson," Hurlbut called out as he approached.

"Thought I mentioned I wanted to be alone," Ezekiel growled.

"Sir, I've been trying for some time to find a moment alone with you. I realize that you avoid me like the plague, and I can't say I blame you. When we last spoke privately, I derided Mormonism and warned you against it. Now I have embraced it. I must seem like a hypocrite to you."

"You, Philastus, a hypocrite?" Ezekiel said sarcastically.

Hurlbut laughed. "I don't suppose I'm more of a hypocrite than any other man."

"Yes, you are." Ezekiel narrowed his eyes. "You don't believe in this church, not like my sons and Lyman. I don't know why you have joined the Mormons, but I suppose you have your own plans."

"Of course I believe it, sir. What sane man would join such a despised sect if he did not believe it?"

"I need to get back to the inn." Ezekiel stood and began to walk away.

Hurlbut came up to his side and thumped him on the back. "Like I said, Mr. Johnson, I have wanted for a long time to apologize to you." Hurlbut reached into his pocket and retrieved a handful of coins. He handed them to Ezekiel. "Please accept my apology by allowing me to buy you a drink."

Ezekiel shook his head brusquely. "I've enough money to buy a drink for myself."

Susan sat alone in the room at the inn waiting for her father to return. She went to the small desk, picked up a quill and paper, and began a letter.

*Dear Mother and all,*

*Today I met the Prophet of God. How difficult it is to find the words to describe my feelings. Outwardly, he is an appealing looking man—tall with a high forehead and light brown hair which he combs back. He has a noble deportment and looks strong and able. He has a quick, easy smile. Yet his inner qualities surpass his fine looks. His*

*actions and speech are not rehearsed like so many preachers*
*I have heard. There is honesty and compassion about him.*
*Father was favorably impressed. Perhaps Seth is right.*
*Perhaps meeting Brother Joseph will change Father's heart*
*and unite our family. Tomorrow morning we travel to*
*Amherst. How I look forward to seeing Annie and Sixtus*
*after such a long time. I will meet tiny Sariah. I wish Seth's*
*heart was not so set on Father's redemption. Though we all*
*hope for that end, Seth will be bitterly disappointed if it*
*does not work out so.*

A knock sounded at the door. Susan looked up from the letter. She felt uncomfortable answering it when she was alone in the room. The person on the other side knocked again. The room, already warm, now felt suffocating.

"Miss Susan?" Sue recognized Philastus Hurlbut's voice.

Susan did not answer.

He knocked again and said loudly. "Miss Susan, are you awake in there? If you don't answer, I'll get a key from the innkeeper and make sure you are not ill."

"I'm awake now, sir," Susan called back, "but busy presently."

"Your father is downstairs drinking. Lyman and Seth are meeting with the brethren. The pleasant duty of looking after you falls to me. Open the door please."

"No, sir."

"Come, you must be thirsty. I have a glass of cold cider for you."

"No, thank you."

Moments passed. But Susan did not hear Hurlbut's footsteps walking away. She wondered if he were watching her through the keyhole. She stood up and walked to the dresser where there was a pitcher of water and a glass. As she poured herself a drink,

Hurlbut's voice hissed through the crack in the door. "Come, we are a man and a woman, both in need of company."

"I prefer my own company," Susan said loudly.

Hurlbut did not speak further, but a full ten minutes passed before Susan heard him walk away.

An hour later, Susan lay on the bed, a shaft of moonlight shining through the window. She was cold with fear and anger despite the heat. She heard a key in the door. Susan sat up in bed and took old Betsy off the table beside her. Her father entered, his husky form illuminated by a candle he carried.

"Papa," she cried out in relief. The candle flame wavered, telling Susan that Hurlbut had spoken the truth. Her father had been drinking.

"How's my black-eyed Susie?" Ezekiel said loudly. He saw the black shape of the gun in Susan's hand. "This town makes no sense. A man having visions. Your own daughter pointing a gun at you."

"I thought it might be someone else," Susan said carefully as she set the gun back on the table. Sue felt utterly alone. Maybe her mother was right. She shouldn't have come without another woman. Yet she had met the Prophet.

"Susie, you always were a wise lassie. But a gun won't do. You need a pa and brothers to protect you. Not every lass has a pa or brothers. Did you know that?"

"Yes, Pa." Susan stood up and walked over to her father. "Go to sleep, Pa. Tomorrow we see Joel and Benja," she said as she briefly kissed his cheek. Susan carefully took the candle from him and put it on a candlestick.

Ezekiel stretched out on the floor. Susan knelt down and gently covered him with a blanket. Ezekiel patted her knee. "This world's an ugly place, Susie. You can't be too careful. You know that, don't you?"

"Yes, Papa."

"But Papa'll take care of you. I'll always take care of you."

"I know, Papa." Susan stood up, went to the door and bolted it. She blew out the candle, walked over to the window, and looked outside at the low full moon. It was lovely the way the clouds streamed around it. She thought of Electa Sherman, Lyman's sister. Electa was nineteen months younger than Susan and almost as pretty as Almera, though in a different way. Electa was petite with light hair, blue-green eyes, and a bow-shaped mouth. She had spent last spring with Lyman and Delcena. She was bright-eyed and quick-witted. Susan liked her a great deal. She wondered if Electa knew that her cousin Philastus was a snake.

# 14

*Our barque is tossed upon the waters dark,*

*Where snags and wrecks in wild confusion lay,*

*With not a beacon, its lone path to mark;*

*No light but heaven's electric, piercing ray.*

—JOSEPH E. JOHNSON, FROM "LINES WRITTEN DURING A STORM ON THE
MISSOURI RIVER IN 1851"

When Cornelia Sherman announced to her mother that Lyman and Philastus had come, Asenath Hurlbut Sherman dropped her knitting and ran to the door. "Lyman, hello!" Asenath warmly embraced her son. At fifty-two years old, she was a short woman with a keen eye and quick feet. Her husband had died many years earlier. She had once lived in Kirtland but had moved to Erie County to live near her brothers, Asel and Ansel. Asel provided a small cabin for her on his property. Out of the eight children Asenath had borne, two daughters still lived with her—twenty-year-old Cornelia and sixteen-year-old Electa.

It had been over a year since Asenath had seen Lyman. In that time, her son had lost a child and been baptized a Mormon. She observed joyfully that a confident, able man with a firm, sure step had replaced the idealistic, bright-eyed boy she had raised. After welcoming Lyman, Asenath turned to her nephew. "And look at you, Philastus," she declared. "What a handsome man you've become."

"Handsome is as handsome does," Cornelia commented wryly.

Philastus chuckled and bowed. "Dear aunt, you and your daughters are as lovely as I remember."

"And you are ever the charmer." Asenath laughed. "It's good to see you boys."

"It is good to see all of you," Lyman returned. Asenath herded the group into chairs, and as they settled in, Lyman turned to his sister. "Cornelia, you look well."

"Looks can be deceiving, Lyman," Cornelia responded. "I have been plagued with headaches all summer." Cornelia was tall and blonde with a rectangular face and sharp features. She was matter-of-fact and not shy about it. The fact that she did not possess Electa's beauty or vivacity bothered her more acutely with each passing year. Cornelia continued. "It has been a long time since you have come to us. I suppose Delcena has kept you busy. How is she?"

"She is with child and has been ill," Lyman responded. "But with the Lord's blessings, it won't be long until we are all settled together in Kirtland."

"Where is my hug, Brother?" Electa asked with a sweet, petulant smile when she came to the door.

"Waiting for you." Lyman stood up and opened his arms.

Electa laughed and ran to him. Lyman thought of how his baby sister, the darling golden child, had become a dazzling young woman.

"We are all baptized now, Lyman," Electa announced after the hug. "Cornelia too."

Lyman grinned at his sisters. "Jared Carter told me." Asenath and Electa had accepted the gospel six months prior, but Cornelia had initially been reticent toward the new religion. "What changed your heart, Nelia?" Lyman inquired.

Cornelia focused on her brother. "I stopped listening to the many contrary opinions and read the entire Book of Mormon. I prayed about it and felt peace and assurance."

Lyman looked warmly at his sister. "I'm very happy for you."

"It has been difficult," Cornelia commented, "with the talk about Solomon Spaulding's manuscript."

Lyman nodded thoughtfully.

Philastus casually leaned back on two legs of his chair and pressed his hands together with the fingers pointing upward. "I know nothing of this Solomon Spaulding manuscript. What is it?" he asked casually.

Lyman quickly related the details.

Asenath watched her nephew. As a child he had been self-willed and precocious but intelligent and handsome. She counseled Philastus, "Brother Erastus Rudd and others read Spaulding's work years ago. It is a fictional romance about a group of Romans that washed ashore on the Americas. It is far different from the Book of Mormon. You may want to ask Brother Rudd about it."

Philastus clapped his hands and sat upright on his chair. He grinned at his aunt and cousins. "I don't doubt Joseph Smith's prophetic gifts. I should like to get my hands on the fellow who is promoting this false rumor and wring his neck."

Asenath chuckled at her nephew. "His name's Henry Lake, and he is a hard nut to crack. Better stay away from him, Philastus. He's a big, strong fellow—dead set against the Church and hungry for a fight."

"Ha!" Philastus grinned. "He sounds like a worthy opponent."

Electa laughed. "I should like to see Cousin Philastus thrash Henry Lake. Can you imagine, Mother? Henry Lake, humbled at last."

Philastus's eyes rested on his lovely cousin. All thoughts of Almera and Susan Johnson dissipated. Here was sunshine and beauty, a blooming yellow rosebud. He had two objectives while in Erie County. First, charm Electa. He wouldn't compromise her virtue. It wouldn't do to pick this young flower prematurely. Instead, he must wait until she was in full bloom. His other quest was to make contact with Henry Lake and Nehmiah King. He was curious to know their point of view, to see if he could discover the genesis of Joseph Smith's claims. He longed to know what made the man tick. If he knew the secrets, he would be able to needle his way into the leadership circles of the Mormon Church.

"Ben, convince Susan to come fishing with us." Almon grinned. Almon held out his hands two feet apart and winked at Susan. "The trout we catch in the Black River are this long."

Susan's face became hot.

"Come with us, Sue," Ben cajoled.

Susan stammered. "I-I can't leave Annie with the children to put to bed and the dishes to do."

Annie laughed as she stood up, bouncing the fussing Sariah on her shoulder. "Go, Susan. I have Father Johnson to entertain Sixtus. And look, Seth has already cleared the table. I'll set Joel to work while I feed Sariah."

Ezekiel, who had Sixtus on his knee, looked at his daughter. There was color in her cheeks. This trip was good for her. Ezekiel remarked, "Susan, every maid should go fishing once in her life."

Ben grinned. He was glad to have his father, brother, and sister visiting. It had been lonesome at Joel's during the past four and a half months. If it weren't for Almon's friendship, he would have been desperate to go home. He looked at his sister. "Come on, Sue. Watch me out-fish Almon."

Almon affectionately thumped Ben on the back. "'Tis highly unlikely, little brother."

Susan looked away from Almon and Ben, wishing that Almon could no longer make her heart beat so quickly. Annie saw her discomfiture. She handed Sariah to Joel and put her arm around Susan. "Stay here with me, Susan, if you'd rather not go."

"It's not that," Susan said uncomfortably. "It is just that this is my only clean dress."

"I'll give you a cloth to put down on a log before you sit," Annie suggested.

Ten minutes later, Susan headed out with Benjamin and Almon. Ben was unusually talkative. As they left Joel's property, he pointed out the crops he had planted and told Susan about how much his foot had hurt on the trip to Amherst. He described how hard he had worked for Joel during the spring and summer. Susan listened carefully to everything Benjamin said, determined to ignore her feelings at Almon's nearness. Sue could tell that Ben was very glad to see her, and this warmed her heart. At home, with so many in the family, she sometimes wondered if she were really very important to anyone. Would all go on as usual if she were gone?

At the river, Susan laid the cloth down then gathered her skirt beneath her and sat down on a log to watch. She observed how Benjamin and Almon had vastly different fishing styles. Benjamin baited his line carefully and lowered it into the deep pool near the shore. He squatted with his pole in his hands, staring at the line for any movement, his complete attention focused on fishing. In contrast, Almon cast his line out, then wedged his pole between three large rocks so that it would stay there without him holding it. Leaving his pole there, he walked over to Susan.

"Your brother wants to catch the first fish today," Almon announced loudly, baiting Ben. "But he tries too hard. I, on the other hand, am free to read or snooze. Whatever suits my fancy. And I'll still win the contest."

"We'll see about that," Benjamin retorted, still staring at his line.

"Miss Susan, which line would you wager on?" Almon laughed.

"Benja's," Susan commented. "His fish won't get away."

"Unless he tries to hook him too quickly and scares him away." Almon smiled knowingly as he raised his eyebrows. "If my line twitches, I'll let the bait tease the fish a bit. My fish is bound to swallow the getup whole—worm, hook, and all."

Susan did not respond but kept her eyes on Benjamin. Almon shuffled his feet. Then he sat down near Susan. He tapped his knee with his finger. "How is your mother?"

"Very well." Susan could not think of anything else to say.

Almon kept tapping. "And Almera?"

"Fine."

"Is Almera over Elijah Handy?"

"Almost. This week she is helping Delcena."

"Is Delcena well? And Nancy?"

"Delcena is with child and has not been well. But she is getting better. Nancy is stronger than she has been for many years."

"Good." Almon stood up and paced around the log. Then he changed the angle of his wide-brimmed hat. Susan wondered if he ever held still. "And the others?" Almon asked, "Joe and Mary? The little boys? Esther and Amos? Have any been sick with ague?"

"No. They are all well," Susan said.

Almon continued pacing, but seemed to be at a loss for words. Susan noted that he had not yet asked about Julianne. Susan looked toward the river. "Almon, your line is moving," she exclaimed.

Almon glanced over. "It's only the breeze." Then he snapped his fingers. "Julianne. She is the one I'm forgetting. How is she? I would have thought she would have come here with you to see the Prophet."

"Juli is busy at home," Susan said quietly as she looked down at her hands. They were folded in her lap. She was too still and quiet for Almon. She had to accept that. It was Juli he cared for.

Almon's foot nervously tapped the ground as he nonchalantly continued. "Busy with what? Is she being courted?"

Susan shrugged. "A new convert from Fredonia has called."

The next question came out in a gust. "Does she like him?"

"Juli is of marrying age and must consider every offer," Susan said quietly. She did not mention that the man was a bald, forty-year-old widower with six children.

Almon suddenly whirled around to face Susan. He squatted down and looked her squarely in the eye. His green eyes were alive with passion. It pained Sue to know that the passion was not for her. She felt her face turn crimson. Almon spoke. "After harvest, I will be going to Cincinnati to find out about studying law there. It won't be long until I am licensed to practice in six states. I am not so young and inexperienced as Julianne supposes."

"Almon! Your line!" Ben yelled. Susan and Almon's eyes turned toward the fishing pole. They both saw the quick sporadic bounces.

"Land her for me, Bennie." Almon yelled. "I'm busy talking with a pretty girl."

Ben laughed and shook his head. "No, sir! I've a bite too!"

Almon shrugged to Susan. He ran to his pole. But as he lifted it up, the fish was gone., the hook sucked clean. He looked back at Susan and punched the air with a fist. "I've been skunked by a fish!"

Down the river twenty yards, Ben jerked his line and set his hook. The trout flipped ferociously as Benjamin landed it on the muddy bank. Its silver body gleamed with the colors of the river. Benjamin ran over to it and held it up like a trophy. "Ha, Almon! Susie, look!"

Susan clapped. "It's a fine fish, Benja."

"You might have caught the first fish, but I am apt to catch the biggest," Almon challenged.

Ben threaded his fish on a stringer and the two young men fished on. This time, Almon stayed close to his line. As the sun set, the trees became shadowy silhouettes with crimson sky behind them. Neither Ben nor Almon had another hit. Finally, Almon threw his hands in the air. "Let's go home."

"Almon, you usually make me fish until you win. How come you're giving up so easy today?" Ben said with a tease in his voice.

"Don't get cocky, Ben. I'll win next time." Almon gathered up the fishing paraphernalia while Benjamin sliced open the trout with his knife and gutted it. Ben rinsed the fish in the river water.

On the way home, daylight dimmed as the moon and stars appeared. Almon walked close to Susan and pointed out an owl winging by. The summer night was cool and still. Susan listened to the frogs and crickets. She felt a strange and lovely sensation—as if she were a part of the earth and sky. For the girl who spent so much time inside working, the moment was a gift from a loving Heavenly Father. When they neared the house, Benjamin ran ahead, anxious to brag about his fish.

At the cabin door, Susan lingered outside a moment, wishing she could tuck this moment away somewhere and bring it out again whenever she felt cold or alone. She glanced at Almon and saw that he was watching her carefully with a slight frown. His arms were folded and his brow knitted as if he were examining her and she wasn't quite making the grade. Her feeling of peace evaporated.

She reached to open the latch, but Almon sprung forward and positioned himself between her and the door. "Susan, I will speak with you."

Susan's heart pounded.

Almon's eyes darted past her out to the moonlit night. Did he have the look of a trapped animal, or was it Susan's imagination? Then he looked in Susan's eyes and stoically took her hand. Susan swallowed as Almon spoke. "Meeting your family in Pomfret was the best thing that ever happened to me. I admire you very much. I think you would make an excellent wife and mother. In a year, after I have studied law, I plan to move to Kirtland. I should be able to rent a place and make a living."

"Don't!" Susan ejected. "Please don't!" She pulled her hand away and stumbled back as if she had been slapped. How could the words she had dreamed of hearing feel so insanely wrong? How could she listen to his proposal when she knew he loved her sister? She shook her head as tears rushed to her eyes.

Frustration filled Almon. "I see that I have violently offended you. I'll never do so again." Almon turned on his heel.

"Wait," Susan called out. Almon stopped in his tracks but did not turn around. Susan fought back tears and with great effort steadied her voice. "Almon, you love Julianne, not me. I know it. How can you court me when you love my sister?"

Almon slowly turned around and looked at Susan. Her declaration had surprised him. Almon let out a gust of breath as his shoulders sagged. "Julianne sees me as a child. Someone is courting her. There is no hope there for me. I thought you and I might grow to love each other."

"Juli admires you, not the new convert courting her. In time, I think she will love you."

Almon gaped at Susan. "Are you certain?"

"Almost entirely," Susan whispered.

"But she didn't come here like you did. And she has told me she is too old for me. And she hasn't written me."

Susan spoke. "Perhaps she thought I admired you, Almon. Perhaps she didn't want to spoil things for me. But I love you like a brother, not a beau. You are too lively for me. You suit Julianne."

"But when will I see her again?" Almon cried out as he walked toward Susan. "How can I convince her that I'm not a child?"

"The same way you convinced me," Susan whispered. "By telling her your plans."

"Will you help me, Susan? Will you talk to her for me and dissuade all other suitors?"

Susan wiped her tears and nodded.

"Then there is hope," Almon shouted. He rapturously picked Susan up and swung her around. After putting her back down, he said, "I always knew there was more to you, Sue, than you ever let on. You are the dearest sister to me."

"You are dear to me as well," Susan said quickly. Then she turned and hurried into the house, closing the door behind her. She left Almon on the doorstep wondering why Susan had forgotten to invite him in. He considered knocking, but then thought better of it and strode home whistling.

In the shadowy kitchen, it took all of Susan's strength to stop the sobs threatening to seize her. She doubled over, and her breath came out in tremulous gulps. Ben's voice floated in from the small adjoining sitting room where he triumphantly detailed his fishing techniques. In the kitchen, the only light was a fire in the hearth where the fish was being boiled in a pot. Susan heard Annie's footsteps. She straightened and wiped her eyes with her sleeve.

The door to the adjoining room opened, and Annie entered the kitchen carrying a candle. The light illuminated Annie's face and auburn hair but left Susan in shadow. "Sue, I heard you come in," Annie said cheerfully. "Has Almon gone?" Without waiting for an answer, Annie bent over the table and used the candle to light the kitchen's candlesticks.

"Yes," Susan replied, trying to keep her voice level.

"That's too bad. Everyone wants a taste of Ben's fish. It should be done now."

"I'll help you serve it," Susan offered.

Susan stayed with the group for twenty minutes. First, she served the trout and then ate a portion herself. Finally, her feelings were too intense to bear company any longer, and she excused herself by saying that she was tired and needed to rest. Annie watched Susan walk out. She wondered what had happened with Almon that evening and if Susan were upset. She wasn't like her sisters. Annie had been close to Delcena and Julianne. In a similar situation, they would have hugged Annie and told her every detail. If need be, they would have cried together. But not Susan.

After Susan went to bed, Joel read aloud a copy of some of the revelations that would soon be published. Benjamin and Annie listened attentively. Seth repeatedly glanced at his father, trying to read Ezekiel's reaction. Joel read on, "Behold I will reveal unto you the Priesthood, by the hand of Elijah the prophet, before the coming of the great and dreadful day of the Lord. And he shall plant in the hearts of the children the promises made to the fathers, and the hearts of the children shall turn to their fathers. If it were not so, the whole earth would be utterly wasted at his coming."

Ezekiel stood up, thinking of how his heart would never turn to his father. Never. Joel stopped reading. "I'm going out," Ezekiel said briefly.

"Where to, Pa?" Seth questioned anxiously.

Ezekiel looked away from Seth's intense brown eyes. "To the tavern."

"But you were favorably impressed by the Prophet. These are the Lord's words to him," Seth said earnestly.

"I'm more in need of a drink than the Lord tonight."

"But you believe Joseph Smith is telling the truth."

"I believe that the boy thinks he is telling the truth," Ezekiel corrected. "That doesn't mean all those things really happened."

"Pa." Seth stood up. His hands trembled. His voice became louder with each word he spoke. "You must ask God. You must stop drinking. The Holy Spirit cannot guide you when you are inebriated. Your salvation depends on it. Your children depend on you. Mother depends on you. If you do not turn your heart to us, how can we turn ours toward you? The earth will be wasted when the Lord comes! Lives will be wasted! You must turn from the path you are on this night! Do not give the devil power over your soul! Pray for strength, Father! Pray for a new heart to replace the one blackened by drink!"

Ezekiel gaped at Seth. His eyes narrowed. His calm, gentlemanly son was shaking with emotion. Or was it rage? Ezekiel's stepfather's words from long ago echoed in his mind. *The devil has worked beside you, boy! Pray, you misbegotten child! Your heart is black! Pray for your soul!* Ezekiel breathed raggedly. Everyone in the room was utterly silent. Finally, Ezekiel spoke between clenched teeth, "Boy, I've accepted you the way you are, even when you talk like a fool. It's high time you accept me the way I am." With those words, Ezekiel Johnson turned and stalked out of the cabin, slamming the door behind him.

It was four in the morning when Baby Sariah's crying awakened Benjamin. Ben heard footsteps in the master bedroom. The bed creaked. Then Sariah was quiet again, and he knew Annie was feeding her. Ben rolled over. The bedroll next to him was empty. Ben's eyes searched the dark room for Seth. He saw his father's form in one corner and heard the familiar snores. Ben vaguely recalled Seth leaving sometime in the night. He had assumed it was to use the privy. He remembered his father coming home at some later point and slumping into bed. Had Seth been there then? Ben strained to remember but couldn't.

Ben wandered into the kitchen and lit a candle in the hot ashes. He lifted the candle up. The room was quiet with deep shadows in the corners. He pulled his boots on and walked outside. A light wind had kicked up in the night. The slice of moon was high and the stars brilliant. A raccoon scuttled by. Ben walked out to the privy and found it empty. Ben stood still, listening to the night noises. Leaves rustled in trees. He heard no footsteps, no human sounds—just wild emptiness. Ben went back inside. He knocked on the door to Joel and Annie's bedroom.

While feeding Sariah in bed, Annie nudged Joel to awaken him. "Someone's at the bedroom door," she whispered.

"What on earth?" Joel said, still half-asleep. Sariah whimpered and quieted. Joel limped sleepily to the door in his crumpled trousers. Joel unlatched the bedroom door and cracked it open. "What's goin' on, Ben?"

"Seth's gone," Ben said worriedly. "I don't know where he is."

Seth stumbled forward as he ran toward Kirtland. Flames blazed inside of him. He smelled the smoke and felt the heat. They sliced into his consciousness like a beast lurching toward the heart of its prey. The flames had taken his father's soul to fuel their hunger and threatened his brothers and sisters. He felt them screaming. Was there nothing he could do? Was there no escape? His legs churned onward in a waking nightmare. Dust and ashes fell behind him. Black night and blazing daylight loomed ahead of him.

It was late morning when Seth arrived on the edges of Kirtland. As the road emerged from the woodland, rays of light illuminated the ripening cornfields. Seth stopped for a moment and could not remember where he was or why he had come. He crumbled to the ground from utter exhaustion. As his eyes closed, the image that brought him here filled his mind. It was of Joseph Smith calmly smiling and patiently teaching in the midst of the flames—as untouched by them as Shadrach, Meshach, and Abed-nego.

Joseph Smith, Emma, and their two-year-old daughter, Julia, were having an early lunch in their rooms off of the Whitney store when there was a knock at the door. Joseph answered it. "Good morning, Don Carlos." Joseph grinned at his youngest brother. "Have you come for some of Emma's cooking?"

A smile illuminated Emma's features. Don Carlos was her favorite of Joseph's siblings. "Carlos, come eat with us. Here's eggs, bread, and melon for you."

Don Carlos shook his head. As they looked more carefully at him, both Joseph and Emma could tell something was wrong. Joseph spoke first, "Carlos, what has happened?"

Don Carlos sat down at the table in an extra chair and explained. "A fellow brought David Johnson's brother Seth to the house this morning. He found Brother Seth unconscious on the outskirts of town. At first, this man thought Brother Seth was a drunk. But there wasn't the smell of liquor about his person and he found a page of *The Star* in his pocket. When he discovered Brother Seth was Mormon, he brought him to us. Brother Seth is conscious now, Joseph, and asking for you. It seems he traveled all night from Amherst. He is most distressed in his mind."

Joseph looked at Emma. Their time together was constantly interrupted. He worried about her. She was with child once more and had not been sleeping well since the mob violence in Hyrum. "Go, Joseph," she assured. "I understand."

Joseph kissed his wife and little girl. "Bye-bye, Pa-Pa," Baby Julia chattered between bites of food.

When Joseph arrived at his parents' home, his mother directed him to the small bedroom. The Prophet found Seth sitting in a chair with his face buried in his hands. The two were alone together. There was an untouched plate of food and a glass of water on the desk in the corner that Mother Smith had provided. Seth looked up at Joseph. His eyes were bloodshot. The Prophet was shocked at the difference between this disheveled man with exhausted, driven eyes and the intelligent gentleman he had met a few days ago. Joseph knelt down in front of Seth's chair and took his hands. They were hot and damp. "Brother Seth, what is wrong?"

"I seek your wisdom," Seth proclaimed as he stared at the Prophet. "My father is lost! He will not be redeemed. I fear to lose my brothers and sisters, for they will not be allowed to gather to Zion. I see the flames of hell before my eyes, consuming my family. I have labored for them all my life. That life's mission is in flames. Brother Joseph, I fear my mind is broken. I see these flames rising before my vision. I can smell them. I have run through those flames, seeking you, the Prophet, whom the adversary cannot destroy."

"You have run the whole night? From Amherst?" Joseph questioned as he gently let go of Seth's hands and stood on his feet. He was amazed at the physical endurance of this man.

Seth sank deeper into his chair, weeping. "Yes. I find no escape."

"You've had no food, water, or rest?"

"I can't sleep nor eat."

Joseph gently laid his hand on Seth's shoulder. He felt Seth tremble. "Brother Seth," Joseph said, "as I listen to you, I find myself thinking of that day long ago, when as a boy, I went to the grove of trees behind our house to pray vocally for the first time, to offer up the desires of my heart to God. As I began to ask God which of all the sects was true, I was seized by a power which entirely overcame me and bound my tongue so that I could not speak. Thick darkness gathered around me, and it seemed I was doomed to sudden destruction. Despite the terror, I exerted all the power of my spirit to continue to call upon God for deliverance. But my strength failed. I was about to give myself up to destruction, not to some imaginary ruin, but to the power of some actual being from the unseen world. At that moment, a pillar of light appeared exactly over my head, above the brightness of the sun. I was delivered from the enemy that held me bound. When the light rested upon me, I saw two personages, whose brightness and glory defy description, standing above me in the air. It was our Father in Heaven and his Son, Jesus Christ."

The prophet was silent for a moment as he remembered. Seth closed his eyes. When he spoke, his voice was barely audible. "Brother Joseph, you are God's anointed. But I am not. The flames do not recede."

"Brother Seth," Joseph said, his voice clear and filled with compassion, "it seems that Satan desires to weaken your spirit, to fill your intelligent mind with fear. But it shall not be so. The Lord of Heaven gave His life for you." With those words, Joseph laid his hands on Seth's head and poured his soul out in a blessing rebuking the power of the destroyer, promising Seth guardian angels to watch over him until his mind was whole once more. After the blessing, Seth trembled.

The Prophet laid his hand on Seth's shoulder until the trembling ceased. "Eat, dear brother," Joseph said as he looked at the plate of food his mother had placed on the desk. "I'll go now and speak to my family."

When Joseph entered the kitchen, his mother and brother turned to him. "How is Brother Seth?" Mother Smith asked.

"He is under great strain," the Prophet answered. "But the Lord will be with him." Then he turned to his brother. "Carlos, after Brother Seth has eaten, could you go with him back to his family in Amherst? In his current condition, I don't think he should travel alone."

Don Carlos quickly nodded.

"He needs to rest first," Mother Smith said, "or he won't have the strength to travel."

Seth stood in the doorway. The Smith family turned when they heard his voice. "I must leave immediately," he said. "I must get back to my family in all haste."

"Did you eat?" Mother Smith asked. "You need strength for the journey."

Seth nodded. "Thank you."

After Mother Smith packed a knapsack full of food, Don Carlos followed Seth out the door.

An hour later, Don Carlos was astounded at Seth's pace as the two traveled the road through the woodland. His mother needn't have worried about Brother Johnson. At that moment, Seth appeared to have an overabundance of strength.

As the two men moved onward, Seth stared at the forest he had run through the previous night. There were stately shadowy trees in full summer leaf—maple, oak, pine, and aspen. The undergrowth was thick with shrubs, seedlings, and wildflowers. Seth's eyes stung with tears. His mind still burned. If he did not keep moving, he feared that the flames would engulf his vision. Last night they had overcome him. He had felt the heat, smelled the burning, and heard the screams. Yet they were illusions. He must call on God and hold to the promises voiced by the Prophet.

The next morning in Amherst, Ezekiel stood outside Joel's cabin, staring at the trail that edged into the woods and forest beyond. He, Joel, Ben, and Almon Babbitt had followed it yesterday, tracing Seth's footprints to the point where the trail came out of the woodland and joined the road outside of Amherst. But the road had been dusty, sun-baked, and travel-worn leaving no additional clues to tell them which direction Seth had gone. On the edge of panic, Ezekiel dug his fists into his trouser pockets. They had knocked on countless doors and searched barns and fields. Shortly, men and dogs were coming to help them search the woods. Ezekiel took out his watch. It was nearly ten. Seth had been gone for a day and a half.

A branch cracked. Ezekiel looked up. Two figures emerged from the woods. At first glance, it looked as if a man were helping a drunken friend. But Ezekiel knew the form of the slender, stumbling man. He called Seth's name and ran forward. It was his son who staggered on the arm of a tall, young stranger. As he ran, euphoric relief flooded Ezekiel.

Ezekiel wanted to embrace Seth, to tell him how glad he was that he was all right. But he stopped short when he saw the strange, confused look in Seth's eyes. "Seth, where've you been? What's happened to you?"

"He's exhausted, sir," the stranger said. "When we camped last night, he could not sleep. He has had very little food and no rest for two days."

"Seth, what's goin' on?" Ezekiel asked again.

Before Seth could answer, Ben and Susan ran up. Joel followed with Sariah in his arms. Annie trailed behind, holding Sixtus's hand.

Ill and exhausted, Seth could not think. His eyes darted from his father to his siblings. "I saw flames," he tried to explain. "All around here. Everywhere. I smelled them. All was lost! I ran to find the Prophet."

Ezekiel gaped at his son. Seth's mind was broken, Seth's beautiful and intelligent mind. Shock and horror filled Ezekiel. "There's been no fire," Ezekiel shouted in agony. Seth looked frantically around as if he were about to bolt.

Benjamin ran to Seth and wrapped his arms around him. The boy began to sob. He had been so afraid Seth was dead somewhere. Here was his older brother, his mentor, the man he loved and respected with his whole soul, the brother who had always comforted and watched over him. Seth had been Benjamin's strength, and Seth's frailty terrified the boy.

Seth put his arms around Benjamin, and his blood-streaked eyes met Joel's. "Joel," his voice grasped for something to hold on to. "It was the illusion of hellfire, Joel. The Prophet blessed me to be well, but the fire still licks at my heels."

"Come inside, Seth," Joel said as he handed the baby to Annie. His voice was very firm and very calm, the same tone he used to soothe a frightened animal. "You need sleep. After you've rested, you will tell me all."

Susan stepped forward. Although socially shy, there was a part of her as strong and pliable as molten steel. "I'll go in with Seth. Joel, you stay here and talk with this gentleman." Sue nodded toward Don Carlos. Her black eyes were moist, full of love and sorrow. Her voice was very soft. "Seth, I'll get you something to eat and make up a bed for you."

Seth looked into Susan's eyes and nodded. As Don Carlos watched Susan take Seth's hand and walk with him toward the house, he thought of David. His heart ached for David's bewildered brother, whom he had always heard was a gentleman and a scholar. He was equally touched by the compassion of David's gentle sister.

"What happened to my son?" Ezekiel addressed Don Carlos. His voice was defensive.

Carlos shrugged sadly. "I'm not sure, sir. A stranger found him unconscious outside of Kirtland yesterday morning."

"Kirtland?" Ezekiel gaped at Don Carlos. "What makes you think my son was in Kirtland? He was here the night before. Kirtland's fifty miles away."

"That man brought Brother Seth to my parents' home," Don Carlos said steadily. "We live in Kirtland." Then, he held out his hand and shook Ezekiel's. "My name's Don Carlos Smith, Mr. Johnson. Your son, David, is my dearest friend. I know Brother Joel and Sister Annie well."

Joel stepped forward and embraced Don Carlos. He had been so stunned by Seth's appearance that he had not welcomed his young friend. "Carlos, thank you for bringing Seth home. We are deeply obliged to you. Yet we are shocked at his state of mind. He seemed whole when he was with us yesterday. Father, Don Carlos is Joseph Smith's youngest brother."

Ezekiel bit his tongue and turned brusquely. His instinct was to strike out at Don Carlos for the Mormon insanity that had infected his son. But he knew this was not fair. "I'm goin' to tend to Seth." He turned and hurried toward the cabin.

Inside, Susan sat on the bed next to Seth and helped him drink a glass of water. After the water, he looked at his sister. "It was an illusion, yet I saw it with my own eyes. Everything burned, Susan," he whispered. "Our father, our home, the love of our family. All I have toiled for. Ruined. Turned to ashes."

A quote from Shakespeare that Seth had made his students learn back in the Pomfret schoolhouse came to Susan's mind. She gently smoothed Seth's hair back from his forehead and said quietly, "'And ruin'd love, when it is built anew, grows fairer than at first, more strong, far greater.' All will be well, Seth. God is with us."

Susan continued to stroke Seth's hair as she hummed a hymn. The door of the room was slightly open. Ezekiel stood behind it and watched Susan and Seth.

# 15

*Will they kindly look over my actions*
*And say, though his faults were not few,*
*He never intended to wrong us,*
*His heart was still loving and true?*

—George W. Johnson, from "Will They Miss Me"

The air was cool and moist under a gray, hazy sky in the early morning two days following Seth's breakdown. Ezekiel, Susan, and Seth prepared to board a schooner and begin their journey home. Joel and Benjamin, concerned about Seth's emotional state and feeling the pains of a visit that was ending much too soon, accompanied them to the dock. Ben fought back tears as he told Seth good-bye.

"I'm sorry, Bennie. I'm sorry," Seth said as his younger brother clung to him. Tears filled Seth's eyes. He knew that his mind was not whole and that his breakdown had injured Benjamin. Images of fire still haunted Seth at night and unpredictably blurred the edges of his vision during the day. It took great effort to think clearly.

"I'll miss you," Benjamin gulped. The previous night, Susan had explained to Benjamin how Seth believed that unless their father accepted the gospel, Ezekiel would further surrender to numbing drink and the family would suffer. She tried to help him understand why that anxiety triggered Seth's mania. Regardless of the reasons, Ben could not accept that his stalwart brother's mind was now frail. How could God let this happen? The very thought stunned Benjamin. Ben's mouth quivered as he stepped back from Seth.

"I'm sorry, Bennie," Seth said again.

Joel cut in. "We'd best finish our farewells before the boat leaves." He embraced Seth quickly. "God will be with you," Joel assured. Then he turned to his father, "Good-bye, Pa."

Ezekiel shook Joel's hand and bid him farewell. Then he embraced Benjamin. "Take care, son. Someone will come fetch you after harvest."

Susan kissed both of her brothers on the cheek. "Good-bye, Joel. Good-bye, dear Benja."

Ezekiel turned to Seth, pained by his pale face and exhausted eyes. "Seth, Susan, let's go," he ordered brusquely. Susan put her hand on Seth's arm, allowing her older brother to guide her up the plank even as she steadied him.

While Susan and Seth went to find a place to sit down, Ezekiel remained on deck. He took a plug of tobacco out of his pocket and popped it in his mouth. He chewed it as he watched Joel's and Benjamin's figures recede into the distance. He thought about the decision he had made to leave Ben in Amherst through the harvest. Benjamin hadn't been particularly happy about it, but the decision was based on two facts: first, Joel could use the extra help with the crops; and second, Ben was extremely upset by Seth's illness. Ben's anxiety seemed to make Seth more nervous. Susan, on the other hand, had the opposite effect. She would lay a quiet hand on Seth's arm and he visibly relaxed. Seth was able to talk with Susan as he attempted to make sense of his ordeal. Her quiet voice and searching eyes steadied him. Ezekiel spit the tobacco into the water.

A husky, blond young man strode over to Ezekiel and struck up a conversation. "Hello. My name's Tom Perkins."

"Ezekiel Johnson."

"Are you from these parts?"

"No. Just visiting."

"Me too. My older brother Wesley lives in Amherst. My wife and I are from New York City. I'm looking for a place to settle."

The young man's search reminded Ezekiel of his early marriage when he and Julia had traversed wilderness, searching for the best place to build a life and raise their children. Did this bright-eyed young fellow have any comprehension of the trials in store for him? "The soil is rich enough here," Ezekiel commented. "Good for cane, fair for wheat."

Tom Perkins nodded. "I'm considering it. I'll visit Fort Dearborn before I make a decision. They're building a town there—calling it Chicago. Means *strong* in Indian. The land's been platted. They're selling quarter sections at a decent price. I'll head there come October. Pork's more expensive though, up to thirteen dollars a barrel."

"What do you think you'll find in Fort Dearborn that you won't find here?" Ezekiel questioned. "When I was a young man, I wasted a lot of time looking for paradise. It doesn't exist."

Perkins looked at Ezekiel carefully, then spoke. "You ain't Mormon, are you?"

Ezekiel shook his head, but he did not elaborate. He wished he could think of a way to escape this conversation. Tom Perkins went on in a low confidential tone. "There's no Mormons in Chicago. But they're all over here. My brother thinks their headmen, Joseph Smith and Sidney Rigdon, are led by the devil and ought to be lynched. The simple and weak-minded gobble up their doctrine. Wesley says that at one of their meetings, a young girl was possessed, shaking and having strange visions. Reverend Ezra Boothe knows the details and sent the paper in Ravenna a bundle of letters."

Ezekiel's jaw went rigid. He spoke between clenched teeth. "Boy, I have two things to say to you. First, lynching Joe Smith would be murder, pure and simple. Second, if I were you, I'd move my family to Fort Dearborn and keep them as far away from the Mormons as I could. Not only the weak and simple-minded are prone to embrace their doctrine." Without another word, Ezekiel turned and stalked away.

"Mister, I meant no offense. You said you weren't Mormon," the young man called after him.

Ezekiel turned around and glared at Tom Perkins. "I ain't Mormon. And never will be. But I've met Joseph Smith. He's no more of a devil than me or you."

Throughout the remainder of the journey, Ezekiel watched Seth's painful battle to appear well. There wasn't much liquor onboard, and Ezekiel longed for a drink to escape the bitter reality that bored into him. Religious fanaticism in the form of Mormon doctrine had driven his handsome, intelligent son to the brink of madness. Like one lamb following another, Seth had followed Joseph Smith off the cliff to insanity.

They arrived at the Dunkirk port two days later at dusk. Ezekiel decided that it would be best to spend the night at the local tavern and travel home early in the morning. After Susan and Seth had retired to their rooms, Ezekiel went downstairs to get a drink. As he sipped a brandy, thoughts about his family's insane religiosity pounded in his mind. Ironically, he had named Seth after his own mother, Sethiah. Ezekiel had suffered as a child because Sethiah's religious fanaticism kept her in bondage to a cruel husband. This Mormon religion had divided him and his wife. Joseph Brackenbury had died while away from his loved ones because of religion. Seth was on the brink of losing his mind due to his obsession with God and hell.

Ezekiel's fingers tightened around the drink in his hand. He could endure it no longer. There would be no more victims in his family. Whatever the cost, he would get them away from the influence of Joseph Smith and the Mormons! He would sell his farm and move his wife and children. When the farm was gone, they would start again. He and Julia weren't young anymore, and it would take every ounce of their strength to carve out a new life.

Only one thought haunted him. *Julia would not understand nor accept this move.* Forcing her could cost Ezekiel any shred of love she had left for him. And he loved her. There was no escaping that fact. Ezekiel lifted the glass that quivered in his hand. But there was no escaping another fact as well. Ezekiel's brow furrowed and his eyes hardened. He had to regain his place as head of his family. He had to get his children away. They would thank him someday. Ezekiel finished his drink, then asked the bartender if he knew anything about the new city Chicago.

The next morning, Susan felt unwell and broke out in a cold sweat. Ezekiel rented a wagon and mule so that she would not have to walk the five miles to Pomfret. Upon their arrival home, Julia immediately put Susan to bed, concerned that she was sick with ague. While Ezekiel and David went to return the wagon and mule, Julia noticed that Seth's eyes were bloodshot and he seemed nervous and distracted. She wondered if he was getting sick as well.

Julia didn't have a chance to talk with Seth immediately, for it was a busy day. Seth went outside to help Joe and Mary in the garden. In the sitting room, Nancy was working with George and Will on ciphering. Julianne and Almera had gone to the Shermans' to help Delcena and had taken little Esther with them. This left Julia alone to perform the momentous tasks of house-keeping and cooking for a large family.

As Julia went about her work, three-year-old Amos grew irritable and incessantly tugged at her skirt. She wished she had time just to sit and tell him a story. Her baby boy was her darling, blond and dark-eyed like Mary, smiling and sensitive like Joe. On most days, Amos entertained himself by following his brothers and sisters, but today he was difficult to please. Julia picked him up and hugged him. She kissed his forehead. It was cool and damp. Julia hoped that Amos's irritability wasn't a sign that he was becoming ill too.

In the late afternoon, Julia went outside to take the linen from the clothesline. Amos followed her, then crawled into a nearby hammock and fell asleep. Julia sighed with relief as she looked at her beautiful babe. She would have some peace while she fixed supper. When she went inside with the fresh-smelling linens in her arms, she found Seth standing near the mantel. There were beads of sweat on his temples as he nervously drummed his fingers. Julia placed her hand on his arm. "Son, are you well?"

"I will be, Mother," Seth said. "How is Susan?"

Julia put the linens on the table and folded them as she talked to Seth. "I went upstairs an hour ago, and she was sleeping peacefully. I think that Susan will be better tomorrow. Perhaps she was simply tired from the strain of the trip."

Seth nodded. "That's likely." He continued to drum his fingers.

Julia looked carefully at her son. He was no longer looking at her. It was as if he stared at something she could not see. Julia spoke. "Son, a few days ago we received a letter that Susan wrote while in Kirtland. In it, she said that Father was favorably impressed with Joseph Smith. Is that still the case?"

Seth turned to Julia briefly and shook his head. There was great pain in his eyes. Julia did not question him further. She continued folding the napkins, her own disappointment welling in her throat. Seth looked away from his mother and the drumming of his fingers turned into a nervous throbbing. A few moments later, Julianne, Almera, and little Esther arrived home from the Shermans'.

"Hello, Seth." Julianne greeted her older brother with a cheerful smile as she walked through the door. Seth's hand stilled as Julianne hugged him. She kept talking, "We knew you were back. Pa and David are at Delcie's. They stopped by on their way back from returning the wagon. Where's Sue?"

Julia looked over at her daughters. "Susan's upstairs sleeping. She felt ill this morning but seemed much better this afternoon."

Julianne grinned at Seth. "Seth, how are Joel and Annie?"

"Well," Seth said shortly.

Julianne's brow furrowed slightly.

"Is Lyman at home?" Seth asked.

Julianne nodded. "David is staying there for supper. He and Lyman want you to come over." Julianne put her hand on Seth's arm and spoke lightly, trying to break her brother's mood. "But I wasn't going to tell you, Seth. I wanted *you* home tonight, telling me all about the trip. I suppose I'll have to wake up Susie."

Julia cut in. "Let Sue sleep," she said. "There will be time enough to hear the details after supper."

"I was only teasing," Julianne commented.

"I must talk to Lyman," Seth interrupted. "Mother, can you spare me tonight?"

Julia nodded. This exhausted, distracted young man was so different from the son who had left her four weeks ago.

"Just rush away without telling us anything about meeting the Prophet," Almera blurted, clearly annoyed at her brother's uncommunicativeness. Seth seemed not to hear. He was already out the door.

"What's wrong with Seth?" Almera asked. Julianne's eyes echoed the question.

Julia looked toward the door that Seth had just walked out of. "I'm not certain. But he indicated that there is no hope for your father's conversion." Then, Julia spoke more to herself than to her girls, "Will Zeke come home for supper or spend the evening at the tavern?"

"Pa said to tell you he'd be home," Julianne said, her brown eyes thoughtful. "There's always hope, Mother. Remember the story about Pandora? Hope is the thing left at the bottom of the box."

That evening, while the girls cleaned the kitchen and the children played games in the yard, Julia sat down on the porch bench next to Ezekiel. She took his hand. "Is it good to be home?" she questioned.

Ezekiel turned and looked at his wife. She was beautiful to him, and it pained him that circumstances would cause him to hurt her. "Yes. Delcena seems much stronger, and the crops are doing well."

Julia nodded. "We'll have a new grandchild by November."

"And Susan. Is she better?" Ezekiel asked.

Julia nodded. "I think so. She's been fast asleep for the past four hours."

"When's Seth coming home?" Ezekiel's voice was suddenly tense.

Julia shrugged. "I don't know. Didn't you see him on your way?"

Ezekiel shook his head briskly. "I stopped by the tavern on a business matter."

At the mention of the tavern, Julia's hand tensed in her husband's. Ezekiel knew it was the drinking that concerned her. But he had not gone to the tavern to get drunk. He had gone to put out the word that his farm was for sale.

"We don't even know if Seth made it to Delcena's safely," Ezekiel said, his voice clearly frustrated.

Julia studied Ezekiel's demeanor carefully. He might have had a drink, but he was certainly not drunk. She asked the next question carefully. "Has Seth been ill, Zeke?"

Ezekiel turned abruptly to face Julia. His fingers tightened around her hand. His voice rose as he spoke, the frustration he had kept inside now boiling over. "Yes, Julia, Seth is ill. But the sickness is in his mind, not his body—a mania caused by Joseph Smith and the Mormon religion! Last week, he ran fifty miles in a night, from Amherst to Kirtland, thinking he was chased by a fire. There was no fire! He came back to us wild and deranged, ranting about the fires of hell destroying us. Julia, this religious insanity must cease! It is a disease that first infected young Joseph Smith, an honest, decent fellow. It is like diphtheria, moving from one victim to the next. There will be no more talk of Mormonism, angels, or hellfire in this home. I will not have it! It has taken Joseph Brackenbury's life and driven our son insane. You have defied me in the past. You will not defy me again!"

Julia stared at her husband. She pulled her hand away. If her son's mind was broken, it was not because of the gospel of Jesus Christ but because of the strain Seth felt due to his father's drunkenness and unbelief. And she knew that Ezekiel would not accept nor understand this. She felt deeply frustrated and defensive. "You will lay blame wherever you choose," she said as she quickly stood up. There were tears in her eyes as she challenged her husband. "But I am under an edict from heaven to teach my children Christ's gospel. If our son is as ill as you claim, it is blind of you to blame it on the Church. It is cruel of you to force me to disobey God. I cannot—I will not—stop teaching my children. Not even for you!" With those words, Julia stood up and hurried into the house.

"Julia," Ezekiel shouted after her. "You misuse me! I am not a cruel husband! We are moving far away from here!"

In her room, Julia cried to her Heavenly Father. Her concern for Seth and her sorrow at Ezekiel's reaction felt like a dagger in her heart. Would Ezekiel really move them even farther away from the Saints? In tears, she prayed for the comfort of the Holy Spirit and for the wisdom to know how to safeguard her children.

David, Seth, and Lyman walked together in the warm twilight. They slapped at mosquitoes as Seth confided in them his complete ordeal, explaining that he prayed without ceasing and strove to trust in the Prophet's blessing but found little relief. He shook his head briskly as if he were trying to empty it of the flames that tortured him. "Furthermore," he moaned, "this disease in my mind is causing Father's heart to further harden."

"You must not blame yourself for Father's hardness nor let it destroy your peace," David countered. It felt strange to David, giving Seth the same advice Seth had given David in the past.

"But how can I control these images raging in my mind?" Seth cried out.

Lyman stopped walking and turned to Seth. "Dear brother, Delcena and I are planning on going to Jamestown for a time. The local Saints are gathering there in preparation for the move to Kirtland. Philastus has room for us in his house. Would you consider staying here while we are gone? It's quiet and restful."

David added, "Nancy or one of the others could keep you company."

Seth was silent for a moment. He looked from his brother-in-law to his brother. Lyman had such inner peace and wisdom. David looked so strong and fit. "What do you think, David? Can you handle Father's intemperance without me at home?"

"I can now," David said.

"You have grown stronger, David," Seth commented, "while I have broken like a weak link in a chain. The Prophet's blessing is my hope."

"Then let that hope work toward your healing," David said as he put his arm around Seth's shoulders. "I must write Don Carlos and thank him for taking care of my big brother."

"I would that I never needed his care," Seth said dismally.

The next morning at breakfast, Seth told his family that he would be living at the Shermans' cabin while they were gone. An argument immediately ensued about who would go to keep Seth company. If was finally decided that Nancy and Joe would stay with him. With these plans, Julia felt some peace. Perhaps getting away would help Seth to heal. Ezekiel remained silent and did not voice his opinion. His mind was focused on his own plans to move his family. But he had decided not to speak of it again to Julia until he had a buyer for their home and was certain about where he was going to take them.

During the following weeks, Ezekiel and Julia were too busy with the harvest to confront the issues that divided them. The crops had proved fruitful. When the days came to harvest the wheat, Lyman rode to Pomfret to help. David and Lyman reaped while Ezekiel and Seth bound the wheat into sheaves. The four men worked in unison, any division between them bound and set aside by the cords of necessity.

While the men worked the wheat fields, the rest of the family harvested and husked the corn. The children also picked apples and gathered nuts to store for the winter. The bruised apples were made into cider and preserves. Julia also supervised the making and storing of cheese. After the wheat was in and the corn was husked, the men slaughtered the bullock and hog. The women salted and preserved the meat. There was no time for contention. The larder had to be filled so that the household could survive the winter.

One Sabbath evening in mid-October in the Shermans' cabin, Seth sat on a chair near the parlor fire. Nancy reclined on a cot near him. Nancy read aloud from one of the Prophet's latter-day revelations that Lyman had left for them to study. "Fear not to do good, my sons, for whatsoever ye sow, that shall ye also reap; therefore, if ye sow good ye shall also reap good for your reward."

Troubled by this passage, Seth stood up, walked to the hearth, rested his hand on the mantel, and stared into the flames.

Nancy stopped reading. "Seth, what are you thinking?"

Seth turned to his sister. During the past weeks he had told her the details of his ordeal. "I have tried to do good. I have loved the Lord and served my parents and brothers and sisters. Yet these thoughts of despair will not completely leave me. Many mornings, I awaken in a sweat, fearing the flames will return." Seth sat back down in the chair. His eyes looked dismayed, but not restless or haunted as they had looked weeks ago.

Nancy gazed steadily at him. "Flames can purify as well as destroy, Seth. Could those flames in your mind become your refiner's fire? You are so much better than when you first came home."

Seth sighed deeply. "I don't know. It feels like I'm locked away in this little house like an invalid. Mother insists I stay until Christmas, and David threatens to thrash me if I come back too soon. I am useless. When I'm at home helping with the harvest, Mother smiles, tells me all is well, but I perceive tears near the surface. I don't know if they are because of my weakness or because Father is threatening to move the family. For the moment, the entire household is under strict orders to be as cheerful as Julianne—at least when I am around. If I could get Susan off by herself, she would tell me all, but the rest keep a constant eye on me. They're conspiring to protect me. Me! The brother who used to be their schoolmaster and protector. I'm no longer wise or strong in their eyes. This weakness in my mind has rendered me useless."

"I know how you feel," Nancy said quietly, thinking about her own broken body.

Seth exhaled sharply. "Here we are—the two who promised to stay by mother and the children—to help them forever."

"I try, Seth," Nancy countered. "I help the others as much as my strength permits."

Seth stood and moved quickly to Nancy. He sat down at the edge of her bed and put a hand on her shoulder. He had not meant to insinuate that she too was useless. He looked into her gray eyes. "You are a strength to the family, Nancy. As much as when you were whole. And now your task is to keep your crazy brother company."

Nancy chuckled. "Crazy is as crazy does, Seth. And you don't seem too crazy to me. You are still doing more than your share—helping with the harvest and taking care of your crippled sister. But, Seth, you cannot be everything to everyone. Mother and Father must work out their own problems. Pray for them, Seth, and help them, but let the Savior bear their sorrows. We must try to be like Him, try to lighten the load of others, but also allow others their own choices and struggles. As I have spent long hours imprisoned in this body, I have realized that this is the plan. We must not imagine ourselves so much like the Savior that we take on burdens that are not ours. Instead, we must lean on the Savior's arm and take His yoke, for His burden is light. You know that, yet you persist in a futile effort to save us all from pain and to bear all of our family's burdens and bring order to all of our lives. It is not right, and you, like anyone who depends on themself and not the Savior, collapsed under the weight. We cannot save them, Seth—only Jesus can. He is the only being capable and loving enough to bear all. Seth, let go of your own strength and find peace in His arms once more."

Seth closed his eyes and put his hand to his forehead. "Nance, you should have seen the confused and sorrowful look in Benjamin's eyes when I left him in Amherst. My frailty caused that. It weighs on me."

Nancy continued, "Your mind is nearly healed, Seth. Father mentioned that it is time for Ben to come home. Go get him. Show Ben that you have weathered this storm. It would be good for both of you." She lifted the paper resting on her chest. "Let me read you more of the Lord's words to the Prophet. They pertain to all of us: 'Therefore, fear not, little flock; do good; let earth and hell combine against you, for if ye are built upon my rock, they cannot prevail. Behold, I do not condemn you; go your ways and sin no more; perform with soberness the work which I have commanded you. Look unto me in every thought; doubt not, fear not. Behold, the wounds which pierced my side, and also the prints of the nails in my hands and feet; be faithful, keep my commandments, and ye shall inherit the kingdom of heaven.'"

"You will inherit the kingdom of heaven, Seth," Nancy said softly. "We all know that. But you must let the rest of us find our own way to Zion's gates. The God who governs eternity, who knows each star in the sky and numbers each sparrow, knows how to guide each honest soul toward eternal life. I remember you telling Benjamin that long ago when he was worried about Father. Take your own counsel, dear brother. Lay your burdens at the Savior's feet, Seth. Just let them go."

Seth unexpectedly smiled. "Nancy, you give as good a lecture as Mother." Then his face became serious, and he closed his eyes once more. He took Nancy's hand tightly in his. He repeated the words in the revelation. "'Fear not, little flock; do good; let earth and hell combine against you, for if ye are built upon my rock, they cannot prevail.' Thank you, my dear sister. You are an angel to me. I will strive to lay my burdens at the Lord's feet. Pray for me, for I still fear that this mania will return."

"I always pray for you, Seth," Nancy whispered. "But I don't fear its return. The Lord is turning your weakness into strength." Then she added, her voice growing strong, "And you shall be a golden shaft in the Lord's bow, an elder of Israel sent forth by the Master, the Son of God."

"I pray so," Seth whispered.

Two weeks later, Nancy moved back home, and Seth left to accompany his mother and sisters Julianne and Almera to Jamestown to help with the birth of Delcena's baby. He planned to stay in Jamestown a few days, then travel to Ohio to get Benjamin.

On a cold, clear morning, Delcena gave birth to a healthy baby boy whom they named Albey Lyman Sherman. During the labor, Lyman and Seth went outside with Lyman's two little girls. As Seth watched Lyman play with his daughters, he thought of Delcena and of how life was a crucible of pain for both men and women. Yet women were blessed, for their crucible brought life into the world. Then a strange and comforting thought entered Seth's mind like a shaft of light—that his crucible would yield a gold so refined that it would shine as a star guiding his brothers and sisters toward eternal life.

After the delivery, Lyman and Seth were called inside to see Delcena and the baby. Delcena was bright-eyed, and the child was pink and healthy. As Lyman held his son, he remembered the beloved little boy he had lost. He thought of the little girls he treasured. He felt great awe for his wife. He thanked his Heavenly Father for His bounteous mercy and love and for the restored gospel that enriched their lives. With a prayer in his heart, Lyman handed the baby to his brother-in-law.

Seth placed his smallest finger into the grip of the newborn babe. Seth grinned at Lyman. "Your son is a golden child. And my friend, the fire within me is doused at last."

Too joyous to speak, Lyman put his arm around Seth, and they both watched the child as tears of joy softened their eyes and moistened their cheeks, which were wind-burned and tanned by the harvest sun.

The day before Seth was to leave for Ohio to get Benjamin, Ezekiel rode to Jamestown with three purposes in mind. The foremost was to see his grandchildren. Second, he was following Nancy's instructions. Nancy had sewn matching stock ties and bonnets for each member of Delcena's and Joel's families. The tiny, pale blue cravat for Delcena's infant and the miniature baby-blue bonnet for Annie's little Sariah were especially cunning. Ezekiel was to present Delcena her gifts as tokens of Nancy's love and congratulations. He was to give the other gifts to Seth to take to Joel's family. Third, Ezekiel had decided to tell Seth that he had sold the farm. Ezekiel no longer had the heart to keep his plans secret.

Ezekiel knocked on the door and heard Delcena call for him to open it and come in. He opened the door and found Delcena sitting in the rocking chair holding Albey. Ezekiel bent down and kissed Delcena's cheek. He admired the sleeping infant in her arms. Fifteen-month-old Mary toddled up to him. Three-year-old Alvira tugged on his trouser leg. He picked both little girls up and held them close. A few moments later, he put them down, took the infant from Delcena, and cradled him in his arms. A sense of loss and sorrow filled Ezekiel's heart. Would Julia ever forgive him for taking her away from these little ones? Could he bear it himself?

Before leaving that morning, Ezekiel pulled Seth aside. He unapologetically told him that he had sold the farm.

"Then you are moving, Pa," Seth said awkwardly. "You're actually doing it."

Ezekiel nodded. "The first of March, I'll sail up the lakes to Chicago and buy a quarter section of land. I'll send word for your mother and the children as soon as I have a place for them. The move will likely take place in May. We have to give up occupancy by the first of June."

"Does Mother know?" Seth questioned.

Ezekiel shook his head.

Seth's eyes studied his father. Seth had no desire to argue with his father or try to force his hand. He sighed deeply. He had to put his trust in God. "When will you tell Mother?"

Ezekiel shrugged. "In a day or two. Seth, you're welcome to tell Joel while you're at his place. I know you might decide to settle in Ohio with Lyman and Joel. Whatever you choose, I'll continue to honor you as my son."

"And I honor you as my father," Seth said. Yet as he spoke, his eyes burned. Seth was not surprised by his father's announcement of the move, but he knew what a blow it would be to his mother.

The next day, as he boarded a steamer to go and bring Benjamin home, Seth resolved to have faith, to do what he could to soften the blow, and to find a way to help his brothers and sisters make their way to Zion. Two days later, he disembarked at Fairport, Ohio, and headed to Kirtland before going on to Amherst. He knocked on the door of the Prophet's apartment in the early evening.

Joseph greeted Seth with a joyous grin. "Brother Seth," Joseph said as he shook Seth's hand and embraced him. "It is good to see you looking so well. I knew there was great strength within you. Come in, come in. Emma and I have wonderful news."

As Seth stepped into the room, Joseph went into the bedroom to invite Emma to join them. Emma came out holding an infant in her arms.

Joseph introduced them. "Brother Seth, meet my wife, Emma, and our son, Joseph Smith the third. Our little girl, Julia, is not here but is currently staying with her grandparents. Little Joseph joined us two days ago."

After Emma and Seth exchanged greetings, Emma added with a smile, "When you go to Amherst you must tell Sister Annie the happy news—that Emma's prayers have been answered, that the miracle has at last come forth, that the Lord has blessed her. She has her sturdy, baby boy and is overcome with gladness."

Seth smiled at Emma as he admired the baby. "This will bring Annie and all of us joy. Congratulations."

"Come sit down, Brother Seth," Joseph said as he motioned Seth toward a chair. "I'm anxious to talk with you. How is your family? Has your father's heart softened? How is your mother? How is the branch in Pomfret? The Saints in Jamestown?"

"Joseph," Emma chided with a laugh, "ask Brother Seth one question at a time, rather than a dozen at once."

Joseph chuckled good-naturedly. "I forget myself sometimes. Emma keeps me in line. Brother Seth, tell me all."

Seth exhaled and began talking. "Brother Joseph, I regret to say that my father's heart has not softened. He plans to move the family to Chicago in the spring. Mother does not know these details, though she expects this is coming. She prays continually that all her children will gather with the Saints someday. Now, to answer your third question. The Church in Chautauqua County does well under the guidance of Elder Lyman Sherman. There have been six recent baptisms."

"Ah, Brother Lyman Sherman," Joseph said thoughtfully. "I recall that he is married to your sister. When I met him, I perceived seeds of greatness in him."

"He is truly the best of men and the wisest and most loyal of friends," Seth said.

"Those are compliments indeed," Joseph mused. "I hope to get to know Brother Lyman better."

"You shall be seeing a good deal of him. He and my sister will be in Kirtland soon."

Joseph smiled and nodded. Then he looked directly into Seth's eyes. "Brother Seth, my thoughts turn toward your mother, even though I haven't yet met her. I believe that your mother will be blessed for bringing such a large family into the Church. Tell her to have faith. A way will open for her to gather with the Saints. For the time being, could you tell your brother Joel to come visit me soon? He is planning to move to Kirtland, and I know of some land that he might be interested in. A short distance from here, near the schoolhouse, there is a house and property that may come up for sale this spring. It is big enough to house a large family. You may want to take a look at it on your way out of town. A lovely orchard extends behind the house and partly up the hill. The creek could be harnessed and a sawmill built. Brother Joel may also be interested in some wild land on the edge of town."

Seth felt great peace as Joseph spoke. He prayed silently that he would retain that faith. "Thank you, Brother Joseph," he said. "God bless you for your kindness to us."

"And may the Lord bless you, dear Brother Seth. You have an inheritance in Zion and a great mission to fulfill as an elder of the restored Church of Christ. I am certain of that."

After saying farewell to the Prophet, Seth walked to the small schoolhouse where the Prophet often taught. It was a cool fall day, and the setting sun was as brilliant as the colors of the trees. Fall leaves crunched under his feet. He looked beyond the schoolhouse to the house that the Prophet had mentioned. It was a brown frame house, two stories high and solidly built. It was too big of a house for a family as small as Joel's. A hill extended upward behind it, the only hill on the Kirtland flats. A large oak tree shaded the yard. Seth pictured the leaves turning green in the spring. He pictured a swing hanging from the oak tree and Esther pushing Amos on it. He pictured his brothers Benjamin and Joseph helping Joel build a sawmill on the creek. He saw in his mind David and Don Carlos Smith pulling sticks in the yard and Almon Babbitt calling on his sisters. He saw his mother and Nancy in the windows of the house, sewing and cooking as they discussed the gospel. He pictured Mary, George, and William running each morning to the schoolhouse that was hardly more than a stone's throw away. He saw them all hearing the word of God at the feet of Joseph, the Prophet. These images in Seth's soul were clear and joyful, heaven sent. But even as his heart felt great peace, a part of his soul ached. He searched through these pictures in his mind for one more person, for his beloved father, Ezekiel. But he could not find him.

# ✑ NOTES ✑

PROLOGUE

Jonathan and Sethiah King were living near or in Ashford, Connecticut, when Ezekiel left home, based on deeds of land purchased in 1776 by Jonathan King and the 1780 census record (Cluff & Gibson, 40).

There is confusion as to when Ezekiel was actually born and what his age would be at this time. The story Ezekiel told his family is not consistent with research done after his death. Ezekiel told his family that he was born on January 12, 1776, and that his father died in the Revolutionary War after he married his mother (B. F. Johnson, 1). There is no record of his birth in the Uxbridge Vital Records. However, recorded county court proceedings for September 1773 read as follows:

> Bethiar Gansee of Uxbridge in the County of Worcester [Massachusetts] spinster comes into court to answer to a presentment found against her by the Grand Jurors for said body of this county for that she did on said last day of May Anno Dom 1772 at Uxbridge aforesaid commit the crime of fornication with a male person to the said jurors unknown whereof she there afterwards had a [illegitimate] child born of her body against the peace to which she pleads guilty. (Clara S. Johnson, Ezekiel Johnson and Julia Hills, *A Report of a Research Trip Made in 1960,* [Salt Lake City: Committee of the Ezekiel Johnson Family Organization, 1961], 9)

Based upon this research, it is now believed that his birth was in January or February 1773 and that his mother and father were never married.

Family tradition refers to Ezekiel's mother as both Bethiah and Sethiah. Historical documents list Ezekiel's mother as Sethiah (as we have chosen to use),

Bethiah, Bethiar, and Sethiar. These differences result from the penmanship of the time period. S and B were very similar and sometimes indistinguishable. We have chosen Sethiah because it appeared that she may have signed her name Sethiah (or Sethiar) King on court documents concerning her father's will. Sethiah's last name of Guernsey was also possibly referred to in historical records as Ganzee, Garnsey, Garfeel, Gansey, etc. These differences likely resulted from the handwritten record keeping of the time (Cluff & Gibson, 36).

Ezekiel Johnson never told his children very much about his father (B. F. Johnson, 302). Earlier family research identified about five Ezekiel Johnsons who could possibly have been his father based upon proximity, age, and date. In this fictional account, we have chosen Ezekiel Johnson born June 25, 1750, to be the unknown father of Ezekiel. This Ezekiel was from Grafton, Massachusetts, and filed the intention to marry Rachel Merrifield in 1773. Strangely, there is substantial proof that they never married. Rachel Merrifield gave birth to a son, Levi Johnson, in March 1774, which was believed to be this Ezekiel Johnson's son also (Cluff & Gibson, 40). Our choice of Ezekiel's father is not arbitrary but consistent with new information that has just recently been discovered by Preston Johnson, a descendent of Ezekiel and Julia's tenth child, Benjamin Franklin. On October 23, 2004, at a Benjamin Franklin Johnson family meeting, Preston presented the results of a DNA research study that he has conducted to find the father of Ezekiel Johnson. Through his DNA research, it is determined that there is a very high significance and probability that this Ezekiel Johnson of 1750 was the unknown father of our Ezekiel (Benjamin Franklin Johnson Newsletter, December 17, 2004).

It is also likely that, as portrayed in the story, "baby Ezekiel" was not named immediately after birth. When Sethiah was brought to court in 1773, she would not name the baby's father. However, in January 1776 a child named Ezekiel Johnson is recorded as residing with his unmarried mother Sethiah Guernsey, her mother and stepfather, and Sethiah's siblings. Sethiah's intent to marry Jonathan King was also recorded in 1776 (Massachusetts Vital Records, as researched in Cluff & Gibson, 34).

It is fact that Ezekiel ran away because of mistreatment (R. D. Johnson, 16). His promise to never beat or harm a living thing is based on his son Benjamin's words: "with no other blow than words was he ever known to strike anything living" (B. F. Johnson, 9).

Ezekiel did take the purse of James King when he left home. It contained several receipts from various places. One of the receipts was from a man, Jon Pilling, in Albany (Cluff & Gibson, 4; R. D. Johnson, 17–18). Selling cowbells in Albany is based on business papers from Albany, New York, 1797, found in his wallet. Two of the papers were notes from one man, each for 12 cowbells at 12 shillings a bell. The notes were never redeemed (R. D. Johnson, 16).

Census records place Isaac Chapel and his family living next to Jonathan and Sethiah King in New London, Connecticut, 1840. Family research has found an Elizabeth King married to Isaac Chapel. It is possible that Elizabeth King was the daughter of Jonathan King from a deceased wife (Cluff & Gibson, 42).

It does seem possible that Esther Hills Forbush may have known Sethiah and been aware of her pregnancy and circumstances involving court because of the close proximity of Grafton and Uxbridge (Cluff & Gibson, 5). Members of the family of the father of Ezekiel (Ezekiel Johnson, 1750) were buried next to Joseph Hills, father of Julia, in Grafton in the same cemetery where members of the Forbush family were also buried (Clara S. Johnson, *Ezekiel Johnson*, self-published, 10–11). The names, ages, and general demographics concerning Julia's family of origin are taken from family group records.

## CHAPTER 1

Pomfret Township, Chautauqua County, New York, is the location of the family home. Descriptions of home and family life were taken from the poetry of Joseph and George.

Ezekiel's drinking was a problem in the Johnson home (B. F. Johnson, 2).

There were many newspaper articles written about Joseph Smith and his religion during this time period. The article referred to, dated August, 27, 1829, from the *Niagara Courier,* is a reprint of an article from the *Palmyra Freeman.*

Most of the pet names for the siblings used throughout the book were created by the authors. However, Julianne did refer to Benjamin as Benja. This greeting was found in an original letter to Benjamin from his sisters while on his mission to the Sandwich Islands.

Philastus Hurlbut historically played a significant role in LDS Church history, promoting the theory of the Spaulding manuscript with the purpose of discrediting Joseph Smith and the Book of Mormon. It is certain that Philastus Hurlbut was related to Lyman Sherman, perhaps even a first cousin.

CHAPTER 2

Joel Hills Johnson's patent for his invention of a shingle cutter was registered as Patent #39 on December 8, 1829, by Andrew Jackson, president of the United States (Mary Julia Johnson Wilson, *Ancestral Sketches and Memories of Mary Julia Johnson Wilson of Hillsdale, Utah*). The details of being cheated out of some of the rights are not explained in detail, but Joel writes about the destruction of his sawmill and the debt thus incurred and reasons for his move to Ohio in his journal (J. H. Johnson, Diary, 5).

Benjamin wrote that Ezekiel's drinking, "the fiend of unhappiness," would "break the bonds of union between our parents, and . . . destroy the happiness of their children" (B. F. Johnson, 2). Ben's sober and sensitive personality, as presented in the novel, is supported by his recorded statement, "my heart at times would seem almost ready to burst with sorrow and grief" (2).

It is unknown whether Seth Johnson ever married or not. He was single at the time the family lived in Pomfret and Kirtland. However, the intent to marry between a Seth Johnson and a Sophia Stone dated April 4, 1824, was recorded in the marriage records of Dana, Worchester, Massachusetts.

Family events that historically occurred between the years 1828 and 1830 were combined into one year's time period. This causes some minor discrepancies: the death of Joel and Annie's baby girl and the birth of their son, Sixtus, actually occurred on July 18, 1829, and October 8, 1829.

CHAPTER 3

The gold watch and the Bible sitting on a stand in the house are referred to in George's poetry (G. W. Johnson, *Diary of George W. Johnson,* 37, 30), and Julia did have a gold chain as remembered by her children.

Ezekiel's restlessness, moving and settling in several locations in their early marriage, is based on the writing of the children (R. D. Johnson, 20; B. F. Johnson, 2).

Mrs. Bull is a fictional character. However, the family name Bull was taken from the Johnson family research that located a farm near the Johnsons' property owned by a family with the surname of Bull.

The characterization of Hurlbut is historically based on reports of his character found in several different sources. He is described as "conceited, ambitious, and ostentatious . . . of a low moral status" (B. F. Johnson, 17) and "a man of fine physique, very pompous, good looking, and very ambitious, with some energy, though of poor education" (*History of the Church* 1:355). Philastus was not a doctor of medicine; however, he was, for a short time, a member of the Methodist clergy in upper New York. He was dismissed because of his immoral character (Winchester, 5).

## CHAPTER 4

According to family research, Delcena and Lyman had two children born around 1830; the daughter's name was Alvira, and the baby boy died sometime before July 21, 1831. His given name was unknown (Julia Johnson, letter to Diadamia Forbush, July 21, 1831).

Joe studied herbs as a child and, as an adult, continued growing herbs for medicinal purposes personally and professionally (R. D. Johnson, 1–2).

The hymn "I Know My Redeemer Lives" was well known in the time period. We have used the lyrics as they were presented in the first hymnal compiled by Emma Smith in 1835.

The retelling of Joel's boyhood experience living with his uncle Joel Hills and almost drowning is recorded almost word for word from his diary (J. H. Johnson, *Diary,* 2–3).

Joel and David first became familiar with the new "Mormonite" religion in Amherst. They became friends with Almon Babbitt during this time period (B. F. Johnson, 5; J. H. Johnson, *Diary,* 6–7).

The incident of Parley P. Pratt and "Stu-boy" is recorded in his autobiography (*Autobiography of Parley P. Pratt,* [Salt Lake City: Deseret Book, 1973], 50).

## CHAPTER 5

The sorrow in the family is seen in Benjamin's description of his feelings at this time: "It almost seems that I was born to be a child of sorrow; for such was my love for both of my parents, my heart at times would seem almost ready to burst with sorrow and grief; and a feeling always seemed with me to wish . . . that I never had been born" (B. F. Johnson, 2).

Annie was the first member of the family to embrace the gospel. Although Joel would not attend meetings for a period of time, he allowed Annie to go. He writes that he "never would abridge any ones [sic] liberty in religious matters" (J. H. Johnson, *Diary,* 6). He did use his personal Bible to compare the teachings of this new sect to the ancient Church of Christ. The actual words, the four different points of comparing doctrine, are taken from his journal (J. H. Johnson, *Diary,* 6). David also joined the Church at this time.

Joel stated that Annie attended a meeting where Samuel Smith, Lyman Wight, and others came (J. H. Johnson, *Diary,* 5). David's and Don Carlos Smith's friendship is historically based; however, the time they first met is not recorded. Gideon, Jared, and Simeon Carter were well-known residents of Amherst, Ohio, and members of the Church (Jared Carter, *Journal of Jared Carter,* Brigham Young University Special Collections, 1, 3, 8).

The incident concerning the cruel rumors about Alvin Smith's body being dissected are based on an announcement by Joseph Smith Sr. printed in *The Wayne Sentinel,* September 30, 1824.

## CHAPTER 6

Joel H. Johnson, in his personal history, states he was baptized on June 1, 1831, by Sylvester Smith and that Annie was baptized a few days earlier (J. H. Johnson, *Diary,* 7). Although the date of David's baptism is not recorded, Benjamin states that both of his brothers, Joel and David, were baptized in Amherst (3).

Jared Carter, a Mormon missionary, tells of David's disappointment in his baptism because Edson Fuller "was under the influence of an evil spirit" and, in a short time, "was cut off from the Church of Christ" (Carter, 11).

The meeting in the Barney's barn is based on a historical account found in Jared Carter's journal where "John Whitmore" attended. "Whitmore" was probably misspelled, and it was most likely John Whitmer, one of the three witnesses, who came to speak. The miracle in the barn was also recorded by Carter: "The cloud come up and rained considerable all around the barn, but rained not on the barn to wet us" (Carter, 6). His account also includes being called to go to a feverish Almon Babbitt "to pray for him" and then walk with him three miles after he was healed (6).

Reactions to the baptism of Annie, Joel, and David in Pomfret are based on historical information. Benjamin writes: "This news came upon us almost as a horror and a disgrace" (B. F. Johnson, 5).

The letters from Seth and Julia are accurate except for minor details incorporated for clarification. A typed copy of the actual letters is found at the University of Utah. The possibility of Seth's involvement in court is mentioned in a postscript on Seth's letter to Joel.

## CHAPTER 7

Joel met Joseph Smith Jr. at a conference in Orange, Ohio, a town about 18 miles from Kirtland and 35 miles from Amherst. When Joel was introduced to the prophet, Joseph Smith described himself as a "great green lub[b]erly fellow" (J. H. Johnson, *Diary,* 11).

Records and notes of the Orange Conference, October 24–25, 1831, were found in *History of the Church* 1:189–90, *Journal History* (October 25–26, 1832), and *Far West Record* (19–26). Joel Hills Johnson's name is listed as attending this conference. Since a congregation of Saints met for the last session (*Far West Record,* 26), it is possible that Almon, Annie, and David may have been there.

Many of Joseph's words and conversation in this chapter are taken from excerpts found in *History of the Church.* Joseph speaks of their prayer for Zion and revelation, which describes Zion and the area of Independence, Missouri (1:189–99).

As presented in the chapter, the conference consisted of four sessions. It seems that the first three were for the priesthood holders, where certain early ordinations and callings were issued. In attendance were Joel, Joseph Brackenbury, and Edmond Durfee (*Far West Record,* 19–26). The first three sessions included statements of testimony and commitment by many of the priesthood leadership of the Church, including Joel. "Br. Joel Johnson said that he had professed religion for a number of years, also felt to bear testimony of the goodness of God, and to consecrate all to the Lord" (22).

The call of certain elders to the high priesthood during the second session, their rebuke by Sidney Rigdon during the third session, and that Joseph Brackenbury and several others "received the rebuke in meekness" is recorded in the minutes of the conference (*Far West Record,* 26).

The general body of the Church attended the fourth session. The speakers (Sidney Rigdon, Oliver Cowdery, Hyrum Smith, and Orson Hyde) at this general session were assigned during the third priesthood session (*Far West Record,* 26).

CHAPTER 8

The textual details that the older members of the Johnson family studied the Book of Mormon while Ezekiel was living away in Fredonia, received a testimony of its truth, and, upon discovering Benjamin and Joseph listening in secret, allowed them to participate, is recorded in family records (B. F. Johnson, 5, 6; R. D. Johnson, 39).

The Book of Mormon scriptures referenced in this work are quoted from a replicated printing of the 1830 version of the Book of Mormon.

The exact time when Joel, David, and Almon went to Pomfret is different in the various histories. B. F. Johnson records that in the fall, his brothers and Almon come (5), whereas Joel records that in January 1832, he went with Almon to visit friends in Pomfret (J. H. Johnson, *Diary*, 12).

The quote from the newspaper article concerning Martin Harris was published in the *Niagara Courier*, Thursday, August 27, 1829.

CHAPTER 10

The townspeople's persecution of the family because Nancy was not healed actually occurred. In *My Life's Review*, Benjamin states that priests were "asking why my sister Nancy, who then walked upon crutches, was not healed?" if this religion was all it claimed to be (6). It is also mentioned in the newspaper article reporting Brackenbury's death that the missionaries professed to heal the sick but could not heal Nancy Johnson, a cripple who had fallen from a horse (*The Fredonia Censor*, Vol. XI, Fredonia, NY, Wed, January, 1832).

Joseph Brackenbury's death and last words are based on Joel's account:

For our beloved brother Joseph [Brackenbury] was taken sick with what was supposed to be bilious colic and remained in great distress, which he bore with fortitude of a saint for one week and expired with an unshaken confidence in the fullness of the gospel which he had preached, and a firm hope of a glorious resurrection among the just. (J. H. Johnson, *Diary*, 12)

Some sources suggest Elder Brackenbury was poisoned (*Far West Record*, 250; *Journal History*, Nov, 15, 1845). However, no members of the Johnson family in their records state that poisoning was the cause of his death, but an illness (B. F. Johnson, 6) and bilious colic (J. H. Johnson, *Diary*, 12).

## CHAPTER 11

The names of Joe's friends in this chapter are taken from a series of letters with Mrs. Blanchard Darby of Pomfret, New York. In these letters, he asks about Morris Cook's family, Willard Lewis, and Blanchard Darby. The actual name of the woman he is writing to is not revealed in the letters, as she consistently refers to herself as Mrs. Blanchard Darby. The fictional name of Rachel Risley is used to portray this friend and the close relationship Joe may have had as a youth with a young girl whom he will later correspond with regularly. These letters are dated January 15, 1865, October 22, 1865, and November 8, 1868, and are found in "The Papers of Joseph Ellis Johnson (1817–1882)," a manuscript collection found in the Special Collections Library at the University of Utah.

The section of Joel's letter to Annie relating information about Elder Brackenbury's death is taken from Joel's actual words (J. H. Johnson, *Diary,* 12).

Benjamin records his trip with Joel to Amherst in the early spring, and the misery, pain, and weakness in his ankle is as he describes. "Traveled on foot over 200 miles in one week, carrying my bundle of clothing. The year previous I had cut my ancle [*sic*] with an axe, took cold in it, and for a time it was feared I would lose my leg. The ancle was still weak; and the misery of that journey can only be known by my good angel and myself" (B. F. Johnson, 7).

Annie gave birth to a baby girl, Sariah, on February 18, 1832, in Amherst, Ohio.

## CHAPTER 12

The Sabbath meeting in Pomfret is recorded in Jared Carter's journal. It includes who spoke and that the spirit instructed him to "confine the congregation to a choice" (Carter, 11).

David was rebaptized as recorded in Jared Carter's journal. Carter gives the following insight: "He felt dissatisfied with his former baptism . . . and it also was the case that David Johnson had lived unworthy of the communion of the Sacrament." Jared's response in the text of the chapter is taken from the following entry in his journal: "Now this to us was a case as we had not before experienced but we, after praying to our heavenly father [*sic*], concluded to leave it to him. He then said he would be baptized" (Carter, 11).

Historically, Jared Carter's companion in Pomfret was Mr. Calvin Stoddard who did not continue with Jared for the remainder of his mission.

CHAPTER 13

Ezekiel, Susan, and Seth went to Kirtland and met the Prophet that summer. Seth felt "extreme anxiety to see [his] father converted to the truth and redeemed from intemperance," and it appeared to the rest of the family that Ezekiel's response to meeting Joseph Smith was favorable (B. F. Johnson, 7).

Joseph Smith recorded the experience when he was poisoned in May 1832, while traveling from Missouri to Kirtland with Newel K. Whitney. He wrote, "I raised large quantities of blood and poisonous matter, and so great were the muscular contortions of my system, that my jaw in a few moments was dislocated" He was instantaneously healed after a blessing by Whitney (*History of the Church* 1:271).

Words from *The Evening and Morning Star* that Joel, Seth, and Lyman read are found in *History of the Church* 1:273–77.


CHAPTER 14

The origin of the Spaulding Manuscript as presented in this chapter is historically based. Henry Lake and Nehmiah King, of Erie County, claimed that Joseph Smith's idea for the Book of Mormon was taken from a story written by Solomon Spaulding.

Seth's mania is reported in Ben's writings:

While in Amherst, at my brother Joel's a mania seemed to come over Seth . . . Apparently this was because of his extreme anxiety to see our father converted to the truth and redeemed from intemperance. Our first intimation of this mania was the discovery that he had left the house in the night; and when, after anxious searching and waiting for him he came back about 10 o'clock a.m. next day, his mind in a wild and deranged condition, we found he had traveled near 100 miles in that short period of time. (B. F. Johnson, 7)

CHAPTER 15

Seth went home to Pomfret with Ezekiel. Ben stayed in Amherst, most likely to help with the harvest. Seth traveled to Ohio in the fall and brought Ben home. Ben wrote, "He [Seth] returned home with my father, and remained weakened in mind for a few months, but was the same fall able to come to Ohio, from which place, after a short stay, I accompanied him home; after which he became to all appearance perfectly sound in mind" (B. F. Johnson, 7–8).

Tom Perkins historically represents the relative of a Wesley Perkins who wrote a letter about moving to the Amherst area. This historical letter provides insight into the feelings of the non-Mormons in Ohio regarding the Mormons and their religion. Ezra Boothe, an early apostate during the Kirtland period, wrote a series of letters to the local newspapers. The date of the Perkins's letter is February 11, 1832.

> As it Respects Religion in this Town there is Considerable Stir at Present The Mormon Religion excites the greatest curiosity at Present Joseph Smith & Sidney Ridgen is the head men in this Business thare god is the Devil non but the Simple will imbrace thare Doctrin . . . it is paid no attention to only By those that are possessed of a weak minds. (Wesley Perkins, Brigham Young University Special Collections)

The house that Joseph Smith suggests that the Johnsons buy is the home that Joel actually purchased in May 1833. On the land records, the home was in Joel's name first (May 1833), then Seth's (August 1834), then Joel's again (February 1835), and then finally in Julia's name (May 1837). It was located on the Kirtland flats, close to the schoolhouse, with an orchard and hill behind it (B. F. Johnson, 8; R. D. Johnson, 50–51; Kirtland Land Records of Tract 1, Lot 18, Parcel B). This original home still stands and is owned by the Church. It has been significantly changed through the years and is now a little blue house near the Visitor's Center, close to the rebuilt schoolhouse. It is recorded that Joseph Smith "counseled" Joel to buy property in Kirtland (J. H. Johnson, *Diary*, 12–13).

SELECTED BIBLIOGRAPHY

Cannon, Donald Q. and Lyndon W. Cook, ed. *Far West Record: Minutes of the Church of Jesus Christ of Latter-day Saints, 1830–1844.* Salt Lake City: Deseret Book, 1983.

Cluff, Judy L. and Franklin K. Gibson, comp. *Johnson Gems: The Life Story of Julia Hills and Ezekiel Johnson.*

Johnson, Benjamin F. *My Life's Review, Autobiography of Benjamin Franklin Johnson.* Provo, UT: Grandin, 1997; and Provo, UT: Benjamin F. Johnson Family Organization, 1999.

Johnson, George Washington. *Diary of George W. Johnson.* Provo, UT: Brigham Young University, 1940.

———. *Jottings by the Way.* St. George, UT: C. E. Johnson, 1882.

Johnson, Joel H. *Diary of Joel Hills Johnson.* Provo, UT: Brigham Young University, 1945.

Johnson, Rufus D. *J.E.J. Trail to Sundown, Cassadaga to Casa Grande, 1817–1882, The Story of a Pioneer: Joseph Ellis Johnson.* Salt Lake City: Deseret News Press, 1961.

Le Baron, Dale E. *Benjamin Franklin Johnson, Friend to the Prophets.* Provo, UT: Grandin, 1997.

Winchester, Benjamin. *The Origin of the Spaulding Story, Concerning the Manuscript Found.* Philadelphia: Brown, 1840.

The Papers of Joseph Ellis Johnson, Special Collections. University of Utah.

# ABOUT THE AUTHORS

Marcie Gallacher, a graduate of Brigham Young University, is the author of four novels: *Amaryllis Lilies, Fixed Stars, Whispers of Hope,* and *Homeward.* Her publication credits include an article in the *Ensign* and stories in the *New Era* and the *Friend.* She especially enjoys reading and writing novels, participating in equestrian sports, and doing family history research. She and her husband, Gray, reside in Wilton, California, with their four children, Jamie, Matt, Brett, and Michelle.

Kerri Robinson, a licensed clinical social worker, is a part-time counselor and has written professionally. LDS Church history is one of her lifetime passions. She and her husband, Brent, live in Alpine, Utah, and are always busy with their blended family of nine incredible children, Josh and Sarah, Andrea, Tim, Erik, Mark, Scott, Ryan, Julianne, and Cassidy.